DETROIT PUBLIC LIBRARY
3 5674 05668531 7
P9-AOB-999

THE DEATH OF DENMARK VESEY

A novel of the Charleston Slave Revolt

PRAISE FOR
The Death of Denmark Vesey

“Modeled on the historical fiction tradition of Gore Vidal, and the moral irony of Graham Greene, James Paul Rice’s *The Death of Denmark Vesey* creates the turbulent world of slavery in antebellum Charleston, South Carolina with a cast of characters who embody the dichotomies of racial strife that still plague the South today.”

Wesley Lee Edward Moore III, English Chair, Porter-Gaud, Charleston, SC

"Now more than ever, the story of Denmark Vesey begs to be told. Rich with carefully researched historic detail, James Paul Rice’s book brings Vesey’s world to life. The star is Lucinda, a young slave whose distinctive point of view delivers the story in a new and absorbing way."

Charlie Geer, Author of *Outbound: The Curious Secession of Later-Day Charleston*, winner of the Regional Fiction Independent Publishers Award.

THE DEATH OF DENMARK VESEY

A novel of the Charleston Slave Revolt

JAMES PAUL RICE

KNOX ROBINSON PUBLISHING
London & Atlanta

KNOX ROBINSON PUBLISHING

34 New House
67-68 Hatton Garden
London, EC1N 8JY
&
3104 Briarcliff RD NE #98414
Atlanta, Georgia 30344

First published in Great Britain and the United States in 2017 by Knox Robinson Publishing

A CIP catalogue record for this book is available from the British Library.

ISBN HB 978-1-910282-58-8

ISBN PB 978-1-910282-67-0

Printed in the United States of America and the United Kingdom

www.knoxrobinsonpublishing.com

for Wesley Lee Edward Moore III
A true Charlestonian

Don' hol' nuttin down deep een you heart.
Ain' God gi' you mout fo talk 'em?

Gullah Proverb

"He was said to be a man of superior powers of mind
& the more dangerous for it."

Writing about Denmark Vesey, from a letter by Mary L. Beach, Charleston, South Carolina to Elizabeth L. Gilchrist (German Town, Pennsylvania) 5 July 1822

"Look like the innocent flower,
but be the serpent under't."

Shakespeare, Macbeth

Flowing Like the Dark River

This was where the river changed. Here the waters of the Ashley River slowed and darkened to the color of tea, flowed and ebbed with the ocean tides, then spread in miles and miles of marsh and sweet grass, far as you could see. Here the deer tracks ended, for downriver the brackish water was unfit to drink. The smell here was like no other place, the smell of salt and fish and swamp rot. Most days the sun was hot an hour past daybreak as the river gave up to the sky the nesting birds. Kingfishers swooped and plunged, long-legged cranes waded with a high step, yellow canaries chirped from the shade along the riverbank. Here a half-day's fishing and a half-day's trawling could feed a hundred men, like the good Lord Jesus worked his miracle and fed the multitudes with loaves and fishes. Water oaks along the river were black and thick as a tangled dream. Grey beards hung from every branch.

The Yamasee Indians claimed the trees were home to wise spirits, and the Indians used the bark in their potions and treatments. The conjurer Gullah Jack said the Yamasee were powerful in their knowledge of spells and magic, of charms made from crab claws, crushed nuts, and parched corn used to guard secrets and distil protection. Reverend Morris Brown, when he taught from the Scriptures, said the water and trees and stones have spirits that serve the Voodoo gods or devils. There was a spirit here that moved across the face of these waters, like a soul wrung from the body of a man or a work song lifting from the labor in the fields.

Half a morning from here by riverboat, at the mouths of the Ashley and Cooper rivers, was the harbor town of Charleston. A place could have an influence on you even if you had never been there, and Lucinda had been influenced by Charleston all her life, although she had never set foot off Radcliffe Place Plantation. The plantation's slave men who served under Master Radcliffe's nephew selling and buying provisions regularly travelled to Charleston. They told stories of so many church steeples rising toward the heavens that Charleston was called The Holy City. They told of houses the colors of pale flowers; of white-sailed ships at anchor in the harbor; of smoke billowing from a steamboat chugging upriver. She tried to picture it all in her mind: wharves stacked high with barrels of rice, cotton bales, and pallets of timber; docks where busy black hands and sweat-streaked backs loaded and unloaded cargo. She imagined carriages drawn by fine horses jaunting along the streets of crushed oyster shells and white sand, streets glistening pearly white like the Gates of Heaven.

Lucinda's heart soared at these tales and snatches of talk by Master Radcliffe and his family at dinner, which she overheard while she was tending the table. Thousands of slaves were brought in ships from Africa and the West Indies and sold in the Charleston slave markets. There was a church with thousands of members, the African Methodist Episcopal church, just for Negro folk. There were black people who were not slaves at all, but free to work for money and have their own possessions. These things seemed marvelous to her and she longed from an early age to know if they were true, to witness all of it with her own eyes, ears, and heart. Although she was taught that the Lord does not answer selfish prayer, she sometimes slipped and let pass from her silent but mouthing lips this indiscreet request.

How her heart beat fast and a surge of shock and surprise rushed over her when she learned her prayers were answered!

"Massa Radcliffe gonna move us to Charleston, chile" her mama told her. "You say you wish't you be a town slave. I reckon yo' wish come true."

The year was 1821. Autumn.

Mama told Lucinda Master Radcliffe's sister's husband died. So Master Radcliffe determined Lucinda's mama, who was one of the best house niggers on the plantation, and who could cook, clean, service, sew, and grow flowers and garden vegetables if need be, was to move to Charleston for his sister. And Lucinda was to go with her mama to learn the ways of a town slave.

"How old am I, Mama?" Lucinda asked.

"Let's see, chile, you been born plantin' time in ought-four. That be two summers after Miss Elizabeth." Mama held up her closed fist and extended each finger as she counted the years to make sure. "I reckon you be 'bout sixteen. Why you ask?"

"I want to remember how old I was when we went to Charleston."

A fine Indian summer morning in November dawned gold and indigo the day Mama and Lucinda set out by Master Radcliffe's schooner for

Charleston. High up in the tree tops, the raucous crows cawed loudly like gossips. In the distance, a solitary hawk floated on an early morning updraft, eyeing for prey. All around them, the marsh grass stretched tall and golden green in water the color of a pewter cup. Master Radcliffe sent on the journey some of his strongest and most trusted slaves, along with his nephew, Master Jimmy Johnson, whose mother they would serve in Charleston.

"I ain't ever been on the river, chile!" Mama said as they stood waiting on the dock. "The alligators scares me!"

Lucinda took Mama's hand, steadying her as she stepped into the boat.

"Come on, Mama," she said, "No alligator's gonna trouble us," although the alligators frightened Lucinda too.

The boat bore provisions from the plantation for their new household: barrels of dried corn, sacks of rice, potatoes and yams, smoke-cured and salted hams, fresh harvest collard greens. They also had extras to exchange at the Charleston market for needs of the plantation: salt, pepper, coffee, sugar, vinegar, tobacco, rum, tubs of molasses, and gunpowder. Lucinda had packed her trunk with her few belongings: a coarse Negro cloth grey dress she wore most every day, and a fancier Negro cloth blue dress for when guests came to Radcliffe Place or that she wore for Sunday church services; her Bible, a gift from Miss Elizabeth; a cracked hand mirror Elizabeth had given her instead of throwing it away; and a pair of still-too-big cow leather shoes . . . a special treat for a young slave given to her by Mistress Nelly, as she said, "for being such a fine little pickaninny, always willing to help her mama and learn about the kitchen and the garden."

Lucinda's heart beat with fear and excitement. She tingled inside. This was such a special day! She felt so many feelings flow through her, flowing like the dark river, as she turned and watched the plantation Big House and the river landing dock, the slave cabins and the slaves at work in the fields, the gold of the harvest checkered here and there with the indigoes, mauves, and purples of the canals and the ditches, the rice fields with their silvery ponds, the cotton fields, then the shadowed woods and the groaning lumber mill all slowly disappear from sight. She knew one day she would return to this, the only place she had ever known. Yet somehow she also knew there was a bigger world waiting for her to discover, like a curious child hoping to find the attic filled with chests of toys and playthings.

She sat leaning up against a sack of rice, daydreaming in the warm sun as the boat caught the river's current, and the sails caught the wind.

The sluggish alligators sunning on the river bank seemed as docile as an old worn-out coon hound taken in as a pet, but Lucinda had heard tales of more than a handful of hounds in the vigor of their prime eaten alive by a vicious alligator.

"Abra'm," Mama cried, pointing at the riverbank, "the alligators. See 'em?"

"I sees 'em," Abraham replied calmly.

The deep green of the forest, the lurking shadows of the cypress swamps, a half-dozen plantations carved out of the wilderness, the wooden sloops, barge flats, and boats on the river, beaches of driftwood and palmetto trees, open spaces of water against a sky blue as a robin's egg, all glided by one by one, slipping away like time itself. Lucinda was charmed by the feeling of floating on the water, of travel, a new feeling, almost of freedom!

Mama, Lucinda could tell, though her mama would never admit it, was more uneasy than Lucinda was about leaving the plantation for a new life in town. Mama wore a bright patchwork dress and head scarf she had worked on for years using snatches of cast-off cloth from sewing repairs or quilting bees . . . attire more suitable for a visiting minister's occasional Sunday service for the slaves than their trip down river.

In the few days after being told they were to move to Charleston, Mama sewed a dress and head scarf for Lucinda. Lucinda had wondered how Mama found the time or the fabric until she learned Mama had begged Miss Elizabeth to sell some cloth and candles to work by, promising to pay for them by hiring herself out as a seamstress on Saturday afternoons in Charleston. Indigo blue, sunset gold, brick red, cypress green, the dress which Lucinda now wore was a bright patchwork of colors, and Mama had crafted it to fit Lucinda's still-girlish waist with now womanly hips and breasts. Mama said they must impress their new mistress, and in her new dress which fit so wonderfully, Lucinda felt not like the common plantation slave she was but instead like an African princess!

Mama jabbered all morning in high-pitched Gullah, a voice almost like that of a young girl, to Abraham, the chief slave among them. She asked all kinds of questions. Abraham paid her little mind, only once or twice answering with a nod of his head and a low moaning uh-huh or un-huh.

"Mary, there be heaps an' heaps o' Africans," Abraham finally answered Lucinda's mama. "Heaps an' heaps."

Mama had brought some rice cakes wrapped in oiled paper, and she handed some to each of them, making sure Master Jimmy Johnson got the biggest piece so he would not tell she had sneaked food from the plantation kitchen. But now the calming rocking of the river and the warmth of the unblinking sun had drained Mama's energy, and she snored loudly beside Lucinda on the rice sacks.

Mama once told Lucinda she was the keenest little nigger girl on the whole plantation, the way Lucinda could at a young age mimic white folk's talk, or remember the ingredients to a pumpkin pie, down to the three pinches of cloves and cinnamon spice, and the color and the amount of wood coals in the oven needed to get the pie to bake clean through just right, or which herbs from the garden went in tea and which, when cooked with venison, helped take the gameness out, or how she remembered Bur Rabbit or Bur Fox tales her grand mammy told her long ago. Mama said she knew Lucinda was special from the day she was born. Luckily, Lucinda paid no mind to Mama's sayings because if she had she'd have been thought the sassiest and most uppity little nigger girl ever lived. And Mama's mood could change fast. More than once when she thought Lucinda had sassed her, Mama raised thick blood welts on Lucinda's bottom with the swift lashings of a bamboo switch.

Lucinda had heard a dying man's life will flash before his eyes at the moment of his death, and so it seemed to her now, as Radcliffe Place Plantation grew further distant up river, she could suddenly recall her whole life. The boat drifted gently downriver like a blue heron feather floating in a stream. Lucinda closed her eyes. Her mind drifted too as she recalled memories and moments of her life on the plantation.

In a dark room, Lucinda reached out for a candle on the wooden pine table next to her pallet. She blazed a broom straw from the embers in the fireplace and lit the candle. The flame's flickering light cast dancing shadows on the cabin walls. Mama's pallet was empty. She's already up and at the Big House kitchen, thought Lucinda. She hurriedly dressed in her grey work dress, tied her hair up in a scarf, and put on a clean apron, tying it in place tightly around her slender waist. As she dressed, she said a prayer, "Sweet Jesus, bless us this day. Look over Mama and me. Watch over the Africans as they go about their tasks." Then she added, "Bless Master Radcliffe and Miss Elizabeth and the white folks too."

She hurried from the cabin across the plantation yard. The sky was grey with clouds, a dull pearl of light rising up in the east. The morning bugle call echoed across the plantation. The roosters crowed in answer. Several Africans were already at their tasks, dark figures hard to see in the gloom, calling out "mornin'" as they passed. They carried buckets to milk the cows, mixed slop for the hogs, gathered hoes for the fields, and fetched feed and water for the mules and horses.

She made her way to the kitchen at the back of the Big House. She entered and saw Mama bent over stoking the fire in the cook-hearth.

"Mama, why you not wake me up?" Lucinda asked, rubbing her eyes with her hand.

"I reckoned you wanted a li'l extra shut eye."

"Thank you, Mama."

"That's alright, chile." Mama handed Lucinda a plate of hominy and roast pork and a cup of clabber. "Here be some breakfast for you. Now you hurry and finish up and run to the springhouse and fetch a jug o' milk. Uncle Jacob say Massa Radcliffe and Massa Johnson and Miss Elizabeth goin' fox huntin' this mornin' and they gonna want they breakfast soon enough."

The cool, sweet-smelling springhouse was down by the creek, and as Lucinda walked along the path, she could see the rice fields off in the distance. The last of the harvest had been taken in as it was almost November and the field stubble was being burned before plowing under and working the fields for next year's planting. The morning mist climbed off the rice ponds, and the water gleamed like a silver tea set.

She balanced the jug of milk on her head, holding it with one hand as she toted it back to the kitchen. The morning clouds had begun to break. She looked out over the plantation. The mule and horse barns, oxen stockyard, hen house, pigsty, pens for goat, sheep, and hunting dogs, and the corn, potato, and cotton fields spread out in all directions from the Big House. The blacksmith's shop, which also served as the cooper's and the wheelwright's workplace, was halfway between the Big House and the slaves' cabins. Although she was not to go there, she had more than once stuck her face up to the cracks between the sideboards and witnessed the hissing heat that fumed from the iron works and the loud bang of the blacksmith's hammer as he wrought some wagon wheel's tongue or ploughshare. The slave cabins were grouped in rows like a little town. The slaves called it the Settlement. The older slaves said Radcliffe Place's slave dwellings were once built in the wattle and daub way from Africa, but new slave cabins were constructed at the time of the rebuilding of the Big House following the fire. Hundreds of extra bricks were cut and fired for the cabins. The Africans' dwellings were now made of cypress boards and brick, raised pine lumber floors, fireplaces with fires, which burned winter and summer because it was bad luck to let the fire go out, shuttered open-air windows, wooden front porches, and swept-clean dirt yards. Slave garden plots of squash, yams, okra, greens, and flowers grew close by.

The slaves who worked Master Radcliffe's horses stood with five of the hunting horses saddled and gathered in the yard. The slaves brushed the horses' manes, coats, and tails, tying the tails with strips of leather. The horses' tan coats glistened in the morning sun. The fox hounds had been released from their pen and the pack moved about the yard as one, circling and turning back near the horses, baying with deep raspy barks, tails lifted skyward. "Whaooo," one of the slaves called to the dogs as they darted between the horses, barking roughly, their noses to the ground. The dogs hushed at the command. In a dark lair somewhere in the woods a fox awaits discovery and death, Lucinda thought as she watched.

She returned to the kitchen with the jug of milk.

"Go help Uncle Jacob serve the table before Massa Radcliffe's breakfast," Mama told her. "When you's finish that, go up and help Liddy make the beds."

The dining hall was one of Lucinda's favorite rooms in the Big House. A great mahogany buffet brought from England by Master Radcliffe's father had been saved from the fire that nearly destroyed the house many years back, and the buffet reached from one side to another along the back wall in the dining hall. Silver serving trays and a silver tea set with bone china floral-patterned tea cups were set on the buffet. A marble fireplace measured the narrow wall, carved cornices embellished the ceiling, and the walls glowed in burgundy and teal. Across from the buffet a huge mirror in a fancy gold frame hung above the wainscoting, reflecting the entire room. Midday dinners, in the brief moments before anyone entered the room, the reflection in the mirror of the table lit by flickering candelabras and set with platters of pork, turkey, oysters, bread, rice, okra, sweet meats, perlow, fruit pies, and cut flowers, awakened within her a haunting feeling as if all life were suddenly stilled, and time itself had abruptly ceased.

This morning, Master Radcliffe sat at the head of the grand mahogany table dressed in a black hunting jacket, white breeches, a white vest, and long black riding boots. His black riding helmet was on the table beside him. Master Jimmy Johnson and Miss Elizabeth were dressed the same except they wore red jackets.

"We'll be back late morning," Master Radcliffe was saying to no one in particular, his salt-and-pepper colored hair handsome against his hunting jacket and vest. "Otherwise the heat will be too great for the horses."

"Father," Miss Elizabeth said to him, "spare the fox this time, won't you? Don't let the dogs get him."

"What's the use of hunting if you spare the fox?" Master Johnson asked.

"Why, it's the pleasure of the morning ride, the thrill of the chase," Elizabeth answered him. "Father knows that, Cousin."

Lucinda carefully removed their plates when the meal was over and returned to the kitchen. She heard the hunting horn sound and saw through the open door Master Radcliffe and Miss Elizabeth and Master Johnson ride away with two slaves on horseback behind them.

"Look as though the weather gonna be good for washin' today," Mama said. "Now go upstairs and help Liddy and start gettin' things ready. And don't you forget to empty the chamber pots."

With the beds made and the rooms cleaned in the Big House, Lucinda and four other slave women went to the well to draw water, returned to fill the big cast iron wash pots and build a fire. When the water was hot, they took turns working a wooden pestle to churn the lye wash. They repeated the process with fresh water to rinse the wash clean. They then hung the clothes on the line to dry. Later they would be taken inside to iron.

Lucinda's daydream waned, swept away like drift wood carried along by the river. She watched the water flow as her thoughts filled with other images and memories of the past.

Master Radcliffe seemed not to care about events outside the plantation, but he often had visitors who would talk with him and seek his advice. Before Lucinda and Mama were moved to Charleston, his Excellency Governor Thomas Bennett and an elderly man, the Honorable Charles Pinckney, visited Radcliffe Place Plantation. The old man wore clothes and a tri-folded hat like the painting of Master Radcliffe's father that hung on the library wall. While she helped the old house slave, Uncle Jacob, serve at the dining room table, then later take tea and rum glasses into the library where Master Radcliffe and his guests had retired, Lucinda overheard part of their talk.

"Gentlemen," Master Pinckney said as she went about removing a tea tray, "slavery must not only stand, but continue to expand in territory. Otherwise, the very survival of our means and way of life is at peril. But it is the unfettered movement of the free Negro which is our greatest threat."

There was a long silence in the room. Outside the crickets echoed throughout the wilderness. Something had excited the hunting dogs and their raspy yelps carried from their pen across the field to the plantation house. Inside the library, there was the soft tinkling of cups as she and Jacob cleared the table.

"Congressman," Master Radcliffe finally broke the silence as after deep reflection, "I concur with your sentiments completely. However, as a planter, I must tell you I am afraid it's we who have sown the seeds of our predicament."

Lucinda heard voices come from downriver, awakening her from her reverie. She sat up and looked about her. A barge flat loaded with barrels and manned by a handful of Africans appeared ahead of them at a bend in the river. Abraham called out in greeting as the schooner sailed past. Mama still slept soundly. Lucinda looked straight up. The sky was still a radiant, crystal blue, so clear it was as if she could see forever. She seemed to be still while the sky moved past her overhead. She leaned against the sacks and closed her eyes again.

She was serving in the dining room. Mistress Nelly had seated herself alone at the table waiting for the others. Lucinda reached for the pitcher of buttermilk when her hand accidently slipped. The pitcher spilled to the floor.

"You foolish girl," Mistress Nelly shrieked and with the table's silver candlestick she struck Lucinda hard on the wrist. Lucinda's hand went limp. Tears filled her eyes. At that moment, Miss Elizabeth walked into the room.

"She's made a terrible mess and hurt herself in the process," Mistress Nelly said. "Get someone in here to clean this up. And find out what's wrong with her."

The doctor was sent for in Charleston. No one ever asked Lucinda what happened, not even Mama. From then on, Mistress Nelly only spoke to Lucinda to give a command and she avoided looking Lucinda in the eyes.

While waiting for the doctor, Miss Elizabeth had taken Lucinda aside.

"Lucinda," Elizabeth said sternly, "Mother says she doesn't know what crazy ideas you've gotten in your head. We taught you to read the Scriptures for your own betterment, for the salvation of your soul, and for you to serve as a good influence on the other slaves. You will do what my mother tells you. Make no mistake about it. Or you'll be whipped for being disobedient. Remember the verses from St. Paul, 'Servants obey in all things your masters with all fear, according to the flesh, not with eye-service, as menpleasers, but in singleness of heart, fearing God.' And Saint Peter wrote, 'Servants be subject to your masters with all fear, not only to the good and gentle, but also to the forward.' You must accept your condition no matter what and show us the utmost loyalty and obedience."

"Miss Elizabeth I didn't . . ."

"I don't want to talk to you about this ever again. Do you understand?"

"Yes'm," Lucinda said.

Lucinda's recollection dissolved like a spoon of sugar stirred in a cup of tea. Her river of memory rolled on, shifting to other vivid images of her past.

Elizabeth sat at her vanity table. "Come brush my hair," she said. She looked at herself in the mirror as Lucinda came and removed the tortoise shell hair combs one at a time until Elizabeth's dark tresses fell across her shoulders and her back. She shook her head, bowing forward, exposing the nape of her neck, the skin white as fresh cream. She moved and sat on her bed. Lucinda took the brush and held Elizabeth's hair in her hand as she gently pulled the brush through the strands.

"Get up on the bed and lean against my back so you can reach," Elizabeth instructed her. Lucinda obeyed.

The room grew dark. Lucinda glanced toward the windows. Black clouds had gathered in the sky and blocked the sun. A roll of thunder rumbled overhead as the wind suddenly threw rain up against the windows and splattered on the roof above them.

"No, harder," Elizabeth said in a husky whisper. She took the brush out of Lucinda's hand. "Like this," she said and pulled the brush firmly, forcibly through her hair.

The rain whipped up against the house in a dull roar. A blue flash lighted up the window, followed by a loud clap of thunder rolling away in the distance.

Lucinda brushed the hair, tugging at the ends, pulling out the tangles. Then she brushed near Elizabeth's head, pulling hard, taking the brush all the way down past her shoulders. Elizabeth's hair began to soften and glisten, drawing fine and silky. Lucinda could see Elizabeth's face in the vanity mirror. Her eyes were closed. Her face wore a look Lucinda had never seen before. Elizabeth bit down slightly on her bottom lip. Her eyes remained shut. Lucinda continued to stroke with the brush, leaning up against Elizabeth's back, taking the brush and starting at the top of her head and pulling the brush hard down through to the ends of her hair. Elizabeth's breath came in short, shallow pants. Lucinda thought she heard her moan, but then decided it must have been the wind creaking against the house. She thought Elizabeth had gone to sleep and Lucinda paused for a moment but Elizabeth turned her head slightly in expectation. She brushed until her arms were tired, and she continued to brush, and brush again, one long caress at a time. The hair was soft as silk in her hand and seemed in the darkened room, as black as molasses.

The room grew quiet. The rain had ended.

"Miss Elizabeth," Lucinda whispered.

"Mmmm," Elizabeth whimpered softly.

This must be what she looks like when she's sleeping, Lucinda thought.

"Miss Elizabeth," she whispered again.

The blue eyes opened and Elizabeth looked around as if waking from a dream. She climbed down off the big rice planter's bed and patted her clothes into place. She took a step forward and slapped Lucinda across her face with her open palm.

"Leave me," she said, not looking at Lucinda's face.

Lucinda was so stunned she stood for a moment frozen in place. She then turned and quickly left the room, the tears stinging in her eyes. They had grown up together almost like sisters. At least like friends. Then to have a wall build up to separate them, one the master, the other the slave, one with utter power over the other, the other subservient until the end, the strangest of relationships.

Her reflections on Miss Elizabeth faded away like field mist in the morning sun. Lucinda peeked to find Master Jimmy Johnson standing in the front of the schooner looking at her. The riverbank passed by so quickly she grew dizzy from watching. She reentered the shadowy world of memory.

Sometimes in the evenings after the day's tasks were done, when it was not too hot or not too cold, she and Mama would sit outside on their cabin porch steps and weave baskets of sweet grass. Sometimes they worked quietly without speaking; sometimes they talked.

"Mama, why are we slaves?" Lucinda once asked. She often wondered why the Africans were servants to the whites.

"I don't know, chile," her mama answered. "I ask myself that question sometimes. Some things the Good Lord don't want us to know, I reckon. We just got to be thankful for what we got. One day Jesus'll come and take us home and then we's be free." That was all Mama said.

Sitting on their cabin porch steps, her nimble fingers weaving the dry sweet grass into baskets to fan rice or hold bread or store seeds until planting time, Lucinda looked about the yard. Some of the slaves were still busy with their evening meals and she could see them in their cabins through the open doors. Slave children ran and hollered, skipped rope, or played marbles. Some of the African women weeded and hoed the slaves' vegetable patch. Somewhere across the way, she could hear the plucked strings of the qudugudo and a woman singing to her children.

"What was the plantation like when you was a little girl?" Lucinda asked Mama.

"The slaves suffer more then," Mama said. "Massa Radcliffe's pappy, he been the Massa and the plantation ain't this big. The crops be rice and yams and corn and a li'l indigo. Not so many slaves. Most of the field hands they be from Africa. Massa Radcliffe's pappy he been hard on the slaves. More whippins. Work day and night. The slaves barely had 'nuff to eat. Me and yo' grand mammy had it good 'pared to the others. We's worked in the Big House like we's do. The Big House not this big. This been afore the fire."

Mama wasn't always so talkative, so Lucinda probed further.

"What about my pappy?"

"He been born in Africa," Mama answered. "He been made a slave there and sold and put on the boat from Africa to Charleston. The ol' Massa Radcliffe buy yo' pappy at the slave market. First yo' pappy talk just in the Afric' way and that's how come I get to know him. At night I learnt him some of the Eng'ish words and way of talkin'. He been keen, like you. No time he been a field driver. He hate doin' that. He hate to work the Africans so hard." Her mama's face suddenly squeezed up and she looked like she was going to cry. "If it weren't for that snake bite and then the fever."

"You miss him, Mama?"

"Well, that been a long time now, chile. You been just a li'l baby gal then," Mama said. "But I ain't knowed another man since."

"Mama," Lucinda asked, "is it true what they say, that when we die we go back to Africa to be with our ancestors?"

"That what yo' grand mammy say," Mama said. "Maybe we's go to Africa afore we's go to heaven." Her mama twisted on the porch step, then stood up stiffly. "You full o' questions, chile" she said. "Time for bed. Mornin' come mighty quick."

Lucinda opened her eyes. The black-barked oak trees leaned from the riverbank over the water's edge. Spanish moss hung thick from the branches, grey and ghostly as a spider's web. She closed her eyes again.

She remembered being taught to read. Every morning, Mistress Nelly practiced a daily devotional with her daughter, which included reading the Bible aloud. Lucinda began to join them.

"Mother," Elizabeth said to Mistress Radcliffe one day, "Lucinda wants to learn to read. Don't you Lucinda?"

"Yes'm."

"I guess there's no harm," Mistress Neely said. "She needs some Bible learning." The daily lessons began. As Elizabeth learned and improved, so did Lucinda.

"Now you try it," Elizabeth said to Lucinda.

"In the be-gin-in' God cre-at de . . .

"Cre-a-ted."

"Cre-at-ted de . . . "

"The," Mistress Nelly said. "Look, Lucinda, put your tongue between your teeth like this and blow out. The. The."

"The heaven and the earth."

"Good!" Elizabeth said excitedly.

"She's a smart little pickaninney," Mistress Nelly said.

Miss Elizabeth even gave Lucinda a Bible as a gift. As Lucinda grew older, she began to read to Mama aloud from the Bible each night before they went to sleep, no matter how tired they may have been. And whenever she could, she studied Miss Elizabeth's spelling book and drilled with a quill.

The memory slipped away, replaced by the childhood recollection of her grand mammy.

Her grand mammy sat on a crude wood chair by the fire. Lucinda climbed up in her lap and snuggled up against her, clutching the black-faced rag doll her grand mammy had made for her.

"Grand mammy, tell me a story."

"Tell you a story, chile? How 'bout how come Bro Cooter tote he cabin on he back?" '

"Yeah!"

Her grand mammy began. "Time been Bro Cooter no tote he cabin on he back. He been living with the other creaters on the marsh in he cabin down by de river. One day Buh Cooter eh spy Buh Alligator when he been on the river bank."

"'Brother Alligator' say Bro Cooter, 'yous got the biggest mouth and the sharpest teeth all the God creaters. How come yo mouth so big and yo teeth so sharp?'"

"'Me eats the marsh grass,' say Bro Alligator. 'My teeth be big an sharp for to chaw.'"

"Now Bro Cooter, he eat marsh grass. He mouth not big an he teeth not sharp like Buh Alligator. He afraid Bro Alligator be too schemey. So Bro Cooter, he say to himself, next time me go where Bro Alligator be on the bank of the river, me tote my cabin on my back. That way, need be, me hide in my cabin. Me no worry bout Bro Alligator and he big mouth and he sharp teeth.

"Sho nuff, by and by Bro Cooter he crawl by Bro Alligator, an Bro Alligator he chop down on Bro Cooter with he big mouth and he sharp teeth. Bro Cooter, he hide safe in he cabin. He cabin on he back hard er the rock and some Bro Alligator teeth they break off. Bro Cooter he jus' keep on acrawlin'."

"'Look what you do, you break my teeth,' Buh Alligator holler."

"Say Buh Cooter, 'Me not break 'em, Brother Alligatur. You break 'em when me you try eat.'"

"An that be how come till this day, Bro Cooter tote he cabin on he back where ever he go."

Lucinda's eyes fell shut when her grand mammy finished, and she slept peacefully in her grand mammy's arms, still holding the doll to her chest.

Mama shifted her weight on the rice sacks. She was still asleep, her snores like the drone of the plantation lumber mill. Lucinda kept her own eyes closed. She slipped back into her memories of Radcliffe Place.

She remembered the last day of her grand mammy's life. Her grand mammy had been sick for many days, and at the end, she was stricken to her straw mattress where she lay weak and helpless. Mama had spent every moment she could at her bedside. A grey, cold dawn broke over the plantation the day her grand mammy died.

"Oh, Lord, she gone" Mama kept saying. Mama cried and cried, and when she cried so did Lucinda.

Lucinda asked, "Mama, where did grand mammy go? Did she go back to Africa?"

"Yes, chile," Mama said between her tears, "she go back to Africa."

"Will we see her when we go back?" Lucinda asked.

"Yes, chile, we's see yo' grand mammy when we's go back."

The death of a slave was not uncommon, but only as Lucinda grew older did she grasp how death was like a coon scratching round the door at night, always searching for a way to slip in. A slave died most every year, sometimes more in winter. Most were babies lost to the fever, or old slaves too weak to live. When a slave died, the Africans gathered for all-night dances and chants, singing and lamentation held until early morning light. They prayed to the African gods for the dead soul's safe journey back to the land of their ancestors.

They buried the Africans in a field near the edge of the big woods. Lucinda shied away from the graveyard because she was afeard of haints, but sometimes she gazed from a distance and wondered how many slaves were buried there. She wondered if God knew each one's name because there were only axe-hewn pine headboards with no names on some of the graves and some graves weren't marked at all. Her grand mammy and grand pappy and pappy were buried there, somewhere, maybe with a pine slat for them but she did not know. She guessed no one but God knew. She thought one day she would be buried in that field, and she wondered if a marker would head her grave, and if anyone would remember her before the angel Gabriel blew his horn to wake the dead on the morning of Judgment Day.

Not all of the slaves' singing was for sad occasions like funerals. The Africans also sang in the fields as they worked or as they went about their tasks. The lead singer would sing a few words, and then the whole of the slaves in the field would sing back. This was how the slaves kept time together as they struck with the hoe in the rice fields, or struck with the hoe in the cotton rows, or thrashed the rice with their sticks. Sometimes music was for merry making when the slaves could carve out time. Christmas Day the Africans would gather for someone to play the Yoruban qudugudo or molo or banjo and washboard. They sang spirituals at prayer meetings, some she remembered her grand mammy singing. Mama said when she was little the slaves made drums from hollowed out logs and stretched hides and beat out chants and dances like they do in Africa. Warm nights when a full moon glimmered in the blue-black sky, Mama said the drumbeats echoed from plantation to plantation up and down the river. But the masters of the plantations stopped it all. The masters said the slaves were using the drums to talk to each other, perhaps to stir up a slave insurrection.

Echoes of drumbeats mixed in her mind with memories of the screams of a tortured slave.

"One o' the field hands done gone up and run away," Mama had confided to Lucinda. The news of the escape had passed among the slaves like the spread of a wildfire through drought-dry pines. "Massa sent the bounty man after him." Mama rolled her eyes heavenward. "Lord look after him if they catch him."

Within a week, the runaway had been captured. Lucinda heard the slaves in the yard begin to talk excitedly. She halted her work, and went to a window to peer out. A man on horseback was riding through the gate of the plantation with the slave on foot in chains beside him. The man on the horse nudged a rifle into the back of the chained man, prodding him in short halting steps, the chains dragging in the dust between his feet. As the man and the slave came across the yard, it seemed every slave on the plantation turned and watched. No one dared speak or move. Slowly, the slaves returned to their tasks. The captured man's feet linked to his chains by iron hoops around his ankles, his hands shackled in front at his wrists, an iron collar fitted around his neck, secured to his waist and his hands and feet. The man on the horse, and the captive slave cast long black shadows on the ground across the yard as the late afternoon sun burned down on them.

The bounty man handed over the slave to one of the Irish overseers, and the slave's chains fastened to iron-hooks on the side of the barn. A whip had been fetched for all to see the lashing. One of the other field hands, a great black hulk of a man, had the grim task of administering the thrashing, his face without expression, like a rock on the ground or the face of a dead man. The overseer stripped off the runaway's torn shirt. The big, black arm of the punisher raised the whip to strike, catching at its highest point a glint of sunlight on the metal tips of the cat-o'-nine-tails, which winked at Lucinda before flashing down in a swift movement. The snap of the whip on the naked flesh was like a gun shot fired across the plantation. A flock of black crows in the trees at the edge of the yard suddenly rose in the air and winged their way off into the distance. The whipped slave cried out and drew up in pain. He turned his head and grimaced with terror at his abuser. His brow ran with sweat. The shot of the whip sounded again. His cries of whimpering and pleading echoed across the yard. Twenty times, Lucinda counted, the whip struck the slave's back and each time he cried out until he finally sank against the wall of the barn and was still. The ground at his feet was dark with sweat and blood. At the end, they dragged him away to one of the cabins.

Lucinda fought back her tears as she watched. She knew whippings were reserved for the most serious offenses; stealing and running away. This was the first she had seen so up-close and so brutal. She cringed each time the whip slapped against the slave's back. Her stomach knotted up with a sick feeling.

She often wondered why God made some folks slave and some folks free. She thought she understood in heaven we would all be the same and praise God as one. But she did not understand why things were different here on earth. The ministers who visited the plantation always told the slaves to obey their masters and be content with the life in which God had placed them. She did not then understand the cruelty men would go to to achieve their ends or to protect their way of life, their families, their property, and their riches. For the first time in her life she felt afraid, and cast with a burden of vague dread that gnawed at her insides like the worm rotting the apple from the core.

Lucinda looked about the boat. Mama's snores rattled up against her.

"Uncle Abraham," Lucinda asked, "how much longer till we get there."

"A li'l ways yet," was his answer.

Master Radcliffe strictly forbade knowledge of female slaves by the men of his household or his overseers, unlike so many other slave owners, as she was soon to see when she found a large number of yellow or light-colored mulattos in Charleston, and so she still had her honeycomb intact, having been under the watchful eye of her mama or the Radcliffe family, and never alone long enough with any of the slave men for deflowering. In the year after the birth of his child, Master Jimmy Johnson had looked at her more than once, especially when he did not think she knew he was doing so.

And there were times recently, in the quiet stillness of hot late afternoons, after the morning's house chores were done and the noon meal had been served and cleared away and the kitchen cleaned, when the household took a brief respite from the toil and the heat and Mama was granted a quick nap with her head resting in her hands on the kitchen table, when Lucinda would steal away to their narrow sleeping quarters and quickly undress and in a luxurious comfort take the cracked hand mirror Miss Elizabeth had given her and hold it in front of her face to view the woman she had become. Her long hair, long for a slave, had curled into locks and she always tied it back with a calico cord unless she was sleeping. Her skin was dark chocolate, almost black, and her red lips, although full, were not thick and shaped like a little heart at the top. Her eyes looked back at herself like twin suns that shone with a dark light. Her eyelashes were long and silky, which gave a sleepy softness to her face, and her skin, because she didn't work outside and ate the same food and meat served at the Radcliffe's table, glowed. Her teeth were good and gleamed white against her face and pinkish mouth. Her throat was longish and slender, like her grand mammy's, and her slender shoulders and arms sloped smoothly to her breasts, somewhat large for her slender frame. She would hold the cracked mirror so that she could fully see their curves and shape, her dark nipples large as an expensive coin and the color of hazelnut. Her nipples would harden as she worked her hand over her breasts, now sensitive and warm against her palm. Afterwards she would cling to this glorious and refreshing feeling until the very final moment, then quickly dress and leave to awaken Mama, still snoring with head down and dreaming of who knows what at the kitchen table.

The boat made a sudden quick jerking movement, snatching Lucinda up from her fancy. The river had opened into a great expanse of water. "Oh ya!" Abraham called out. "Oh ya," the men called back as they moved quickly in place to work the sails and oars. She had never seen so much water, which seemed to go on forever. The waves became bigger and her stomach was like a butter churn going up and down, up and down, up and down. She tried not to be sick. Mama too had a sick look on her face and sang softly,

"*Walk on the water, sweet Jesus,*
Jesus save my soul.
Walk on the water sweet Jesus,
Jesus carry me home."

The men sailed the boat toward the shore. There where the sky met the land and the land met the water was Charleston! She could almost reach out and touch the city with her hand. She thought of Miss Elizabeth's box of jewels with gold and precious stones white and green and blue and red. That was how Charleston looked to her, like brilliant jewels spread out in rows upon a table. She could see the spires of the churches reach up like arms trying to touch the heavens. A big bridge crossed over the Ashley River. Edifices and big houses crowded almost to the water, overlooking the marsh and the river bordered with trees of oak and pine. What she saw reminded her of the rows of cabins of the Settlement at Radcliffe Place, but the houses and buildings in Charleston were so big and grand!

Master Radcliffe's schooner sailed up the Cooper River and rounded the land toward the wharves. Sunlight glared off the water. The wind blew steady. Ships with unfurled sails floated at anchor. Schooners and clippers, flying flags of so many patterns she could not count them all, flocked in the harbor like swans displayed on a lake. Wharves extended into the water where warehouses lined the edge. The stench of tar and pitch smoke charged the air. The wharves were crowded with men at work unloading barrels and bales. She could hear their swarthy shouts carry across the water.

Abraham and the slaves carefully worked the boat up to one of the wharves crowded with dugout canoes, schooners, and barges, and tied it to the wharf by rope. Lucinda and Mama stood up on shaky legs. Master Johnson went to send for a wagon to take them to their new mistress and the slaves began unloading the provisions from the boat.

Two black men stood near them on the wharf. One of the men was little and wore big side-whiskers. The other man watched her with dark, probing eyes. She had never seen a black man with such a bold stare.

She walked past them and saw as they stood next to each other the little man made the other man look taller than he really was. The man who stared at her was thick chested, round as a cooper's barrel, his shoulders broad like his waist. His thick forearms showed solid beneath his shirtsleeves, arms of a man who worked with his hands. His head was bald up front, and his wiry hair was grey like the color of sheep's wool, his short whiskers and moustache almost white. The face round-shaped, his skin dark black, weathered like an old horse saddle. His lips hung thick and meaty on his face. He watched with his dark eyes, eyes like the eagles she had seen high in the tree tops of the woods at Radcliffe Place Plantation, eyes watching warily each smallest movement on the forest floor. His clothes were the same grey coarse Negro cloth the slaves wore, but his face, his manner, had nothing of the slave about them. There was something different in his bearing: pride.

"*Qui est-tu, Mademoiselle*?" the man spoke but she did not understand his words, and was unsure if he was talking to her. Lucinda and Mama and the slave men walked down the wharf to where the road began and their wagon was waiting.

"Who be those men?" she asked Abraham.

"Chile," he answered, "the big 'un be the luck'est nigger man ever live, got a pack with God o' the devil, one o' the other! Ole man Denmark Vesey he name. Won the lott'ry afore ye born, 'n' buy he own freedom. Now the fanc'est free nigger carpenter in all of Charlestown. The other one the conjurer Gullah Jack." Abraham gave her an all-knowing look. "Best ye be shy o'them."

She climbed on the back of the dray wagon and snuggled between Abraham and Mama. The reins snapped, and the wagon creaked and shuttered to a start, the hooves of the mule began their *ca-plop, ca-plop*. Mama's eyes were big as an owl's eyes and she gestured this way and that way and kept saying to Lucinda in Gullah, "Look! Lucinda, Look!" Lucinda too stared all around with her own big eyes as she silently pondered the start of her new life in Charlestown.

The Holy City

On a drizzly spring morning in April 1670, the British frigate *Carolina*, overfilled with ninety-three British settlers, navigated into the natural harbor where two rivers came together as they flowed into the Atlantic. A clenched-fist-shaped peninsula jutted between the rivers' confluence. Winding up a creek, which narrowed between marsh grasses and tall pines, the ship anchored and the passengers came ashore some distance from where the city would be later built. The colonizers christened the original settlement Albemarle Point. The settlers named the rivers for Lord Ashely Cooper, the chief Lord Proprietor for the Carolina Colony. In August, the first slave arrived from the colony of Virginia, described as "one lusty Negro man." Other slaves soon followed in growing numbers.

The investment Proprietors in England, to help ensure the King would remain interested in the venture soon choose the name Charles Town in honor of the Crown. A hundred-fifty years later, in 1820, the city was the sixth most populated in the Republic. The census of that year counted over twenty-five thousand: just less than half the city's population was white, a little more than half, African slaves, with almost fifteen hundred free persons of color.

Major harbor towns are populated by transients from the world over. In 1822, so was the seaport of Charleston. Rambling through the filthy alleyways, imbibing rum in a tatty grogshop near the docks, or wandering at the wharves where men worked under the yoke of bondage, the creole lingoes of the West Indies, and tongues of Europe and West Africa confronted your ears. Port cities were where ideas and schemes were exchanged along with the trade of goods. Revolts, plots, conspiracies, revolutions, *coup d'états*, and murders hatched in harbor towns. Abolitionist ideas and anti-slavery pamphlets entered Charleston's harbor through the hands of black sailors, pamphlets sent by those in the North, or England, or Sierra Leone opposed to slavery.

The Charleston authorities exercised their power to prevent such publications from reaching and influencing the slaves. Since 1740, punitive laws were imposed in the colony to thwart slaves from being taught to read and write. The sole purpose was to discourage the spread of ideas of freedom. The effort was now led by the city's Intendant James H. Hamilton, Jr. But the authorities were not always entirely successful.

The Intendant complained to South Carolina's Governor, Thomas Bennett, "Numerous slaveholders in this city ignore the law."

"A slave who can read and write is often more beneficial to his master," the Governor stated matter-of-factly, "especially, if the slave is employed or hired out in a mechanic craft." The governor was one of the largest slaveholders in the city, and employed hired-out slaves at his lumber and rice mills. "Some owners out of Christian sympathy wish for their slaves to be able to read the Bible. There are slaves who do all they can to learn to read on their own. The African Church even teaches black folks to read."

"And should be stopped from doing so," the Intendant said firmly.

"How can we serve impracticable fines on every slaveholder in the city who allows a slave to learn to read because it increases the slave's worth?"

"Nonetheless, something must be done," the Intendant said firmly, "for one day there will be a price to pay."

"If you're ever questioned, show the Patrol this," Mistress Johnson instructed Lucinda. "If you wish not to be punished, don't lose it."

"Yes'm."

Lucinda read: *My servant Lucinda has permission to be on errands and go to the markets for provisions. Sarah Johnson.*

"Tuesday will show you where the markets are. Pay attention how to get there."

"Yes'm."

When Lucinda went for victuals or to the cisterns to fetch water, she walked as fast as she could, taking the extra time she made to explore about her. After a few weeks, she had been from the Battery nearly to Hampstead, from South to East Bay, and from the wharves on the Cooper River across the city toward the bridge over the Ashley. The city reflected a *mélange* of different influences, many new to her: English architecture in classic columned Doric and Ionic style, bright colors of the West Indies, the sea-borne plantation homes of Barbados, flowers and gardens in tropical lushness, all spun with the syncopated Negro rhythm of West Africa.

This morning Lucinda stood at the crossing of Broad and Meeting streets where she could see the Custom Exchange at the end of Broad, a great building beside the Cooper River which housed Charleston's post office and where ships entering the port were registered and fees collected. She walked toward the Exchange, past slaves unloading mule-drawn drays and stacking barrels in front of shops, past the grand houses with balconies overlooking Broad Street, past the grogshops, past the grocers. Structures on both sides of the street, facades of brick or stucco or cypress, rose up around her, some weathered and grey; others painted white, indigo, or cream. The stink of garbage dumped on the street made her stomach squeamish. "Mornin'," Lucinda greeted the African women who passed by her with filled baskets balanced on their heads. Palmetto palms and live oaks hung with Spanish moss offered her shade from the sun. A wary dog watched her, scratching at its flea-ridden half-starved ribs with one hind leg. Carriages and wagons jostled noisily down the dusty street. She heard the clamor of voices coming from beside the Exchange. She walked closer.

"A prime gang of Negroes!" shouted the auctioneer, "Accomplished in rice and cotton cultivation!"

A slave auction! Lucinda tried to stay hidden from view, and watched. A long platform stood in the middle of the street, some Africans in loincloths displayed on it, exposed to the bidders.

"These Negroes are very orderly and well-disciplined and have been organized and worked as a gang," the auctioneer exclaimed.

A score of planters and gentlemen dressed in fancy swallowtail coats and tall hats crowded up to the table. One planter signaled the auctioneer to let him have a closer look and pointed to one of the women slaves, who was made to step down off the table. The bidder examined her carefully, turned her around, poked her with his cane, and peered into her open mouth. Two auctioneers, one at each end of the table, called out the biddings and egged on the bidders, chanting the praises of their goods. The five slaves, three men and two women, sold for $3,100. Lucinda was amazed and felt a strange pride that the Africans commanded such a large sum.

One man in the crowd was selling his horse. Another man drove around in a circle, bawling out to the spectators to make an offer for his carriage and horses. Next, a family group of four slaves stood upon the table, a man and woman with two young children who clung to their mama's legs, wide-eyed fear fixed on their faces. The auctioneer called out for bids: "Do I hear an offer of $1,000?" Several of the bidders signaled their desire. "I have $1,000 bid for the drove. Do I hear $1,100?"

Then what Lucinda thought must be a husband and wife brought no bidders as a pair, so the auctioneers sold the man by himself, then the woman, each to different buyers. Like animals, Lucinda grieved, they buy and sell us like pigs, or oxen, or mules. She rushed away to her errands. She could not rid her mind of the way the Africans looked as they stood on the platform, the sculptured shapes of their skulls, the thick black curly hair cut close, the wide-eyed whites of their eyes stark against the sable glow of their faces. The idea that one day she might be sold, that one day she could be forced to work in the fields, terrified her. She imagined herself in chains, stripped and exhibited on the auctioneers' table, her future uncertain, abandoned to the fate of the auction block. She asked herself repeatedly, why are we slaves? Is it God's work or is it men's? She wondered at the stories she had heard at the Radcliffe House. Elizabeth told Lucinda the Bible tale of the curse of the sons of Ham. Elizabeth read from the book of Genesis, 'a servant of servants shall he be unto his brethren.' "Your black skin, that's the sign of the curse," Elizabeth said. "The Africans are doomed to a destiny of slavery."

Lucinda hurried down the narrow street by the river. Rows of warehouses crammed the waterfront. Men stared at her while they worked. They whistled and hollered. Suddenly she filled with panic. She had somehow become confused and lost her way. She walked quickly, almost at a run, and darted away from the river at the next street. Out of her sight until she turned the corner, two members of the Patrol stood at the edge of the building. She bumped up hard against one of them, her forehead banging his chin. Lucinda tumbled to the ground, the sweet-grass basket in her hand knocked loose, rolling into the street. Before she could say a word or get to her feet, the Patrol drew his bayonet and raised his arm, ready to strike.

"No, Massa," Lucinda cried, "Massa, don' kill me!" Even in her fear, she knew she should play the simple kowtowing slave.

The Patrol lowered his arm, but continued to grip his bayonet tightly in his hand. "Get up," he growled. She struggled to stand. No one helped her. The Patrols stood silently, inspecting her, their crisply pressed uniforms a faded blue from many washes. One of the Patrols looked quite young, not much more than a boy, Lucinda thought, but wore neatly trimmed goatee whiskers. The other Patrol, the one Lucinda bumped hard against, wore a blotchy, wrinkled face set with red bloodshot eyes, moist and filmy, the face of a man fond of his rum.

"Fo'give me, Massa," Lucinda begged, "I didn't . . ."

"Just where you going in such a hurry?" the older Patrol's question interrupted her.

She fumbled with her words. "A task to the market fo' my Misses. I didn't mean to . . ."

"Who's your Mistress," the younger Patrol asked.

"Misses Johnson. Misses Sarah Johnson . . . o' South Bay."

"Show me your permission paper," the older Patrol commanded.

"Yes, Massa," Lucinda said, reaching with trembling hands into the pocket of her apron. She handed the paper to the Patrol.

The older Patrol stood silent, rubbing his chin, which had begun to turn red. He stared at the paper for a long while. Finally, he handed it to the younger Patrol. "What do you think?" he asked.

"Seems in order," the young man said matter-of-factly. He gave the paper back to Lucinda.

"No slave's allowed to run in the streets unless to announce a fire or such calamity. Let us catch you again and it's off to the Magistrate and the Work House for a little sugar," the older Patrol said. "Do you know how many lashes are charged for striking a white man? Even more for assaulting a member of the Patrol. Now get about your errands."

"Thank ye, Massa. Thank ye." Lucinda bowed as she spoke. "Where be Meetin' Street?"

"That way," the young man pointed.

She walked slowly, not daring to look back. She would never be able to explain to Mistress Johnson or to Mama what happened if she had been taken up. When she reached Meeting Street, she sneaked a backward glance. The Patrols sauntered down the street behind her.

The grittiest parts of the city were near the docks where the dram shops and dance halls abounded, grimy alcoves recessed in the little alleyways and dirty lanes by the Cooper River, the hovels, the stables, the shanties where the hired-out slaves often slept. In the evenings, when a weathered, wooden saloon door swung open and a drunken sailor or two or three stumbled out into the night air, the sounds of loud voices suddenly flooded into the street, a pandemonium of shouts, curses, threats, laughter, and bragging in half-a-dozen languages, mixed with the blue smoke of pipe and segar tobacco, the sweet stench of rum, and the reek of human sweat. Sunup to sunset, the docks and wharves groaned with the lift of chains and ropes loading and unloading cargo from ships flying flags of a dozen foreign ports. The boom of signal cannons roared loud from the harbor.

The back alleyways and crowded lanes choked toward the center of the city, fouled by rotting food missed by the vultures, and the stench of piss built up with trash in the corners. Rats scurried from their dank hiding places, stopped still to rise propped on hind legs, their noses twitching feverishly as they peered about and sniffed the rank air. As workmen were emptying cargo, rats from the ships would hide in the cargo pallets and when the pallets were set down on the dock, the rats would jump out from their hiding places and race toward the dry bank. The men used clubs to try to kill the rats on the wharves, and the man who killed the most each day got a drink at sundown at the expense of his work mates. Killing rats, and drinking, with incidental support of brawling, gambling, swearing, and telling lies were the chief sources of entertainment to distract from the drudgery of labor.

The fish market near the wharves displayed fresh fish, shrimp, and oysters early each morning, the fish lined up like soldiers, the open fish eyes looking up inspecting the buyers. Oranges from Florida, plantains from Cuba, and vegetables from lowcountry plantations overflowed the bordered tables of the produce market. Hucksters called out, "picked this mornin'!" exaggerating their goods. Lucinda filled her basket carefully, inspecting each purchase, haggling over the price, for her mistress was most strict and demanded Lucinda be thrifty or suffer punishment.

The butchers at the meat markets in Cow Alley constantly sharpened their knives, wiping their hands on their bloodstained aprons. The circling vultures dropped down to the markets and the wharves, their retarded heads dipping to snatch a morsel of dead fish or flesh, so tame from their constant scavenging they mingled freely through the crowd, tolerated because they kept the markets clean. The birds scared Lucinda: she hated them. They were the ugliest creatures she had ever seen. The slaves called them Charleston eagles.

In the genteel parts of the city, the houses stood two or three stories high, some layered with pastel blue or tan or cream-colored stucco, and fitted with green or black window shutters. The broad porches of the grand houses captured the harbor breeze. Lucinda peeped to see the kitchens, slaves' quarters, and carriage houses sited at the backs. Flower gardens shielded behind wrought iron gates and iron and brick fences nearly hid from her view. Slave shacks squeezed at the back of some yards. The shops up and down Broad, Elliot, Meeting, and Tradd streets displayed their wares: tailors, cobblers, jewelers, gun shops, harness makers, saddles, and cabinetmakers. St Phillip's and St. Michael's churches boasted tall steeples and huge columns as big around as an oak tree. She remembered it said Charleston was the holy city because of so many churches. There may be many churches, Lucinda thought, but the more she learned of the Charleston men and their drinking and horse race gambling, their dueling, and relations with their women slaves, or the women who hung around the grog shops near the docks waiting for the sailors, the less certain Lucinda became.

The white sand and crushed shell streets sparkled in the sunlight or collected rain puddles that wet her feet. The rain steamed up in a humid mist with the smell of animals and wet leather and the sea and rotting things. The streets were soiled by horse-waste until the slaves came and cleared the manure away. A few lanes were paved with cobblestone and rattled loudly under the turn of carriage or wagon wheels. Slaves conducted much of their business in the streets, and each day the streets were crowded with black faces and noisy with the calls of black voices. A fishmonger's wagon creaked noisily along pulled by a floppy-eared mule. A barefoot black boy drove a goat pulling a cart loaded with sweet potatoes, a young man in a fancy, frilly shirt and tall black hat rode on a white horse.

The land facing the harbor was blocked by a sea wall, the Battery. Palmetto palms with bark that peeled back on itself and fronds like large green fans swayed back and forth in the breeze. Oak trees, green year round, were hung with Spanish moss. Mistress Johnson told Lucinda Charleston possessed shabby gentility.

Lucinda saw so many, many people lived in Charleston, more than she could have ever imagined. Most came from different lands across the sea. Some whites, like the Radcliffe family, had come from England or plantations in Bermuda or Barbados. There were different Africans like Angolans or Ebo, slaves who spoke African tongues, slaves brought from the West Indies, or slaves from the Sea Islands who spoke Gullah as she could. Some folks, slave owners and slaves who came from Santo Domingo, the French Negroes, talked French, and there was a French church for them. There were Jewish people who had come from Spain, and German settlers, with shops on King or Tradd Streets. Occasionally a Yamasee Indian, a trader, could be seen in the streets. The voices of the city spoke to her like the lapping of the harbor against the sea wall; or like the distant howl of a lone wolf far at the edge of the plantation wilderness; the soft whisper of young lovers beneath the moonlight; or like the moody lamentation of a Negro spiritual.

Charleston was an old city, recurrently ravaged by nature and time, earthquakes, hurricanes, and fires. Every few decades, a storm of severe destructive strength blew through, inundating the streets, the wind breaking and blowing out un-shuttered windows. Whole plantations could be devastated. Only fires spawned more fear by white Charlestonians. As for the Africans, the order of fear was fires last, then hurricanes, then God. But the most feared of all by the slaves in Charleston was Denmark Vesey. The Intendant of the city later wrote of him, “his temper was impetuous and domineering in the extreme, qualifying him for the despotick rule, of which he was ambitious. All his passions were ungovernable and savage; and to his numerous wives and children, he displayed the haughty capricious cruelty of an Eastern bashaw.”

“Mama, how you like our new mistress?” Lucinda asked. Mama was ironing and Lucinda folded the ironed pieces carefully before putting them away.

“I ain’t complainin’,” Mama said. “She be right kindly. Least she get to bed early and ain’t ringing no bell callin’ for somethin’.” Lucinda laughed.

Mistress Johnson helped Mama acquire seamstress work, and Mama did her extra sewing at night or on Sunday afternoons. Mistress Johnson took half of all Mama earned. Mama had to get a special badge that cost two dollars so she could take on tasks for other people, and Mistress Johnson paid for the badge, but Mama paid the two dollars back after being hired out.

Lucinda had picked up the badge from the table in their room and turned it over in her palm.

“I wish I could hire out and do tasks to make money,” Lucinda complained.

“You’s a li’l young yet for that, chile,” Mama told her.

Lucinda inspected Mama’s badge closely, the gleaming copper tarnished blue-green in places. It read *Charleston, N. 347, Servant, 1821.*

“I want to earn money to buy our freedom, Mama.”

“You won’t live that long, chile,” Mama said soberly. Lucinda knew it would take her longer than her whole lifetime to earn that much money and she sullenly resigned herself that they would always be slaves.

“Mama,” Lucinda said as they switched tasks, for it was now Lucinda’s turn to work the heavy stove-hot iron, "ask Mistress Johnson if we can go to the African Church. All the other slaves go there." Lucinda struggled with the hot iron, nearly burning her hand. She set the iron on the stove and licked the hot skin on her fingers. "The minister's a free black man, Mama." Lucinda resumed ironing. "Reverend Morris Brown. They say the church started when Reverend Brown and his disciples left the white Methodist church." Lucinda carefully gripped the iron by its handle wrapped in a damp padded cloth and pressed it against the laundry, pushing and pulling to iron out any wrinkles. "They say the church here is sister of a church up north in a city called Philadelphia. A place with no slaves, Mama." Lucinda handed the finished piece of laundry to her mama to fold. She hated ironing. "We never heard a black preacher."

Mama wasted no time. That night as they prepared Mistress Johnson's bed for her retirement, Mama said, "Mistress Johnson, we's would like to attend the African Church this Sunday if that be alright with you."

"The African Church?" Mistress Johnson asked. She sounded surprised.

"Yes'm," Mama replied. "We's would like to worship with our own folks."

Lucinda was afeard Mistress Johnson would take offense at Mama's bluntness, but Mistress Johnson only asked, "Wasn't there some kind of trouble there with the Charleston authorities?" She wore her long hair pulled back at night when she prepared for bed and her longish face and long ears reminded Lucinda of Master Radcliffe's.

"We's know nuttin' 'bout that now," Mama said.

The slaves at the market told Lucinda the church was once raided, some members charged for disturbing the peace, and Reverend Brown and others arrested. Lucinda had not told this to her mama.

"We's be good and cause no trouble," Mama said, and turned to look at Lucinda. "Ain't that right chile?"

"Yes, Mama," Lucinda answered as she fluffed Mistress Johnson's bed pillow.

"Let me ask around about it," Mistress Johnson said to them.

A few more days of pleading by Lucinda and Mama, and Mistress Johnson finally said yes, they could go to the African Church.

"Where's this church?" their mistress asked.

"Hampstead," Lucinda answered.

"How will y'all get there?" Mistress Johnson queried.

"We'll walk," Lucinda answered. "It's not so far."

"Don't tell my brother," Mistress Johnson said. "It'll be best if he doesn't know." And if there was ever any trouble, she told them, they would never get to go again.

Mistress Johnson wrote a special pass to carry with them in case they were stopped and questioned by the Patrol. The African Church in Hampstead was outside the city lines, so they started out early Sunday morning. The weather was warm for December, but they wore the coats their new mistress had given to them anyway. They bowed to every white person they passed on the streets just as Mistress Johnson told them they were supposed to do.

They saw some slaves walking in the same direction.

"Where's the African Church?" Lucinda called to them.

"We going there. Come with us."

They were told the church had been built by the slaves with money sent by abolitionists and white churches up North. Lucinda was awestruck when they finally got there. She could see the spire on the top as they approached. The steeple stretched skyward like a black hand reaching toward heaven. Hundreds of black folks packed the sanctuary. She searched to see any faces she might recognize from the market place or the streets of Charleston. She was surprised to see Denmark Vesey sitting near them in one of the crowded pews. He seemed to notice her looking at him. She hoped he remembered them from the day at the wharves.

Reverend Morris Brown stood on the pulpit. He raised and slowly waved his arms in front of him. "Children o' Jesus!" he cried out in a loud raspy voice. The congregation murmured and shifted noisily in the pews. "Our Lord told his disciples: 'Let not your heart be troubled; ye believe in God, believe also in me.'"

"Amen," the crowd replied.

"Our Lord told his disciples: 'In my Father's house are many mansions: *if it were* not so, I would have told you. I go to prepare a place fo' you.'"

"Hallelujah," the congregation cried out.

"Our Lord told his disciples, 'And if I go and prepare a place fo' you, I will come again, and receive you unto myself; that where I am, *there* ye may be also.'"

"Amen."

"The Lord be gone to his Father's house . . . "

"Hallelujah!"

". . . to prepare a place fo' you . . . "

"Amen."

". . . a place at His Father's banquet table. Jesus sits at the head. Brother Tuesday on your right. Sister Sarah on your left. Brother Abraham across from you. Where the Lord be, so y'all be!"

"Hallelujah!"

"A place at the Lord's table fo' everybody!" Reverend Morris reached out his arms. "A place fo' the sick. A place fo' the weak. A place fo' the weary!"

"Amen."

"The Lord told his disciples: 'Let not your heart be troubled!' Be happy, children o' Jesus. The Lord watches over you, watches day and night. The Lord Jesus always there, in time o' trouble, in time o' desperation, in time o' need. Fo'ever is the eye of the Lord on His children."

"Hallelujah!"

"Our Lord told his disciples: 'In my Father's house are *many* mansions.' No freezing cold to bear, brothers and sisters, no blazing burning sun, no soaking rain pouring down on you."

Moans broke out in the chamber. The congregation began to clap in rhythm.

"Sit at the banquet table. Feast together, children o' Jesus!"

"Amen, Lord Jesus!"

Then the church folk began to sing and shout. Lucinda and Mama stood up with the others. Some of the Africans jumped in the aisles, lifted their arms, shook their hands in the air, danced and cried out, "Hallelujah, Lord Jesus." Lucinda felt the bliss of the Holy Spirit came down and take hold of the worshipers. Mama closed her eyes. She swayed back and forth and lifted up her arms. The rafters of the church creaked and shook as the Spirit of the Lord sank deeper and deeper in the hearts of the worshipers. Reverend Brown shouted out the words and the assembly called back:

When we all get to heaven,
What a glory it will be.
When we all get to heaven,
Lord Jesus, we'll be free.

Reverend Brown told them how much Jesus loved them, how their heavenly home would be their reward for all the suffering and woes of this world, and how happy they would then be for all of time. Mama even put five and a half cents in the offering basket from the money she had made from her seamstress work. They were putting on their coats after the service to walk back to South Bay when Denmark Vesey came up to them.

"Welcome to the African Church," he said. "I'm Denmark Vesey, one of the Church Class Leaders." He seemed to Lucinda almost a different man than from the day she saw him at the wharves. He now wore a dark suit with a vest, and a fancy laced cravat tied about his thick neck. "Did I see the two of you at the wharves not long ago?"

Mama looked at Lucinda. Lucinda answered, "Yes, we had just come to Charleston."

"Just come?"

"Our Master's James Radcliffe. We lived at Radcliffe Place Plantation on the Ashley River. Now we live in Charleston."

"I know Radcliffe Place."

"You do?"

"Oh yes, I've been there, often," Denmark Vesey said. "The day I saw you at the wharves I thought from your dress you must be French Negroes from the Santee."

"Mama sewed those dresses for us," Lucinda said proudly.

"What are your names?"

"My name's Lucinda. This is my mama, Mary."

"Would you like to meet Father Brown?" Denmark Vesey asked.

"We's would!" Mama said excitedly.

"Come with me," Denmark Vesey said. They followed toward the front doors of the church. Father Morris Brown stood outside shaking hands, talking with members of the congregation as they made their way out. Lucinda and Mama waited in line with Denmark Vesey until it was their turn and as they got up to Father Brown Denmark Vesey said, "Father, this is Mary and her girl Lucinda."

Father Brown took Mama's and then Lucinda's hand, the sleeve of his black robe with red piping falling over Lucinda's arm. Once she was close, Lucinda realized from the warm brown tone of his skin, and the shape of his face, that Father Brown was a mulatto. He was a tall man, four hands taller than Denmark Vesey. Morris Brown's dark solemn eyes imparted a drift of sadness to his face, Lucinda thought, the line of his mouth turned down at the edges. He was quite bald, his creased forehead rolled back to where his black hair began and which he wore long in the back. "Let me see," he said to them with a questioning look on his face. "Have we met before? I don't seem to remember."

"No, Father Brown," Lucinda told him. "This is our first time here. Our master's James Radcliffe, of Radcliffe Place Plantation."

"Oh yes, I know who he is. A very powerful man."

"Powerful?" Lucinda asked, unsure what Father Brown meant.

"Yes, powerful, with many friends," he said. "So, you come the way from Radcliffe Place?"

"Oh, no," Lucinda explained. "We now live here in Charleston at Master Radcliffe's sister's house, Mistress Johnson."

"I see." Father Brown said to them. "Well, Mary, Lucinda, thank you for worshiping with us today. God's blessings on both of you. We hope y'all come again soon."

"We's be here nex' Sunday," Mama promised him.

Denmark Vesey walked a few steps with Lucinda and Mama as they began their journey home. "We hold a prayer meeting and Bible study with some members of the church Wednesday evenings at my shop on Bull Street," Denmark Vesey said. "It's not a large gathering, but you're welcome to join with us. Do you wish to come?"

Mama again looked at Lucinda.

"Yes," Lucinda answered Denmark Vesey. "We will if we can. I often read and study the Bible."

"You can read?" Denmark Vesey asked with some surprise in his voice.

"Yes," Lucinda said. "Miss Elizabeth Radcliffe learnt me."

"Good," Denmark Vesey said to them. "Good. We hope to see you Wednesday evening 'round sunset. 20 Bull Street. Can you find it?"

"Yes," Lucinda answered. "We'll ask our mistress if she'll allow us to come."

Lucinda was thrilled when Mistress Johnson gave them her say so to go to the Bible study associations at Denmark Vesey's shop. They told Mistress Johnson they would get all their tasks done before leaving and do them the very best they could. All day Wednesday, they worked extra hard. Lucinda was in such high spirits. The time for them to go to Denmark Vesey's finally came, and she cradled her Bible in her arms as they walked from South Bay through town to Bull Street. Mistress Johnson told them which way to go and Lucinda looked for the brass plaques on the building walls with the names of the streets. She told Mama the street names. Denmark Vesey's house and shop, painted white, faced the street with its narrow side and had a false front like many of the Charleston homes. A long porch on the side of the house provided entrance and the roof of the house sloped like the other shops in Charleston so you would know it was a mechanic's workplace. A small sign on the fence at the street read Vesey's Carpenter Shop, 20 Bull Street.

Denmark Vesey greeted them as they came to the door. "I see you brought a Bible with you," he said looking at Lucinda.

"Yes, it was a gift to me from Miss Elizabeth."

"Would you read from it aloud as part of our study tonight?" Denmark Vesey asked.

"Well," Lucinda hesitated, unsure what to say, but then answered him with more resolve, "If you want me to."

"Yes, I would, very much," Denmark Vesey said.

Nearly a dozen people had crowded in Denmark Vesey's shop.

"This is my wife, Beck," Denmark Vesey said. "That's Monday, and Peter, and Quashiba. This is Mary and her girl Lucinda. And Gabriel and Ruth and Mingo. And Minda and Phebe. They're sisters. And Gullah Jack."

The men pulled a long wooden bench from adjacent the back wall to the center of the room. Denmark Vesey stood in front. The women wedged on the bench beside one another. Their long, coarse Negro cloth dresses, ruffled by their mistresses' cast-off petticoats beneath, draped together to the sawdust-littered floor. Scarves of the same bland cloth covered their heads. Only Lucinda wore a brightly colored calico headscarf. The men stood behind the bench facing Vesey. They had taken off their hats and fingered the brims as they held them in their hands. Lucinda could smell the men's sweat from the work pants, overalls, and brogans they wore.

"Let us bow our heads in prayer," Denmark Vesey said. "God, bless this gathering tonight. Look over and protect each one here. Let us be attentive to Thy Word. Amen."

They all said, "Amen."

Denmark Vesey then took a well-thumbed Bible in his calloused, rough hands, and said to them, "Now tonight I'm going to read to you from the book of the Old Testament called *Exodus*, from the 3rd chapter, where God speaks to Moses as a flame of fire out of the midst of a burning bush. Let's begin with verse 7 where we read 'And the Lord said, I have surely seen the affliction of my people which are in Egypt, and have heard their cry by reason of their taskmasters, for I know their sorrows.' And continuing with verse 8, the Word of the Lord reads 'And I am come down to deliver them out of the hands of the Egyptians, and to bring them up out of that land unto a good land and a large, unto a land flowing with milk and honey.'"

Lucinda had opened her Bible to the book of *Exodus* where Denmark Vesey was reading and looked down at it, following the words along as he said them.

"'The affliction of my people,'" Denmark Vesey repeated, "'their cry by reason of their taskmasters.' Jehovah hears your cries, my brethren. Jehovah despairs at your deplorable condition, my sisters.

"You're of the Lord's chosen people. Lucinda is one of His chosen people and has with her tonight her own Bible, which she's going to read for us. Lucinda, would you read *Exodus* chapter 3, verses 19 and 20?"

A feeling of fear coursed through her when Denmark Vesey called her name, but Lucinda said a quick silent prayer asking God to give her strength as she found the verses and began, "And I am sure that the king of Egypt will not let you go, no, not by a mighty hand. And I will stretch out my hand, and smite Egypt with all my wonders which I will do in the midst thereof: and after that he will let you go."

Lucinda looked up. All eyes in the room were on her. She turned to Mama with tears in her eyes, and Mama leaned over and put her arm around her.

"The Word of God tells us how things were and prophesizes the future of how things will be," Denmark Vesey said. "Do you hear the voice of the Lord telling you how things will be? When the Lord speaks to us, we're commanded to listen. We're commanded to follow the Word of the Lord. Moses said to the Pharaoh, 'God says let my people go.'"

The room was quiet. Each face stared at Denmark Vesey as he stood with his Bible open in his hand. No one said a word or made a sound until one of the women began to sing, soft and low:

"Moses said to the Pharaoh . . ."

Everyone sang back, *"Let my people go."*

"Moses said to the Pharaoh . . ."

"Let my people go."

"Aaron's rod a serpent became . . ."

"Let my people go."

"Aaron's rod a serpent became . . ."

"Let my people go."

"Aaron's rod turn water to blood . . ."

"Let my people go."

"Aaron's rod turn water to blood . . ."

"Let my people go."

"A plague of frogs upon the land . . ."

They continued their singing, reckoning all the pestilence God placed on the Egyptians, the lice, and swarms of flies, the slaying of Egypt's cattle, the curse of painful boils of the flesh, hail and fire, the plague of locusts, darkness so thick it could be felt, all the firstborn dead, until the Pharaoh's hardened heart was made soft and he let God's chosen people go.

Denmark Vesey shifted on his feet and leaned back, straightening his shoulders as he lifted his head. His thick, solid chest swelled up, round as a cooper's tub. He then said, "Jehovah has spoken as a flame of fire to the Black Moses. Jehovah has commanded to lead his people on an exodus to the Promised Land of freedom. Amen."

He looked about the room, examining each face. "We're going to conclude tonight's Bible study with three other verses from the *Book of Exodus*," he said. "Chapter 21, verses 23 through 25, which tell us the Laws God commands we must live by. The Lord's Word says, 'And if any mischief follow, then thou shalt give life for life, eye for eye, tooth for tooth, hand for hand, foot for foot, burning for burning, wound for wound, stripe for stripe.' So says the Word of the Lord. Amen. God's Law says all sinners be punished for their sins with like," Denmark Vesey exclaimed. "Prepare for the day when the sinners, the enslavers, will receive their punishment." Denmark Vesey stopped and the center of his eyes darkened to an intense black.

Then he said, "Let us pray. God, deliver these, your people, from their bondage as you delivered your chosen people from their captivity in the land of Egypt. Smite their enemy as you smote the armies of the Pharaoh. Reveal to your children the Promised Land flowing with milk and honey. Lead them to the land of freedom. Amen."

The group repeated, "Amen," and raised their heads and looked at Denmark Vesey. Lucinda watched as a thick bulging line in his neck throbbed in time to his heartbeat. The whites of his eyes protruded large against the black of his face. Drops of sweat rolled off his forehead and face, and fell to the floor.

"Gullah Jack has conjured a potion," said Denmark Vesey, "to protect you on your journey home tonight. Taste some now. He'll give you some to take with you."

Gullah Jack went around to each of them and from a small sack tied at his waist he took a pinch of bitter-tasting paste in his fingers and placed a little on their tongues. He mumbled softly some Voodoo spell as he measured out the potion. He then handed some of the physic to each of them in pieces of folded paper. The Africans knew Gullah Jack as a Negro doctor, a conjurer who made powerful potions to heal the sick or ward off evil spirits. The slaves said Gullah Jack brought a bag with him from Africa with herbs and charms, which he always carried with him. He was leader of the Gullah Society, a group from Angola. They said Gullah Jack could not be harmed, that no bullet could kill him, and he knew how to work charms to make others invulnerable. He was a small man, not fit for fieldwork. He wore big bushy whiskers on the sides of his face. His off-kilter stare pierced like a butcher knife plunging in a side of pork. He was a woodworker at his master's lot at the wharves, his master employed him for errands, deliveries, and like chores, and Lucinda often saw Gullah Jack when she went to the markets. He acted as if he was not quite right in the head when he was around the whites, but he was not that way with his fellow Africans. Then he was most serious. He was a member of the African Church, and Lucinda had seen him there too, often in the company of Denmark Vesey. Gullah Jack finished handing out the potion and sat down, his head bowed, still muttering a Voodoo prayer in a soft voice.

Long after dark, Lucinda and Mama started their walk back to South Bay. All slaves were supposed to be off the streets by sunset and the beating of tattoo. The bells in the tower of Saint Mark's had tolled nine times, but enforcement by the Patrol was not very often, especially before ten and there were still other slaves on the streets hurrying home like them. Mama was quiet as they walked and Lucinda knew she was thinking of something. Then her mama broke her silence.

"Ol' man Vesey," Mama paused before she went on, "he hate the whites."

"Why you say that?" Lucinda asked her.

"Jus' do."

"How you know?"

"Jus' can tell," Mama said. Then for the first time in Lucinda's life Mama said something Lucinda didn't expect her to say, "that's alright, Lord fo'give. I hates 'em just like."

Once back at South Bay, Lucinda lay on her pallet unable to sleep, even as she was tired and the hour was late. Mama snored loudly from across the small room. Why did Denmark Vesey so hate the white man? Lucinda wondered. She had sensed the feelings among the men in Denmark Vesey's shop, the powerful emotions, anger and hate, thick as green wood smoke, hard and heavy as a blacksmith's hammer. Did every slave hold such anger, such hate in his heart?

The cowbell on the shop door clanged as two white men entered. Two slaves trailed a few steps behind. Denmark Vesey stood engaged in conversation with the shopkeeper's son.

"Why, it's all in the Bible, Benjamin Ford," Denmark Vesey was saying.

Vesey moved his head slowly and glanced at the men, his eyes dully focused on them before turning back to the boy. The white men edged closer, expecting Denmark Vesey to stop. But he kept talking.

"Who were our first parents?" Denmark Vesey asked the boy.

The two slaves stepped back and stood quietly near the door, their eyes clung to Denmark Vesey.

"Do you not read the Good Book?" Denmark Vesey asked, still ignoring the white men. "Who were the first man and woman?"

"Adam and Eve," the boy replied. He looked helplessly at the white men, rolling his eyes as if to say 'bear with me', for there was something about Denmark Vesey that did not make it easy to interrupt him.

"And we're all descended from them," Denmark Vesey said fervently, and swept his arm about the room. "All of us. Black and white. We're *all* their children. We're all equal. All men have equal rights. No one should be the master of another man," and now Denmark Vesey turned and fixed his eyes on the other men in the shop. "That's what the Bible says." He stood silent for a moment. "The laws of slavery are ridged and strict and the blacks have not their rights which come from God," Denmark Vesey said. "But know this, boy, everyone has his time in the sun, and the time for the blacks will come."

With that, Denmark Vesey turned toward the door, nodding his head in greeting to the slaves as he made his way out to the street.

"Who the devil was that?" one of the white men questioned the boy.

"Oh, his name's Vesey, Denmark Vesey," the boy said. "He's a free black, a carpenter. His house and shop's just down the street."

"He's dangerous," the other white man said.

"Oh, he's not dangerous," the boy said. "He comes in here all the time talking like that. Don't pay him no mind. He's just crazy. A crazy old nigger, that's all. One whale of a carpenter though. What can I do for you men?"

The cold rainy days of winter began to fade like a painful memory forgotten slowly. As January turned to February, the air was warmer, the sun brighter, and the sky bluer. The grey of winter lifted away like an onion, peel by peel. Lucinda saw early blooming crocuses, tulips, and daffodils color with purple, scarlet, flamingo, and yellow the flower boxes of Charleston. In the gardens, soft-faced camellia blossoms attended as an early signal to spring.

February was the social season for Charleston's and the lowcountry's elite. The city was crowded with plantation masters and their families. Lucinda worked her way through the noisy streets, bustling morning until late night with people and carriages. The markets too were crowded and she had to shout and wrangle with the sellers to get a good price so her mistress would not punish her for paying too much. Shops on King and Tradd streets filled with buyers, for there was money to be spent after the season's crops were sold. Slaves hastened about their tasks. Ships sailed in and out of the harbor. Bales of cotton stood six high on the wharves. At the back of the Customs Exchange and in the auction houses, slaves constrained in chains stood naked on the block as auctioneers haggled for the highest bid.

The city was gay. Charleston's wealthy reveled in extravagant parties and lavish balls night after night after night. Music drifted in the air, waltzes and dances called by the timbre of violins and the croon of horns. *Débutante* balls presented the planters' young unwed daughters to the Charleston gentry. Families arranged marriages for economic and social gain. The indulgence of the city was at its height, displayed in dress, jewelry, horses, carriages, parties, music, gambling: the errant opulence of leisure. On the surface old Charleston seemed as calm and predictable as ever. If anything, the slaves were more willing and cooperative. The early stages of the conspiracy of forces united by Denmark Vesey under the cover of dark night lay quietly hidden, known only to a very few.

On a mild February evening, Lucinda stood with Miss Elizabeth on the top portico of Mistress Johnson's big house overlooking the harbor. She attended to some finishing details with Miss Elizabeth's hair. The row of flaming street lamps along South Bay was like a valley of rising moons. The western horizon, opposite the grey-blue water of the harbor, burned with a fading tangerine sun against streaks of turquoise sky.

"Oh Lucinda, isn't Charleston so lovely," Miss Elizabeth exclaimed.

"Yes'm," Lucinda answered, "Lovely as you, Miss Elizabeth." Lucinda had long learned what was expected of her.

"Lucinda, do you think so?" Elizabeth cooed. "Tell me, how do you find this ballgown?" Elizabeth twirled in front of Lucinda, the low-cut top revealing the white skin of her shoulders and neck, the broad matching azure skirt spinning round. "Father says it was made in France. The French are the best for fashion, you know."

"You look beautiful, Miss Elizabeth."

"Oh, I'm so looking forward to this evening," Elizabeth sang. "This is my favorite time of the year." Lucinda stopped trying to fasten the combs and ribbons in Elizabeth's hair.

"We've three galas to attend tonight, Lambkin!" Miss Elizabeth said as she twirled. "One's a masquerade!" In each hand, she held a mask of *papier maché*, one painted gleaming gold, the other velvety black. "Which should I go as," she asked Lucinda. "Black Midnight or Golden Noon?" She held the masks to her face, alternating them back and forth.

"Black Midnight, Miss Elizabeth," Lucinda answered.

"Do you think so? Oh Lucinda, we went to the theatre last night!" Miss Elizabeth said breathlessly, her eyes suddenly open wide as she stared at Lucinda. "Speaking of black midnight, we saw Shakespeare's tragedy *Macbeth*. Bloody, bloody, with horrible witches and ghosts and murder." Miss Elizabeth shook her head as if to chase the images from her mind. "You would have been terrified, Lucinda! I suppose you're glad that blacks and slaves aren't allowed to go to the theatre." Lucinda stood silent. "Oh, Lucinda, the British actor Junius Brutus Booth played Macbeth. He's so striking! Father says he's known in Britain as the greatest tragedian actor. The evening was simply divine, Lucinda, all the ladies in their lovely gowns and the men in their cravats, their top hats and their suits."

She stopped twirling and let Lucinda work on her hair.

"Do you think I'll catch me a beau tonight, Lucinda? Don't you think that's what I need," Elizabeth asked, "a suitor to come to father and beg for my hand? A handsome, wealthy lowcountry planter's son, now that's what I need, Lucinda, that's what I need."

The jewelry at her throat twinkled in the fading light. Elizabeth's face was plain, like her mother's, and she had applied rouge to add color to her bread-dough complexioned cheeks, but the gown was magnificent, and Elizabeth glowed with confidence. Lucinda was shapelier, hidden beneath her slave attire, with a West African face, the big dark eyes, silky lashes, black, black onyx skin, soft ruby red lips, and her slender neck.

In the street below, the challises and four-horse carriages filled with party goers paraded in front of them, the ladies in their gowns of muslin, silk, and linen, the planter gentlemen attired in gloves, hats, cravats.

Tuesday pulled up in front of the mansion, dismounted from the carriage platform and opened the carriage doors.

"Oh, Lucinda," Elizabeth said as she hurried off the portico and into the mansion through the open French doors, "I must go." Mistress Nelly called to her from the downstairs. "Coming mother, coming," she cried as she disappeared down the curved staircase.

Lucinda watched as Tuesday snapped the reigns and the horses came to attention. The carriage bunched with Master Radcliffe, Mistress Nelly and Elizabeth, Master Johnson, Mistress Ruth, and Mistress Johnson lumbered away down South Bay. She stood and watched as long as she could see the carriage make its way in front of the columned white mansions facing the harbor. She heard faint echoes of music from a nearby gala, and the raised voices and laughter from the men as they gambled and drank their rum. The sounds floated up to her over the tops of the palmetto palms. She imagined the playful talk of the single young ladies like Elizabeth as they sipped their Madera wine, curtsied and blushed, accepted the hand of a gentleman suitor and stepped gracefully onto the dance floor, the wide skirts of their gowns swirling in time to the music, the eyes of their suitors fixed on them with an enchanted gaze. She thought how no slave would ever have a life filled with such elegance and luxury. A slave could only serve the whims of masters going about their extravagance. She watched with a lonely and hollow emptiness inside, her own slave heart craving with a young girl's longing and desire.

Denmark Vesey stood inside the door of the grogshop as his eyes adjusted to the dim light. "Denmark!" He recognized the voice calling to him and turned to face a handful of slaves who sat hidden in dark shadow in the back corner of the saloon rolling dice and gambling in a game of *rolae polae*. "Mingo," Denmark Vesey said, "What's new?"

"Oh, ain't much, Denmark."

"What you doin' here?" another of the black men asked Denmark, "You don't partake of strong drink."

A burst of loud cheers and curses by a gang of men riveted by a gamecock fight erupted abruptly from a back room, then died away.

Denmark Vesey ignored the disruption. He continued to address the group of slaves. "I go wherever men are gathered so I can spread the news,"

Denmark said. "And they gather in grogshops!" Denmark's sharp white teeth showed as he grinned. He leaned his thick-chested torso against the bar and propped a leg on the bar step. "A cup of clabbor," he said to the bartender.

Several white men stood at the bar talking. Denmark drained his drink in a few rapid gulps. The talk of the white men was of the drop in the price of lowcountry cotton and rivalry from cotton grown in the upcountry.

"But the price of slaves hasn't declined," one of the men at the bar said to the others, "not one bit."

"You shouldn't have to pay anything at all," Denmark Vesey said, and the men at the bar looked at him with curious surprise.

"That right?" one of the men asked doubtfully.

"Yep, there shouldn't be any price at all for a man," Denmark said, just loud enough so that both the white men and the slaves heard him, "because no man has the right to make another man a slave."

The white men stared at Denmark. Unblinking, Denmark stared back. The slaves near the back grew quiet.

"That's what Senator King of New York told the Legislature in Washington when they were debating about the admission of Missouri to the Union," Denmark said coolly.

The bartender most any other time would have paid no mind to Denmark Vesey's proselytizing, for the free black was known in most every saloon in the city for his outspoken views; but the barkeep was now afraid the white men were going to take real offense at Denmark's boldness.

"You gents want another drink?" the bartender asked.

Just then, the men who had been engaged in the gamecock fight spilled from the back chamber, boisterous and noisy, crowding between Denmark Vesey and the other men. The one with the victorious bird held the gamecock tenderly beneath his arm, the rooster's head covered with a sleeve of burlap to keep it still. The loser clutched his dead gladiator by the neck, a black and gold crown of feathers with bright red blood on its claws. He opened the saloon door and tossed the limp body into the street for the vultures. The gamblers gathered at the bar. They argued loudly, rehashing their gaming, ordered and downed three-finger tall pulls of rum. One day they will be silent, Denmark thought. He reached into his pocket for a ten cents piece and plopped it on the cypress bar for his clabber. He turned to the group of slaves in the corner. "Mingo, you all take care," he said and walked with sure step out the saloon door and onto the street.

"I've read to you from abolitionist and anti-slavery pamphlets, from speeches before Congress by Senator Rufus King," Denmark Vesey said to Jack Purcell. Jack leaned on Denmark Vesey's workbench while Denmark busied himself with shaving and shaping a piece of cypress wood. "We're not alone in our cause." Denmark Vesey halted and faced his friend. "Jack, I've read to you from the newspapers about events in Santo Domingo. Don't you think it's high time for the uprising there to spread to the slave states of America?" Jack considered with his mulatto yellow-brown eyes, his face with something of the white man about it. "God helps those who help themselves," Denmark said. "You've heard that said, haven't you, Jack?"

"Yes, God helps those who help themselves. I don't doubt that's true," Jack answered.

"Senator King will continue to speak and write and publish pamphlets against slavery as long as he's alive, until the Southern States consent to emancipate their slaves. But we must do our part. We must help ourselves. Slavery is a disgrace to the country, Jack, and we must do what we can to right this situation."

"How can you be so sure you'll be successful?" asked Jack.

"What do the others say about me, Jack?"

Jack took his time. He did not like to go fast. "That you're a man of great capacity."

"Just so," Denmark Vesey said proudly. "And I wouldn't attempt a plan so fraught with danger if I wasn't certain my actions were ordained by God." Denmark Vesey stopped his plane, and turned to meet Jack's stare. "You believe in miracles, don't you Jack?" Denmark Vesey asked.

"I say I reckon I do," Jack answered.

"God parted the waters of the Red Sea?"

"Yes, He did," Jack affirmed.

"Didn't the Lord go before His chosen people by day in a pillar of a cloud to lead them the way from Egypt to the Promised Land; and by night in a pillar of fire, to give them light to go by day and night?"

"Amen, Brother Denmark. God worked His miracles," Jack agreed.

"Didn't the Lord rain down bread to feed their hunger? Didn't Moses strike the rock and water sprang forth to quench their thirst?" Denmark Vesey continued.

"That's right," Jack said. He studied Vesey's round, grizzled face. "But how will you do it, Denmark? Do you have force enough? Where will you get men?"

"We'll find men fast enough," Denmark Vesey said. "Men aplenty. We expect men from the country and town."

"Where will you begin?"

"On Boundary Street."

"At what hour?"

"At 12 o'clock at night, or early in the morning. As soon as the Patrols are discharged."

"How will you manage it?" Jack asked.

"We'll give them notice and they'll march down and camp round the city."

"But what will they do for arms? The whites have the Patrol, guns, and horses. The blacks have not."

"We'll find arms enough. They'll bring down their hoes and axes."

"That won't do to fight with here," Jack said dismissively.

"Let us get candidates from town and with arms and then we'll take the Guard House and the Arsenal in town, the Arsenal on the Neck, and the upper Guard House, and supply the country people with arms."

"How will you approach the Arsenals?" Jack asked, still doubtful. "They're guarded."

"Yes, I know that," Denmark Vesey answered, "but what are those guards . . . one man here, one man there. We won't let a man pass before us."

"Well, how will the black people from the country and the islands know when you're to begin?" Jack asked. "Or how will you get the town people together?"

"We'll have settings up, that is night meetings for prayer and there notify them when to start."

"But the whites in the back country, when they hear the news, they'll turn to and kill you all. And besides you may be betrayed."

"What of betrayal? If any do betray us, we'll cut out their tongue and end their life. If one of us gets hanged, we'll rise at that minute." Denmark Vesey fixed his hard gaze on the face of the brown man. He knew he needed every strategy to solicit his soldiers: religion, threats, Voodoo magic, fear, anger, hatred, the example of Santo Domingo, the promise of reward, the allure of freedom.

"A risky business," Jack Purcell said, shaking his head, "I ain't sure .

. ."

"God will guide us, Jack. Guide us as He guided his children to the Promised Land. But we must first break the yoke."

Jack pondered all Denmark Vesey had said. He knew the free black carpenter's word held a powerful influence among the slaves. If any man could lead the blacks to rise against the whites, it was Denmark Vesey.

"Tell me, Jack. Do you want to be free?" Denmark Vesey asked.

"I do, Bro' Denmark."

"The revolt in Santo Domingo shows the way," Denmark Vesey said. "Once the insurrection began there, the slaves joined in great numbers. What was done in Santo Domingo, can be done in Charleston."

"But how will we organize ourselves?"

"We'll use the African Church to recruit our numbers," Denmark Vesey said. "We'll send men to the country and bring down the country blacks. Jack, we have but to strike a spark and the flame will burn into an unstoppable conflagration just as in Santo Domingo. Remember the fable of Hercules and the Wagoner whose wagon was stalled. The wagoner began to pray, and Hercules said, you fool, put your shoulder to the wheel, whip up the horses and your wagon will be pulled out. If we do not put our hand to the work and deliver ourselves, the blacks will never come out of slavery. We must meet and mature our plan. We must prepare. "

"Men could die, Denmark," Jack said bleakly, "black men."

"Which is better, Jack? For some men to lose their lives so that the rest will be free, or for all to live but all remain slaves?" Denmark Vesey picked up the cypress board and inspected his work, holding it out at arm's length and squinting with one eye to make certain it was straight. When he was satisfied, he put the board on the workbench. "The American War of Independence from England, the French Revolution, the revolt in Santo Domingo. Don't you see? This is a new era of freedom, of liberty. Our day has finally come."

The crowning event of the winter social season was Race Week at Washington Race Track.

"The races are each year in late February," Miss Elizabeth told Lucinda.

"We'll stay in Charleston for the entire week," Mistress Nelly told Mama. "And we have two guests coming from Savannah. You and Lucinda will go to the races to serve and look after little Jeremiah."

"We're members of the Jockey Club," Master Radcliffe said at breakfast to their guests, the Moores, from Savannah. "We've eight seats in the stands. And we'll place the carriages as close as we can outside the track fence." Master Radcliffe nodded his head toward Lucinda as she tended the table. "My servants will be there to serve you. You should be quite comfortable."

"Whatever will be fine," Master Moore said. "We appreciate the invitation. I look forward to some exciting racing."

"I've six of my best horses here, including my prize Arabians," Master Radcliffe said with a hint of pride. "I hope for a big purse winning week."

A rutted, often muddy wagon trail ran from Radcliffe Place Plantation along the Ashley River to the bridge at Charleston, a trip that consumed the better part of a day. Master Radcliffe had his horses, carriages, and livery slaves brought along the trail for Race Week. Each day of the races, the slaves wiped the carriages clean of dust, polishing their glossy black finish until they gleamed like ebony. Master Radcliffe stabled some of his horses at the course, but he boarded his most beloved animals at the stables in Charleston. Every morning, the slaves walked Master Radcliffe's horses through Charleston with other horses stabled in town. Lucinda, Mama, and Uncle Jacob walked with them. People crowded the streets to watch. As the entrants passed, throngs of children, black and white, cheered them. Lucinda tingled with excitement as the crowd along the streets shouted out to them and clapped as they paraded by.

Jockey Club Race Week was like nothing Lucinda had seen before. She could hear the buzzing of the crowd like the sound of a nest of honeybees as they walked toward the raceway. A grey cloud of dust hung over the field, stirred up by all the people and the horses led in all directions. Carriages crowded around the outside of the track fence. Young boys, black and white, leaned against the fence, peered inside at all they could see, or scampered about trying to earn a penny by errand or chore. Tavern keepers had rented houses near the track, converted into restaurants, bars, and inns. Wooden stands served as tables, displayed with liquors, turtle soups, and foods. The gentlemen and ladies dressed in finery for the occasion. The gamblers, slaves, traveling salesmen, and others excluded from the refined areas inside stood on the outside of the course, drinking their liquors and wines, voices raised, the air thick with loud laughter and cat calls.

"You know," Lucinda overheard Mistress Johnson say as Master Johnson helped his mother dismount from the carriage, "for years

Washington Race Track's isolation has made it a popular place where gentlemen come and duel to settle their offenses. Several men have been killed here defending their honor."

Lucinda helped Ruth with Jeremiah. He cried as they put him in a push carriage the slaves on Radcliffe Place Plantation had made for him.

"Father helped start the Jockey Club," Elizabeth said proudly over the noise. "People come from all over, even other states, to see the races."

The Jockey Club's wooden stands stood on the finish line side of the track, the seats tiered so the races' spectators could see over the heads of those in front of them. Master Radcliffe's seats were near the front for a full view of the course. Lucinda and Mama stood in the field near the stands when they weren't busy running back and forth to the carriages outside the course fence when Master Radcliffe or the family needed something.

At the sound of a bugle, the jockeys pulled tightly on the reins and guided their horses to the starting post. The crowd grew hushed. The horses stomped about nervously, turning sideways and twisting about. The riders pulled harder on the reins. Once the horses were calm, the starter pointed a black pistol up in the air. "Ready," he shouted. He fired the pistol with a cloud of white smoke, and at the blast of the shot, the riders began digging their heels into the horses' sides and striking their horse on its hind parts with a short whip to make it gallop as fast as possible. The horses lunged forward toward the first turn, bunched tightly together. The jockeys hit with their whips and dug with their heels. Tails and manes flew in the wind as the horses raced around the course. Dirt sprayed from the horses' hooves, churning the track. One horse, a chestnut-colored filly, muscles flexing in front and rear, edged out a length lead and the throng roared their approval. Lucinda could see why the crowd loved the races so much. They were so exciting! Her heart pounded as she watched. No other animal was as majestic and beautiful as a horse. As the horses rounded the second turn and raced along the backstretch of the track, the pack began to spread out. The horses' legs were a blur of motion. Lucinda could hear the hooves dance in rhythm . . . gal-lop, gal-lop, gal-lop. Toward the third turn, two of the horses trailing near the back began to edge up and passed ahead to gain nearer the lead as the field came out of the fourth and final turn of the track. One horse and rider began to lose ground and fade back. As the horses charged along the home stretch, the frenzied crowd waved their arms and shouted out frantically, urging their favorite on. Two horses challenged for the lead as their riders madly whipped their mounts' sides trying to gain advantage. Closing in to the finish line, the lead horse was on the outside, but at the final second the horse on the inside, Delilah, burst home with a sudden bound and won the purse by inches. The crowd roared with a great swell of cheering lifting up from the field. The men who had won their bets whooped and hollered, hopping up and down like children at play, holding on to their hats to keep them from popping off. Lucinda heard Master Jimmy Johnson in the stands call loudly, boasting he had won his wager.

Sleek with sweat after the race, grooms brushed down the horses. Other slaves ran out on the track with rakes and spades and leveled the places where hooves had churned up the dirt. The men bet on every race, their pockets crammed with money notes and they would take out a fold and pay their losses or stuff their winnings into their pockets. Lucinda kept her eyes peeled to the ground hoping to find a dropped bill, but she had no luck.

Lucinda spent her days at the races taking care of Jeremiah. She was amazed at how much he had grown since she last saw him in November. He could now walk and talk. Lucinda had to constantly watch him to make sure he didn't wander off or to keep him from getting into something. She wheeled him in his perambulator near the stands at the fence, sitting down in the shade to rest. She looked up and saw Master Johnson walking toward them, his face flush with drink.

"How are you doing with him?" Master Johnson asked, smiling at her as he approached.

"He doesn't seem to ever get tired, Master Johnson," Lucinda said.

"He'll sleep some sooner or later," Master Johnson said.

"He's so big now!" Lucinda said. "I can't believe how much he's grown!"

"When are you going to have one?" Master Johnson asked, knelling down and playing with his child's toes that stuck out of the pushchair.

"When I'm married, I guess."

"You don't have to be married," he said, looking at her. And then he winked.

"Why are we slaves, Uncle Denmark?" Lucinda asked. She and Denmark Vesey were walking back to Charleston from the Sunday services of the African Church at Hampstead. The sky above them was a shifting tableau of black clouds against brief clearings of blue and bright sun, a windswept afternoon. She held tightly to her Bible in her arms.

"We're slaves because the white man has made us slaves. Made us slaves by murder, by torture, by the whip," Denmark Vesey said. He looked at her charily. "Do you want to be free?"

"Yes," Lucinda answered. She hesitated for a long moment. "I want to be like you, a free black, Uncle Denmark," she said shyly.

"I was once a slave," he told her. "I was a slave for longer than you've been alive." Denmark Vesey considered before he went on. "And though I'm now free, I'm not satisfied with my own freedom. Not when our people live in such misery and chains."

They entered into Charleston, passing the Lines, the earthen wall of fortification built by slave workers in 1812 to protect the city against incursion by the British. Carriages in the streets returned white residents from church services. Slaves on foot dressed in their finest Sunday attire gathered and filled the market place. Monday Gell, Gullah Jack, Jack Purcell, Peter Poyas, Rolla and Ned Bennett . . . Denmark Vesey's chief recruits . . . began to make their way to his house and shop on Bull Street for their appointed rendezvous. The wind pushed against Lucinda, the black clouds continued to build and scurry across the sky.

"There are those in England and in the North who wage a crusade against slavery," Denmark Vesey said, "who work to see slavery abolished, for all slaves to be freed. But the whites here will never set the slaves free."

She did not speak.

Denmark Vesey said, "Before the American colonies warred with England, Thomas Jefferson and others wrote the Declaration of Independence. It states that all men are created equal by God, all men have certain rights. The white man has no right to enslave the blacks. Slavery is counter to the law of man and the Law of God. Study the scriptures, child." Denmark Vesey gestured toward her Bible. "It's against the commandments of God to enslave another man.

"God created Adam and Eve, our first parents. We're all descended from them. We're all created the same. The Bible says we must take hold of our situation and fight for our freedom."

"But how, Uncle Denmark?" Lucinda asked.

"We must rise up and overthrow the white man."

Denmark Vesey let his words pierce their mark. He prayed to God to safeguard him.

"Have your masters ever hurt you?" he asked.

"Mistress Radcliffe broke my arm once," Lucinda said, pointing to her wrist. "She struck me with a silver candlestick for spilling a pitcher of buttermilk."

"The beginning of more to come," Denmark Vesey said. "If you had seen the mistreatment of slaves as I have, you would know what I say to you is true. Would you fight for your freedom?" Denmark Vesey asked.

"If I had to I would," Lucinda said firmly, "if I couldn't escape or run away." Then with doubt in her voice she said, "I'm just a girl. I'm just a slave, Uncle Denmark."

He thought back to so many years ago when he was her age. Yes, he had always hated being a slave, and he had dreamed many times of escaping and running away. If he had run away back then, he knew he would not have known how or where to go. His experience was, once you're imprisoned in slavery, once you're captive of another man, there's a torpor which takes hold of you. As much as your heart longs to be free, as much as you think you want to be free, the inner strength you need, the outer measures you need, are greater than what you have to escape and become free. Sometimes a man's soul wanders lost without direction. So it was before he came to trust his fate to God. That's why he had to help the slaves in Charleston. That's why the Israelites needed Moses to lead them from their bondage in Egypt to their freedom in the Promised Land. That's why he was called by God to help the slaves overcome their fear, to escape their misery, to break free from their chains.

"What you are is a young woman with a brave heart," Denmark Vesey said to her. "You have more strength than you know, Lucinda. You have you. That's something worth fighting for, something that no one can take away."

She walked along in silence before she asked, "What's it like for the Africans in other places?"

"There's an island in the West Indies," he said. "Santo Domingo. The slaves there rose up and won their freedom by overcoming their French masters and defeating the French armies. It's now a country where all black men are free."

"But Uncle Denmark, what can I do?"

"Alone? Perhaps nothing, child. But we can band together. If the Africans are united, if we're as one force like the people in Santo Domingo were, then we have power, we have strength. Look about you. Charleston's more like a Negro country than a country of whites. If there's any place the slaves can join and fight for freedom, it is here in Charleston. Charleston is the African city of this country."

She was again silent for a long while. Then she said, "Ever since I was a little girl at Radcliffe Place, I dreamt of Charleston. I thank the Lord I'm here now. I like the African Church."

"That's the great good of the African Church," Denmark Vesey said. "The Church has brought the Africans together, made us see we're one, whether Ebo like Monday Gell, or Mandingo like Mingo Harth, or from Angola like Gullah Jack, or from Guinea like me. Unity. Solidarity. That's what it'll take to overcome the whites. And that's what the African Church has learnt us."

"And I got to know you, Uncle Denmark. I now know of things I never heard of before."

They walked through the streets of Charleston toward the edge of the city. Finally, she whispered, "Uncle Denmark, do you mean the white people must be killed for us to be free?"

"This is how it was done in Santo Domingo," he answered her. "If the blacks are going to be free here, we must follow the same path that led to freedom there."

"But Uncle Denmark," Lucinda hesitated, "the Bible says thou shalt not kill."

"Unless charged by God," Denmark Vesey said, and he turned his head so he could see her face. Her bright eyes radiated with the sheen of polished ebony. "There are times when God commands us to do battle in His name. When God warned Moses the Egyptians' first born would die at the hands of the mighty angel of the Lord, God sanctioned death. Samson destroyed the Philistines because God willed it and gave Samson the strength to bring the pillars down. God commanded Jericho be utterly destroyed except for Rahab and her family.

"The prophet Zechariah says: 'Behold the day of the Lord cometh, and thy spoil shall be divided in the midst of thee. For I will gather all nations against Jerusalem to battle; and the city shall be taken, and the women ravished; and half of the city shall go forth into captivity; and the residue of the people shall not be cut off from the city. Then shall the Lord go forth, and fight against those nations, as when he fought in the day of battle.'

"Don't you see, child? Scripture prophesizes such a day will come. No matter how good the treatment is by your masters, no man should be enslaved by another, and we must fight with the fist of force, just as they did in Santo Domingo. The day will come when the blacks will rise up, when we will fight for our freedom. Only blood atones for blood."

Her mind spun round like a fast-turning waterwheel. "When will that day be, Uncle Denmark?"

"Sooner than you think, child."

"How will I know?"

"Word will be spread. You'll know," Denmark Vesey answered. "Say nothing of this, child. Our secret must be guarded with the greatest care. Or all of us will suffer."

"I won't say anything, Uncle Denmark," she said, "I promise. Never. Not to anyone."

Could she murder, she wondered? She was afeard, but unsure what she feared. She knew most slaves would willingly kill their masters to gain their freedom. She knew they loathed the whites with a hatred that could erupt into blood and death. Yes, she had always wanted to be free. Wasn't freedom the dream of every slave? But to kill the whites? On the plantation, her stomach had turned at the slaughter and sight of gushing animal blood; she could not even witness the butchering of a hog. Murder, warfare, bloodshed were the domain of men, she reckoned, like whipping a slave to inflict punishment, or the hunting of game in the wild.

As if knowing her thoughts, Denmark Vesey said, "You've not to worry, child. You'll not be asked to kill."

"I'll do whatever God commands," she told him.

"God has something to do with it," said Denmark Vesey, "for we have gone four years in our plan without discovery." Denmark Vesey looked at her. She stared straight ahead. She would never betray me, he thought. "Let us hurry," he said, "the blind seer is waiting for us."

Denmark Vesey stood and spoke to the Bible study group: "We have someone new with us tonight."

A young man almost a head taller than Denmark Vesey stood up beside him. "Friends, this is David Walker," Denmark Vesey said. "David's a free black man from Wilmington. He has come to Charleston looking for work. He came to our service at the African Church Sunday and I asked him to join us tonight. Make him feel welcome."

"Welcome, David," Lucinda said with the others. She looked at him closely. There was a determined, dogged look in the set of his jaw: his quick, intelligent black eyes ranged carefully across the room, absorbing all, the skin of his face muted black. His body seemed all bones, lanky, thin, and sinewy. He shuffled his long-fingered hands nervously, unsure what do with them as he stood before the group. He looked to be in his early twenties. He's not much older than I am, she thought to herself. She wondered how it was he was a free black, and not a slave. She then recalled the night the Governor and Master Pinckney had come to Radcliffe Place to have dinner with Master Radcliffe. Master Pinckney had said, "It is the unfettered movement of the free Negro which is our greatest threat."

The group sang a spiritual and Denmark Vesey said a prayer to close their meeting. David Walker came up and spoke to her.

"Would you like some company on your way home?" he asked.

"You're welcome to walk with me," she answered, "but it's not far."

"I'd like to walk with you," he said.

The Bible study group made their goodbyes, and Denmark Vesey saw each member off into the evening. A few walked some of the distance with Lucinda and David until everyone had gone their separate ways, leaving the two alone.

"So you've always lived in Charleston?" he asked when they were by themselves.

"Well, no. Only since a handful of weeks before this past Christmas." She spoke softly, more than a hint of shyness in her voice, for she had never before been courted. "Master Radcliffe moved Mama and me from Radcliffe Place Plantation when his sister's husband died. Our new mistress lives here."

"Living here is different from the plantation, I suspect."

"Oh yes," she said, "here we have more . . ." She halted, searching for the words.

"Freedom?" he asked her.

"I was going to say time. Freedom?" she hesitated. "I guess." Then she added, "Whatever freedom is. I'm not sure I know."

"Freedom is the ability to make your own decisions about your life," he said.

She reflected on his words. She was certainly not free, for she had never made her own decisions.

Some of the houses on Meeting Street had windows and shutters opened to let in the night air and the faint playing of a piano and violin, sad music of love and loss, reached them in the street.

"How is it that you came here," she asked him, "to Charleston, I mean?"

"I came looking for work. I left Wilmington 'cause I had no future there. Charleston's the Mecca for free colored people up and down the Georgia and Carolinas coast."

"Mecca," she said, "where the followers of the prophet Mohammed face to pray." He looked at her with surprise. "Some of the Africans on Radcliffe Plantation worship the god Allah."

"And the city where the Mohamedeans are to journey in pilgrimage sometime during their lifetime," he said to her.

The early March evening was unseasonably warm. The flames in the street lamps burned with a golden glow that radiated like a hallo around the globes, reflecting bronze-like on David's and Lucinda's faces as they passed in and out of the shadows. The sky above was a fabric of blue velvet lit with the twinkling of countless stars. Strangely, she was nearly as new to Charleston as he was, yet she felt like some ancient inhabitant of the city.

"This way," she said, turning the corner off Meeting Street onto South Bay. "How did you become free?" she asked. "Were you ever a slave?"

"My papa was a slave on a plantation near Wilmington, but my mama was a free black woman. So I was born free. Or as free as a black man can be in this country."

"And you're on a pilgrimage?" she asked.

"Yes," he answered, observing her, "Yes, I guess I am. I came to see what it's like here. I want to travel across this country, to see and learn everything I can. I want to find out for myself what the condition of the black man is at different places. I'm like Denmark Vesey," he explained. "I want to work to free our people from slavery."

She did not say anything, so he too grew silent. He noticed to his surprise they were walking in step together.

"Has Denmark Vesey talked to you about slavery, about freedom?" he asked.

"Uncle Denmark says we're enslaved under the burden of our taskmasters like the Israelites were held in bondage in Egypt," she whispered.

"Do you believe what he says is true?"

"I don't know," she said slowly. She looked around to be certain no one was nearby. Then she added, "I believe it's not right for the whites to treat us like they do. And the more I see, the more I believe like Uncle Denmark says the whites will never set us free."

"Denmark Vesey speaks the truth," he said to her. "You'll never be free unless you do what you can to make yourself free."

They walked along together in silence again, the water sounds of the harbor reaching them from the darkness.

"Do you go to the African Church every Sunday?" he asked.

"Yes. And most every Wednesday we attend the prayer meetings and Bible study at Uncle Denmark's. My mama comes most times, but tonight she had some sewing tasks to do."

"Are you free to come and go when you want?" he asked.

"Only to church and to the meetings like tonight. And I go on errands to the markets most mornings. That's what Mistress Johnson permits me to do. She wrote out a pass for me."

"I went to the gathering of the slaves at the market last Sunday afternoon," he told her. "Do you go there?"

"Yes. I can go there. Mama has gone more than I have, but I've been before," she answered.

"Would you meet me there Sunday after church?" he asked.

She looked straight ahead, her eyes focused on some undeterminable point in the darkness. Her heart raced. Yes, she wanted to scream. Yes, I'll meet you there.

He seemed to take her silence as an offer of acceptance, for he said, "I'll meet you this Sunday. Look for me at the entrance to the market."

"We're almost there," she spoke to him gently. "I can walk the rest of the way myself."

She turned and stood for a moment facing him, unsure what to think or what to do. She stood very still, looking up into his face and into his eyes. He put his arms around her shoulders.

"Lucinda, you're beautiful," he said pulling her closer to him. No one had ever told her that before. Was that what she was now? A beautiful black woman? What happened to the little nigger slave girl she had always been? He leaned forward and gave her a kiss, a brief, simple kiss. Her heart beat loudly. "I'll see you Sunday," he said and turned away, disappearing slowly into the night.

Sunday seemed as if it would never come. All week as Lucinda did her tasks or ran her errands she thought of meeting David Sunday afternoon. At the Sunday church service, she looked about but could not find him in the congregation. When the service was over, she looked again, and not seeing him, she told her mama, "Mama, I'm going to the market. I'll be home before dark."

Mama gave her a questioning look, but only said, "Be's careful, chile."

"I will, Mama."

As Lucinda walked toward the market entrance, she saw David standing to one side waiting for her. She could feel her heart beat fast at seeing him again.

"I wasn't certain you would come," he said, stepping close to greet her.

She did not answer him. He took her hand. She held to his.

"It's good to see you," he said, looking into her eyes, black bottomless pools of light.

She said, "I looked for you at church."

"I looked for you too," he said, "then I came here." He paused. "Let's walk to the Battery. It'll be quieter there."

She mouthed a silent prayer of thanks, for it was a sparkling day, the sky deep blue and almost cloudless, with a fresh breeze scooping off the water. Hand in hand, they wandered in slow step together. Behind the wrought iron gates, the gardens of luscious-flower azaleas had begun their early bloom, purple, red, and fuchsia.

"Do you like it here in Charleston?" she asked him.

"Yes, I do," he said.

"Would you stay? Live here for good?"

"I don't know yet," he answered. He then asked, "You said the other night you'd only been here since before Christmas. You said you came from Radcliffe Plantation?"

"I was born on Radcliffe Place Plantation up on the Ashley River. Mama and myself lived there until we were sent here. We were servants in the Big House. Mama told me the Radcliffe's daughter, Miss Elizabeth, was born two planting seasons before me. We were raised together. When I was a little girl, I didn't know I was a slave. Mistress Radcliffe read the Bible to us and learnt me to read like they learnt her."

"They learnt you to read?" he asked.

"Yes. They were good to me then. Whenever I could I studied Miss Elizabeth's spelling books and schooled myself with a quill. But the older I became, the more tasks I was made to do. Mama and myself were forced to work day and night. They stopped treating me special. I heard Mistress Radcliffe tell Miss Elizabeth slaves are created for work, not love, and that it was a squander of warmth and care to bestow it upon a slave."

"Such is the life of a slave," he said.

"Life is meaner for the field hands," she said. "They work in the heat of the summer sun and the rain of fall and the cold of the winter frost. The overseers beat them with a whip if they don't work hard enough. They can never rest."

"Everywhere I've been, the blacks are forced into such wretched conditions," he said. "That's why we must do something. We must stop it."

"That's what Uncle Denmark says," she said. She decided to say no more about Denmark Vesey. Instead, she continued, "It's better for Mama and myself here in Charleston. We almost always get our tasks done by sundown and our Mistress doesn't often call for us after dark."

"Do you know anything about your people, about your ancestors?" he asked her.

"My grand mammy was born in Africa," she said.

"Did you know her?"

"Oh yes. She died when I was young. But I remember her. She sometimes comes to me now in dreams. She tended me when I was little. I remember stories she told and songs she sang to me. She said she came in a ship from Africa to Barbados and from there to Charleston where she was sold to Master Radcliffe's father. I remember my grand pappy too. My pappy died before I was born."

They reached the Battery.

"Africans aren't allowed to walk along the Battery," she told him. "The Patrol will take you up and the Magistrate will have you whipped. Let's not go any closer."

The March wind tugged at them, the water choppy in the harbor. A steamboat chugged up the Cooper River, smoke from the chimney snapped by the wind. Several schooners scooted across the grey foam and a freighter off in the distance made its way toward them. A fast-sailing three-mast clipper raced from the bay. David reached and placed his arm around her shoulder.

"I don't know why I'm telling you about my grand mammy and all," she said, looking down at the ground.

"I want to know," he said. "That's why I asked you." His tone changed. "Why do you bow and step aside when you pass a white person?"

"That's what we're to do," she said. "Mistress Johnson said we must . . ."

"There be laws of God, and there be laws of man," he interrupted her. "We must obey the laws of God, but we can choose whether or not to obey the laws of man. We have choices. We can decide."

"But you were born free. I was born a slave," she said to him.

"But you can be free. Isn't that what Denmark Vesey says? Don't you see?" he asked. "The whites hold the Africans in ignorance. I went to a Camp Meeting. I embarked in a steamboat from here and having been five or six hours on the water, we at last arrived at the place of the hearing, where there was a great concourse of people who were collected together to hear the Word of God. Myself and my boat companions, having been there a little while, were all called up to hear; I among the rest went up and took my seat. Being seated, I fixed myself in a complete position to hear the word of my Savior and to receive such as I thought was authenticated by the Holy Scriptures. But to my no ordinary astonishment, our Reverend gentleman got up and told us colored people that slaves must be obedient to their masters, must do their duty to their masters or be whipped, that the whip was made for the backs of fools." David paused. "Our gospel is that of peace and not blood and whips."

"Miss Elizabeth told me I must be obedient, and used Scripture that says so," Lucinda told him.

"They are false Christians who abuse the black man," he exclaimed. "Jesus preached a message of love . . . 'Love thy neighbor as thyself.'"

"How you know these things?" she asked.

"I spent much time reading books and the Bible," he said.

"Who learnt you?" she asked. "Where did you get books?"

"My mama was a free black woman, like I said. She was employed as a house servant for a white man in Wilmington who was a lawyer. He had no slaves. He was an opponent of slavery, the only white man I've ever known who had such beliefs, an abolitionist. The whites in Wilmington hated him. He had a large library of books . . . law books and histories about ancient Greece and Rome, plays, and the writings of Thomas Paine. He taught me to read and encouraged my use of the books in his library."

"Shakespeare?" she asked.

"How do you know of him?"

"Like I said, Miss Elizabeth, Master Radcliffe's daughter, and her mother, Mistress Nelly, learnt me to read. Miss Elizabeth and myself read some of Shakespeare's plays aloud, *Romeo and Juliet*, *A Midsummer Night's Dream*, and *The Tempest*. I played Caliban!"

"You're so fortunate to be treated in such a special way!" David said.

"I was their pet. It's not so now. I'm just another slave expected to do every task they demand."

She had never in her life known anyone like David. Not even Denmark Vesey was like him. Suddenly a great empty space within her was filled, and the feeling overwhelmed her, a feeling all so new. They stopped and sat on the ground together overlooking the harbor. She looked out at the water. He watched her dark smoky eyes, her silky-fine eyelashes, her lips black-red, curved, her slender throat curving downward.

"Come with me," he said suddenly.

"Where can we go?" she asked, surprised.

"Philadelphia, New York, Boston."

"What?"

"Run away with me. Escape. Leave Charleston. Be my wife. Leave this behind."

"David, I can't do that."

"Why not?" he asked.

"I couldn't leave Mama like that."

"I thought you wanted to be free?"

"I do . . . "

"But?"

"Not like that. You don't know what they'd do to me if I tried to escape. Punish me. Torture me if we were caught. And they'd treat you worse. They'd kill you. You'd be hanged."

"I'm willing to take that chance," he said, looking into her eyes, dark as midnight. "Do you want to be with me?"

"Yes."

"Then come with me. I can counterfeit your papers of manumission. We can take a steamboat from the harbor all the way to Boston. I can protect you."

"David," she said and the tears built up in her eyes. Without thinking, she placed her head on his shoulder. Should she tell him how she sometimes felt so lonely? How she prayed for God to send someone to her just like him. How at night she lay on her pallet unable to sleep, wondering what it would be like to love someone. She had wondered if slaves were supposed to have such feelings. Now here was someone who could do what he wanted because he was free. And he was asking her to join with him, to run away, to escape, to be together. How was she supposed to know what to do? Would God let her know? What kind of sign would He give her? Was this it now? That she was here, that David had come into her life, suddenly dropping like manna from the sky. Or was it temptation? Was the devil trying to steal her away into his corruption? How could she know? How could she be certain?

"You said freedom is making your own decisions," she said, pulling back from him. "How do you know what's the right thing to do?"

"You just know," he said. "You have to follow your feelings."

"Sometimes I don't know how I feel," she said. "I get confused."

"Faith in Christ can lead us out of confusion," he said.

She wanted to feel his body against hers. She wanted to place her flushed cheek against his cool face. She wanted to share in his freedom. If only she knew how, she thought.

The shadows had grown long around them. She wiped the tears from her eyes with the back of her slender hand.

"I have to go," she said to him. "It'll be dark soon."

"When will I see you again?" he asked.

"I'll see you at Denmark Vesey's Wednesday night," she said, and then asked him, "Where do you stay?"

"In a crowded boarding house," he said. "at 20 Limehouse Street. I have a bed in number 6, upstairs." He gestured toward the direction of the river. "Limehouse crosses Tradd. Not far from the Cooper River." Then he said apologetically, "They don't allow women in the rooms. The sailors, you know, they . . ." he said.

"Yes," she said, "I understand."

"I'll walk with you," he said, standing up. He took her hands in his and pulled her to her feet. They silently made their way along South Bay, the setting sun over their shoulders stretching long shadows in front of them. The open water of the harbor spread out to the near horizon, dark and grey-green where the rivers came together, the sky darkening blue above the line of the sea.

Wednesday evening Mama went with Lucinda to the prayer meeting at Denmark Vesey's.

"Mama," Lucinda said when he sat down beside her, "this is David Walker."

Mama slid a glance from the corner of her eye.

When the prayer meeting was over, David asked, "Would you like for me to walk home with you?"

"Mama," Lucinda said, "David wants to walk us home."

"We's much obliged," Lucinda's mama said to him, "but that's alright."

"That be who you go see Sunday?" Mama asked as they walked through the streets.

"I met him at the market and we went down near the Battery for a while, Mama," she answered. "That's all."

"Who he be?"

"He's a free black man, from Wilmington. He came to Charleston looking for work. He's only been here for a few weeks. I met him last Wednesday night at Uncle Denmark's. Uncle Denmark met him at the African Church and invited him to the prayer meetings."

"You sweet on him," Mama said. "You be careful, chile."

Sunday Lucinda once again searched for David in the crowded church congregation. She could not find him. She decided to go to the market. Again, as she walked up to the entrance he stood in the same place waiting for her.

"Do you want to walk down to the Battery again?" he asked.

"If you want to," she told him.

Neither one of them spoke, until finally he said, "Did you consider further what we talked of?"

"About escaping with you?" She whispered the words.

"Yes."

"Yes, I considered it," she said, searching his face. "I thought very much of it. David, it's too dangerous. Master Radcliffe has had slaves run away before. He sends bounty men to capture them and bring them back in chains. They're always found. And they're harshly punished. Master Radcliffe wouldn't stop until we were caught. When he sets his mind to something, he proceeds at all cost. All my life I've seen the way he is." She looked into David's eyes. She reached for his hand. "Can't you stay here? Be in Charleston as a free black man? I'm a slave, but at least we can be together."

"What kind of life is that?" he asked.

"It's the only life I know," she said. "It's the only life I'll ever know." She began to cry, choking back her tears.

"It doesn't have to be this way," he said bitterly. "A day will come when this country will split apart. A day will come when the whites will pay with blood for their mistreatment of the blacks."

"I don't know what else to do," she said.

"The whites don't even recognize marriage of slaves," he said. "Your master could sell you at any time."

"Master Radcliffe wouldn't do that."

"You lack experience, Lucinda. I'm not trying to be unkind, but I want you to understand how things are. I've seen families torn apart, husbands and wives sold to different masters and shipped off in different directions, never to see each other ever again."

She sniffled but said nothing. She knew what he told her was true.

"And every child you bear born into slavery, destined to enrich and serve the white man, to be sold off at any time. I've given much solemn consideration to our plight," he whispered to her. "Running away is the best course of action. This could be the only chance you'll ever have. I thought every slave desires to be free. If not, then they have no soul. Their inner light has been put out. I don't believe you're that way. I think you burn with an inner light."

"I'll do it," she said, staring at him through her tears, surprised to hear her own voice. "I'll run away with you." He leaned over and kissed her. "But I must tell Mama first," she said wiping the tears from her eyes. "I could never leave without telling her."

"We must leave as soon as we can. It's dangerous if we wait too long," he said.

When she was alone with David, it had been easy to say yes but now Lucinda had no idea how she was going to tell her mama. She knew it would not be easy. Finally when she was certain they were alone, she blurted out, "Mama, I'm leaving Charleston."

"You what!" Her mama stopped dead still and stared, Mama's eyes bulging from her face. "What you say?"

"I'm leaving. I'm running away, Mama. I'm going to escape up north."

"You done lost ever bit o' sense I reckon you has!"

"I'm serious, Mama," Lucinda said.

"You be serious dead, that what you be!"

"Don't talk so loud," Lucinda whispered. "Someone will hear you."

"I don't care who hear. You talk crazy talk."

"I made up my mind, Mama. I want to be free."

"You wanna be dead! They catch you and punish you, brand you with a hot iron on yo' fo'head, brand you like they do the cows so that you be marked fo' life and never try to 'scape again. It be all that talk Denmark Vesey put in yo' head."

"It has nothing to do with Denmark Vesey."

"Then it be that man David Walker! Cause he and ol' man Vesey be free they thinks everybody can be free."

"You told me you hate the white man."

"So! That don't mean I stick my neck out fo' them to put in a noose. You get this nonsense out o' yo' head."

"You can't stop me!"

Mama slapped her hard across the face. "Don't you sass me!" Mama cried. She slapped Lucinda again. Lucinda's cheek stung with pain. "You the only thing I got and I ain't gonna lose you."

"I thought you'd be happy for me," Lucinda tried to get out between her tears.

"I be happy that you alive," Mama said. "I don't wanna hear no more o' this. Till you get that in yo' head you ain't goin' to Denmark Vesey's house and you ain't gonna see that man no mo'. You push me and I tell Massa Radcliffe. You understan' what I'm sayin' to you, chile?"

Lucinda turned and ran to their room. She threw herself on her pallet, covered her head with the blanket, and cried herself to sleep. Her mama did not wake her until the next morning.

Sunday morning came. "We's goin' with the Misses to church this mornin'," Mama said, making no mention about Lucinda's red, puffy eyes as they prepared breakfast. Lucinda rode with Mama and Mistress Johnson in the carriage, the livery servant Uncle Tuesday on the coachman's platform urging the horses along through the crowded streets.

"I'm so pleased you wanted to attend my church this morning," Mistress Johnson said to them as they made their way. Lucinda remained silent. At the church service, Lucinda and Mama sat in the balcony along with the other black members of the congregation. Lucinda barely listened to the priest's sermon. All she could think about was David. She wasn't sure what to do. Her mama had never treated her this way. Then all week Mistress Johnson sent Mama to the markets. Lucinda realized she was trapped. There was no way she could get to David. It was too dangerous for her to sneak out, for she was under constant watch by her mama and Mistress Johnson. If she was caught she would be harshly punished. Mistress Johnson even took her written pass. Wednesday came and went. They did not go to Denmark Vesey's. What would David be thinking? Mama made no more mention of him. Lucinda ached with helplessness.

After nearly five weeks, finally one morning Mama was busy upstairs and Mistress Johnson sent Lucinda on an errand to the market. She walked as fast as she could, afraid to run. She went straight to Denmark Vesey's house. Fortunately, he was home. "No, I haven't seen David for a while now," Uncle Denmark told her. In desperation, she hurried to the boarding house toward the Cooper River where he leased his room. She entered the building. No one was in the hallway. She sneaked up the stairs to the room number David had told her. She knocked softly. No one came to the door. Then a man came out into the hallway from another room.

"You look for someone?" he asked. The man spoke with an accent. She thought it might be Spanish but she wasn't certain.

"Yes," she said, "his name's David, a black man. Do you know him? This is his room." She gestured toward the door.

"He leave," the man said.

"Leave?"

"How you say? Move on. Move out. Three, maybe four days."

"Are you sure?"

"I see him before. He say he go north. Boston? Sorry. This I know."

Her heart sank. She was weak in her knees and thought she might fall to the floor. How could she have been so foolish? Why had she not been brave and run away with him at once, escape from Charleston forever regardless of what Mama said. Did he know how much she cared for him? She wandered slowly through the streets toward the market, dazed and hardly aware of where she was going, hoping somehow she would find him returning to get her. She found herself near the wharves, knowing it was not the place for her to be. It was late. She knew she must return to South Bay. Mama would be furious. Or afraid something had happened to her. Mistress Johnson would be angry she had taken so long to return. She might be punished. The tears flowed from her eyes. She gave up her search and rushed to the market, then made her way home. There was a black spot of hatred in her heart for her mama. She was plagued with guilt at her hatred but she could not rid herself of it. She sneaked in quietly without seeing Mama or Mistress Johnson. She put up the provisions in the kitchen pantry and tried to dry her tears.

The next time Lucinda saw Denmark Vesey he said to her, "I received a letter for you." Her heart leapt up. "It's from David Walker." Denmark Vesey reached in the pocket on the inside of his vest and handed her two folded, sealed pages. In a very good hand and in large-size letters she read on the back of the pages *Lucinda Radcliffe, c/o Denmark Vesey, Carpenter, Charleston, South Carolina.* The letters read from *David Walker, 4 Liberty St., Boston, Massachusetts.* "I don't get much mail," Denmark Vesey said to her. "I was by the Exchange and just happened to check. He also sent a letter to me. Should I keep an eye out for mail to you?"

"Yes," Lucinda said eagerly. "If you could, Uncle Denmark. I would so much appreciate you doing that for me."

She lifted the letters to her nose and sniffed, wondering if there was anything of David's smell about them. Her heart beat wildly. She wanted to tear the letters open then and there but she dare not do so. She clutched the papers in her hand, holding to them like a precious object, like a priceless gold jewel or a manumission of freedom.

When she was alone at Mistress Johnson's, Lucinda opened the wax letter seals with a butter knife. She unfolded the pages. The letter was written in the same neat hand as the outside. Her own hands trembled as she whispered aloud:

25th April 1822

My dearest Lucinda,

I have departed Charleston and am now living in Boston, Massachusetts. I tried every way I knew to find you after we last met at the Charleston market. You did not come to the African Church for weeks. You did not come to the market place. You did not attend the class meetings at Denmark Vesey's house. I looked for you day after day at all these places. I walked several times by your Mistress' house on South Bay, hoping to catch a glimpse of you, but with no success. What has happened to you? I pray you are safe and well. I am so fearful you are sick or have been hurt or something is terribly wrong. I heard there were many sicknesses in Charleston over the last year.

Did I do anything to hurt you, to cause you to lose your love for me?

After over a month had gone by, and not being able to find you, I decided you must have had a change of heart. I repeatedly asked Denmark Vesey if he had seen you, but he said he had not, and he too was concerned and worried about you. I could no longer bear the thought of knowing you were in the same city as I was, that my bosom craved to have yours next to mine, and I longed to see the softness of your face, the crystal sparkle of your black eyes, but that your affection and your love for me had faded. I saw no choice and decided I must renew my journey throughout America without you, as much as I now regret my actions, however sad I am and however much I wish it was not this way.

Lucinda, I meant what I said to you with all of my heart. But the only way I saw us as truly being together was for you to run away with me, to escape the chains of slavery which hold you back in Charleston. I thought you were ready to take this great leap for your freedom. I know such a choice would have placed you in dire danger, and you could lose your life if you were caught . . . both of us could lose our lives. Or I could have stayed with you in Charleston, myself as a free man and you as a slave. I prayed and prayed over this. I am unsure I could ever be the man you deserve if our love was constantly constrained by the bindings of slavery. I pondered and pondered how empty and tragic my life would be if you were ever sold and taken from me. How empty and tragic my life is now that I am not with you. Has fate worked against us in either case?

Please forgive me. You are forever in my thoughts and prayers, and in my heart.

Your love,

David

She tried to control her tears. She sneaked and took a sheet of letter stationery, a quill, and a jar of black ink from Mistress Johnson's mahogany writing desk. She had never stolen anything from her masters, except maybe an extra rice cake from the kitchen once or twice, and she felt guilty for taking the letter sheet. The quill and ink she would return. She said a long prayer of forgiveness. She thought after all she had no choice, it was just one sheet, and she could do something special for Mistress Johnson to make up for the theft.

Lucinda read well, but she wrote slowly. She gripped the quill tightly, styling out every letter of every word.

My dearest David,

Your letter is wet with my tears. My fears have come true. You thought I had forsaken you. And now you have gone away.

I told Mama I was going to run away with you, and she did everything to stop me. She said she would tell Master Radcliffe. Mama told Mistress Johnson something. They would not let me go from the house for weeks. I could not go to the African Church, to the market, or to Uncle Denmark's class meetings. They watched me night and day.

Finally one morning Mistress Johnson sent me to the market because Mama was busy. I went to the place where you said you rented a room.

A man told me you had moved away.

I am so sorry. Will I ever see you again?

I love you.

Lucinda

She folded the sheet and sealed it with Mistress Johnson's seal, using melted wax from a candle as she had seen Mistress Johnson do.

The next errand she ran, she took the letter to the post office at the Custom Exchange. The postage was twenty-five cents. That was all she had, twenty-five cents. Most had been given to her in pence coins by Miss Elizabeth over the years.

Two weeks passed. She saw Denmark Vesey at the African Church.

"Uncle Denmark, did I get another letter?"

"Yes," he said, pulling it again from his vest pocket. "I went by the Exchange yesterday, or the day before."

When the church service was over, she stole away to the house on South Bay, hid in the pantry and read the letter.

8th May, 1822

Dearest Lucinda,

I received your letter. I am glad to know you are safe and that you are well. I was concerned about you.

I have made friends with a group of free blacks here who share my interest in working for the freedom of our people and improving our lot. We are going to publish a journal, and distribute it here in Boston, in New York, and in Baltimore. We are going to see if we can pay sailors bound for Charleston to pass it among the blacks there. We will work to abolish slavery, and for the emancipation of all slaves in the South.

I have become involved in a church here. In Boston, I can be married under the sanctity of the church, and recognized by the laws of the land.

I have considered our fate, Lucinda. William Shakespeare has a character in one of his dramas say "The fault, dear Brutus, is not in our stars, but in ourselves." Our lives are not products of destiny, Lucinda, but of our own will.

I pray God watches over you. May Jesus bless your soul and may all be well in your heart.

David

She knew David was gone from her life forever. He has found someone else to love, she realized, someone he could marry, truly marry, a marriage sanctified by the church, a marriage accepted by both God and man. She blamed Mama. She would never again trust her with secrets. She blamed herself for not keeping plans of her escape unspoken. Should she cast blame on David? He had waited weeks and weeks for her. How could she expect him to do more? Tears wet her face. She gathered herself and knelt on her knees. "Dear Jesus," she prayed, "come into my heart. Caste out the demons that torment me." She felt no will of her own, regardless of David's letter, only that she was born a slave, born in chains, fixed by fate. She would never be free. Only God can save me now, she thought. "In Jesus name I pray. Amen."

An assembly of nearly twenty black men jammed the hot, noisy workroom of Denmark Vesey's shop. Denmark Vesey stood talking with several of the men. He repeatedly pulled out a rag to wipe the sweat from his face, then stuffed it back to dangle from his back pocket. Sandy Vesey, Denmark's son, along with Monday Gell, stood near the open door to the room. A large book like the Bible lay open before them on a table. Sandy Vesey pointed to a letter inserted between some of the leaves of the book and said to Monday Gell, "look here Monday, see how they are making fun of us. Denmark says not to worry. We will fight without the aid of an army from Santo Domingo if we must."

Gullah Jack watched the front door. He called to Denmark Vesey, "Denmark, more men." Denmark Vesey worked his thick-chested frame across the room to greet Perault Strohecker and an unknown companion as they entered the house.

"Denmark, I have brought someone with me," said Perault.

"What's your name and who do you belong to?" Denmark Vesey questioned the stranger.

Perault answered for him, "Bacchus belonging to Mr. Hammet."

"Which Hammet?" asked Denmark Vesey.

Bacchus answered, "Mr. Benjamin Hammet, the gentlemen who put old Lorenzo Dow in jail, and is an officer in Captain Martindale's company."

Seemingly satisfied, Denmark Vesey said, "Come with us," and Bacchus was led by Perault and Denmark Vesey into a side room. Denmark Vesey stood not speaking and studied the face of the man.

"Bacchus, I have some particular thing to say to you," Perault volunteered.

"What's that?"

"We're going to have a war and fight the white people, and you must join with us."

Bacchus Hammet stepped back and forth about the room.

"Perault, I'm sorry that you brought me into this business," he finally said. "And you better let it alone."

Denmark Vesey's hard stare into the eyes of the man before him did not change. "Does your master treat you well?" Denmark Vesey asked.

"Yes, I believe so."

"Believe so? Tell me, Bacchus, do you eat the same as your master?"

"Yes . . . sometimes . . . but not always as well as my master."

"Does your master sleep in a soft bed?"

"Yes."

"Do you sleep on as soft a bed as your master?"

"Well, no."

"Bacchus," Denmark Vesey asked, "Who made your master?"

"Why, God."

"Who made you?"

"God."

"Then aren't you as good as your master if God made him and you? Aren't you as equal and free?"

"Yes."

"Then why don't you join and fight your master? Does he whip you when you do wrong?"

"Yes, sometimes."

"Then why don't you turn about and fight for yourself? You are as free as your master."

"Bacchus, you need not fret. You may as well join us," Perault said.

Then Denmark Vesey added, "Any person who doesn't join us must be treated as an enemy and put to death."

Bacchus' eye began to twitch. "If that's the case, well, I'll join you."

"Can you get arms?" Denmark Vesey asked.

"Maybe an old sword."

"No matter. Any arms. Whatever you can get bring them to me."

They returned to the large room. Denmark Vesey held his Bible in his hand as he stepped up on a wooden box so that his head rose above the level of the crowd. Peter Poyas and Gullah Jack called for silence.

"Friends, I have an important secret to communicate to you," Denmark Vesey said, almost at a whisper. "You must not disclose it to anyone. If you do," Denmark Vesey now spoke more loudly and paused to emphasize his words, "you will be put to instant death." The faces of the men in the room showed that not a one doubted Denmark Vesey's warning. Denmark Vesey held his Bible up in the air. "Hold up your hand and swear you will tell no one. Repeat after me, we will not tell if taken by the whites, nor will we tell if we are to be put to death."

Each man dutifully repeated Denmark Vesey's words.

"We are free but the white people here won't let us be so," Denmark Vesey began. "The legislature in Washington has made us so. It is high time we had our liberty and I can show you how you might obtain it." The men shifted slightly on their feet. The room was quiet. "The only way is to rise up and fight the whites."

"Amen," responded several of the men.

"We must unite together, as the people of Santo Domingo did, never to betray one another, and to die before we would tell upon one another. The blacks are deprived of their rights and privileges by the white people. Our Church was shut up so that we could not use it. It is high time for us to seek our rights. We are fully able to conquer the whites if we are only unanimous and courageous as the Santo Domingo people were."

"How will we do it?" one of the men asked.

"We intend to make the attack by setting the Governor's lumber and rice mills on fire and also some houses near the water, and as soon as the bells begin to ring the alarm for fire the servants in the yard should kill every white man as they come out of their houses. We will take the Guard House and the Magazine to get arms. Afterwards the white women and children must be killed."

There was a slight murmuring among some of the men. "Why kill the ministers and women and children?" one man asked. "Is that not a sin?" another man asked.

"No, to do so is *not* a sin," Denmark Vesey insisted, "for it is commanded in the scriptures, decreed in the Law of Moses." Denmark Vesey held his Bible in his hand and opened it. "Listen to the Word of the Lord from the 20th chapter of Deuteronomy. The 16th verse reads, 'But of the cities of these people, which the Lord thy God doeth give thee for thy inheritance, thou shalt save nothing alive that breatheth.' And verse 17 says 'Thou shalt utterly destroy them, namely the Hittites, and the Jebusites; as the Lord thy God hath commanded thee.' So God said to Moses. Listen to the word of Joshua 6:21, 'And they utterly destroyed all that was in the city, both man and woman, young and old, and ox, and sheep, and ass, with the edge of the sword.'" Denmark Vesey looked about the room. Sweat ran down his face. The men stared, silent and still.

"It is not safe to keep one white alive," he cried, raising his hand with the Bible above his head for all too see, "but to destroy them utterly as commanded in these scriptures. That is how it was done in Santo Domingo." Denmark Vesey turned the pages of his Bible to where he had marked the place. "And Deuteronomy, chapter 2, verse 34 says, 'And we took all his cities at that time, and utterly destroyed the men, the women, and the little ones, of every city, we left none to remain.' In the 31st chapter of Numbers, God spoke to Moses saying, 'Avenge the children of Israel of the Midianites.' Numbers 31, 13 says, 'And Moses was wroth with the officers of the host, with the captains over thousands, with captains over hundreds, which came from the battle. And Moses said unto them, have ye saved all the women alive? Behold, these caused the children of Israel . . . to commit trespass against the Lord . . . Now therefore kill every male among the little ones, and kill every women that hath known man by lying with him. But all the women children, that have not known a man by lying with him, keep alive for yourselves.'"

Denmark Vesey closed his Bible and looked about the room. He reflected for a long moment. "Keep the virgins for yourselves if you must," he said. "We can sell them as slaves in Santo Domingo."

"Are we to stay in Charleston after it's over?"

"Once we take all the specie from the banks, the goods from the shops, the spoil of our plunder," Denmark Vesey said, "we will hoist sail to Santo Domingo. The ship captains shall not be killed, for they will sail the ships. I expect the Santo Domingo people will send troops to help us.

"We shan't be slaves to these damn rascals any longer. We must kill everyone that we can and drive the rest out of the city."

The men in the room began to talk loudly among themselves. Denmark Vesey kicked the box he stood on.

"Men, men. We have a friend who is to go into the country to raise the country Negroes to come down. All who can must put in money to raise a sum to pay his master wages while he is gone. We must have arms made, pikes like they use in Africa for the blacks on the country plantations. Those of you that've got it, put in 12 ½ cents for that purpose." Gullah Jack took his hat in his hand and stood by the door.

"Some of you have come from the country," Denmark Vesey said. "Those of you who must journey tonight, God be with you."

The room was suddenly empty, save for Monday Gell, who dragged a chair to where Denmark Vesey sat on the wooden box he used during the assembly. Denmark Vesey's shirt was dark with sweat; his bloodshot eyes sagged, his thick lips meaty on his face.

"How goes it, Denmark?" asked Monday, spreading his muscular and lanky limbs in the chair.

"I believe all bodes well," answered Denmark Vesey. His probing eyes scanned to inspect every crevice of the room. "Where did you get the holy book of the Mohamedeans?" Denmark Vesey asked, nodding his head toward the table where the book still lay.

"From Africa, the Koran," Monday Gell said, "guarded by Allah on the long journey over the sea."

"Jehovah, Allah," Denmark Vesey said, "the same God of Abraham. The Africans who are Mohamedeans know this, Monday."

The two men sat quietly in the hot room.

"Been mighty hot of late," Monday Gell finally broke the silence.

"That's good," Denmark Vesey said. "Makes Buckra suffer."

The bells sounded from the church tower, striking twelve tolls, midnight in the old city.

"Where will you go after this is ended, Denmark," Monday Gell asked, "When the slaves of Charleston are finally free?"

"Where the Lord's will takes me." Denmark Vesey's voice was grave. He pulled the rag from his hip pocket and wiped his face. "I reckon I'll go to Santo Domingo and see what it's like there. Then perchance back to Africa. After all, Africa's my home. As it is yours." Denmark Vesey turned his eyes on Monday Gell before looking away again. "Such a long time ago since I was taken away. I wonder if I still belong there. I've sailed to most every port from Africa to the Americas. I wonder if I still have a home," Denmark Vesey said, more to himself than to his companion in the sultry room.

The next Sunday after church, Mistress Johnson's livery servant, Tuesday, hooked up the horse and carriage and Mistress Johnson, and the visiting Miss Elizabeth, Master Jimmy Johnson's wife Ruth, and young Jeremiah all climbed in and trotted off for a Sunday afternoon of social calls in the city. Lucinda's mama had completed her sewing and took off to the slave gathering at the market place. Lucinda was alone in the house. She heard the front house door open and the sound of heavy footsteps through the downstairs, then the footsteps come up the stairs where she was checking on a task she'd almost forgotten to do. She turned, surprised to see him. "Why Master John . . ." she tried to say before his quick hand clasped tightly over her mouth, his breath exhaling the sweet stench of rum. He thrust his hot face against her cheek and whispered in her ear, "If you say so much as a word to anyone, you'll regret the day you were born. Do you understand me?" His mouth was sticky against her face. He tried to kiss her. He pushed her with his strong hands gripping her arms, forcing her down onto the divan. He lifted up her dress and pulled down her underthings. He turned her over on her stomach. "You nigger wench," he slurred to her roughly, and smacked her hard with his hand across her bare bottom. She was frightened and thought he might hurt her. Her mind swarmed with wild thoughts she could not control. She struggled to fight but it did no good. He penned her down with his weight. When he was finished with her, he stood and took a handkerchief from his pocket and wiped himself, then folded it carefully and returned it back to his pocket.

"Clean yourself up," he said with a strange hint of gentleness. "Leave no trace of blood." He leaned down and kissed her.

She waited until the sound of his steps on the stairs reached the front door and she heard the door close behind him. She then pulled her dress down and picked up her underclothes from the floor. The tears streamed down her cheeks as she hurried to clean away the blood.

In the days that followed, she went about her tasks with a dark mood, her feelings numb and cold.

"What be wrong with you, chile?" Mama asked her.

"Nothing, Mama."

"Then why you mopin' 'round here wearin' that long face. You sick?"

"No, I'm not sick."

"Somethin' wrong, and don' tell me it ain't. You be still missin' that man David?" Mama asked.

"No, Mama. I'm alright."

She tried her best to hide her feelings. She questioned how she had changed. Before, each day in Charleston had passed faster than a hummingbird's wings beat in blurry motion as it feeds upon a flower. She wondered where the time had gone since the day she first saw the city from the harbor. So much had happened, she reflected. Now her days dragged on in a slow gloom of anticipation. She knew it would happen again. She knew she was unable to stop it.

What was she supposed to do? She was just a slave, she reconciled to herself. Should she give in to him? Let him have his way with her? Was this what was expected of her, to serve his lust, to be his concubine? Should she tell Master Radcliffe? Or Miss Elizabeth? Would they even believe her? If she told, would Master Johnson make her life miserable? Would he punish her? It was all so new to her. Or could she find in her new status a source of influence over Master Johnson. Could she now glean special treatment, special favors from him?

She beheld herself in her mistress' vanity mirror, listening carefully to make certain Mistress Johnson or Mama was not nearby. The face that reflected in the mirror stared back at her with big dark eyes. Was she beautiful, she wondered? Did David, did Master Johnson, truly think so? She could still feel the hot contact of Master Johnson's sticky mouth against her cheek, the rum smell on his breath. She shivered as she examined her reflection. She felt a sickly frailty. She was torn by sadness and shame, yet haunted by urges of desire. Did she hate Master Johnson for what he had done to her? She knew she was not the only slave in such a plight. In her nightly Bible readings she turned to the *Songs of Solomon*. 'I am black, but comely,' she read, 'O ye daughters of Jerusalem, as the tents of Kedar, as the curtains of Soloman.' She was a slave, she was chattel, she belonged to someone else. She prayed to God for mercy and strength.

The next time was two weeks later. He came to Charleston on a Sunday along with a handful of slaves from Radcliffe Place. His mother had been picked up by a friend's carriage and was out for the afternoon. He made sure Lucinda's mama and Tuesday were going with the other slaves to the slave gathering at the market place. He whispered to Lucinda when he was able to get alone with her, "Come to the carriage house at three. Don't be late."

The house was empty and she heard the quarter-hour calls from St. Michael's steeple. She changed to the brightly colored dress and matching headscarf she had worn the day she first came to Charleston. She did not put on any underclothes.

She went out back and entered the carriage house. The room was dark and cool. She climbed into the carriage. She heard the carriage house door open.

"Where are you?" he called out, not loudly.

"Here," she answered softly.

He opened the carriage door and smiled when he saw her in the carriage seat. She turned her head, preferring not to look at him. She did not put up any resistance. She knew it was useless. She pulled up her dress to her waist, leaned back, closed her eyes, and waited for him.

He was gentler with her this time. Afterwards, as he buttoned up his pants, she boldly asked, "Why did you force yourself on me before?"

"I had drunk too much rum, much too much." he said. "I could no longer contain my passion for you." Then he added, "I would never hurt you, Lucinda."

"You could've spoken to me of your feelings," she told him.

"That would've frightened you even more, would it not?" he asked.

"No," she said. "I've seen how you look at me sometimes. You could've had me simply by asking. I would not have refused you."

"I'm most pleased to know that," he said. He kissed her gently on the mouth. "You'll be glad you've made such a decision."

After losing David, she determined never to lose again, no matter what. She craved for someone to love her. After all, she thought, Master Johnson was handsome for a white man, young and lean and muscular, with a glint of wildness in his eyes. You had to search to see but it was there to find if you looked closely and she had seen it. The number of yellow and brown skinned mulattos she saw in Charleston made it clear to her it was common for masters to be with their female slaves. She knew some Charleston gentlemen's slave lovers lived in their master's abode with the white family, but these were generally very light-skinned girls, quadroons and octoroons, not full-blooded Africans like herself. Sometimes she would see them on the streets, sporting parasols to block the sun, dressed in silk stockings and dresses and jewelry, selling baked sweet potatoes or fruits to the passersby. They laughed and dallied and appeared happy and carefree.

I'm like these other slave women, she reasoned, I'm the mistress of my master. He wasn't actually her master except as she allowed him to be, she thought. She would tell no one, especially Mama, but she wondered what Denmark Vesey would think if he knew. It didn't matter, she decided. She would make her own choice, a choice of submission, even if she was not free. She knew there were those like Master Radcliffe who viewed such affairs as the worse sort of treatment of a slave. But what if it was what she wanted, she decided. She struggled with the irony that as Master Johnson controlled her, yet she somehow exercised a free abandon of her own. She then felt least like a slave. Strange to her, there was a feeling of freedom in her surrender. It was the only way she knew—to give herself—the only way she knew to realize some misshapen, some shadow of freedom, freedom that came by her sufferance.

She needed someone she could trust, and she felt she could trust him. If anyone ever found out he had everything to lose. She decided she would do whatever he required of her. The more he dominated her, the more she would surrender and submit to him. The more submissive she was, the greater her feelings. She would be his special slave. No one would ever know. He was her secret, she was his. Her surrender, his desire, their shared passion, deepened the tangled, murky, unspoken master and slave bond between them. Her instincts guided her through the maze.

As for him, he wanted to be with her as often as he could, to drive out his lust by taking her in every possible way. She was ripe for the taking, deliciously ripe. She waited for him to teach her everything.

He was often in Charleston. He sent Mama to the market. Mistress Johnson went out to the garden to admire the roses, now in glorious bloom. He went upstairs. He and Lucinda squeezed into a corner beside the armoire as not to be seen from the room door. Lucinda lifted her skirt and quickly removed her undergarments.

"Master, we shall surely be heard," she whispered to him as he pulled her close.

He cupped his hand over her mouth. She tried to cry out in pleasure. He pressed his hand harder.

He reached the bottom of the stairs just as his mother came in from the garden.

He rented an apartment off an alley in the heart of the city. Once a week he would appear at his mother's house on South Bay with a list of provisions needs for the plantation, and send Lucinda out to the markets, telling her to make certain she found and purchased each item, the list bearing the shops likely to have the provisions and how much she should pay. He gave her coins to pay for a goat-cart to haul it all back, when he had actually already acquired everything and had the supplies waiting to go back with her afterwards. She would walk straight to the apartment where he would be waiting for her.

"Tell me what to do, Master," she said.

He bought her clothes, fine things he brought in a leather travel bag, and she would dress for him, able to wear them only when they were in the room together, silk stockings and silk *lingerie*. She felt like a daughter of Babylon. There was an excitement, which thrilled her along with the guilt, and she was confused and afraid she was now damned by God. The corruption of the city had corrupted her. Her mind and her body, her heart and her soul were bound to his. She was swallowed up in the excesses of the sinful city.

"Do I please you, Master?" she whispered to him.

"Very much," he said.

In so many ways, he could not have been more different than she, his blond hair straight and near to his shoulders in length, his green eyes bright as marbles, the fair skin of his face faint with freckles, more visible after he was out in the sun. His neatly trimmed blonde moustache crowned his upper lip. His skin was smooth as a piece of combed Sea Island cotton to her finger tips, his hands not calloused from work like her own. Sometimes he would take a riding crop and whip her, only on her *derriere* and never hard enough to make her cry; and she was careful never to let her mama catch sight of her unclothed backside. She was moved at the sight of his white skin against her black skin, the image forbidden yet erotic, exotic to her. Her soul had become lost in a dark, aching place beyond redemption.

She ran her fingertips across his chest. "Are we like other lovers?" she asked him.

"No," he said. He then paused before saying, "We're different."

"How?" she asked.

"We're just not the same," he said.

"Good. I don't want to be like others," she said. "Is it because I'm black and you're white?"

"I don't think so," he answered her.

"So it's not this way with your wife?" she questioned him.

"No," he said.

"Even though you have a child?" she pressed.

"You're young and curious. No more questions," he said.

"I'm almost seventeen," she said. "I'm a woman now."

"I've been asked if you are for sale," he told her.

She froze. A spike of panic plunged in her breast. The look of fear must have covered her face like a caul, for he quickly said to her "You've nothing to fear, Lucinda. I told them you're not."

He decided to buy her a gift, a gift to show her he truly cared for her.

"If I gave you a gift, what would you most like?" he asked her.

"Oh, Master," she said.

"I'm serious," he said.

She thought for a moment.

"Miss Elizabeth has an emerald and diamond gold necklace Master Radcliffe gave her one Christmas. Is that what you mean?"

"We shall see," he said.

The next time they were together, he took out a small silk purse from his travel bag and handed it to her.

"Go ahead," he said, smiling. "Open it."

She stared at him with a surprised look on her face, her eyes big, her mouth opened. She carefully untied the purse, and reached in and took out an emerald and diamond necklace. The necklace had three emerald stones in a row with a diamond on either side, all set in gold and on a gold chain. The jewels sparkled magically. Lucinda reached and put her arms around him.

"Oh, Master!" she cried, and her eyes blurred with tears.

She sat on the edge of the bed and undid her blouse and her undergarments, removed them and turned toward him. She took the necklace and clasped it around her neck above her round breasts, like she clasped Miss Elizabeth's necklaces when she helped put them on her mistress, the emeralds and diamonds falling into place at Lucinda's throat. She stood and looked at herself in the mirror, reached up with her slender hand and touched the jewels with her finger tips as they glistened against the sheen of her black skin.

"How does it look, Master?" she asked, turning toward him.

"Beautiful," he said.

If she had lived a thousand years, she would never have dreamed she would have such beautiful riches. She turned her head and her shoulders back and forth, looking at herself in the mirror, the jewels shimmering in the light like a pool of crystal and shining deep-green water.

"African girls don't wear necklaces until they become a woman," she said to him.

He inspected her dazzling face carefully.

"You're the only one I could ever be with this way," he said.

She turned and looked at him. "Why me, Master?" she asked. "Why did you seek out me?"

"I don't fully know," he said. "When you came to Charleston I couldn't think on anything else. My mind was about you all the time. I think about you all the time now. You're different from the other slaves. You make me feel so alive when I'm with you. Even the first time I saw you at Radcliffe

Place when you were still just a girl, I knew then one day when you had grown up we'd be together like this. And then you came to Charleston and it seemed as if it was fated. That's all I know. That's the God's truth."

She wanted to believe him. "Even though I hated you for taking me the first time as you did?" she asked.

"When I came to the carriage house that Sunday afternoon," he said, "I'd decided that if I had to force myself on you again I wasn't going to do it. I was so happy when I found you there waiting for me. You're my special slave, Lucinda," he said, coming close to her, "The one I tell my secrets to, the one that knows me better than anyone else. The one who loves me, the one who hates me. After all," he said with a strange smile, "love and hate intermixed are more powerful that either alone."

Lucinda was late in meeting Master Johnson. She hurried along the street, and ducked into a narrow footpath between two buildings to enter the apartment from the back. She heard the sound of someone behind her. She turned and a man stood blocking the way.

"Where you going, sweet?" he asked, viewing her with his yellow eyes, his unshaven face and yellow stained teeth scary with a look of malicious intent. He took a step toward her.

"Don't touch me. I'll scream!" Lucinda cried.

"Now, why would you do that?" the man asked sarcastically, "Especially when I'll slice your throat if you do." He turned his wrist so that she could see the knife he held hidden in his hand. "You seem reasonable, sweet. Make it easy on yourself. You know a nigger slave can't bring charges or testify against a white man."

Just as she began backing away and started to let out a yell she saw Master Johnson enter the gap between the buildings.

"Master Johnson," she called. "He has a knife!"

Master Johnson quickly moved through the narrow space toward them. The man turned his head to look behind him, and as he did so, Master Johnson pivoted on his foot as he approached and with the full force of his weight hit the man across the face with the back of his fist. The man dropped back and wobbled on his legs. A stream of blood flowed from the corner of the man's mouth. Lucinda stepped back. The man steadied himself and swiped with the knife as Master Johnson swung with his other hand. He hit the man again. The blade of the knife caught Master Johnson under his arm, and cut through his vest. Lucinda could see from where she stood a red stain quickly blot Master Johnson's side.

The man tried to strike Master Johnson again, but Master Johnson reached with his right foot and tripped the man, who fell banging his head against the side of the building. He did not get up.

"Is he dead?" Lucinda asked running toward them.

Master Johnson spit on his fingers, bent down, and held them under the nose of the man.

"No, he's breathing. He's alive." Master Johnson said.

"Master Johnson, you're hurt!" Lucinda cried as Master Johnson stepped over the man and came to her.

"It's nothing," Master Johnson said. "He just barely snagged me. Are you alright?"

"Yes, Master Johnson." She moved and gently put her arms around him.

"You're trembling," he said. "Let's get out of here before someone sees us. Go inside."

"What in the world happened?" Master Johnson asked Lucinda as she unbuttoned his shirt and cleaned the wound, placing a bandage cloth in place.

"I don't know," she said. "I turned into the alley and suddenly there he was behind me. How did you know I was in trouble, Master?"

"I was watching you walk up the road from the window," Master Johnson said and he winced, looking down at his bandage as she tied straps of cloth to hold it in place. "Then I saw you go between the buildings. He was on the street and moved to follow you. I figured he was up to no good so I went out to make certain you were safe."

"Thank you, Master," and she kissed him on his face. "Are you not hurt?"

"The bleeding has already stopped," he said, looking down at the bandage she had made. Then he said, "He might've done all sorts of things to you. I've heard tales of thieves who kidnap slaves off the streets and sell them to be sent to places like New Orleans. You'd fetch a pretty penny there, I imagine. Or maybe he wanted you for himself. Or both. You must be cautious, Lucinda. Never go where you cannot be seen from the street."

"I was in a hurry to get here," she said. "I'm sorry, Master. I'll not be so careless again." She sat on the floor and put her head in his lap. "You risked yourself for me."

"Because I want you all for myself," he said. Then as if to soften his words, he said, "I don't want to lose you."

When they were again together, Lucinda pulled two masquerade masks from her apron pocket. "Elizabeth left these at South Bay after the February balls," she said. "I've reminded her to take them back to Radcliffe Place but she always forgets. I borrowed them for us. Which are you, Master, Black Midnight or Golden Noon?" and she held the two masks up to his face.

"You're the Golden Girl," he answered, reaching for the black mask. "The gold mask makes your necklace all the more brilliant."

She put the mask on her face. "I'm your golden slave, Master," she said as she moved close to him in the fold of his body. She was his to do with as he wished. "How may your golden slave serve you?" she whispered to him softly.

Denmark's Journal

Tuesday, Christmas Day, 1821

I know I am placing myself in grave danger by taking up this quill and keeping a journal, a journal to contain my thoughts, all the revelations which have been made known unto me, and the names of those who will unite with me in revolt against the whites. Should this ever be found it would certainly mean my death at the end of a hangman's noose and the like death of others. I have thus made a special hiding place in the wall of my shop. I pray for God's will it never be discovered during my lifetime. I pray for strength for what is to come.

Today is Christmas Day. I am alone here at my shop and my house. One of my wives, Beck, has gone to see one of my sons. All morning I have reflected on what has occupied my thoughts for these past four years. I have searched the Scriptures for a sign. God has spoken to me through the words of the prophet Zechariah, Chapter 14, Verses 1, 2, and 3: "Behold the day of the Lord cometh, and thy spoil shall be divided in the midst of thee. For I will gather all nations against Jerusalem to battle; and the city shall be taken, and the women ravished; and half of the city shall go forth into captivity; and the residue of the people shall not be cut off from the city. Then shall the Lord go forth, and fight against those nations, as when he fought in the day of battle."

I have now come to know my calling and my fate. Mine is a vengeful and wrathful God, God of an eye for an eye, God of a tooth for a tooth. I have foreseen in a sacred vision of revelation the fury and wrath of my God. The blacks in Charleston will never be free unless we make ourselves free. The uprising in Santo Domingo has showed the way. There the slaves killed their masters, torched the sugar plantations and coffee, cotton, and indigo settlements. Zechariah's prophesy has revealed to me that God not only wills we rise up and overthrow those who enslave us, but His Word commands that we do so. Does not the Book of Exodus, Chapter 21, Verse 16, charge: "And he that stealeth a man, and selleth him or if he be found in his hand, he shall surely be put to death." What was done in

Santo Domingo must be done here. We must poison the water wells, set fire to Charleston, storm the arsenals and shops for weapons, seize the city by arms, murder every white soul, every man, woman, and child, loot all the gold and specie, then escape by sail to the shores of liberty in Santo Domingo or Africa. The Negroes' situation is so bad I do not know how they endure it. I am astonished they do not rise and fend for themselves. The waters of the Ashley and the Cooper rivers must run red with the blood of our oppressors.

I have not come to this end without much prayer and deliberation. I have been a Free Black Man in this city since I was over thirty years old. I am now well beyond fifty. I have lived here for nearly forty years. My hair is white. The blacks call me Old Man Vesey. Most of my life is past. I have for years considered how freedom for the blacks can come about. The older I have become, the angrier I have grown. I have seen slavery in many different lands, under the Danes on St. Thomas, the French on Santo Domingo at *Cap François*, at all the ports of the West Indies, and here in Georgetown, Charleston, Beaufort, and Savannah. Slavery is the same in all these places. My eyes have witnessed whippings and tortures, the crimson blood streaming to the ground from the naked body of a flogged slave. I have seen ears lopped off, tongues cut out, foreheads branded with a red hot iron, masters heartless to pleading cries for mercy, slaves cruelly abused to the edge of death, and beyond. No mercy was offered then. I have no mercy now. I have seen endless slave galleys sail into this harbor, thousands of slaves sold on the auction block. Before 1808, before importing slaves was said to then be illegal, slave ships packed the Charleston wharves waiting to unload their wretched cargo to feed the jaws of cotton growers. No matter that I have gained my own freedom. I cannot rest until each of my black brothers and sisters is free. A conflagration burns within me. I am ripe for revenge and retribution.

I show my contempt for slavery whenever and wherever I am able, whether to the whites or to the slaves. If I am in a grogshop or on the streets and can engage a white in a conversation that all can hear, especially the slaves, I bring up the topic of slavery. I tell them all men have equal rights. I quote from the Scriptures and the speeches of New York Senator Rufus King and the American Declaration of Independence to show slavery is counter to the laws of God. I ask do they not know God heard the cries of His people in the land of Egypt under the burden of their taskmasters and forced the Pharaoh to let God's chosen people go. I repeat to them from the book of Exodus, the 2nd Chapter, Verses 23 and 24 "... and the children of Israel sighed by reason of the bondage, and they cried, and their cry came up unto God by reason of the bondage. And God heard their groaning, and God remembered his covenant with Abraham, with Isaac and with Jacob."

I refuse to bow to any white person I pass on the streets. I rebuke my fellow blacks who do so, telling them God created all men equal, that this country was founded upon such truth, and I am surprised they would degrade themselves so with such conduct. I will never cringe to the whites. No one who has the feelings of a man should ever do so. I tell every slave, "You are as good as any man." "But we are slaves," they reply. "And for saying so you deserve to remain slaves," I tell them. When they ask, "What can we do?" I tell them, "Go and buy a spelling book and read the fable of Hercules and the Waggoner. The Waggoner's wagon was stalled, and he began to pray. Hercules told him, 'you fool, put your shoulder to the wheel, whip up the horses and your wagon will be pulled out.' If you do not put your hand to the work and deliver yourself, you should never come out of slavery."

What does it mean to be a man? A man respects himself, a man stands up and fights for what he believes, wages war for his God. A man possesses the will and the courage to battle his enemy. To be merely a slave requires nothing of the measures of a man. He is not a man who heeds not the call of freedom. The life of a slave is the life of a beast. Death is preferable, for what difference is there between slavery and death?

We must cut off with a bloody blade the white hands that bind us. Yes, some will say my plan is bloody and savage. Savage only to those who have never suffered as a slave, for what other can we do under such oppression and tyranny? Our only means of ever becoming free is to rise up and destroy those who enslave us. This is the message I preach. I do not always expect the slaves to understand me, but I do expect them to do what I say.

I have commanded to my memory the words of the *Declaration of Independence*. I repeatedly tell the slaves the founders of this country wrote, "We hold these truths to be self-evident, that all men are created equal, that they are endowed by their Creator with certain unalienable Rights, that among these are Life, Liberty and the pursuit of Happiness." I also tell them the Declaration reads, "when a long train of abuses and usurpations, pursuing invariably the same Object evinces a design to reduce them under absolute Despotism, it is their right, it is their duty, to throw off such Government." I affirm to the slaves we are bound by this duty to free ourselves from bondage. Both the Law of God and the Law of Man command it. If we do not act, the Declaration is but a dirty rag. Was not the revolution in France fought for the Rights of Man? I have been able to acquire a print of *Le Declaration des droits de l'Homme et du Citoyen 1789*, written by The Marquis de Lafayette with aid from Thomas Jefferson when he was envoy to France. This is one of my most prized possessions. I keep it safeguarded in my secret hiding place. The Declaration was made good in France during the revolution before Napoleon, and in the uprising of the slaves on Santo Domingo. The first article states *Les hommes naissent et demeurent libres et égaux en droits.* The second article maintains *Ces droits sont la liberté, la propriété, la sureté et la résistance à l'oppression.* The slaves in Charleston are not free and have no rights, have no liberty, no property, no security, or resistance to oppression. The words *liberté, equalité, fraternité* shall have no truth until we rise up and make them true.

I have read with great interest in the Charleston newspapers of the debates in Congress over Missouri's admission to the Union. America is a cloven country: half built on freedom, half built on slavery. I have read the antislavery speeches and pamphlets by Senator Rufus King of New York. He is a friend of the Negro. I was able to acquire his pamphlets as smuggled into Charleston by Negro seamen docked at the harbor. The simple fact of my having Senator King's writings could mean my imprisonment, for they are considered dangerous documents for blacks. I tell the slaves that in his speeches over slavery's expansion into Missouri and the Western Territories, Senator King said, "I have yet to learn that one man can make a slave of another. If one man cannot do so, no number of individuals can have any better right to do it. And I hold that all laws or compacts imposing any such condition upon any human being are absolutely void, because contrary to the law of nature, which is the law of God, by which He makes his ways known to man, and is paramount to all human control." I often repeat these words to myself and repeat them often to the slaves. I have read in his pamphlets where Senator King said, "All men being by natural law free and equal, and the formation of society being for the purpose of procuring by the union of individuals safety and other advantages for each and all the Members, as in their individual and antisocial Condition one man could not rightfully make another his slave, so in their social state, they could not confer on others a Right to do what they themselves could not do—hence it follows that no Prince or Government can make and hold slaves." Senator King is one of few men in the government to speak out so against slavery. His enemies, the guardians of slavery, made the Missouri constitution for statehood include slavery and require the exclusion of free Negroes and mulattoes within Missouri's borders. I swear, as the color of my skin is black like the night, the whites of this city of Charleston intend to enforce restrictions on free Negroes and mulattoes here. They want every free Negro banished in exile or sold back into slavery. I am free here in name only, constrained by the color of my skin, by the land of my birth. I must carry my papers of manumission with me at all times. I can be detained and questioned without cause. Should I breach any law or fail to pay the two-dollar tax charged to a free Negro of this state or fail to obtain a badge and pay the ten dollar fee required for all free blacks who hire themselves out, I can be arrested and sold back into bondage. I could be abducted and sold into slavery, for no laws protect me. Who can say what future chains await me and the other free Negroes here, with even worse woes for the bonded slaves? Henry Clay and others swayed Missouri's legislature to pledge the limitations in their constitution are "never to be construed to authorize the passage of any law impairing the privileges and immunities" of any citizen of the United States. These are but empty words. It is an hypocrisy, which makes me want to vomit blood. Free blacks are not recognized as citizens.

I tell the slaves Congress has made them free. I tell them they are in bondage here contrary to the laws of the land. The slaves must first think they are free before they become so. Their mind-forged manacles must be unshackled. I did not think of myself as free for years after I purchased my freedom. Or feel I was equal and had as much right to liberty as any man. Blacks are not inferior to the whites, as the whites often claim. I now know I am as courageous and as intelligent as any man, braver and smarter than most; but some slaves think of themselves as less because they have been told and told by the whites this is so. Slavery is more than bondage of the flesh. Slavery degrades a man, debases his soul, diminishes his emotions to that of a brute, steals his pride, and leaves him empty inside.

I now see my life has been but a preparation for this moment. I was born in the ancient land of Guinea in West Africa in the year 1767, if Captain Vesey's reckon was exact that I was fourteen when first he saw me so many years ago in Saint Thomas. Do not think I was a boy of some poor man, sold off by an impoverished papa in a year of no rain. My father was Assa Mubi, son of Motubu, from an old and distinguished royal tribe.

My family was captured or killed in a bitter battle with our enemy. They came by surprise to our place with a large army, burned our village to the ground, butchered my father and many men, women, and children. They took all others to sell as slaves. In this way, I was commandeered into slavery.

We walked for days without food and little water to the coast of the great sea. There we were held captive in a fort on an island until sold and loaded into a Danish slave ship. We were traded in exchange for cloth and clothing, strong drink, iron bars, objects of copper, and brass, guns, and gunpowder. We began the voyage from Africa to the islands of the West Indies. My mother did not survive the three-month passage. A foul stench, the smell of piss and shit, of death, permeated every nook and cranny of the cargo hold of that ship. I can never forget it to this day, no matter how I have tried to do so. Our feet were shackled together most of the day and all of the night. We had but rice to eat. Each morning the sailors walked through the crowded hull and took those who had not lived through the night and dumped their naked bodies overboard. Men with guns watched us each time we were taken on the deck of the ship. More than a few slaves threw themselves overboard to a watery death to escape the horrors and uncertainty.

Three long months and every day the same. The sun rose over the horizon of the sea and beat down like an angry fist. Dark storm clouds blackened the sky and threw down rain in great torrents. The ships tossed about in the waves, the putrid stench of vomit from the seasick Africans choked the air in the cargo hull.

Each morning I watched the sailors work. I listened to the tongues they spoke so I could begin to learn and understand. The end of our voyage was the sugar cane plantation island of St. Thomas in the West Indies. Most of the slaves on St. Thomas had been brought from Africa, many from Guinea, while others were born on the islands of the West Indies. There I lived in slavery and grew from a child to a man. In St. Thomas I was first taught by Moravian missionaries the Christian faith and words of the Bible. I was perhaps fourteen years old when sold at the slave market of St. Thomas along with a gang of almost four hundred other slaves to the Bermuda guinea captain, Joseph Vesey. We boarded his ships, and delivered to the port of *Cap François* on Santo Domingo. On the voyage to *Le Cap*, Captain Vesey and his officers were struck by my beauty, alertness, and intelligence, or so they said, making a pet of me like an animal, taking me to the cabin, changing my apparel from the rags I wore, and by way of distinction calling me Telemaque. Others over time have misspoke my name, sometimes as Telemak, or Denmark, as I am now known. Captain Vesey once told me the Greek sailors many hundreds of years before spent their lust on boys. Africans would never practice such savagery. I will one day have my revenge against the buggers. A slave is but on object of abuse, or of desire.

Regardless of how they treated me on that voyage, when we arrived at *Cap François*, they sold me along with the other slave cargo. I was to work in the sugar cane fields like a beast of burden under the lash and the noonday sun. There I first learned the art of cunning. I feigned epileptic fits and according to the custom of trade in that place, I was placed in the hands of the king's physician, who declared me unsound. When Captain Vesey returned to *Cap François* some months later, he was compelled to take me back and return the price paid for me to the planter. I was for nearly twenty years since that fateful day, a most faithful slave and personal servant to Joseph Vesey. I first traveled for two years on his ship, the *Prospect*, making calls at the ports of Barbados, Charleston, Georgetown, Savannah, Saint Thomas, Santo Domingo, Bermuda, Kingston, Tobago, Havana, and Martinique, working the slave markets for the Captain at each of these. We made the voyage to the Gold Coast and Slave Coast of Africa, loading slave cargo at ports like Agah, and Calabar, Pram Pram, Salt Pond, and Williams Fort. Strange are the twists and turns of fate. There I was, almost a decade after I had been forced into slavery and made the journey from Africa across the sea to the West Indies, now working a slave ship on the same journey. I have taken seven wives in my life, beginning years ago at those locales. Captain Vesey settled in Charleston in 1783, soon after the American War with England. He maintained his livelihood as a slave broker and then as a ship merchandiser. He lives here today. I have not seen or talked with him in years. He is the whitest white man I ever saw, his face as pale white as the full moon high in the nighttime sky.

I came to Charleston as a slave in Captain Vesey's household. I became his personal servant and did his biding. In December 1799, I drew a prize of $1,500 in the East Bay Lottery. This changed my fate forever. Many slaves in Charleston took their meager earnings, or scrimped and saved as they could, to buy a ticket in hopes of winning monies to purchase their freedom. I thought then I was one of the rare lucky ones. I now know it was an Act of God. Before the year's end, I was able to buy my freedom from Captain Vesey's wife for $600, yes, less than I was worth, but my years of obedient service to him, and their need for money, granted me this special providence. I was unable to purchase the freedom of my wives and children.

I had become skilled at the craft of a carpenter. This trade provided me the greatest amount of mechanic's work, and I made $1.50 a day. I gained a freedom of movement, some independence for my own time, and the freedom to see and think as I traveled throughout the countryside of Charleston from Marsh Island to the Santee to up the Ashley River to the different plantations and lumber mills in my work. In this way, I saw the lives and the hardships of the slaves in the lowcountry of South Carolina. I have lived the life of a Free Black Man in this city of Charleston where my brethren, nearly all of my fellow blacks and Africans, are hopelessly bonded by the cruel chains of slavery.

I have begun to seek out those who will join with me to lead the revolt. I have spent many an hour in prayer, long in the night, searching for God's guidance and His will in leading me to those who are destined to rise up and free our people. The African Church has proved to be ripe for gathering recruits. Many of the people I know are members or teachers and leaders there. I thank God for Reverend Morris Brown. He is much too meek to press the blacks to violent revolt, and I will forever keep secret from him the plans of our uprising. But it was Morris Brown, almost on his very own, who started the African Association in Charleston, using Richard Allen's separation from the Methodist Episcopal Church in Philadelphia as his guide. The Charleston authorities have twice stormed our church and arrested members on trumped up charges of disorderly conduct. In June of 1818 Reverend Brown and four of the church's ministers were sentenced to thirty days in the Work House or be exiled from the state. Each served his thirty days. Eight other Class Leaders and ministers, including myself, received sentences of ten lashes or paid a $5 fine. I paid the $5 fine. Morris Brown holds the trust of all his members. I am able to use that trust and the church for other of the Lord's purposes.

I know I must choose my lieutenants for the revolt carefully, using God's direction and His inspiration. The country blacks on the plantations have little time of their own to spread the news and plans of the revolt. They do not often leave the plantations, and are most time under watch by the overseers or the Patrols. The country blacks, in their great numbers, will overpower and murder the whites on the night of the revolt. But to build the foundation of this business I must first have men from the city, men who have their masters' approval to hire out their services, men whose masters trust them so they will be under little suspicion and less likely to be thought untrustworthy or unhappy and dangerous. The slaves who hire themselves out have more control over their own time. They do not always have to account for themselves and their whereabouts. Some work in their own shops. They can come to meetings, work to obtain weapons, spend time advancing the insurrection. The carters, draymen, sawyers, porters, laborers, stevedores, mechanics, those employed in lumberyards, these are the men I must secure, men who have certain allotted hours at their own disposal. Such men are not free, far from it; but they are men with just enough of the taste of independence, just enough to wet their appetite, enough of a scrap to crave a feast of liberty. I must have men who are sober in their habits and not tempted by strong drink, for it makes for loose tongues. I hope too for men who can read and write. I thank God the missionaries on Saint Thomas and Captain Vesey gave me to learn to read, and the Captain learnt me the skill to speak the tongues he knew, English, and French, and Spanish. With men who can read and write, we can keep lists of those who sign to join us. I must be directed to men in the city who see many others each day so that we may promote our plan to as many as possible.

One of the men God has led me to is Peter Poyas. He is a fellow member of the African Church. I had begun to question him on his views of his condition and that of the slaves in Charleston when he expressed to me his bitterest hatred of the whites. "I will murder every white man I am able," he promised. He offered his complete loyalty, secrecy, and dedication. He is a ship's carpenter. He works his trade and travels much throughout Charleston. He writes in a fair hand. He will arouse no suspicion. God tells me Peter is fearless and resolute, true to his commitments. He is not to be daunted nor impeded by difficulties. He is a man who considers every possible course before he acts. I offer my prayer of thanks to God for leading me to this man worthy of the struggle for freedom.

I have also conversed with Rolla and Ned, men of the Governor, Thomas Bennett. I was at first cautious, unsure of their hearts. I asked each of them, "What news?" Both replied to me, "None." "Yes, there is news," I told them, "We are free, but the white people here won't let us be so, and the only way is to rise up and fight the whites." How my spirit was lifted and my prayers went up to God as I had but begun to feel out their thoughts when each expressed to me his loyalty to our cause.

Rolla bragged to me, "I will first fix my old buck, the Governor, and then the Intendant." Rolla has great self-control and the discipline to meet our ends. He is bold and not to be deterred from his purpose by danger. Ned is a Class Leader at the church along with Peter Poyas. They can use their standing there to garner other members. Ned's appearance indicates that he is a man of firm nerves and great courage. Rolla and Ned know the habits of the Governor, and are poised to mark his death. "We will take the Governor's daughter as our prize," they boasted. "She will be the light of our Harem."

The other man with whom I have conversed is Jack Purcell. I have known him for many years. Jack is a mulatto, one of the few brown men I hold worthy of taking in my confidence. He has many times over the years come to visit me at my shop. His heart wears no passion, but I know he holds the respect of the others.

There are two other men I hope for, and I pray for God's will they join us. One is the root doctor and conjurer Gullah Jack Pritchard. The other man I wish to enjoin is Monday Gell. He is an Ebo, born in Africa. Monday is a harness maker. He works in town at the shop of his master. He is firm, resolute, discreet, and intelligent. He can read and writes in a fair hand.

These are the men I pray God sees fit to be my principle officers and to lead the revolt. They have the trust of their masters. Some of these men have shops where they work, or their master allows them to hire out. This makes for some liberty of their time. They can work to sign recruits. We can easily meet to discuss this business.

When Gullah Jack and Monday Gell have joined us, we must begin to spread the news to the blacks in the city and in the country. We will begin lists of the names of those who sign with us. The lists must be guarded with greatest secrecy. Each man will have only the names of those they sign. This will keep all from being found out if they are ever questioned or taken up. Each man can destroy his list to avoid discovery. I will keep this book with everyone's name. We must proceed with great caution. We must be able to trust each man we sign, or threaten their lives should they betray us. This business must be kept secret until the final moment or we will be put to an end and our effort all for naught.

As I have thought back to my days onboard Captain Vesey's vessels, I would say I have now set sail on a dangerous voyage with freedom for my people as my destined port of call. I must each hour survey this city as a captain at sea surveys the movement of the sun by day, the movement of the moon by night, and the fixed North Star in the nighttime sky. I must know the will and position of each of my men. I must know the prevailing winds and the pitch of the sails and the swells of the sea. I must extend great care to know the dangerous eddies of the ocean tides, the rocky coves of the coast, and the sand bars in the harbor. I pray a sailor's prayer that the Lord watch over and guide me on my journey.

Tuesday, New Year's Day, 1822

The first day of the New Year! I had as is the custom here New Year's Day vittles of hog jowl with a cup of peas and an earthen mug of clabber. I have marked this as the new year of freedom for the slaves of Charleston. The time for the revolt approaches. I will work tirelessly until my task is done.

Today I met with Gullah Jack. I saw him this morning on the street, and asked him to attend to me here. He came at the appointed hour. I had no fears in revealing to him all my plans. He was quick to join in this business.

"I'm a Gullah," he said to me, "born in Africa like you. My pappy was a doctor and conjurer, and passed the skill down to me. I was captured and sold into slavery like you. No one hates the white man more than I do. Not even you. The whites think because I'm small, that I'm weak. Because I'm not built as you, like a tree trunk bigger round than I can reach, doesn't mean I'm not powerful." Gullah Jack flashed a grin, his big side-whiskers puffing out like a turkey bird fanning its tail feathers. His bad eye looked off in one direction, his other eye off in another. "They'll find out how potent this African doctor is," he said, his words as venomous as the bite of a cottonmouth. "Fifteen years I've practiced my conjurin' here. I'll put a hex on 'em that'll make 'em helpless. I'll strike down two white men with every swing of my sword. I'll make charms that'll protect us and keep us from harm. As long as we carry a crab claw in our mouths we can't be hurt."

I judge Gullah Jack to be one of my most loyal and my most valued lieutenants. He is a conjurer, knows the ways of Voodoo magic, and is much feared by his fellow Angolans and the other Africans. He is believed to be invulnerable, that no white man's bullet or white man's sword can harm him, and he can make others so by his potions and charms. The whites think him simple and foolish. They are the foolish ones, for Gullah Jack is artful, cruel, and bloody. His influence among the Africans is without rival. He speaks Gullah and knows many of the slaves on the country plantations along the rivers, on the islands, and along the coast. Gullah Jack will be in charge of the Gullah regiment. He works at his master's shipyard at Gadsden's Wharf, and is among other slaves at the wharves or at the markets or in the streets. He has unpatrolled time to spread the news and build our forces.

"We must foster our forces man by man," I told him. "We must send men to the country plantations, to the Sea Islands, and spread the news. We are nearly ready to begin. Only Monday Gell has yet to make his decision known to me."

I suppose there are those who will ask why as a free black man of some means I choose to risk my money and my property and my life for the freedom of others. My calling is not my own choosing. I am commanded to this task by the Word of God. Our covenant is to obey God's laws and His commandments. To enslave another man is counter to the Laws of God, as Senator Rufus King has said. God punishes those who break His commandments, as He destroyed the Pharaoh and his army for refusing to free God's chosen people in Egypt. I have heard God speak to me in a voice like a flame of fire. The Lord has chosen me to smite with His wrath. The sword of justice shall be my weapon, the arm of might my crucible to purify my hate. My duty compels me to fulfill God's will. Moses was a Hebrew in foreign Egypt, a stranger in a strange land, chosen by God to free His people. I am an African in this foreign land, a black Moses of my people chosen to deliver them up from bondage. I pray the uprising will spread up and down the coast and throughout the slave states of the South. All blacks in the New World must unite. No matter if they are in Jamaica or Trinidad or Brazil or Santo Domingo or the Southern States of America. We are all children of Mother Africa. Our homeland binds us forever as one. No black man can be free until all black men are free. Every black man's fate is my fate. Every black man's slavery is my slavery. Their freedom is my freedom.

The whites of this city claim the slaves in these Southern States are better off than the laborers in the North who are forced to work long hours for paltry wages. I do not believe this to be so. Yes, it is right to pay a man proper wages for his labor, as I have paid the men I have hired to work for me when I needed aid to fulfill the contracts of my trade, and those in the North be damned for their treatment of the workers there. The slaves here will never be better off than the laborers there. It is not a matter of proper wages. It is not a matter of comforts of the flesh. It is a matter of the state of a man's soul, of his pride. I am erupting with fierce pride, but I am humiliated that my wives and my sons and daughters remain slaves. I cannot purchase their freedom. I have tried to do so without success. Their masters refuse to sell them, or at such prices as to be impossible for me to do so.

The whites in Charleston will never willingly give up slavery. They have too much to lose. Slavery of the Africans is entrenched as the way of life here. The plantations were once vast swamp and wilderness. The lives of thousands of slaves were sacrificed to turn the land into the rich plantations of today, great riches made on the backs of the slaves. America is more our country than it is the white's. We have enriched it with our blood, sweat, and tears. The white planters reap profits, while the blacks are left with unmarked graves. Santo Domingo tells all. Today it would still be an island of slaves had not the blacks risen up and overthrown their French masters.

Yes, I hate Buckra . . . with every jot of my being. I did not always hate the white man. I was learnt to hate him. Why do I hate him now? I hate the whites for believing they are superior to the blacks. I hate the whites for enslaving the Africans, for taking us from our homeland, for treating us as chattel, as animals, working us as beasts of burden, for the centuries of cruelty and mistreatment, for the abuse, the torture, the murders, and the deaths. I hate the whites because they have denied us what they have no right to deny. The whites have taken from us what they have no right to take. I hate the whites because our church was shut up so that we could not use it and it is high time we seek our rights. We finally had something of our own and the whites tried to destroy it. I hate Buckra for his rape of our women. I long for the day we reap revenge and reply in kind. I hate the whites because they refuse to free the blacks. I do not like to have a white man in my presence. Buckra can burn in hell. I am too proud not to hate. Any black who does not hate the whites is a coward.

The more freedom a man has, the more freedom he craves. The misused slave hopes for a good master, the slave with the good master wants no master at all. Now that I have my own freedom, I crave freedom for my wives and my children and all of my fellow blacks. God lends His helping hand to those whose hands are busy with their own work. I work to destroy this city and gain the freedom of my fellow Africans.

There are those who propose a back-to-Africa movement. There is Freetown in Sierra Leone. The black Methodist missionary Daniel Coker started a settlement there in 1820. Some free blacks have left the Americas to start a new life there. I could have gone, alone, without my wives and my children. But I did not go with George Creighton to Africa, because I did not will it. There is nothing I can do for the blacks here if I go to Africa. I am called by God to stay and see what I can do for my black brothers and sisters in Charleston. As it is today, Sierra Leone is a choice only for the free blacks. We Africans did not abandon our countries to come to the Americas like many of the whites. We were captured, enslaved, and brought here by force. If the free blacks do wish to return to Africa, who will pay? What help is to be provided to those who leave their lives here and return to our homeland? Only when we are free men with the riches of our spoils, then we can all return to Africa if we so choose.

We wander like the Children of Israel in a desert of misery and bondage. The Promised Land beckons in the distance. I stand like Moses on the peak of Mount Pisgah and scan the horizon, knowing my people will soon be delivered there. We will make our own exodus and cross the sea to the promised land of freedom in Santo Domingo or Africa.

Monday, January 7th 1822

This morning as I passed by the door of Monday Gell's harness shop, I determined to call in on him.

"Monday," I told him, "We have known each other for many years. We have worshiped together at the African Church. You know I hate how the white man has enslaved and exploited the blacks. For years now I have let every man within the sound of my voice, whether slave or white, know how I feel. I wanted to do something back in June of 1818 when they raided our church."

I looked at Monday closely. He is a tall Ebo, wiry and lean on a muscular frame. His bright eyes shone like polished onyx, his features laid hard upon his black clean-shaven face. He has lived here for nearly fifteen years and is in his prime years as a man. I knew how angry he had been back then when the African Church was shut up.

"I'm satisfied with my own condition, as I am a free man," I said. "But all my children are slaves. I wish to see what can be done for them. You know, as I know, the slaves will never be free unless we do something for ourselves." Monday didn't look at me and he did not speak. He continued to work a leather strap on a horse harness at his worktable, sewing a strip of leather in place. "I'm trying to gather the blacks to see if anything can be done to overcome the whites." I told him. I said nothing else until he looked up. "You're an Ebo. The Ebo are a proud people. The Ebo are a warrior people." I stopped again and studied his face. "Will you join in with us?" I asked him.

Monday halted his work. "What is your plan?" he asked.

"My plan is straight enough," I said to him. "We'll use the association of the African Church and the Black congregation membership of the other churches to reach out to those who will join in our cause. We'll build our forces from there. There are more Africans than whites in this city. We'll have no problem attracting forces. Then we'll go to the country slaves and bring them down."

"Who has joined with you?" Monday questioned. "How many folks do you have who back you?"

"I've got Peter Poyas, Ned and Rolla Bennett, Jack Purcell," I said, "and the conjurer Gullah Jack."

"Is that all?" Monday asked.

"There will be others," I told him. "Many others. We'll garner one man at a time." I gave him time to reflect on what I said. "What do you say, Monday? Are you with us?"

"I don't know," Monday said. "It sounds like a risky business. I'll have to think on it."

I departed, leaving him standing there in his shop, at work on the harness.

There is no reason for concern, I thought to myself as I walked down Meeting Street toward the Battery. He will join us yet. Men will risk all for their freedom.

Sunday, 20th January 1822

This morning Monday Gell joined our army of revolt. I saw him at the service of the African Church at Hamstead. Monday said to me, "I'm in it with you until the end." He took longer than the others to declare, but he has now signed. I am established with the men who will lead our Lord's work.

Monday, 28th January 1822

We met this evening at Monday's shop. All of my other lieutenants were there: Peter Poyas, Jack Purcell, Gullah Jack Pritchard, Ned and Rolla

Bennett. We gathered just after dark. Monday pulled the shop door tight, locked it shut, then looked out the window to the street to make certain no one was about. An odor of leather and sweat and wood smoke filled the closed-in room. The fire had burnt down in the hearth, and Ned bent over it, adding a log and working the embers with a poker. Sparks lifted and flew up the chimney as the log caught fire. Monday's tools hung on the walls and covered his workbench. He stood at the bench, his nervous hands rearranging the tools.

"Monday, you're as skittish as a colt being fit with its first bridle," Ned told him. The men laughed. Even Monday flashed a big grin.

"You have nothing to fear," Gullah Jack said to the men. "I have charms made of crab claws to keep us safe."

I studied the face of each man. Peter Poyas with his square-cut jaw and bright eyes; Gullah Jack with his big side whiskers and eyes that looked in two directions at once; the brown skin and white hair of Jack Purcell; the strong, lanky frame and intelligent but nervous face of Monday Gell; the hard features and black skin of Ned; the bulging black eyes and grisly beard of Rolla.

"Let us begin with prayer," I said to the men. They bowed their heads. "God, we strive to do our duty, to obey your commandments," I prayed. "Guide us in our efforts. Lead us as we follow your Word. Amen."

"Amen," the men said.

"Now that you know God has chosen you as His leaders of the revolt," I said, "we must begin to mature our plan and decide the best way to build our forces." Each man sat with his shoulders squared, each face serious and somber. "We must spread the word and recruit our members one at a time. We must be careful and proceed with great caution. Trust no one until you're certain they will protect our plans."

Peter Poyas spoke up. "Take care and don't mention our plan to those waiting men who receive presents of old coats from their masters, for they'll betray us. I will speak to them."

"As you go about signing recruits, ask this question," I instructed them. "Ask 'What news?' When they answer, 'Nothing new,' tell them, 'Oh yes, there is news. Have you not heard? We are free!' They are sure then to ask, 'Who makes us so?' Tell them they are already free, that the legislature in Washington has made them so, but their masters refuse to grant their freedom. Gather their thoughts, ask how they feel about their standing, ask are they not unhappy with their lot as a slave. Tell them, if they say they welcome such news, that the time has come to claim their freedom. Tell them 'I will show you the man!' Bring them to me if need be. When we find them to be trustworthy, we'll include them in our movement.

"When a man says yes, write down his name and keep a list of those you sign. This way, we will know how many are aligned with us and bear out the pledge of each man. When the time comes, we'll need to employ our forces by how many we have signed. Only you will have your list to keep all from being found should you be discovered and taken up. I'll keep a list of all who sign. We will, in this way know our numbers, and how to best use them the night of the revolt.

"You must be brave," I said. "There is great danger if we are found out." The room was quiet. No one spoke. The fire crackled in the hearth. "Freedom will not come easy. But we have much strength. We have God on our side."

"We are brave, Denmark," Peter Poyas said. "That's why we're here."

"We're superior in numbers," I said to the men confidently. "There are more blacks than whites in the town of Charleston, on the plantations in the country, even more so. We're certain to be victorious with such numbers. Surprise will be our greatest asset. We cannot be too cautious. We must choose each man we sign with great care. Our greatest danger is our secret will be exposed before the day of reckoning; some Judas will betray us for the white man's pieces of silver. Tell them if any man spills word of our plan he will surely be watched day and night and will certainly be put to death. As the Gospel of St. Luke 11:23 says, 'He that is not with me is against me.' They know to fear my word. Or they'll soon learn to do so.

"We will send men with word into the country to the plantations. Gullah Jack has use of his master's canoe to journey to the islands and along the river waterways."

"The African gods will show us the way," Gullah Jack said. "Once the uprising begins, all the slaves will join in with us. Let us assemble a sufficient number to commence the work with spirit and we'll not want men, they'll fall in behind us fast enough."

"Or they too will die," I said. "If any black does not join us once the killing begins, they will be dispatched along with the whites.

"I have begun to consider how we must proceed on the night of the revolt," I said. "The country blacks will come into the city in great numbers. We will need draymen to ride into the country on horseback and round up the blacks. Those on the coasts and the river plantations can use their masters' canoes and boats to make it to the wharves in Charleston. We must surround the city and storm in from all sides. Every slave must be armed to the teeth. Gullah Jack knows men who can make spears for us, pikes like the warriors in Africa use. I have begun to study the caché of arms stored in the arsenals and the Guard House. I have studied which shops on King and Market Streets have guns, ammunition, and arms of every sort for sale. We will break down the doors, storm the shops, and get hold of arms. We will sound the alarm of fire and as the whites come out of their homes to escape to safety, we can butcher them on the spot. The more we kill the better. We will dispatch to hell every white man in the city.

"The slaves in Santo Domingo overthrew their masters," I told them. "We will do the same. I've considered how General Toussaint Louverture marshaled his black army in Santo Domingo. I've conversed with every French Negro in Charleston I can. I've questioned them about the Santo Domingo revolt. I've marked in the harbor ships with flags from Santo Domingo and questioned the sailors to see what may be learnt. The uprising began with secret meetings by the slaves on the plantations, just as we are doing here tonight. In August 1791 a Voodoo ceremony served to initiate the start of the insurrection." I gestured toward Gullah Jack. "Jack will use Voodoo rites here to initiate our revolt.

"The slaves in Santo Domingo banded together, rose up in arms, and killed the overseers and masters on the sugar cane plantations. The slaves went in riot from plantation to plantation, spreading the revolt. They set fire to the fields, burned the plantation houses, murdered the whites. The fires leaped up to the sky and could be seen for miles. Over two hundred plantations were destroyed in over a week. Thousands and thousands of slaves rose up in defiance of their masters. The same will happen here. We must recruit a thousand men to our cause. The Lord willing, more than a thousand. Many thousands. Louverture battled the French, the Spanish, and the British, his rivals and enemies in Santo Domingo. We've not so many challenges here. Napoleon sent his army, but God sent the country fever and destroyed them. Huge numbers of Frenchmen died. I was told a raging river of blood could have flowed until there was but one red drop of slave blood left, but the rebellious slaves in Santo Domingo refused to surrender. Jean-Jacques Dessalines, Toussaint Louverture's successor, said his people would prefer extermination rather than lose their place as one of the world's free peoples. The victorious blacks in Santo Domingo abolished slavery, banned racism, and won their revolution against the French and the Spanish. In August 1793, Louverture said to the blacks on Santo Domingo, 'Brothers and friends, I am Toussaint Louverture: perhaps my name has made itself known to you. I have undertaken vengeance. I want Liberty and Equality to reign in St. Domingue. I am working to make that happen. Unite yourselves to us, brothers and fight with us for the same cause. Your very humble and obedient servant.' The French government soon proclaimed the abolition of slavery. We will achieve this here. We will light a fuse to the powder keg that explodes and demolishes slavery in Charleston forever!"

"Amen, brother Denmark," several men said.

"We have much to do," I told them. "We must meet often under the cover of night and mature our plan. We'll mark our movement one day at a time."

"Denmark," Jack Purcell said, "I know a man, Lot Forrester, who wishes to join us. He is hired out by his master, a Mr. Peigne, who's an employee of the State Arsenal. Lot says he can steal some slow match for us."

"Yes," I said to Jack, "I know who he is. He used to be a member of the African Church, but he was turned out. Tell Lot to come and see me."

"We're with you, Denmark," Monday Gell said, standing up, "with you until the end."

The fire in the hearth had burnt down to a dark red glow. The sole light in the room was a whale oil lamp, which gleamed from the table, casting dark shadows into the corners of the room.

"It is late," I said as the quarter-hour call sounded from Saint Michael's Church. "God be with you."

Monday unlocked the door of the shop and the men silently filed out into the near empty street. They headed in their different directions, surveyors dispatched across the battlefield, a small band of soldiers destined to lead a mighty army of revolt and freedom.

Tuesday, 5th February 1822

The time is ripe for me to spread my message to the slaves and to justify from Scripture an uprising in Charleston. The past few years, prayer meetings of blacks, with black preachers as leaders, have become common.

These gatherings receive sanction by the black churches, especially the branches of the African Church. The prayer meetings, and the order they provide, are the way we must use to recruit and put together our forces for the insurrection. I have begun to attend these prayer congregations. They are held in abandoned or empty buildings, which the city authorities do not patrol. I have been able to speak at many of them. I tell the slaves they are already free, Congress has made them so, but they are held in servitude counter to the law of the land. I espouse Scripture affirms our duty to secure our freedom by armed insurrection. I tell the slaves of the revolt in Santo Domingo. I tell them of the speeches by Senator Rufus King. I have been greeted everywhere with open arms and receptive hearts. The feeling of solidarity the African Church creates has made my people aware of the power they possess when they're united as one. I have a small number of members of our church come here to my house each week for Bible study, singing, and prayer. When the time comes these gatherings will be the way to put out the news of the day and time of the revolt.

My rage, my hatred for the whites, has reached a level where it consumes me day and night. I think of nothing else. If I could release my fury now, I would do so this very moment. I crave for the sweet taste of revenge. Revenge is a heady physic. Men will scheme, and strive at all costs, to achieve revenge. Revenge can inspire a man for decades, for a lifetime. Men will deprive themselves; whole families, whole generations, have risked all to achieve revenge. The longer you mull over your desire for revenge, the stronger the urge, the greater the feeling. Revenge is not satisfied by the passion of the moment, but best attained after a long wait. I must be patient. I have waited almost a lifetime. I will wait some longer still. I hate Buckra with perfect patience. Every man has his time, and mine will come around too.

My Creator God of the Old Testament is the Destroyer God of the Flood, the Destroyer God who drowned the Pharaoh and his army in the crashing waves of the Red Sea, the Destroyer God who bestowed Samson with the strength to annihilate the Philistines, the Destroyer God who rained down fire and brimstone to burn Sodom and Gomorrah. Mine is the God of Destruction, the God of Wrath, and the God of Vengeance. I once belonged to the Presbyterian Church, and sought my salvation through the faith of a Christian. Now I have come to see the meek shall inherit the earth as taught by Christ is a false doctrine. The white man will soon know my Jehovah is a God of Justice where the unrighteous are punished. He is a foolish man who thinks he has not the wages of death to pay for his sins. He is a foolish man who thinks he can escape the wrath of the Almighty. The Day of Judgment awaits like the ancient mariners' tales of a yawning chasm at the edge of the seas which tumbles off into oblivion. The sinners of this city must be cast into the bottomless pit of everlasting fire.

I know I am risking all if discovered. At what point is a man's life not worth living if he cannot call that life his own? Is life worth living if lived in misery and in chains? Our lives have meaning only if we are free. The American Patriot Patrick Henry swore, "Give me Liberty or Give me Death." I too am willing to die for freedom. No man can truly be a man when his will is ironbound by that of another. God created man different from the other creatures. God created man with a soul. Better that soul be free and to die a martyr than to suffer under the curse of slavery. I willingly venture all for that which is priceless . . . retribution and freedom.

Thursday, 7th February 1822

Gullah Jack told me of a blind black seer who lives in the city. Jack says the man was born with a caul over his face, and possesses a gift, a species of second sight, which comes to him after prayer or in dreams. Gullah Jack says the man has the skill to foresee the future, a power not even Gullah Jack possesses. Jack took me to see the old blind seer where he lives alone in the upstairs of an ancient house at the edge of the city: a cramped and cluttered, dilapidated room up a narrow set of stairs, with only the weakest of sunlight filtering through a small dirty window on one wall.

The room smelled salty like the sea, and the smell of pent-up air, the musk of mold and damp wood rot. I saw in the dim light the room littered with sharks' teeth, sand dollars, and sea shells, jumbled with dried vulture and crab claws, shed snake skins, the horned bone-skull of a goat, lockets of human hair, turtle shells, hornets' nests like parchment, and a carved wooden statue of the African god Eschu, messenger between heaven and earth. Carved wooden bowls and seven crude voodoo dolls made from husks of corn, colored cloth, and string were perched on a wooden case at one side of the room. A wooden cross hung on the sullied wall, a banjo propped into one corner, a dingy cot squeezed into the other.

"I'm told you have the gift of prophesy," I said to the seer, his deformed eyes with their sightless stare like some tragic curse as he turned his face up to me.

"Yes, Massa" he answered in a voice like the bleating of goats, "my eyes see not this world, but I have visions of the future, things other men cannot see. Surely you're one who understands."

"Tell me then what you see," I said.

The blind man paused for a long while, then mumbled some garbled prayer, his lips trembling as he sounded the words, his eyes like an angry dark night sea, black and impenetrable.

"I see a great calamity," he said finally. "I see the city consumed by raging fire. I see the whites of this city in turmoil and pain. I hear screams of panic and terror. I see God's wrath visited upon the sinners of this city. The sign will be a moonless night." He fell silent, his head bowed to his chest.

"Anything else?" I asked, my heart thumping in my chest. "What else do you see?"

"There is a man. A man of great force," the blind man said. "He is a bugle at dawn waking the asleep."

"Who is this man," I asked him.

"That man is you," he said, then again slipped into silence, his head bobbing side-to-side in rhythm.

I reached for the half-dollar coin in my pocket, took his hand and placed the fifty pence piece in the fold of his palm. His face lit with surprise as he rubbed the coin in his fingers, a strange afflicted face with sightless eyes, and he smiled showing the empty gaps of missing teeth across his mouth.

"Bless you, Massa, bless you," he said.

"No man has an earthly master," I told him, "only God's fate which leads a man to his destiny."

"This seer," I said to Gullah Jack as we made our way down the rickety stairs to the thin street below, "he can be of great value to us. If you need to prove to any men who waver, bring them here to this man. They will see our plan is ordained and prophesized to be. We must be bold, we must be bloody, we must be resolute."

Sunday, 10th February 1822

I have not hesitated to threaten those who hold back on their decision to join in the revolt. I tell them the Negroes live such abominable lives they ought to rise up and change their fate. Frank Ferguson said to me, "I am living well." "Although you are," I told him, "others are not and it is such fools as you that are in the way and will not help them. You have not a man's heart and you are a friend of Buckra. After all things are well I will mark you." I have no forbearance for those who are only about their own comfort and condition.

My threat proved worthy. Frank joined our cause. The ass must from time to time be prodded with the whack of the whip to spur his pulling the load.

Wednesday, 13th February 1822

The members of the African Church who meet here with me for prayer and Bible study just departed. I have not yet taken them into our plan, except the men in our secret society who also come to the study. The time is not yet right. It may never be so. The women are house slaves. Before I include them in our plot, I must be certain they can be trusted like my wives not to tell their masters of our plans. When the time comes, I will know if they are willing to poison or murder to advance our cause. Only then will they learn from me of the insurrection.

Every house slave we approach is told they should fear for their life if they so much as breathe one word of the revolt. As Peter Poyas said, they are not to be trusted. This leaves me uncertain about the young slave girl. I trust my gut to tell me about the steadfastness of a man, but with her, I cannot well apprehend. She seems to be of good judgment. She is strong in her faith. What means may she serve our cause? She could act as a spy or a messenger. Upon occasion, I needed to get a message to Peter Poyas or Gullah Jack or one of the others and was unable to do so. She is out to the market and on errands most every day. She is young and could be molded. She is in the household of one of the planter families who converse with the Governor and the Intendant. Perhaps she can serve as our eyes and ears for news that could be of benefit to us, to know if the whites have any inkling of our plans. She certainly would not be suspected by her age and as she is just a girl. I will question Gullah Jack about her to determine what he considers our best use of her.

I have begun to travel to the country plantations near the Santee, and along the Cooper and the Ashley rivers, spreading the message of revolt and freedom. My years as a carpenter often took me to these places to carry on my trade. I know the countryside of St. John's Island, of Bull's Island, and the areas of the Santee, the Neck, the Ashley, and Cooper rivers of the Charleston District as well as I know the city. I meet with the slaves in small gatherings at night.

I say to the country slaves what I say to the slaves in Charleston. I ask them, are you not unhappy with your lot? I ask them, do you not want to be free? I tell them they have the right to be so. I tell them they have the right to overthrow the whites, to destroy their masters, to gain their rights and freedom. I then tell them they are already free, that the government in Washington has made them so. I ask them, do you not hate the whites, your masters, the overseers, the patrollers? I ask them, do you not want to see your master dead? Well then, I tell them, do something about it! Rise up! I tell them the whites will never give up slavery. I tell them they will never be free unless they make themselves free. I say God has willed our revolt; God is on our side, we march together under the battle flag of the Lord. I tell them we must kill every white, every man, woman, and child. I have been asked, "But what about the children? Shall we kill them too?" I tell them, "What is the sense of killing the louse and leaving the nit?" I tell them the white sinners must be punished and suffer in everlasting misery for their mistreatment of the blacks. I tell them the slaves in the city are ready to rise up, that we are all black African brothers joined together in the struggle for freedom. I tell them many have signed and with our great numbers, we are certain to gain victory.

Whenever I am able, I take Gullah Jack with me. I tell the country blacks Gullah Jack is a Negro doctor and a mighty conjurer. I tell them he is the little man who cannot be harmed. I tell them he is invincible, no white man or white man's sword or white man's bullet can hurt him, his powerful sorceries can keep them from harm. I tell them the government in Santo Domingo knows of our plan and will send armies to fight and ships to provide escape. I write their names and their plantation in my book and I have them sign their mark to show their vow. I call for one man on each plantation to be the one we let know when the date and time are set. He will then inform the others. In Africa the Big Chiefs head the tribes, and every man, woman, and child obeys their command. I am the chief for the Africans here on the plantations. Gullah Jack is my sorcerer. The whites call him a witch doctor; I call him a messenger of the African gods.

Sunday, 17th February 1822

I asked Gullah Jack about our use of the young slave girl. "Take her to the blind seer," Gullah Jack answered me. "He will know her path."

I have much yet to do. We have but just begun. May the Lord give me strength to complete His work.

Friday, 22nd February 1822

I saw in the Charleston newspapers today is the birth date of George Washington. Many of the whites love him still, or the memory of him. Washington was a Southerner, and a slaveholder. He may have fought the British for the liberty and freedom of the white man, but he did not fight for me. Washington's will, so I have heard, set free his slaves upon his death, or in truth to be freed upon his wife's death, but because she was afeard the slaves had a stake in her death, and hence possibly her murder, she freed them herself.

Washington's birthday upholds that every important event in the history of man has required the actions of a major commander. To the Israelites' escape from bondage in Egypt, it was Moses, the American Revolution, George Washington, for the slave revolt in Santo Domingo, Toussaint Louverature. God always selects a leader, a man of fate, a man of destiny. Here God has chosen me for this purpose. I am that leader to free the slaves in Charleston. I am the hammer that drives the nail to build the house. I am the sail that clutches the wind and propels the ship.

Monday, 25th February 1822

Deuteronomy 6:16 reads, "Ye shall not tempt the Lord your God." I do not wish to break my Lord Jehovah's commandments. My God has profoundly blessed me, delivering my freedom by lottery winnings over two decades ago. God willing, I nonetheless pray to be fated to win once more. Today I bought tickets in the Grand Lottery for the Benefit of the South Carolina Academy of the Arts. Should Jehovah's blessings continue to exalt me, the first prize winnings are $20,000, ample enough to purchase the arms and ammunition needed to carry out the insurrection, plenteous enough to serve for an army to fight for the liberty of my people. May the Lord God in his wisdom see fit to reward his dutiful servant?

Tuesday, 26th February 1822

I asked the young slave girl to visit with me last Sunday afternoon. I told her I wanted to take her to the blind seer. I told her Gullah Jack said about her that he believes "she is a blue moon child and may possess the gift for conjuring." I said I wanted her to visit the blind man with me and find out what visions he has of her future.

The girl and I walked through the streets of Charleston toward the edge of the city. The breeze from the sea was up and whipped off the harbor, blowing through the thoroughfares, adding a damp chill to the air. We came to a corner between two ramshackle houses, their grey paint weathered and worn almost to the wood, peeling in hand-sized pieces. The wind chased us and we pulled our coats tighter. This time of year a storm can fast blow in from the sea and turn the weather from fair to foul in a matter of minutes. We made our way down the back alley until we reached the apartment of the seer and climbed up the narrow stairway.

"This blind man, Philip, knows many things," I said to her as the stairs creaked under my steps. "He is gifted with the vision to see the future, of prophesy. Do not be afraid of his weird eyes," I told her. "His eyes are malformed, like a witch's eyes."

The blind man must have heard our coming for the door opened just as we reached the top of the stairs.

"Welcome, Massa," he said to us.

The room was the same as the day Gullah Jack and I were there: the musty smell, the goat's head skull, the sharks' teeth, the crab claws, the banjo propped in the corner, the wooden cross hung on the wall, the voodoo dolls, the wooden carving of Eschu.

"It's Denmark Vesey," I said. "I was here with Gullah Jack a fortnight back."

"Oh yes, I know, Massa," the blind seer said. "I've been expecting you."

"I brought someone with me."

"Yes, I know. Sit down, sit down," he bleated. Two simple wooden chairs rested against the wall, and I pulled them out to the middle of the floor. The seer sat on a stool facing us.

"Seer, this is Lucinda. She wants to know what you see in her future."

The blind man reached without fumble to where her hands were and took them in his.

"She is a centinel," the blind seer said without hesitation. "She will call out a warning to you. I see her bringing forth life." He then fell silent.

"Is that all?" I asked him.

The blind man did not speak for several moments. He sat on the stool without moving, so still it seemed he had turned to stone.

"Death by water," he said at last. "Yes, death by drowning."

"What else?" I asked.

"I don't see any more, Massa."

I took a coin and placed it in his hand.

"Thank you, Massa," the blind seer said, "thank you."

The girl and I threaded our way to the alley below. The forlorn twang of the blind seer's banjo wafted down the stairs from his room. In the street, the bright sunlight glared off the buildings, blinding me as I squinted from being in the dark room.

"What is a centinel?" she asked.

"Someone who watches." I told her. "Like a soldier at an entry."

"What did he mean by what he said," the girl asked. "I don't understand."

"That's sometimes the way of prophesy," I explained. "The future's never clear even when revealed to you." She gave me a puzzled look. "The words of a prophet are like a gumbo stew," I said, and prayed forgiveness to the gods of prophesy for being lighthearted for her sake. "You're likely to find a little okra and some fish and a little squash and some tomatoes and a little pepper spice with a little of most every other food," and give her a wink.

"Oh Uncle Denmark, stop teasing me," she said and smiled shyly. We made our way toward the center of the city, she with a girl's bounce in her step, I with a lingering puzzlement over the words of the blind seer: "she will call out a warning to you."

I met with my lieutenants this afternoon. I told them the girl has become engaged and joined with us. She will serve as a messenger when needed.

Saturday, 2nd March 1822

Sometimes late at night in the darkest of the hours, I pray to God to show me a sign. Some potent unshakable omen as when the angel of the Lord appeared unto Moses in a flame of fire out of the midst of a bush. Some clear mark so that I may know God has chosen me, I am the anointed One. Show me Lord that I may say unto my black brothers, the Lord that art I AM THAT I AM hath sent me unto you. Stretch out your hand, Lord, and smite this city with all your wonders. Give me a rod, Lord, that when I cast it to the ground changes into a serpent, and back to a rod again upon catching it by the tail. Make my hand show sickness and then be healed. Let water taken from the river and poured upon the dry land turn to blood.

Show me a sign, Lord. Amen.

Sunday, 3rd March 1822

I met the most remarkable young black man at the services of the African Church today. His name is David Walker. I espied him in the congregation when he was leaving, and not recognizing his face, I approached to welcome him and issue thanks for his attendance at our service. He said he is a free man of color, born in the port town of Wilmington on the Cape Fear, Carolina of the North coast. His mother was a free black, his father, he said, a slave. He told me he has been in Charleston but a few weeks, had heard others speak of the African Church and sought to attend today. Our conversation grew lengthy, my interest in his words grew great, so I invited him to visit with me at my house and shop this afternoon. I am most astonished at his smartness and his learning. We quickly discovered our mutual interests, for he is as passionate as I am about the deplorable state of our people here in this country. He is learnt, from both the Bible, and Thomas Jefferson, and the histories and writers of ancient Greece and Rome. We conversed for almost three hours!

"I left Wilmington to travel across this land and see all that I can. I want to learn for myself the condition of the blacks in this country.

"The inhuman system of slavery is the source from which most of our miseries proceed," he said to me. "It is a curse to nations. Everywhere I have been, the blacks have been forced into a wretched condition.

"The white man holds us in ignorance, but is much due to our own fault."

I was truly astonished. He sees as clearly as can be seen. The most striking point is his age; he is only in his early twenties.

"The message of the Gospels has been mingled with blood and oppression by the white man. The preachers of the Gospel of Jesus Christ should surely preach against oppression and do their utmost to erase slavery from the country.

"Did not God make us all as it seemed best to himself? What right then has one of us to despise another and to treat him cruel on account of his color, which none, but the God who made it can alter, and particularly in a free republican country.

"They chain and handcuff us and our children and drive us around the country like brutes, and go into the house of the God of justice to return him thanks for having aided them in their infernal cruelties inflicted upon us.

"The whites want to fix a plan to get those of the colored people, who are said to be free like you and me, away from among those of our brethren who they unjustly hold in bondage, so that they may be enabled to keep them the more secure in ignorance and wretchedness.

"The will of God must be done. The avaricious and ungodly tyrants will drag down the vengeance of God upon the whites. When God Almighty commences his battle on America for the oppression of his people, tyrants will wish they were never born."

These are the words I remember him speaking.

I invited him to the prayer meeting and Bible study Wednesday night. He says he knows no one at the church, but I shall ask others to make certain. My bosom and my heart tell me he speaks the truth about himself, but I must be certain. I held my tongue in revealing to him our plans. There is ample time to determine his intentions before taking him into our fold. When he joins, he will serve as a great resource to our cause.

Wednesday, 6th March 1822

The prayer group just departed. David Walker came as I hoped. He revealed more of his knowledge of the Bible at our gathering tonight. His presence seemed to instill a confidence in the others. I have yet to decide when to reveal to him our secret plans.

He seemed especially heart-struck by the young slave girl. I overheard him ask if he could walk her home. I should have known he would find her to his liking.

Sunday, 10th March 1822

Lot Forrester and Frank Ferguson have gone about traveling into the country conveying our plan and swearing secrecy from those slaves they sign on the plantations. We have passed the hat around at each of our meetings and the men have given money to pay Lot and Frank for this purpose. All that is required is for a good handful of slaves on each plantation to know of our plan, for it will be an easy matter for them in the course of the preceding day before the precise night and hour of its execution, or within a few hours of their departure to the city, to induce many others to join them.

For nearly four years now, since the whites first tried to shut our church up, I have met and talked with others about the deplorable condition of the blacks and what we could do about it. God has his hand in it, for we are not yet betrayed.

Thursday, 21stMarch 1822

Gullah Jack came to visit with me today. He had good news. He learnt from talk at the wharves a ship is in port from Santo Domingo. The ship was being repaired at the shipyard at Gadsden's Wharf and is now lying at Vanderhorst's Wharf awaiting return sail to Santo Domingo. Jack talked with some of the sailors onboard. The cook on the ship, whose name is William, will deliver a letter to his uncle so that he may open it and present it to President Boyer in *Port-au-Prince*. God has provided this opportunity to correspond with President Boyer and request Santo Domingo's aid in support of the revolt. It is another sign our plans are dictated by Divine Providence. Monday Gell and I wrote a letter to President Jean-Pierre Boyer. Monday used his quill as he has a better hand than I do. I placed the letter in a cover and Peirault Strobecker, Monday Gell, and I took it to the ship this afternoon and got it to this cook for delivery upon their soon return to the island. I have written out a copy to keep in my journal.

21stMarch 1822
Président Jean-Pierre Boyer
Port-au-Prince
Santo Domingo
His Excellency:

The hommes de couleur and gens de couleur libres of Charleston, in this Southern State of South Carolina in these United States, are subjugated under the cruel hand of the whites of this city. We can tolerate our deplorable condition no longer. We are set to join and rise up against the whites, as the blacks in Santo Domingo overthrew their French masters there.

We appeal to Santo Domingo for aid and support of our cause. The blacks in this city and on the plantations in the country are willing and ready, have sworn their solemn secrecy, and have signed to rise up in revolt. We will loot the banks and shops, storm the arsenals, and seize the gold and specie, arms and weapons. We offer to you this specie for your aid.

We, your black brothers, ask that you grant this petition, send armies to assist our plan, and provide safe sail for our escape to Santo Domingo. We are all children of mother Africa. You have shared our agony of bondage. We submit our like desire to rise up and destroy our masters as you have done. We call out for your aid to help us free ourselves. We await your word and your support of arms.

Your black brothers,

Denmark Vesey, Free black man in Charleston

Monday Gell, Slave in Charleston

Charleston, South Carolina

Tuesday, March 26 1822

I do not want to learn from my mistakes. I want to learn from the mistakes of others. I have studied about the Stono Rebellion of 1739. More than twenty whites were killed, as many as one hundred African brethren. The Africans gathered on a Sunday morning while the whites were at church. They plotted escape, attacked a shop, killed the white owners, seized weapons, powder, ammunition, supplies. Like them, we will break into the stores of Charleston and procure weapons. The Africans of the Stono Rebellion cut off the heads of the whites, and placed them on the shop steps. We will do likewise. The Africans then made for Spanish Florida and freedom.

The gathering for the Stono uprising was of a sudden. There was no studied plan as now. God was not on the Africans' side as He is here, for as the Stono Rebellion rebels marched south, as fate would have it, they were come across by a group of white men lead by the Carolina Lieutenant Governor. The white men spread the alarm and with a horse-mounted army of more than a hundred, returned in the afternoon, and in a surprise attack, killed most of the Africans. The slaves who escaped were hunted down and executed the next day.

Here no white man will remain alive. Here our insurrection will leave nothing to chance.

Saturday, 30th March 1822

I make these entries in my journal, like the prophets of the ancient Israelites wrote down their history, so my people will know the truth

I just returned from Bulkley's Farm on the Neck. Bulkley's is about two and a half miles from here, outside the city lines. It is not heavily patrolled. We gathered there near sunset in the woods next to a field where we could not be seen. There were thirty or more men at our meeting. Peter Poyas and Gullah Jack were there. As I walked through the gate to the farm, a snake slithered across the path in front of me. I took my stick and struck the serpent, killing the creature.

"This is how we'll do it," I said to the men. "We'll smite Buckra with a mighty blow that will leave him dead, like Moses smote the Egyptian for thrashing his Hebrew brother."

I propped up on a log with Gullah Jack sitting on the ground beside me. The men sat in a half-circle on the ground facing me. I studied the grimy faces in the dimming light, faces like those of a man awakening from a deep sleep, slowly becoming aware of his surroundings. Sweat glistened on their brows in the damp heat. The buzz of flies sounded around us. An acrid stench of unwashed flesh stung my nostrils. Some of the men wore no shoes, the sandy dirt showed powdery grey on their bare feet. Someone had ridden a horse, now tied to a tree nearby, the horse's head bent down to the ground as it searched for scrubs of grass, its tail swishing back and forth, its head shaking to chase away the flies. The sunlight slanted in amber tones, coloring the bordering fields. The land was flat, right angle to the plumb, the woods mostly pine with some live oak scattered in. Somewhere not far off, at the edge of the fields, a lone dove cooed in a plaintive call. Many of the African slaves believe in the white man's God, except for the Mohamedeans and their prayer beads. And the slaves believe in our African gods. We believe the trees, the fields, the rocks, and streams possess spirits which are alive, and as I looked out across the distance, I too felt all endued with the spirit gods of Africa.

"Friends," I addressed the men, and they looked up at me, "there is a new day acomin'!"

I knew deep down in the heart of each one of them there burned a bitter hatred for the white man, hatred like hot coals in the heart of the hearth to be fanned into a flame with the softest of breath. Gullah Jack stood beside me as I spoke to the men.

"Are you men of courage?" I asked softly, meeting their eyes. "Have you got anything of a man about you?"

Gullah Jack repeated my words in Gullah and then in Ebo.

"Does your heart hold the pride of a man?" I asked. Their faces were like the face of a man who has been near death, long sick from fever, and beginning to regain his strength, now knowing he is going to get well.

They were, I realized, faces of hope.

I took my hand, closed it into a fist, and beat several times on my chest. "Does your heart long to be free?" I asked them.

"Amen," a few of the men's voices said together.

"Do you know the government in Washington has made you free?" I questioned them. "Your masters keep you enslaved counter to the law of the land. Do you hate those who shackle you in chains?" Gullah Jack again repeated my words in Gullah and Ebo. "There is a new day acomin'," I said again. "The time has come, the time to rise up, the time to overthrow the white man like our black brothers did in Santo Domingo." There was a murmur among the men. "No one will free us unless we free ourselves! We are fully able to conquer the whites if we are only unanimous and courageous as the people of Santo Domingo were. There are more blacks here than the whites. Our strength of numbers is certain to bring about victory. You all know Gullah Jack is a conjurer." I turned and looked at Gullah Jack, holding out my arm in his direction. "Gullah Jack will use his charms to protect you. His magic will make you invulnerable. No white man, no white man's sword, no white man's gun, no white man's bullet will be able to harm you! I have studied the Bible from the Book of Genesis to the Book of Revelation. The white man's holy book wills we rise up and prophesizes we will overcome and destroy our enslavers. God will work His miracle. Our people will be freed and delivered to the Promised Land of Santo Domingo or Africa. The God Jehovah and the African gods demand it!"

"The African gods will protect us," Gullah Jack said in Ebo. "The African gods will help us destroy the white man. The African gods will help set us free."

"We are Africans, if not by birth, then Africans by our sacred ancestors, by the color of our skin," I said. The black faces of the men stared up at me in rapture. An old daddy African with tribal scar marks on both sides of his face is a slave on Bulkley's Farm. He yelled out his agreement in a hoarse war cry.

"Are you men?" I called out. "Do you want to be free?"

"Yeah!"

"Are you ready to fight for your freedom?"

"Yeah!"

"The whites say there are too many of us blacks, and in order to thin our ranks they have resolved to create a false alarm of fire. As we come out of our sleeping quarters in the dead of night they will be prepared to slaughter us like the butchering of an autumn hog." I paused for my words to strike terror in their breasts. "We must act to stop it! An unopened shipment of slave chains was found stored at the wharves. The whites plan to shackle you until the cankerous sores run from your ankles and your wrists!

"We have written to the government in Santo Domingo. They will send forces to help us in the uprising, send ships to help us escape. We will go all around the country and get word to the plantation slaves, into All Saints Parish to Georgetown, as far north as the Santee, round about to Combahee to get people, southward from Charleston as far as Euhaws, James' Island, John's Island, Christ Church Parish, seventy and eighty miles from the city."

"What about arms?" someone from the back of the crowd called out. "What will we use to fight?"

"Any weapons you can get by stealing them from your master . . . hoes, hatchets, axes, spades . . . collect and hide them in a place where they cannot be found, for they will serve well on the night of the insurrection. Any slave who can purloin their master's guns will do so the night of the revolt. We have a blacksmith who is making spikes like they use in Africa," I told them.

Gullah Jack had two spikes the blacksmith had made, and he took a spike in each hand and raised his arms above his head so the men could see.

"These will be mounted on long poles to make pikes," I said. "A hundred of these will be made ready for the forces that march down from here to the city. The night of the revolt, the first thing we will do is to storm the shops in Charleston that have guns and ammunition. We will break into the arsenals. The blacksmith is also casting musket balls for ammunition. In a shop on King Street just outside the limits of the city is an unguarded common wooden store where are deposited the arms of the Neck Company Militia, some two to three hundred muskets and bayonets and a few swords. I have also seen that Dugereron's store in King Street has for sale about five hundred muskets and bayonets. Schirer's store in Queen Street, and the stores of the gunsmiths where some of the militia companies store arms to keep them in working order, are all stocked with weapons. All of these we will seize. We will break into the Arsenal in Meeting Street opposite Saint Michael's Church. There the greatest proportion of the arms of the state are deposited. The Arsenal is on a public street, without even a brick wall in front of it, with doors no stronger than those of many dwelling houses, so the difficulty of forcing it open will not be very great. We will not be in want of arms! We will sweep the town with fire and sword and not allow a single white soul to escape."

I was quiet and the men spoke softly among themselves. The sun had gone down, but a thin streak of blood-red light still glowed in the western sky. Above in the twilight of the darkening sky black bats began to dart and flit, flying in gathering numbers from the thick woods.

"Those of you, who agree to rise up with us against the whites, raise your hands," I directed them. Every arm reached up toward the sky.

"When we're done with the white man," I said to them, "the buzzards which scavenge the Beef and the Fish Markets will grow fat off the carcasses of Buckra."

A throaty accord from the men swelled to me like a sea wave.

"Friends, we're going to pass around the hat and take up a collection. You all throw in seven pence apiece, those who have got it, to purchase dark lanterns for when we break into these stores. The blacksmith who made these pike heads and bayonets hires himself out, and we must contribute toward what he has to pay his master for the time he has spent working on this. Remember, we'll break into the banks and the stores on the night of the uprising and loot all the valuables and gold and specie and then you'll have payment for your efforts and sacrifice."

Gullah Jack took his hat from his head and worked among the men.

"Assume the most implicit obedience," I then said to them. "Let not your hatred show, not in your face, not in your words, not in your acts. Arouse no suspicions. Catch your master unawares when you plunge a dagger into his heart."

There was a stir of consent from the men. I had captured their hearts, and was poised to unleash their wild and naked passions upon their enslavers.

"We must draw on the Voodoo rights at our ceremonies and gatherings," Gullah Jack had told me, "just as the slaves in Santo Domingo did. We must appease the African gods."

The slaves from Bulkley's Farm had built a fire and hung a cauldron of water from the stream over it. Gullah Jack took a tied-up hen and unfastened the legs and the wings, then took the chicken by the neck and began to wring the bird's head with a quick circling of his hand. The chicken squawked in terror until Gullah Jack had wrung the head completely off, a bloody stub of beak and eyes and tissue left in his hand. The chicken fell to the ground when the head came off and it flopped violently in the dust, the wings stiffly engaged in a feeble flap of effort. After a few moments, the bird lay dead and motionless. Gullah Jack took the chicken, placed it in the pot, and stirred with a stick. The water began to boil and after a while, Gullah Jack took the stick and removed the chicken from the pot and pulled the feathers off, now loosened by the boiling. When all the feathers were removed, Gullah Jack placed the chicken back in the pot to rinse it clean, then took the chicken and pierced it with a stick and began to roast it over the fire until it was half-raw. With my knife, he began to cut off pieces of the bloody chicken and passed these around for the men to eat.

"We must be as wild and bloody as what we now eat," Gullah Jack said to the men. "This will make you savage and fearless. Eat this as a mark of our unity."

The men chewed silently until the chicken was eaten by all, then began to whisper among themselves. A few began to moan a spiritual until all had joined in.

"*One fine morn soon be a comin'.*"

Clap.

"*One fine morn soon be a comin'.*"

Clap.

"*One fine morn soon be a comin'.*"

"*Gonna get to the Promised Land.*"

"*One bright morn soon be a comin'.*"

Clap.

"*One bright morn soon be a comin.*"

Clap.

"*One bright morn soon be a comin'.*"

"*Jesus gonna carry me home.*"

"*Moses, Jesus, and Elijah*"

Clap.

"*Moses, Jesus, and Elijah*"

Clap.

"*Moses, Jesus, and Elijah*"

"*Standin' high on de mountain top.*"

The darkness of the night began to fade, and a thin band of color began to lift up in the eastern sky as Gullah Jack and I commenced our journey back to Charleston from the Neck, careful to avoid any encounters along the way.

"My carpentry work has all but come to a halt," I told him. "I am no longer concerned with such pursuits. I no longer wish to build, I wish to destroy."

"And destroy we will," Gullah Jack said.

Sunday, 31st March 1822

I saw two of my wives today. The custom in Africa is for a man to marry as many wives as he can afford. The more cattle and possessions he has, the richer is he, and the more wives he can take. I have had seven different women as wives in my life. All of them slaves. All my children, because they were born to slave women, were born into slavery. In Africa, family lines descend from the mother. Here in America, the white man provides the family name and line for his children; that is, for all of his white children, but not those he yields with his slave women. With those, the African tradition holds sway. Because the children are born to a slave woman, they are born slaves, regardless of their father. Buckra is master of his own slave children!

The white man does not recognize marriage between slaves. The union has no legal sway. But the arrangement is allowed, even encouraged by white masters, perhaps in hopes to create submission among the slaves. There is no ceremony or such: as long as the master of the slave woman approves, the agreement is done. After all, any offspring are the property of the slave woman's master, as chattel slave children add to his riches, property, and wealth.

The whites think nothing of separating these husbands and wives, mothers and children, brothers and sisters, when selling their slaves if it suits the masters to do so. I have often observed the auctions of slaves. Whole slave families are brought in for sale. A mother sold and sent off with a new master in one direction, a child sold and sent off in another. A husband forever lost from a wife, a wife lost by a husband from the ravages of the auctioneer's block. My heart rent by the piteous sobs of a mother who has seen all her children sold and taken from her. The slaves are stripped naked, inspected by the buyers like so many sheep, horses, or cattle, peering in the slaves' mouths at their teeth or tongue, turning the to-be-bought slave to look at their feet and legs, thighs and chests and backsides. The stronger the slave man looks, the more money he fetches; the value of female slaves often judged by different measures.

I am a free black man, but all my wives are slaves. I cannot visit with any of them unless I have their master's approval. Their masters can prevent me from seeing them at any time. They can sell my wives to anyone they want at any time. I could never see them again. Such happened with my third wife.

I took my first wife in Saint Thomas when I had become a man of near sixteen years old. I had been a slave of Captain Vesey for over a year when we sailed with a cargo of slaves from the West African coast to the island. Our ship was to be in port for less than a week. I first saw her at the market of the city. She was perhaps fifteen-years-old, born on the island, she said, a house slave of a rich Danish cane planter. I was smitten by her dark smoky eyes, her black skin, which glowed like polished ebony, her black hair which flowed in soft curls when she removed her headscarf and gently shook her head to further the fall of her hair. I thought at the time Captain Vesey would dock at the port of Charlotte Amalie on St. Thomas some every six months, so taking her as a wife was not unheard of, even for a sailor who was a slave. But I saw her only twice more. Afterwards, Captain Vesey settled in Charleston, and I was unable to visit her again. She was the first love of my life, a plush, soft-voiced girl who did anything I asked. But she and I were slaves, unable to live the life of unchained man and woman, our lives at the whim of a cold-hearted master. I learnt for the first time but not the last the harsh lesson that slaves have no command over their lives; they live only at the mercy of their masters. Whether I have any children by her, I do not know. Slaves they would be.

I took my second wife at the port of Havana, a Spanish Creole speaking girl of fiery temperament. She was *una senorita de statura pequeña y delgada,* but she was as spirited as an unbroken filly too long in the wild. She was always in some scrape with her master's mistress, and her master did most everything to try to break her with frequent floggings and withheld food. For almost a year, Captain Vesey worked the port of Havana, and we docked there for the slave market every few months. One day when we arrived in port, I found her in a trouble. She had been severely lashed by her mistress for what she said they described as her insolence. They had flogged her with twenty hard strikes across her delicate back, and the still bleeding marks were puffy and raw, dark red from the bruising. She cried not a tear. That was all she would say to me about it, "I cried not a tear," her black eyes still dry as a stone. "I would not give them the pleasure to see me cry." Many times over these near forty years, I have considered if it was not solely from her that I learnt to hate and despise the whites for their bitter and wanton cruelty, their hard marks of blood and fury.

I took my third wife soon after Captain Vesey settled in Charleston. She was the slave of a French planter befriended by Captain Vesey who had migrated from Santo Domingo and began a plantation on the Cooper River. The Frenchman too had a slave exchange business in the city. She bore me two children, my eldest, a boy, named Robert, and a daughter, both now slaves in Charleston. One Sunday afternoon I visited her as usual, when she said her master had sold her to be shipped off to New Orleans. Two days later, she was gone. I never saw or heard from her again. The life of a slave can change at the blink of an eye.

I was still young and took a fourth wife soon after. She was the washwoman of one of the largest slave holding families in the city. I saw her often at the water wells of Charleston drawing water and toting it on her head to her mistress's house. She had no duties on Sundays and we were able to meet after services of the First Presbyterian Church where I had become a member. Captain Vesey was agreeable when it came to my seeing my wives and never restricted my doing so on Sundays. We would sometimes take walks by the harbor, the water silted by the river flow, the surf in playful splashes along the shore, the schooners' white sails like outspread wings of a flock of gulls, the sun hot and sticky on our faces but cooled by the breeze from the harbor. There are few moments in the life of a slave which are at peace with the world, but these were moments of peace for me. We would gather with the other slaves in the market place on Sunday afternoons. She dressed in the African way when she could with flowing bright colors and headpiece. She was a great talker, and told stories to the other slaves that made their ears tingle, their eyes light up bright as the glint off Charleston's sand-shell streets, their white-teeth grins flash upon their faces. Her laugh was as free and warm as the morning sun, a laugh as precious to me as freedom. She too bore me two children, another slave son and slave daughter. Her life was hard, filled with drudgery, as is the life of every slave, but it seemed not to affect her. One of my saddest times was when she fell ill, and within but a few days she passed beyond this earth to return to our ancient ancestors in Africa. Her sickness was of a sudden, and no cause ever known. Even her master and mistress, with all of their other slaves, missed her generous soul and her laughter, for they once expressed this to me themselves. Even Buckra possesses a heart, I reckon, stony and hard as it is.

After I gained my freedom, I decided to take as many wives as I wished. I am like the Mohamedeans of Africa who have several wives at once. I married three women over a six-year period, Ruth, Beck, and Delilah. All are house slaves in Charleston. What any one of my wives lacks, another makes up for it. I cannot say I really have a favorite. Now that I am older, I love women in general more than I love any particular one and it suits me to keep several wives at the same time. I do not now often look for women as company, but there are times when a woman fills an empty space, and it is like no other experience in the life of a man. My wife Beck does not visit me here as she once did, but she still comes around ever so often. Another of my wives, Ruth, also lives not so far from my shop in Charleston. These two of my wives I saw today.

Sunday, 7th April 1822

The memory is still so vivid. The green hills of Saint Thomas rose up from the turquoise waters like an oasis floating on a desert sea of sand. We had docked in the harbor of Charlotte Amalie for half-a-day to load a small cargo of slaves and supplies to complete our haul to Santo Domingo, the same journey as a slave I had made near two years before. Captain Vesey had gone ashore on some business. He permitted me to go ashore myself, alone. I walked the dirty streets near the harbor, the heat of the night heavy, sweat built on my brow. The hour was late and the streets almost empty. I crossed a narrow passageway to return to the ship. We were to depart at dawn. I heard sounds of a struggle and repeated blows. I stepped and looked around the corner at the source of the cries. A white man was standing with a club in his hand beating a black man down on his knees, the black man's empty hands open, his arm raised in an act of defense. The white man struck the black man with all of his might again and again. I stepped closer. The white man's back was to me. He was so intent on the man he was beating he did not hear me and did not turn around. I took my knife hidden in my belt and I sneaked up behind him and I reached out just as he turned to me with surprise on his face, his arm raised to strike another blow, and with a quick movement I took my knife, sharp as a razor, and touched it to his neck and swift as a bird with one stroke I slit his throat from one ear to the other. He looked at me in stunned disbelief for a quick moment. I remember the blood sticky and warmer than the night on my hand. I caught the smell of rum on his stopped breath as his eyes suddenly lost their gleam and faded into a dark emptiness. He fell to his knees and then completely prone. The black man he had been beating looked up at me with a look of terror as if unsure if I was going to slice his throat. "Get out of here," I told him and he scrambled to his feet, turned, and ran without looking back. I quickly and quietly made my way to the harbor and to the ship. We sailed away early morning at sunrise. No one but God knows I took the life of another man. I have, like Moses, murdered before. I can murder again.

Friday, 12th April 1822

Monday Gell and Pierault Stohecker say they have never spoken to any person of color on the subject of the rebellion, or know of anyone who has been spoken to by the other leaders, who has withheld their assent. Each day we add more names to our list. Peter Poyas himself has over six hundred names, most of them from the East Bay Street district where he lives. Gullah Jack says there are thousands on the country plantations who are ready to rise up. Peter has the number of all of those who have signed and says it is near nine thousand. Monday said to me if we have that many, why not go ahead and let the revolt begin now. I told him we must wait. We are not quite ready, as we yet have more preparations to do. "Be patient," I told him, "the time will come."

The men have done well in choosing our recruits. I have limited them only two times. I forbade my followers to trust one man because on one occasion he was seen in a state of drunkenness. We cannot risk such peril. The other was a man named George Parker. We came to the resolution that although he is an African, he does not associate with his countrymen, and he is a babbling fellow upon whom no dependence can be placed.

Thursday, 18th April 1822

The young slave girl came to my shop this morning. Her eyes were red as if she had shed tears. She asked me if I had seen David Walker. I told her I had not seen him in a number of days. I suspect he has taken the next leg of his journey of exploration and set forth from Charleston. I pray God watches over him and leads him on his destined path. Alas, I am afraid he has taken the young girl's heart with him.

I have not told her of the wives I have lost to the whims of slavery. If I thought it would ease her pain, I would tell her, let her know she is not alone in her loss. Perhaps someday I shall.

Sunday, 28th April 1822

I have promised my men ample booty once the insurrection is over. We will break into the banks and shops, take everything of value . . . gold, currency, specie. We will arrive in Santo Domingo or Africa as wealthy men!

I have been robbed by the white man my entire life. Now is high time the tables were turned. For twenty years, the fruits of my labor went to my master. Even now, a free black man's labor and skills earn him less than a white man. We are owed as much as we can take with us. Revenge and treasure await!

Saturday, 4th May 1822

I dreamt last night of the insurrection. The Africans danced and chanted in an immense Voodoo ceremony with Gullah Jack at Buckley's Farm. Drum beats echoed along the Cooper and the Ashley rivers, and from John's and Bull's Island all the way to the Santee. The plantation Big House and fields of Buckley's Farm burnt, and the flames and towering billows of black smoke eclipsed the stars in the night sky. The tumult of drums swelled into a senseless frenzy.

The bells of the churches in the city rang twelve midnight.

Throngs of slaves amassed on the city, the night sky torn with their war cries. The slaves came by canoe, barge flat, riverboat, schooner. Slaves on horseback, slaves on foot, armed with axes and hoes, swords and knives, guns purloined from their masters. Faces painted as the warriors in Africa, bloodthirsty hatred in their reddened eyes.

The city burnt. Flames roared up like the tormented cries of hell, houses and shops in the town consumed to dark ashes and dust, thick smoke whirling in the night wind. Bennett's Mills destroyed in a great conflagration. The angel of destruction Abaddon spread his vast wings across the nighttime sky.

In the harbor, a navy of ships flying flags of Santo Domingo floated on the greasy water, garrisoned with armed soldiers to disembark and employ their forces in aid to the insurgent slaves.

Screams and cries of terror deluged the streets of the city. Screams and cries of terror I shall never forget. The slaves savagely dispatched every white person as they came out of the burning houses and onto the streets. Every white person, man, woman, and child killed. The rivers and harbor turned red with blood, strangely visible to me in the dark of the night. The Prophets, robed in white, bearded, and with long locks, Isaiah, and Ezekiel, and Obadiah and Zechariah and Joshua, stood atop the steeples of the churches, orating in the ancient Hebrew tongue.

My eyes scanned across the city and saw the streets strewn with bloody white bodies, mutilated and naked. Pikes with dismembered heads lined the ways.

I woke with banging in my chest like a smith's hammer forging iron and no sleep to follow.

Sunday, 12th May 1822

I returned this afternoon from a visit to some of the plantations in All Saints Parish. I set out from the Charleston harbor last Wednesday morning aboard a schooner loaded with passengers and freight. Traveling up the coast, the wind was up, the white sails whipping and snapping in the breeze, a great dome of blue sky with clouds blowing in from the southeast, flat at the edges against an ocean of white cap swells. The wind made for quick sail but choppy seas. The ship coursed in sight of the shore off the port bow. Sea gulls circled and squawked overhead. In the distance, I could see stretches of empty beach and dunes. A knot of palmetto palms thick before the water's edge. The dark swamps bordered by water fields of sweet grass, stands of live oaks draped with Spanish moss, and cypress groves at the back of the green tidelands, for spring is now in earnest. A white crane stood in the water's edge. The landscape brought to my mind the islands of the West Indies, for there is a hint of the same lushness here along the Carolina coast, enough to make me think of old places after these many years.

Within two-and-a-half hours of Charleston, the schooner was navigating the water into Winyah Bay near Georgetown and docked at Fraser's Point. I disembarked from the ship, shifting my carpenter's workbag on my shoulder and looked about me. Men unloaded several barges and canoes at a wharf. I walked toward them along a wooden plank dock built out over the water.

"Where can I hitch a ride up river, brother," I asked one of the slaves working to unload a barge. He pointed to a dock some yards away.

"See them. They be headin' up river."

I made my way to where a large canoe was being unloaded by half a dozen men.

"A bit for a lift up river," I said to the one who looked like the headman.

"Sho', bro'," he answered me. "We's oblige ye. Wha' you be headin'?"

"How far you going?"

"Rosehill."

"I'll go with you all the way." I figured it best if I went as far up-river as they could take me. I would then work my way back at as many of the bigger plantations as I could. I gave the man the coins I held in my hand, a dime and a two-and-a-half cents piece.

"We's be leavin' soon."

The lead man waved his hand to me they were ready to depart. I carefully stepped into the bobbing canoe and sat down in the back, placing my workbag between my legs. Once filled with the men, the canoe slipped through the channel as effortlessly as a water snake. The men rowed as one, moaning a low work song in time. The canoe entered the river from the open bay, the murky waters of the Waccamaw ghostly reflecting the Spanish moss and riverbank oaks like an antique mirror faded by time.

As memory serves me, there must be thirty odd rice plantations along the Waccamaw River before you get to All Saints Church . . . . there's Calais, Strawberry Hill, Friendfield, Marrietta, Bellefield, Youngville, Oryzania, Alderly, Rose Hill, Forlorn Hope, Clifton, Prospect Hill, Fairfield, Waterford, Hagley, Weehawka, True Blue, Midway, Caledonia. I cannot recall them all, and I could get to only a handful, but I told the slaves on the plantations I visited to spread the news of the revolt. They say All Saints Parish on the Waccamaw River is one of the largest rice growing regions in the world, and I believe it. The river winds broad and shallow south along the coast before it flows into the sea, far enough inland from the ocean for the river water to be fresh. Rice won't grow in brackish water. The rice ponds are built with ditches, canals, and floodgates to divert the fresh river water into the fields. I knew that for each plantation big house the canoe passed on the trip up river, there are hundreds and hundreds of slaves working the plantations. I thought of the thousands over the decades who gave their lives in backbreaking labor to create such wealth and life of leisure for their white masters. The thought was fodder for my hatred. We made good time and reached Rosehill Plantation by mid-afternoon.

"Let me out on the river bank near the horse trail," I told the men. "I don't need to go all the way."

I pulled my carpenter's bag from the floor of the canoe and tugged it up to my shoulder. The bag was heavy and cumbersome, but in such strange territory, it was best to have it with me in case I was questioned by a plantation patrol. And just as I worked my way up from the river bank to the trail, I heard hooves approaching from behind. I knew from the sound it was a lone horseman. I turned as the hoof beats came closer and I saw a man in a gallop pull the reigns to slow his horse as he caught sight of me. He was staring with a wary expression and approached me cautiously, as if I was a snake sunning on the bank of his favorite fishing spot. I knew from his look he must be a patroller or hunted runaway slaves for bounty. He rode up beside me, leaning forward in the saddle as he looked down at me, his hands tightly on the reigns, a long-barreled rifle strapped across his back.

"You a run-away, nigger?" he asked, a snarly look on his face under his hat. That was all he said, then he continued to stare, his dark beady eyes fixed upon me.

"No, I'm a free black man from Charleston," I answered him. "I'm a carpenter looking for work."

"A carpenter, huh."

"Do you wish to see my papers?" I asked him.

"Yeah, I would. Show 'em to me," he said, then turned and spit on the ground, pulling the horse's reigns just enough for the horse to stomp about.

I reached into my carpenter's tool satchel and handed him my documents, my papers of manumission, my work badge, and fee payment papers.

"Vesey. Denmark Vesey," he said still wearing his snarl. "What kind of name is that . . . Denmark?"

"I came from the Danish island of Saint Thomas in the West Indies. They call me Denmark, like the country."

"All right, nigger," the man said, the snarl ridged and pasted on his face as he handed the papers back to me. "You go about your business. You just stay out of trouble, you hear. We keep our niggers in tow up here in All Saints Parish, you understand?"

"I understand," I answered him. At another time, I might have ended his life then and there.

I walked toward the plantation staying close by the woods. I then waited there until near dusk when the slaves were returning from the fields at the day's end. I joined them as they trekked in a slow pace toward the cabins.

"I've come from Charleston," I told one of the men. "I have news for the slaves. I'd like to gather with some of you tonight after dark."

"What news?" he asked.

"News you'll want to know," I said.

"Come to my cabin after sunset," he instructed me. "Watch where I go."

I lingered back from the group, and took shelter in a grove of trees near the slave cabins, keeping close watch on where the man had gone. When the sun had fully set and the night was dark about, I made my way across the yard to the man's cabin. The man sat on the steps of the porch eating his evening meal. I could hear from the cabin through the open door a woman working the hearth and attending to a child.

"Want some hoe cake and a cup of clabber?" the man asked me. I saw it as a good sign.

"I'd much appreciate it," I thanked him. I didn't realize how hungry I was until the man asked, or how long it had been since my breakfast that morning.

He got up from the porch step, went inside the cabin, and returned with a cake of corn bread and a cup with the buttermilk.

"What news have you?" he asked.

"News about your freedom. Gather some men so I can tell you."

The man got up without answering and I watched him walk along the row of slave cabins until he disappeared into the darkness. In short while he returned, a group of ten men or so with him, shuffling restless and curious in the dark. They gathered at the porch where I now sat on the step. I could not see their faces, only a dark glimmer reflected from the cabin fireplace emitting a feeble light through the open door. Not one of the men said a word.

"Some of you may know who I am," I said, almost in a whisper, just loud enough for them to hear me. "I'm a carpenter in Charleston, a free black man. I've come this far because I have news." I stopped and listened closely. The fields and woods beyond the cabins toward the river had come alive with a chorus of sounds; a thousand creatures alive with the night. The golden glow of fireflies flashed gently across the yard. "You've likely heard that Congress in Washington has made you free, but your master refuses to grant your freedom." I paused again to let my words have their effect. "Well, it is so. The slaves in Charleston are ready to do something about it. They want to know if you're ready to join them?"

A quiet stirring issued from some of the men and they shuffled their feet in place as if to help take in what I had said. I knew that for over two years since news of the admission of Missouri to the Union rumors among the slaves had spread all up and down the coast that their freedom had come about.

"That is the news I've come to tell you," I said. I know slaves well enough to know their hearts swelled with hope at my words.

"What can we do?" the man who had given me the food finally asked.

"Word will be sent to you when the time is right. You'll need to come into Charleston by horse, by canoe, by boat, however you can. Spread the word of the news I've told you. But be most careful and tell only those you know you can trust not to tell their masters."

All that needed to be done was to create a spark to ignite the kindling of hatred and the flames of insurrection would rage up uncontrollably. I had set off that spark.

I spent the night in the woods at the edge the plantation. At dawn, the man from the cabin came to me with more food.

"We talked more last night," he said to me. "We're ready to fight. We'll let the slaves on the other plantations know. We'll be careful who we tell."

"What's your name," I asked him.

"Caesar." he told me. "I am called Caesar."

"Caesar," I said. "We'll send a man on horse to you when we are ready."

I worked my way down river each day, catching a canoe or barge when I could, hiding in the woods as not to be seen, and each night at dusk making my way to the slave cabins of a plantation. Each night the slaves were the same. No slave with the heart of a man refuses the chance for freedom. Georgetown will fall within an hour of the commencement of the insurrection against the whites.

Tuesday, 14th May 1822

Bacchus Hammett has stolen a pistol, a sword, and a keg of powder from his master and conveyed these to me. We'll make up fixed ammunition from what he has provided. I've never shot a gun before. I would rather use a blade to hack Buckra to pieces. I hide the pistol in the safe keeping place where I stow this journal. I take out the gun when we have a gathering here of my men and place it on the table in the light of the lamp so that it is within sight of everyone. It seems to comfort the men like a mama's milk calms the crying baby. The sight of that gun by my men works like one of

Gullah Jack's charm potions.

Saturday 25th May 1822

I met here at my shop tonight with a dozen of the men who will bring freedom to the blacks of this city. With me were my chosen twelve: my original men, Gullah Jack, Ned and Rolla Bennett, Monday Gell, Peter Poyas, Jack Purcell, and those others who have been most active, Bacchus Hammett, the Devil amongst women, as he describes himself, Mingo Harth, Lot Forrester, Frank Ferguson, Tom Russell, and Batteau Bennett.

The date of our uprising has now been revealed to me. The night of July 14th. I informed the men of this plan and all agreed it is the right time. July 14th is a Sunday. The slaves gather in the market place on Sunday afternoons, a tradition going back to the early days of slavery in Barbados and other islands of the West Indies. The Charleston authorities will think nothing of the crowds of slaves that are about. The night will have no moon. A blanket of darkness will cover us. July is the time when the white people go to the North or Sullivan's Island or to the upper part of the State to escape the country fever. The city will be thin of men. Many members of the militia, the guard, and the patrollers will be away from the city. July 14th is Bastille Day, the anniversary of the storming of the dreaded French prison, and the celebration of the overthrow of tyranny and oppression, the day of *liberté, equalité, fraternité*.

I opened our meeting by reading to the men the Bible from Joshua 6:21, "And they utterly destroyed all that was in the city, both man and woman, young and old, and ox, and sheep, and ass, with the edge of the sword."

"The day of the insurrection is soon upon us," I told them. "God has worked His will. Our plan is almost complete. Soon all that is in this city will be utterly destroyed, the riches will be ours, and you will be free.

"The slaves from the country plantations will journey to the city Sunday, July 14th by foot, barge, canoe, river flat . . . whatever means they can. The slaves on the plantations close to the city will hide those from Georgetown, the Santee, and John's Island the night before, so all will be near the city at the appointed hour. Sunday afternoon of the uprising, the slaves will begin to move into the city. Sunday is when the slaves in the country customarily come into town. There is a gathering of the slaves in the market place, a practice accepted by the whites. Nothing will appear unusual.

"We have spoken of our plan for the night of the revolt many times," I said to them, "but let us study again. Gullah Jack will provide poison for the wells of the city."

"I will give you bottles with poison to put into your masters' pumps and into as many pumps about town as you can. I'll give other bottles to those I can trust to do the same. Buckra will die from deadly drink."

"And Gullah Jack has made potions and charms to protect you," I said.

"Here is dry food made of parched corn and ground nuts," Gullah Jack said. "Eat this and nothing else on the morning of the uprising, and when you are ready to join us as we pass, put into your mouth this crab-claw." Gullah Jack reached into one of the small sacks he carried on his belt and held up a crab claw for all to see. "With this crab-claw in your mouth, you cannot be wounded. I will give the same to the rest of my army," he said. "If you drop the large crab-claw out of your mouth, then put in the small one." Gullah Jack handed to each of the men a small sack with the corn and nuts and big and small crab-claws.

"Our attack will commence when you hear twelve peals of the bells from Saint Michael's steeple," I said to the men. "The house slaves will slaughter their masters as they dream asleep in their beds. After we seize the arms from the Arsenal and the Guard House, we'll sound the alarm of fire, and as the whites come from their houses, the slaves in the yards will dispatch them on the spot. We will charge all points at once. The country slaves will march into the city from several directions. They will hack and butcher, shoot their way to the heart of the city leaving a trail of blood and the litter of white bodies in the streets. Peter Poyas will lead an army of blacks from the coast and the Sea Islands and seize the state arsenal at Meeting Street and the Guard House."

Peter Poyas stuck out his square jaw proudly. He has been one of my most loyal recruiters, gathering hundreds for our cause.

"Surprise in our attacks is crucial," I said. "I have paid a white barber here in the city to make false white hair and whiskers with the hair of white people. With the aid of these and by painting our faces white, we will in the darkness of night and in the confusion be mistaken for white men."

Peter Poyas said, "I will wear the disguise of a white man's whiskers and hair, and begin by going alone from my house on East Bay and assembling with a party on South Bay."

"Peter's group will be joined by a force of country slaves from the James' Island plantations," I said.

"I will advance in my disguise some distance ahead of my party and surprise and put to death the centinel before the Guard House," Peter Poyas said to the men. "If I can only get a grip at his throat, he will be a gone man. My sword is very sharp. I have made it so sharp I have cut my finger." Peter then held out his hand with his thumb on his finger for all to see. "We will then march and seize the Arsenal and Guard House opposite Meeting Street across from Saint Michael's Church and confiscate the arms."

"This is our most important strike and must be done without flaw," I emphasized to the men. "From this force, a party will then be detached to prevent the white people from assembling at their alarm posts by cutting them off as they arrive. The screams of dying white men will be the sole alarms to be heard!"

"Do we intend to kill the women and children?" Jack Purcell asked.

Rolla Bennett answered, "When we've done with the fellows, we know what to do with the wenches."

Everyone laughed.

"A second body of our men," Ned Bennett said, "made up partly of slaves from the country and partly from the Neck, will assemble at midnight on the Neck and under my command, will seize the Arsenal there."

"A third group," Rolla Bennett spoke, "will gather at midnight at Bennett's Mills. After I murder the Governor and the Intendant, we'll set the mills afire and march through the city or take station at Cannon's Bridge to prevent the inhabitants of Cannonsborough from entering the city."

"A fourth band made up partly from the country and partly of those from that portion of the city," I said, "will rendezvous on Gadsden's Wharf, then march and attack the upper Guard House. A fifth of country and Neck slaves, for whom the pikes have been made, will gather at Bulkley's Farm and seize the powder magazine about a mile from there, then march into the city. Our sixth group will assemble here at my shop at midnight and under my command march down to the Guard House."

"My forces will then join and march with you," Batteau Bennett said.

"We'll join the other slaves as they advance in to meet us," I said. "Neither will we be without horses. We'll send men on horses to the country to bring the people down. Members of the draymen and carters of the city will serve as our horseman. Many of them keep the horses of their masters and there are free blacks in those occupations who own their own horses. Some of the butchers' boys can provide themselves with horses. Some slaves engaged in our plot are slaves at some of the livery stables and at the appointed hour will have the horses saddled, and at the hour will open the stable doors and thus provide their comrades with horses. The slaves whose owners are attached to the corps of cavalry in the city will seize and take with them the horses of their masters. While the attacks are going on, our men on horseback will ride through the streets and kill every white person they might meet."

"My Gullah army will rally on Boundary Street at the head of King Street, and take possession of the arms of the Neck Company, and those in Duquereron's store," Gullah Jack said.

"Once we have seized all arms," I reminded them, "the best way for us to conquer the whites is to set the town on fire in several places, at Governor Bennett's Mills, and near the Docks. Every servant in the yards will be ready with axes, knives, and clubs to kill every white man as they come out when the alarm bells begin to ring. The screams of the murdered whites will fill the streets. Fires will rage. I have seen in the past how the whites panic when there is an accidental blaze. Nothing can be done without fire.

"If any blacks hold back and do not join in by this time, they too must be killed," I emphasized. "As the Bible says in the Gospel of Luke, 'he that is not with me is against me.'

"We will have other arms," I encouraged the men. "Pompey Haig told me the Frenchmen, blacks, are very skillful in making swords and spears, such as they use in Africa, and will help provide weapons to us. I have found a black smithy that will secretly make one hundred pikes. John Vincent has stolen a bullet mold and musket balls have been cast and hidden in sacks throughout the city."

"I will carry the pikes up to Bulkley's Farm," Gullah Jack said, "and hide them there so they will be on hand the night of the revolt."

Monday Gell spoke up. "I have hidden in my shop a keg of gunpowder Bacchus Hammett stole from his master."

Lot Forrester said, "I've obtained a length of slow match from the State Arsenal on Meeting Street."

"We have sent a letter to President Boyer of Santo Domingo," I said. "The government of Santo Domingo will send ships to take us away after we have killed all the whites and freed ourselves."

I pored over the faces in the room. I saw Peter Poyas' face of fierce determination; I saw Bacchus Hammett's face of hope; Gullah Jack's face of anger; but I saw not one face of fear. Only Monday Gell's eyes did not meet mine.

"This is the way we shall do it," I said to the men. "Commit every point to your remembrance. God shall be with us."

I again studied each face.

"We shan't be slaves to these damn rascals any longer," I vowed. "We must kill everyone we can get hold of, and drive the rest of the flesh-mongers out of the city. Once we take control, we will make then our determination of how to proceed. We'll control the fortifications on the Neck and around the Harbor and with our protected position, we can retain possession of the city for as long as we deem expedient. The city's militia will be thin of men that time of the year, and with the country slaves occupying the city in such forces, our strength will serve to protect us. No one will dare attack us from the outside.

"We'll raid the banks of their gold and specie, plunder the city of all that is valuable," I tempted them again. "The ships sent to our aid by Santo Domingo will be our escape there or to Africa.

"Friends, let's pass around the hat for each of you to put in twelve-and-a-half cents to pay that black smithy's wages to his mistress and for buying arms and lanterns and the false wigs and whiskers." Gullah Jack took his hat from his head and walked through the room. Every man dug into his pocket, dropping coins into the hat.

"I've worked many miles north of Charleston, many miles toward Santee, into Saint John's Parish to the south of James' and John's Islands, and to the west beyond Bacon's Bridge over the Ashley River," I said to them. "My life's work is almost complete. Soon you will be free."

Saturday, 1st June 1822 2 AM

We are found out! The young slave girl came to me in the dead of tonight to impart that the Governor and the Intendant visited her master this evening. She overheard them say the slave William Paul has been taken up and is lodged in the Guard House. William spoke with the wrong slave at the wharves, a man named Peter Desverneys Prioleau, and this slave reported plans of the revolt to his master, who informed the Intendant. The girl risked herself at grave danger by stealing away to warn me with this news.

Lord forbid, now the Intendant, City Council, and the Governor know of the insurrection! How much do they know? None of my men or myself were spoken of, from what the girl says. The whites will make strong effort to learn more, and with haste. I pray the protections we have taken will guard us. If others be taken up, I pray they keep their lips sealed and shield our secret with their life. Otherwise, they will die at my hand for their indiscretion. Silence is our salvation and security.

After much prayer tonight, I believe it best to fix upon an earlier date for the uprising. The night of June 16th will serve. That too is a night of no moon, and should give us time for preparations if we move quickly. Tomorrow I must determine whether I should go into hiding. I can stow away at one of my wives if need be. For now, I will keep my journal in its hiding place. If what the girl says is true, the whites do not know the revolt has originated with me. I will seek out Gullah Jack and Peter Poyas this morning to learn what they counsel.

Once the girl imparted her news to me, she turned to the door to make her way back to South Bay under the cover of dark night. I paused for a moment, still uncertain if my course was sure.

"I know you must hurry back," I said to her. "But before you go, let me show you something. It is of consequence."

She looked from the door to me.

"Are you to be trusted with a secret?" I asked her.

"Yes," she answered. "You know I am, Uncle Denmark."

"I have prayed very earnestly, and believe you to be true," I said. I looked at her carefully for a long moment mulling over the question I had long considered. Then I told her, "Come." I walked back to the corner of my shop and gestured for her to follow. We came to a blank section of the wall. "Do you see anything?" I asked her.

She looked very closely at the wall made with planks of wood, trying to figure what I meant.

"What am I supposed to see, Uncle Denmark?" she asked me. I made no answer. She said, "No, I don't see anything."

"Good," I said to her, "good. Now watch." I reached to the workbench and picked up a small blade about three inches long and very thin. "Look carefully," I said. I took the tip of the blade and slid it under the head of a small nail at one place on the wall. The nail pulled out about an inch, and then I did the same with another nail on the wall. I took my fingers and gently pulled out each nail and took the blade and slid it under a small crack between the nails. Suddenly a square of the wall opened up like a trap door and inside the space were my papers and journal.

"If anything happens to me," I said, and I could tell from the troubled look on her face she knew I was most serious, "I'm going to give you a key to this shop and I want you to come here as soon as you can, but make sure you're not being watched or followed, that you're safe. I want you to come and open up this hiding space as I've showed you, take these papers and guard them with all you have and show them to no one. You must not be found with them and they must not be found. Can you do that?"

"Yes," she said. "I'll do anything to help you."

I knew then I had made the right decision. She was the one slave no one would suspect of being involved in the plot. My secret would be safe with her. I was quiet for another moment and looked at her again.

"Here," I said, "take this key to my shop. Safeguard it. Can you store it in a place where it cannot be found?"

"Yes," she told me.

"The blade to pull out the nails will be hidden here under this bench," I continued. "Put the cover back in place and the nails back in like this," and I showed her by fitting the cover and pushing the nails with my fingers into their holes in the wall. When I finished the wall looked like any other section of the walls in the room.

"And you have a safe place to hide my papers . . . if it comes to that," I asked her.

"Yes, I can store them in my trunk at Mistress Johnson's," she said, "They've never searched or opened it and I have had it for many years. They will be secret and safe."

"When do you go out to the markets each day," I asked her.

"It depends," she said. "Not always the same time, but in the morning, whenever Mistress Johnson tells me to go. Why do you ask that?"

"I may at some time need for Gullah Jack to get a message to you," I said. "He can meet you at the market. I'll tell him to look for you there in the mornings." Then I told her, "You must get back," I walked to the window and looked out. "You must be careful."

"Yes, I saw no one when I came. I'll be alright."

"Do not speak of this to anyone."

"I know. But I had to come and tell you now."

"You did the right thing, child. Now go. Be careful."

"One more thing, Uncle Denmark," Lucinda said to me. "Poison."

"Poison?" I asked, for a moment unsure what she meant.

"I'll need poison." Then I realized she intended it for her masters the night of the revolt. "Ask Gullah Jack to prepare a powerful poison for me," she said, and slipped silently out the door and into the black night. I pray to God she saw safe journey.

I shall tell the others I have burnt this journal and my list so she will be under no suspicion.

I turn my face up toward the window. A dull light has begun to glow faintly through the glass. I hear the morning birds begin to warble and chirp under the oak trees in the yard. I have been writing in my journal all night!

Saturday, 1st June 1822 11 PM

The hour is almost midnight. After a night of no sleep, I departed from my shop this morning at dawn to see Peter Poyas at his house before he set out for the docks. He knew William Paul was being held at the Guard House, but he did not know why.

"So you heard!" I exclaimed to him. "He was taken up by the Patrol at my shop yesterday afternoon! Can you believe that? I was not in but it seems solely by chance he was at my place when they found him. No one knew then why he was taken up. The others thought for stealing. I only learned why last night. William Paul made conversation about the insurrection a few days ago at the wharves with a slave named Peter Prioleau, and this Peter then told his master, the Governor, the Intendant, and the Council of the City! I'm going to kill every one of them! Do you know this Peter Prioleau?"

"I believe I know who he is," Peter Poyas said to me. "He's the slave of a Colonel Prioleau, his cook, I believe."

"A damn house cook!" I nearly shouted. "Just as you warned us to take care and not mention our plan to those waiting men who receive presents of old coats from their masters, for they'll betray us. Mark my words, Peter. I swear when I find this man who revealed the secret of our plans, I'll rip him apart with my bare hands. He'll regret the day he was born to a woman!"

"Denmark, if the Patrol took up William Paul and nobody else, the Governor and the Intendant can't know much," Peter Poyas said. "As long as William keeps silent," Peter added less confidently.

"I pray he does," I told him, "Or he'll also die by my hand. I hope for the best. I don't think they know about the two of us. Not yet at least."

"What should we do now, Denmark?" Peter asked.

"The first thing is to destroy your list. Burn it now, this morning, right now, before you leave for the ship yard," I said.

"You're right," Peter said, and he went to the back of his lodging and brought out a sheaf of papers in his hand. He put them in the fire grate and struck a spark. The papers flamed fiery orange and yellow, then melted into black feathery ashes. "Now that's done," he said to me.

"We must gather this evening," I said to Peter. "I'll go about talking with Monday Gell this morning and appoint with him to meet at his shop after sunset. I'll see what I can do about reaching Ned and Rolla and Gullah Jack. If you see Gullah Jack at the wharves today, give him my message.

"As you say, Peter, if the whites know only that William Paul approached this Prioleau cook and said something about an insurrection, we can deal with that, I pray." I continued. "But if anything does happen, say not a word, not a single word. Make light of any charges. Whatever happens, whoever else may be taken up, we must be silent. We must say nothing to implicate others."

"Don't worry, Denmark," Peter said. "If anything happens to me, I'll so convince them that I know nothing, they'll think the whole business was some fantasy William Paul dreamt in a bout of fitful sleep."

"I have prayed very earnestly on bended knee since late last night," I told him, "and I'm of the judgment we must affix an earlier date for the attack, to midnight of June 16th. We have little time remaining. We must get the word out as quickly as we can to the slaves here and in the country, but I think it best. We cannot take the chance of waiting any longer."

"You right, Denmark," said Peter.

"We'll confirm these new plans when we gather tonight," I said. "Say nothing. Know nothing."

I then hurried away to see if I could find Gullah Jack.

I did not find Gullah Jack then but he came by my shop in the day and said Peter Poyas and Mingo Harth had been taken up! How my heart sank. Then Gullah Jack came back to me in the late afternoon and said they had been released!

"William Paul must have identified them and gave information on Peter and Mingo as members of the conspiracy," Gullah Jack said to me. "But Mingo said they were able to convince the Wardens they knew nothing, and having found no other reason to hold them, Peter and Mingo were released this afternoon."

God bless his soul! Peter Poyas was able to use his cunning and fully divert his questioners. Mingo took Peter's cue and was just as crafty.

"We must meet here tonight," I told Gullah Jack. "Let Peter and Mingo know. Tell them to be certain no one is spying on or following them. I'll get word to the others. Poison," I then said to Gullah Jack, remembering the request of the young slave girl. "Lucinda asked that you prepare poison for her. She is getting in readiness for the night of the revolt. She has proved to be a wise choice."

The men . . . Peter Poyas, Mingo Harth, Monday Gell, Ned, and Rolla Bennett, Gullah Jack . . . all attended the meeting here tonight. Except for Gullah Jack, they wore looks of fear and concern on their faces.

"We must be courageous, men," I told them. "We're too far along to turn back now. The Governor and the Intendant can know but very little. I pray my threat of death will keep William Paul from saying more. Even if he does, even if he names another of us, if we remain silent, if we uphold we know nothing like Peter and Mingo did today, they will never be able to find out about us."

"We completely threw off those two Wardens, Wesner and Condy," Peter bragged to the men.

"Peter played deader 'n a possum," Mingo said with a big smile.

"When the Wardens asked me if I knew of any plans for an uprising, I played the Gullah Jack fool," Peter explained. "I hoodwinked 'em better than Jack could have." Peter slapped the grinning Gullah Jack on the back, "I told 'em, 'Do you think I'd take on all the whites of this city? I may be dim-witted, but I ain't that dim-witted!' Then I smiled real big at 'em and looked 'em straight in the eye. 'Do you think I'd risk my good life as a ship's carpenter? I ain't heard talk about such business, and I don't want to hear any. But if I ever do, I'll come to you and my master and let you know,' I said to 'em. They bit the bait and were hooked faster than I could throw the line in the water."

"Worked like one of Gullah Jack's charms," Mingo added.

I could see the looks of relief on their faces at the news by Peter and Mingo, and each man swore his dedication to continue; but in their eyes, I could sense an emotion of fear and concern, especially those of Monday Gell.

"We must be smart like Peter and Mingo. We must be cool. We must be bold," I said. "Now's not the time to be afraid. Destroy your lists. Do so tonight. Burn them. These must not be found."

All agreed the night of June 16th would be the new night of reckoning.

"We must send men to the country on horseback to let the slaves on the plantations know the day has changed. Tell all of those you have signed in the city to be ready," I instructed them. "Now that the time is near, gather in more recruits so that we will be amply prepared, and bring them here to more of our meetings."

I had but one other pressing task. I wrote out today a second letter to President Boyer in Santo Domingo requesting aid. I took the letter to Monday for him to use his quill and his fair hand. Gullah Jack will take the letter to the docks tomorrow to secure safe delivery of it on the next ship bound for Santo Domingo.

1st June 1822

Président Jean-Pierre Boyer

Port de Prince

Santo Domingo

His Excellency:

The insurrection of the slaves against their masters in Charleston has been secretly set for midnight, June 16th.

We again ask you to abet our action with forces and ships for safe sail to escape. We will loot the banks and shops to secure all gold and specie. We offer to you this specie for your aid.

We await your word and the support of your arms and sail.

Your black brothers,

Denmark Vesey, Free black man in Charleston

Monday Gell, Slave in Charleston

20 Bull Street

Charleston, South Carolina

United States of America

Monday wrote out another copy of the first letter sent to President Boyer and put it in with the new one. It matters not. We have sufficient forces without aid from Santo Domingo to carry out the insurrection. We can then readily board ships docked in the harbor and pirate them to Santo Domingo in escape.

Friday, 7th June 1822

We have heard no other news. No one else has been taken up or questioned. We have escaped further detection! The night of the insurrection is but over a week away!

Ned Bennett and Peter Poyas brought new recruits to my house for a meeting tonight. I want to get as many more as possible before June 16th. I am depending upon the others to bring to me those we need.

"Men, I have an important secret to communicate to you," I said to open our meeting. "You must not disclose it to anyone. If you do, you will be put to instant death." I was certain that with my threatening tone, my unblinking stare, and my reputation among the blacks they would well know I was most serious. I made them hold up their hands and swear they would tell no one. I made them repeat, "We will not tell if we are found out, and if they kill us we will not tell anyone."

"Say it is so," I said to the men, and they all did say so.

"We're deprived of our rights and privileges by the white people," I told them. "Our Church was shut up so that we could not use it. It is high time for us to seek our rights. We're fully able to conquer the whites, if we're only unanimous and courageous, as the Santo Domingo people were. We intend to seize the arms and weapons in the arsenals and the shops, then make the attack by setting the Governor's Mills on fire, and also some houses near the water, and as soon as the bells begin to ring for fire, the servants in the yards should kill every man as he comes out of his door using axes and clubs. Afterwards we should murder the woman and children. Those that we don't kill we will drive out of the city. God has so commanded it in the Scriptures." And I read to them from the book of Joshua.

Again, some of the men said they thought it was cruel to kill the ministers and the women and children.

"What is the sense of killing the louse and leaving the nit? It is for your safety not to spare one white skin alive," I told them, "for this was the plan which was pursued in Santo Domingo. The revolt was successful there. We must do the same here. We shan't be slaves to these damn rascals any longer. We must kill everyone that we can get hold of, and drive the rest out of the city. Our revolt must succeed as so many are engaged in it."

I hit and hit with my words like the hammer striking the nail. I repeat my message over and over until the slaves learn it by rote.

Saturday, 8th June 1822

Tonight Peter Poyas, Ned Bennett, Gullah Jack, Frank Ferguson, Adam Ferguson, and Monday Gell came here to meet with me. Frank Ferguson told us he has collected four plantations of Negroes. He said he will start next Saturday to bring them into town. He said he will conduct them into the woods and place them about three miles away until Sunday night.

Tuesday, 11th June 1822

Ned Bennett came to me with a bold idea. His scheme is fraught with risk, but the more I consider, the more marked it seems. We could gain a few precious days of safety by distracting the whites. We might be able to surmise what and how much the whites know. I have talked with Gullah Jack, Monday Gell, and Peter Poyas and they agree Ned should act. We thus gave Ned our endorsement. He is first to go to the Governor and obtain his consent, then go to the Intendant with the complaint that he has heard he was named as a person who had information in relation to an insurrection, and if he is an object of suspicion, he has voluntarily come to solicit an examination. Ned said he would discuss this today with his master, the Governor, and then visit the Intendant.

Wednesday, 12th June 1822

Today I met Jesse Blackwood on Saint Phillip's Street. As we walked to my house, Frank Ferguson joined us.

"Denmark, I have just returned from the country," Frank said to me.

"Well what success," I asked him.

He answered, "I have got two fine men for our purpose on my mistress' plantation who must be sent up to and informed when the people are wanted in town."

I turned to Jesse. "Would you be the man to go?" I asked him. "I want you to go into the country and to enlist as many as possible, and tell them to be in readiness to come down and assist us."

"Yes," Jesse said. "But I don't know the way."

"Frank will tell you," I said.

We arrived at my house and Adam Ferguson was waiting for us here. Frank told Jesse how to get to the Ferguson plantation on John's Island.

"You must ask for John O or Pompey," Frank told Jesse. "They will be waiting to hear from you."

"I've no horse and I have no money," Jesse said to me.

"Come back Saturday and I'll give you two dollars for a horse," I said to him. Frank and Adam threw down on the table 25 cents each. "If you cannot go you must get someone else," the men told Jesse.

They departed from my house with Jesse's promise to do our bidding.

Ned Bennett came to me tonight and told me he went to see the Intendant yesterday.

"My plan worked," Ned said to me. "I think we're safe."

"What did you tell him?" I asked.

"I told the Intendant I had gone to my master and asked for approval to come to see him. I told him if I was under any suspicion I wanted to be examined."

"What did he say?"

"He asked if I had any knowledge of an insurrection of the blacks against the whites. I told him no, I had heard nothing. I told him I did not see how such a thing could ever come to pass. Moreover, I said, as a man of Governor Bennett, my loyalty was to my master, and if I had heard anything, I would have gone straight to him to impart such news. I told him my master would stand up for my character and my faithfulness." Ned gave me a hard look. "Little do they know!"

"Do you think the Intendant knows anything?" I asked.

"I can't be certain," Ned said, slowly pondering my question, "but it seemed to me in how the Intendant looked and asked his questions, he doesn't know anything, Denmark. If he does, they would have taken me up then and there, don't you think?"

"I hope you're right," I said to him. "We need but three more days. Then the hour of reckoning will have come."

Saturday, 15th June 1822

One more day! One more day and all our plans, all my years of work and dedication, the sweat and the toil, the ceaseless effort, will come to final fulfillment. My anguish will be resolved, my bitterness transformed to the sweet taste of revenge, my ambitions to ruin the whites achieved. The slaves of Charleston will then be free! I have each day for these past four years pondered and prayed to God to deliver my people and my children from servitude. I have devoted to it nearly all my waking hours. I asked God for His guidance and His instruction. He has not forsaken me. I am now poised on the verge of triumph and glory. The people of Africa have been shackled in slavery in this land for over seven generations. I await the moment when the bells in the church steeple of Charleston chime twelve midnight and the arsenals are ransacked for weapons, the city burnt and destroyed, and the whites meet their doom and their fate. Our armies will achieve glorious victory. We will march down the streets of Charleston laying waste to every white man, woman, and child. The will of God shall be done. My people are the chosen ones of God. Their years of suffered burdens will be revenged, retribution shall be paid.

A bright flame burns in my chest, a bright flame of hatred, a flame of power, a bright flame of pride. I want to revenge even the smallest of infractions, the most trivial incidents of abuse, the slightest of insults. When the throats of the whites are cut and their blood spurts to darken the ground; or their hearts are speared with pike and they tumble to their knees in agony and pain, eyes slated skyward; or their bodies are sliced in twain with scabbard by our warrior horsemen, I pray God flashes in front of their eyes the scenes of their wicked lives. The blatant harms, the whippings, tortures, chains, the abuse of power and position, these will be rightfully recompensed. Even the most minor, the smallest, most incidental abuses, these transgressions too will be sorely paid. Most of all, if a man has not respected me, that is the greatest wrong. I will demand respect by killing him on the spot without hesitation or regret, an eye for an eye, like for like. One more day, and in the winking of that eye, all shall be righted, the white man shall be the slave . . . of death.

Sunday, 16th June 1822

Jesse Blackwood returned from the country about noon to tell me he was able to get a horse to go and bring down men to fight the white people, and that he was allowed to pass by two parties of the Patrol on the road, but that a third party had brought him back.

"Denmark, the Guard is too strong. The Guard was so strict, I could not pass them without being taken up," Jesse said to me.

I expressed to him my sorrow, for the business is urgent. "We want the country people to be armed," I told him. "We might attack the forts at the same time. We need to take every ship and vessel in the harbor and put every man to death but the ship captains, as we will need for them to sail us to Santo Domingo."

We met today at 4 o'clock, as was our intention as a final preparation for tonight's commencement of the insurrection. But the preparations made by the whites, and the number of troops on duty, told us that the plot has been discovered and the whites are on their guard.

"The Guard is too strong," the men said to me. "They are on horseback at all points around the city, at the bridge over the Ashley, at the docks and the wharves, at the market."

"We have been betrayed by some Judas," I said to them, "who will certainly pay with his life. Do not dare show yourself, whatever might have been our plans. Pass the word as you can." As our hope of success was founded on affecting a surprise, I sent word to those from the country to depart from the city as soon as possible and wait for further orders.

"What can we do, Denmark," Peter Poyas asked with disappointment in his voice.

"There is nothing we can do," I answered. I tried to put up a brave face, but I was afeard myself. "Jesse says the Patrol is too strong. He was able to get past two Patrols, but a third turned him back. The country blacks cannot make it into the city. Go home. Tell all those you can that the insurrection is off for tonight. We shall see how heavy the Patrol is in place. That will tell us how much the whites know of our plans. Tell those that you can we will get word to them soon."

Damn malevolent Buckra!

Tuesday, 18th June, 1822

We have for certain been discovered! Peter Poyas, Ned, Rolla, Batteau Bennett, and others were taken up and are being held at the Guard House. I have destroyed everything but this journal, and will store it in its hiding space. I sent word with Gullah Jack to look for the young slave girl at the market and give her a message to follow my instructions. I told him to tell her she must be most careful in doing so. All else is burnt. I told the men if I am caught I will not tell anyone's name and they must not mention mine.

I do not want to turn back now. The first thing I must do is save my own life if I am to live to fight another day. I am going into hiding until I find a ship destined for Santo Domingo in which to escape. After reaching Santo Domingo, I will organize a navy with the support of the government there, set sail back to Charleston to invade and ransack this city, and incite the slaves to rebellion

Our cause is a glorious one.

Until then all is now ended unless an attempt can be made to rescue those who might be condemned to death by rushing on the people and saving the prisoners, or all dying together in the attempt.

“What News?”

Thursday morning, 30th May 1822 the Intendant of Charleston, James H. Hamilton, Jr., rode in his lavish carriage down Broad Street. The climate had been unseasonably hot for several days and the Intendant removed his top hat and wiped his damp brow with his handkerchief.

He observed the street from the carriage window. Africans scurried about like ants busy with their tasks. Wagons loaded with goods clattered and jockeyed for position in the street. As he watched, the Intendant was proud of what he had accomplished. If only the price of cotton would go back up, and the costs of slaves go down, the future of the city was certain to be promising.

The carriage drew to a halt at the Intendant’s bureau and his livery servant dismounted and opened the carriage door.

“Wait for me here,” the major said, stepping down to the street. “I shan’t be very long.” The Intendant assumed a military bearing. “And refrain from the grog shops while I’m gone or I’ll have you severely whipped.”

“Yes suh.”

The major was met at his bureau door by Warden Dove.

“You have a visitor waiting to see you, Major.”

“Who is it?”

“Colonel Prioleau. He says it’s urgent, sir.”

“Show him in.”

“Major Hamilton,” the Colonel said as the Intendant extended his hand in greeting, “forgive my unappointed presence but I must speak with you. It is a matter of some exigency.”

“Certainly,” the Intendant said. “Please, sit down, Colonel.”

“This morning, Major,” the Colonel said unable to disguise the anxiety in his voice, “I returned from the country where I had been several days conducting business. Upon my arrival in town, a favorite and confidential slave of mine, my mulatto cook, Peter Desverneys, confessed to me a conversation which had taken place at the market on Saturday proceeding between himself and a black man."

James Hamilton leaned forward in his chair and stroked his bearded chin. What was this all about, he wondered.

"Continue, Colonel."

"This conversation provided strong reasons for believing that a revolt and insurrection are in contemplation among a proportion of the black population!" the Colonel declared.

The Intendant felt his stomach turn. The last thing he ever wanted to happen under his watch was a revolt by the slaves, an insurrection that could end in the ruin of his political career and aspirations. Except for a predictable number of runaways, there hadn't been a slave uprising in Charleston since the Stono rebellion in 1739. On the other hand, if what his visitor was saying were true, the Intendant speculated that if he could be instrumental in squashing such a revolt before it began, it might well elevate and spur his political ambitions. He was a man not adverse to risk, as his numerous duel challenges were testimony. The son of a Revolutionary War Continental Army hero and grandson of a member of the Continental Congresses, the greatness achieved by his prominent Revolutionary-era forebears set the standard for all his pursuits.

"What particularly was said?" the Intendant asked. The Major was read in the law, practiced lawyering, and in his reading had not overlooked a single aspect of the slave law acts going back to the founding of the colony.

Colonel Prioleau related the exchange between his slave and the black man at the wharves.

"This demands an immediate summons of the City Corporation," a dogged Major Hamilton stated. "I want them to hear this from your slave first hand." The Intendant reached for his gold watch from his vest pocket. "Colonel, can you have your man here by 5 o'clock?"

"Certainly, Major," Colonel Prioleau answered. "I'm at your bidding. I'll do whatever you require."

The Intendant added, "I'll also solicit the attendance of His Excellency the Governor."

"Your attention to this matter is most appreciated," said Colonel Prioleau, relief in his words.

"Your visit and your information are equally so," the Intendant said. "We'll get to the bottom of this, Colonel. I promise."

Colonel Prioleau rose from his chair and hurriedly departed to retrieve his slave. James Hamilton pulled his quill from its pewter holder, removed the lid to the ink well, dipped the quill, and wrote out the convention notices to the members of the Corporation.

"Warden Dove," Intendant Hamilton called to his aide.

"Yes, Major, coming sir."

"Send out these notices to all members of the City Corporation," Intendant Hamilton said. "And this one to the Governor. This is a matter of the greatest urgency, Warden Dove, so get to work on this right away."

"Yes, Major," the Warden replied.

Within an hour, there was a knock at the Intendant's door. Warden Dove stuck his head into the room. "Major Hamilton, forgive me, sir. The notices are all delivered. And Colonel Prioleau is here."

"What time is it?" Hamilton asked and he again pulled out the gold watch from his vest pocket. "Four o'clock. He's early."

"Colonel Prioleau has lodged a group of slaves in the Guard House, Major," the Warden said. "He wishes to speak with you, again sir."

"Certainly. Send him in."

"Major Hamilton," Colonel Prioleau exclaimed. "When I went back to get my Peter, I examined him again," the Colonel declared excitedly, waving his hat in his hand.

"Sit down, Colonel, sit down," the Intendant said, and he gestured toward the chair across from his desk.

"Thank you, Major," Colonel Prioleau said. He placed his squat build in the chair and took a deep breath before continuing. "As I was saying, when I went back to retrieve my slave I examined him again. He suspects the Negro fellow who communicated the intelligence of the intended revolt belongs to Messrs. J. and D. Paul of Broad Street. Recognizing the importance and urgency of the matter, I went straight to the Paul's and discoursed with them the particulars. We agreed it best to have the whole of their male servants committed to the Guard House."

"You've done the prudent thing, Colonel," James Hamilton commended him. The Intendant tapped his fingers on his desk as he thought. "Before your cook tells his story to the City Corporation, let's have him determine if he can identify the man who accosted him from among them."

Colonel Prioleau's cook, Peter Desverneys, was taken to the cell in the Guard House where the Paul's slaves were being held.

"Look over each man carefully," the Intendant commanded. "Tell me when you are satisfied."

Peter Desverneys Prioleau stood at the cell door and gazed for several minutes at the handful of men in the cell.

"You," the Intendant said, pointing to William Paul when he saw Peter Desverneys nod his head as a sign of recognition, "come closer." Peter looked him over again.

"Yes, sir," Peter Desverneys said to the Intendant, "I'm satisfied."

"Come with me," the Intendant instructed Peter Desverneys Prioleau. They returned to the Intendant's bureau. Colonel Prioleau was called back into the room.

"Colonel," Intendant Hamilton said, "Your Peter says the man who approached him on the wharves was the Paul's William."

"Are you certain?" the Colonel asked his slave.

Peter Desverneys' face reflected his fear. "Yes, Master, I'm certain. He's the man who asked me 'what news?'"

The City of Charleston Corporation assembled at five, with His Excellency the Governor, Thomas Bennett, attending. James Hamilton watched as the color drained from the faces of the Governor and the Corporation members as Peter Desverneys related his tale.

The day was scorching hot for late May with no breeze blowing in from the harbor, and the kitchen and the house of Mistress Johnson were like a three-legged skillet over a raging oak wood fire. Mama finished her tasks early and went out back to bed to escape the heat. Lucinda sat hidden in the corner of the pantry resting before she joined her. She must have dozed off to sleep, for the next Lucinda knew she woke to the sound of footsteps on the veranda and heavy knocks on the front door.

"James Radcliffe, Intendant Hamilton, sir . . . and some of the City Wardens," she heard from the entrance foyer.

"Yes, yes. Come in, come in," Master Radcliffe said.

"You received the Governor's message then, sir?" asked the voice of the Intendant.

"Yes."

Lucinda could hear her heart race loudly in her chest. She dared not move or make a sound. She knew if she were found, no matter what she said, she would be harshly punished with the whip. The footsteps moved to the parlor. She put her ear to the wall.

"Thank you for seeing us at this hour, sir," the Intendant was saying, "but it is a matter of great urgency. The Governor . . . the Governor is on his way. He should be here momentarily, very momentarily."

"Sit, please. A drink gentlemen?" she heard Master Radcliffe ask.

"No sir, thank you," several voices grumbled together.

"Please indulge yourself, sir," one of the voices added, "you'll need a stiff one when you hear what we're about to tell you."

"I myself rarely indulge, thank you," Master Radcliffe replied coolly.

Silence. Then the sounds of the clop and rattle of a carriage halting in the street.

"That must be the Governor now," Intendant Hamilton said.

There was the sound of footsteps on the porch and a knock on the door.

"Thomas, come in," Master Radcliffe said. "Come in, come in."

"Thank you, James."

"It has been too long."

"Yes, it has." The Governor's words and footsteps flowed along the wall at Lucinda's ear. "Oh . . . I see you've been told already."

"No, no. They arrived just now," Master Radcliffe said. "Please, sit down." There was a shuffling sound as Lucinda supposed the men moved places to accommodate the Governor. "What the devil is this all about, Thomas?"

"Are we private?" the Governor asked softly.

"Private?" Master Radcliffe asked. "Yes, my sister's upstairs asleep."

"And your servants?"

"Only three, and long asleep. What the devil is this about?"

"James Radcliffe, prepare yourself," Governor Bennett said somberly, then blurted out, "We have reason to believe there's a slave uprising afoot!"

"A slave uprising?" Through the wall, Master Radcliffe's question hung heavy in the silent room. Lucinda's heart did a rapid skipped beat. She pressed her ear and listened with all her might.

Intendant Hamilton spoke, "Yes, sir. A rebellion. A plot to excite an insurrection among the blacks against the whites . . . "

"How do you know this, Thomas?"

"At the Master Wharf another slave boasted of it to Colonel Prioleau's cook, a mulatto named Peter Desverneys," the Governor responded.

"Boasted of what?" Master Radcliffe asked.

"There is a conspiracy among the slaves, a plot as Major Hamilton says, to rise up and overthrow every slave owner in Charleston!"

"This was told by one slave to another?"

"Yes."

"This happened when?"

"Saturday," Governor Bennett answered.

"This past Saturday, the twenty-fifth of May, sir," Intendant Hamilton clarified.

"And you learned of it when?"

"This afternoon," Intendant Hamilton said. "Colonel Prioleau came to me about three o'clock saying his man Peter had confessed to him."

"Why did his slave Peter not inform the Colonel on the day it happened?" Master Radcliffe asked bluntly.

"Colonel Prioleau was out of town attending to some affairs in the Capitol, and was unavailable," Governor Bennett explained. "Peter did seek the advice of a free black, a William Pencil, who encouraged Peter to inform his Master. Peter, unable to do so, then went to Misses Prioleau and her son, they too telling Peter to alert Colonel Prioleau in full upon his return."

"According to Colonel Prioleau's man," Intendant Hamilton interjected, "he was conducting an errand for his master's mistress at the Fish Market, then walked to Fitzsimmons Wharf, observing some of the boats and the flags they were flying. There he was approached by a slave he did not know. They exchanged some trifling conversation regarding Peter's observation he had seen a flag on a boat with the number 76 before, but never one with the number 96, when the man who approached Peter asked, 'Do you know something serious is about to take place?' When Peter said 'No,' the other slave man said, 'There is and many of us are determined to right ourselves, and we are determined to shake off our bondage, and for this purpose we stand on a firm foundation. Many have joined, and if you go with me, I will show you the man, who has a list of names, and will take yours down.'"

"And you believe him, Prioleau's mulatto cook?" Master Radcliffe asked.

"Oh very much, sir," Intendant Hamilton said. "Colonel Prioleau says his Peter came forth because he was fearful if it was discovered he knew he might lose his life, that he could not remain easy under the burden of such a secret. Colonel Prioleau says Peter told him he was astonished and horrified at such information and is well satisfied with his condition and grateful for his master's kindness and wishes no change."

"What other evidence?" Master Radcliffe asked.

"Intendant Hamilton called a special session of City Council this afternoon and I met with them then," Governor Bennett said. "We were very fortunate in that we learned more in advance of this meeting."

"After my first discussion with Colonel Prioleau, I called for the session of Council to meet at five," Intendant Hamilton said. "But before we met, Colonel Prioleau again questioned his cook Peter. The Colonel came to believe the slave who spoke to Peter at the wharves was one of Mister and Misses J. D. Paul's property, the Paul's, the grocers, at the corner of Broad and King. Colonel Prioleau then went to their residence, told Mr. Paul the circumstances in full, whereby Mr. Paul, of his own choosing and for which we applaud his fidelity and principle, immediately had all five of his male slaves taken up to the Guard House. Peter Desverneys Piroleau there identified the slave at the wharf as Mister Paul's William."

"Peter was brought before City Council at today's meeting," Governor Bennett said, "and related to them the events as he first told his master. I saw him with my own eyes, James. I heard him with my own ears. I believe everything he told us is true."

"William Paul has admitted being at the wharf with Colonel Prioleau's Peter," Intendant Hamilton resumed, "but denies any knowledge of the plot. However, from his demeanor when questioned, sir, we do not believe him. We have him imprisoned at the Guard House, telling him he is to be placed in solitary confinement in the black hole at the Work House."

"We think this threat will loosen his tongue, and we intend to question him further tomorrow morning," Governor Bennett said.

There was a long silence, and when Governor Bennett spoke again, his voice was not the same. "We've known each other for a long time, James. Your opinion's important to me. This is why I asked to see you now."

"This is quite a shocking tale, gentlemen," Master Radcliffe said and Lucinda heard him stand and walk about the room. "If true, it requires great caution. We must not alarm the city without cause."

"Of course," Governor Bennett said.

"When ready," Master Radcliffe continued, "we must be prepared to strike with great speed and diligence." Master Radcliffe paused before he asked, "Who's behind this plot? Who is the man with the list of names?"

"We do not yet know. We believe the plot is a close secret and well-guarded," said Intendant Hamilton.

"Find the top link of this chain," Master Radcliffe replied sharply. "As you say, learn all you can from the slave William. Use whatever means are required. And I mean every means. Keep him in the hole until his tongue is loosed."

"I concur with you completely," the Intendant confirmed.

"Major Hamilton," Governor Bennett said and Lucinda heard them all stand, "take your men and wait for my instructions. We will work our plan of inquiry and begin preparations tomorrow morning after we question further this William Paul. Do not speak a word of this, not one of you, you understand. Do you understand?"

"Yes, Governor. We do."

The footsteps suddenly marched across the room and out into the street and were gone. Lucinda could tell Master Radcliffe and Governor Bennett were still in the room but it was quiet as death.

Then she heard Master Radcliffe ask, "If this is true, Thomas, who could have orchestrated such a thing?"

"James Hamilton believes it has something to do with that Morris Brown and his African Church followers. You know the trouble we've had from them."

"Brown?" Master Radcliffe said. "I seriously doubt it. He has too much to lose. Even so, it's well time his church was closed. Closed forever this time."

Lucinda heard the two men go outside on the front veranda. She knew it was safe then; they could not hear her. Even so, she slipped out without a single grunt from the loose plank on the kitchen floor, and not even a soft mouse-like squeak from the back door hinges. She heard a voice in her head, like Denmark Vesey said Moses heard from the burning bush, and she thought it wasn't her voice, but some other voice, but then she was not sure, that it may have been her own voice. The voice told her what to do, and she knew before the stars were gone from the nighttime sky she had to warn Denmark Vesey.

The evening drum had long sounded at the Guard House commanding all slaves to be off the streets. A high wall to keep them penned at night surrounded Lucinda and Mama's quarters at the back of Mistress Johnson's house. There was a big oak tree next to the wall, and Lucinda knew where Master Jimmy Johnson kept some rope with other tools used by the slaves when they were in the city. She tiptoed in the darkness to the tool bin, took the rope, threw one end over a sturdy limb on the tree, and used the rope to climb up to the top level of the wall. She tied the rope to the tree limb and dropped it over the wall on the outside, making certain it was in shadow and could not be seen, and then she climbed down the wall holding to the rope with all her strength. She walked under the palmetto palms to the back alley crowded with slave quarters in both directions. It was a dark night. The alley was silent and no one was about. She hid in the shadows making her plan, then without a sound, she stole away like a haint toward Denmark Vesey's house on Bull Street. She watched with a most cautious eye to see if anyone was about. She must have been watched too by the eye of God, for not even a dog barked or stirred and she was able to steal through the back alleyways more softly than a whisper. Sweet jasmine scents from the walled-in gardens hung thickly in the night air. She could see the steeple of St. Michael's Church in the distance dark against the starry sky. She knew the watchman was on duty in the steeple tower who called out the quarter hours, so she made sure she was hidden in the shadows and could not be seen. She reached the shop and house of Denmark Vesey without seeing a single soul. A lone lamp light burned in one of the back rooms. The gate to the house was shut and secured for the night, and she thought for a moment her dangerous trip was without cause, but then she saw there was just enough space at the bottom of the gate to slide under. She quietly slipped through and very gently tapped on the shop door. There was a stirring in the house and the door cracked open as Denmark Vesey's large brown eyes peeked out at her.

"Child, what in the Lord's name are you doing here at this time of night," he whispered.

"Uncle Denmark," She whispered back. "I have something to tell you. It's important. But hurry, I must get back."

He opened the door and Lucinda quickly stepped in.

"The Governor came to see Master Radcliffe tonight," she said breathlessly, trying to get all out at once. "He had some other men with him. They told Master Radcliffe they've learnt there's a slave uprising afoot. They're making more inquiry tomorrow."

"How do you know of this?" Denmark Vesey tried to hide his fear.

"I'd fallen asleep in the pantry before they came, and was awakened by their voices. They didn't know I could hear them."

"And what did they say?"

"Only that a slave named William Paul told Colonel Prioleau's cook, Peter, of plans for a revolt. And they have the slave William taken up at the Guard House."

"Did they say who was behind it?"

"No. They said they don't know."

After showing her his journal's secret hiding place, Denmark Vesey whispered as he walked to the window and looked out. "You must get back. You must be careful."

"Yes, I saw no one when I came. I'll be alright."

"Do not speak of this to anyone."

"Yes, I know, Uncle Denmark. But I had to come and tell you now."

"You did the right thing, child. Now go. Be careful."

She walked ever so quietly out of the house and slipped under the gate and moved into the dark shadow of the trees, then more quietly than she had ever done anything she made her way back. She was almost home when she thought she heard someone nearby and she crouched dead still in the darkest shadow and listened but it must not have been anything. The rope was still hidden in place on the wall when she got back and she pulled herself up making sure not to make a sound and untied the rope from the limb and hooked it over to let herself down and pulled the rope to the ground and put it back in the bin. Mama was sleeping soundly when Lucinda slipped into her pallet. She had made the greatest adventure of her life without peril, and in her prayers she thanked Jesus for watching over her, as she fell fitfully asleep.

The next morning the sun came up just as it always had and there was, thank goodness, a cool breeze blowing in from the harbor. She and Mama made breakfast of hominy and slices of roast pork and fruit pie for Mistress Johnson and Master Radcliffe. Master Radcliffe sat reading some papers and showed no sign of his visitors the night before. Lucinda went about her tasks as usual until Mistress Johnson sent her to the morning market to get some fresh provisions. The streets were noisy, congested with horses and mules, carts and carriages, slaves on foot busy on their errands. Everything seemed like any other day. The market was full of the clamor of voices and smells of seafood and sweat and a smell like damp earth on sweet potatoes. The slaves talked all at once, calling out what they had to sell and how good it was or haggling over the prices they had to pay.

She wondered where Denmark Vesey was and what he was doing, but she dared not go near his shop. All her questions came flooding back. Why were the Africans slaves? Did God make us this way? Or was it, as Denmark Vesey said, the evil cruelty of the white man? Did the whites have to be killed for the slaves ever to be free? Denmark Vesey told her many times the whites would not hesitate to save themselves by killing every black person if necessary. Was what Uncle Denmark said true? Did the blacks have to kill the whites in order to save themselves? She thought of Master Johnson. Would he be killed? They had never talked about her being a slave. Somehow, when they were together it didn't seem to matter, even if she was more a slave to him than she had ever been to anyone. Each time the door to the apartment closed upon them, the world outside no longer seemed to be.

She toted the provisions in a basket balanced on her head and hurried along Meeting Street to Mistress Johnson's house. The flowers in the Charleston gardens made the morning air sweet. The crushed shells and white sand in the streets glistened in the sunlight. The sky was brilliant blue. The breeze from the harbor made her feel fresh and alive. Sounds of toil at the wharves and in the merchant and mechanic shops lifted up toward the sky. Most of the faces of the folk she saw in the streets were black like the color of her own face.

She watched the birds fly across the sky. That must be what freedom feels like, she thought, to soar, to lift above the earth, to ride the wind, to travel distant places. Elizabeth had told her some birds fly long distances to hatch their young, to search for food and warmth. Lucinda looked down at her feet on the ground. She would never be able to fly, she thought.

She was trapped by the dark undercurrent of forces of Charleston, ensnared in a tangled web of hatred between slave and master, between black and white, between the bonded and the free. She did not know what to do. She was scared. She was confused. She knew murder threatened to engulf the city in fire and blood and she was helpless to stop the slaughter. Was this the price to be paid for freedom?

She arrived at the house on South Bay, took the provisions and put them in the pantry and helped Mama cook and do their tasks, just like any other day, a day like any other.

Thursday, 30th May 1822 at 7 o'clock in the evening the captive slave William Paul was examined by the Charleston Intendant and Wardens. He first denied having any conversations with Peter Desverneys Prioleau, then admitted to the chatter about the ship's flag, but strongly denied any other discussion. He was not believed. He was held for the night in the Guard House. Early the next morning, Friday, May 31st, he was again interrogated.

"Prisoner!" the warden cried harshly, kicking at the sleeping man flat on the dirty pallet on the cell floor. "Get up! Get on your feet."

The iron chains fastened to the cell wall and fixed to William Paul's hands and legs clanked and scraped loudly as he struggled to get on his feet.

"What do you want to tell me this morning?" the warden asked.

"I got nuttin' to tell," the prisoner said sullenly. He looked down at the cell floor, avoiding the eyes of the warden.

"I believe if I was a man in your situation, facing the gallows and all, waiting for that knotted rope around your neck to tighten up and jerk all quick like when the trap door swings away, and the weight of your body tugs downward and your neck goes snap (the warden clapped his hands) as it breaks and you stand before your Maker for everlasting judgment, why I believe a man in your condition might just have a little something to say this morning." The warden stopped, leaning forward slightly, waiting. He repeated softly, "Again, what do you want to tell me?"

"Like I say, I got nuttin' to tell." William Paul raised his head and his eyes for a moment met the warden's.

"Make it worse on yourself then," the warden said. "It's up to you."

Through the cell's open-air one-foot by half-a-foot iron-barred window near the top of one wall, they could hear the morning birds' chatter and fuss. The warden simply stood, gripping a baton in his hand. He did not move. He did not speak. He must have stood that way for what seemed an eternity.

"Mingo. Mingo Harth," William Paul finally said in a low whisper. His eyes glistened with tears.

"What did you say?" the warden asked gently.

"Peter Poyas."

"Mingo Harth, and Peter Poyas. Are they the ones?" the warden asked soothingly.

"Yes," the prisoner answered, and he began to cry in earnest.

"You've done well," the warden said. "You've done quite well." He paused just for a moment, and then asked, "What else can you tell me?"

"Mingo's got a list. A list of those who signed up."

"Let me get you something to eat, something to drink," the warden said, suddenly scurrying to open the cell door. "I know you must be hungry and thirsty."

"My uncle says there are rumors of an uprising of the blacks against the whites." Master Jimmy Johnson stood staring down at Lucinda as she lay on the bed. "Do you know anything of this?"

"No, Master." She fiddled with the necklace around her neck, twisting it in her hand.

"This is a very serious matter, Lucinda." His green eyes examined her coldly. "I must know if you learn of anything."

"Yes, Master," she said obediently.

"And don't tell this to anyone." There was harshness in his voice he had not used with her before.

"Yes, Master."

"You are being truthful with me, are you not?" His stare was hard and unblinking.

"Yes, Master."

"I would not have you lie to me," he said sternly, "especially of such grave and dangerous matters." He picked up his riding whip, gripping it tightly in his white-knuckled hand.

She said nothing. She reached for his other hand. "Do not speak of such horrid and frightful things," she said. "Come, let me please you," and she tugged gently on his hand until he came to her. She kissed him on the face, and slid down to him.

Afterwards, she walked back to South Bay with a slave boy leading the goat-pulled cart filled with the provisions. The boy held a stick in his hand and from time to time beat the goat to draw the wagon.

What should she do, she agonized. Like a torrent, the questions rained down hard upon her. Denmark Vesey had cautioned her not to speak of the revolt. She knew he was certain to be the leader of any insurrection against the whites. She remembered seeing a pistol among the papers in his hiding place. Should she go to Denmark Vesey and ask him what to do? Or did he intend to tell her when the time was right? Did he think it best that she not know more? The questions piled up in her mind. No answers came. She knew she dared not tell Master Johnson. She knew she had no influence on how he would respond, or to stop him, regardless of what she did. His loyalty was to the whites, her loyalty to the Africans. Would he be killed along with the others? Should she try to protect him? Did the slaves on Radcliffe Place Plantation know of the revolt? Did Mama know?

She knew she would never turn her back on Denmark Vesey. She did not wish to turn her back on Master Johnson. Only if fate drove her beyond all other choices, she thought. She felt the trap of her conflict close in execrably around her, like a hanging noose being tightened about her throat as she waited in dark dread for the foot support to give way and begin to swing loosely, twisting in the wind, hanging like an eclipse blotting out the sun.

James Hamilton's deep-set, sleepy eyes overlooked his slightly hooked nose, the hard-set mouth on his long Scottish face in a thick line above his prominent bearded chin. His broad, high forehead was topped with full hair worn somewhat long in the fashion of the day. His eyes gave a certain look of sadness to his face, as if he had suffered some misfortune earlier in his life and for which he had never fully recovered.

"Thank you very much for seeing me, James," Intendant Hamilton said. "The Governor has asked me to keep you informed." Major Hamilton gestured toward the leather chair across from his desk. "Please, please sit down. Make yourself comfortable.

"Here's where we stand," the Intendant said, and he shuffled some papers on the desk. "Finally, after a number of days in solitary confinement, and some threats and encouragement, if you will, William Paul released more information to us." The Intendant emphasized the word encouragement. "The prisoner named two names which he described as agents in the conspiracy. Peter Poyas, a ship's carpenter, and Mingo Harth, whose master owns a lumberyard. We had these two taken up and their trunks searched. We found nothing, except this enigmatic letter from an Abraham Poyas to Peter Poyas." The Intendant again sorted through the papers on his desk. "I have it right here. I wanted to read it to you to see what you think.

"Dear Sir, with pleasure I give you an answer. I will endeavor to do it. Hoping that God will be in the midst to help his own. Be particular and make a sure remark. Fear not, the Lord god that delivered Daniel is able to deliver us. All that I informed agreed. I am gone to Beacon Hill. Signed Abraham Poyas."

The Intendant reached over the desk and handed the letter to James Radcliffe.

"Not very clear, I grant you," Intendant Hamilton said, "but it seems to me to reek like week-old fish. What do you think?"

"It's difficult to judge," James Radcliffe said, looking down at the letter in his hand. "It could mean most anything."

"It could," Major Hamilton said, "or it could mean one thing." He licked his lips and stared past James Radcliffe's shoulder, his eyes absorbed in his thoughts. Then he collected himself. "The germane matter was how these two, this Peter Poyas and Mingo Harth, responded when they were examined. James Radcliffe, these fellows behaved with so much composure and coolness, and treated the charge alleged against them with so much levity, that the wardens, Wesner and Condy, were completely deceived and had these men immediately discharged. However, it did seem advisable to have them watched, so spies were employed of their own color to give us advises on all their movements.

"City Council," Intendant Hamilton continued, "still being under the conviction that William Paul possessed more information than he had as of then disclosed, appointed a committee to examine him from time to time."

Seven days and seven nights, William Paul was imprisoned in solitary confinement in the Charleston Work House, fed one small meal a day of corn pone and clabber, and used a stinking pot emptied only infrequently. He was given twenty lashes to break his will. The constant image in his brain was of a noose around his neck and his lifeless body swinging from the gallows.

"On June 8th, in an interview with Mr. Napier, William Paul's silence was finally broken," Intendant Hamilton said. "He confessed that he had for some time, as long as three months, known of the plot, that it was extensive, embracing an indiscriminate massacre of the whites, and that the blacks were to be headed by an individual who carried about him a charm, which rendered him invulnerable."

James Radcliffe sat in stunned silence. He could hardly believe what he was being told. Every planter's worse fear seemed to be coming true.

"This has not been an easy inquiry," the Intendant complained, and he suddenly stood and walked back and forth before he sat back down heavily. "However, whatever belief we might have been disposed to place in the unsupported and equivocal testimony of William, it was not thought to be a case in which our doubts should limit our efforts for preparation and defense. As you wisely said when the Governor and I came to see you when we first learned of this plot, 'when ready we must be prepared to strike with great speed and diligence.'

"Measures were thus taken to immediately place the city guard in a state of the utmost readiness. Sixteen hundred rounds of ball cartridges were secured and the centinels and patrols ordered on duty with loaded arms."

James Radcliffe said nothing. He continued to stare in near disbelief. Intendant Hamilton resumed: "Three or four days elapsed and notwithstanding all our efforts, we could obtain no confirmation of the disclosures by William Paul. On the contrary, James, they seemed to be placed in question by the circumstances of one of the individuals, Ned Bennett, one of the Governor's men, who William had named as a person with information about the insurrection. This Ned, with approval from the Governor, came to me voluntarily, soliciting an examination. I must say," and Intendant Hamilton pulled at his beard as if deep in thought, "that was a true strategic maneuver regardless of the source."

"What did he say?" James Radcliffe asked.

"He said to me, if he was an object of suspicion, he wanted to voluntarily come and be questioned. Perhaps in retrospect, all was well, as it may not have been best to prematurely press these examinations, for it might have had a tendency to arrest any further developments.

"At any rate, on the night of Friday the 14th the information of William was finally validated and our worst fears confirmed. At 8 o'clock in the evening, I received a visit from a gentleman, Colonel Wilson, who is well known in this community for his worth and respectability.

"This gentleman, with an anxiety which the occasion was well calculated to beget, stated to me that a faithful slave belonging to his family, a slave who was distinguished alike for his uncommon intelligence and integrity, had come to him and informed that rumors were abroad of an intended insurrection of the blacks. Colonel Wilson said he was told this movement had been traced to some of the colored members of Dr. Palmer's church, in which his slave, George, was a Class Leader. The Colonel had enjoined his slave, George, to conceal nothing, and on that evening of Friday the 14th he came back to his master, and informed him that the fact was really so, that an uprising was contemplated by the blacks. Not a moment should be lost in informing the constituted authorities, George told Colonel Wilson, as the succeeding Sunday, the 16th at 12 o'clock at midnight was the time set for the uprising, which if not prevented, would certainly occur at that hour.

The Intendant paused. He wondered that James Radcliffe seemed surprised the slaves could organize themselves.

"Go on," James Radcliffe said.

"It appears this slave, George, was in no way connected with the plot, but had an intimate friend named Abraham, who was one of his class, and who had been trusted by the conspirators with the secret, and solicited by them to join in. To this, Abraham at first appeared to consent, but, at no time, absolutely sent in his adhesion. It was this Abraham who shared this with his Class Leader, George Wilson. Colonel Wilson said his servant, George, stated that about three months ago. Rolla, belonging to Governor Bennett, communicated to Abraham the intelligence of the intended insurrection, and asked him to join; that Rolla remarked in the event of their rising, they would not be without help, as the people from San Domingo and Africa would assist them in obtaining their liberty, if only they made the motion first themselves. Rolla further told Abraham if he wished to know more, he had better attend their meetings, where all would be disclosed. And at another time, Rolla informed Abraham that the plan was matured, and that on Sunday night the 16th of June, a force would cross from James Island and land on South Bay, march up and seize the arsenal and guardhouse . . ."

"Lord forbid!" James Radcliff exclaimed.

". . . and that another body at the same time would seize the arsenal on the Neck, and a third would rendezvous in the vicinity of the Governor's mills. They would then sweep the town with fire and sword, not permitting a single white soul to escape."

Intendant Hamilton stopped. The noise of the busy street outside the Intendant's open window was the only sound in the room.

"That is how we learned of the intended date and time and details of the insurrection," the Intendant finally said.

"This is unbelievable," said James Radcliffe, trying to collect his thoughts. "I had heard some vague rumors bantered about, but knew nothing of all this. I haven't seen Thomas in a number of days."

"Had it not been for the mulatto slave George Wilson coming forward as he did, we might now be in real peril," the Intendant said. "We might all be dead! God is on our side, James. God is on our side."

The Intendant leaned back in his chair, a trace of pride in his voice. "As the account by Abraham and George Wilson was remarkably similar with that given by William, Mr. Paul's servant, and as the witness could have no possible communication or the story have been the result of preconcert and combination, I immediately and without delay took the sum of this intelligence to his Excellency the Governor and convened City Council. This was laid before the Governor by 9 o'clock on the evening of the 14th, and by 10 o'clock, the commanding officers of the regiments of the city militia were convened by his Excellency's order at my residence. We met again the next afternoon . . . Saturday afternoon, the 15th . . . and measures were determined on by his Excellency as were deemed best adapted to the approaching exigency of Sunday night.

"James, we discovered the execution of the plot Friday night at 8 PM, and by the next afternoon we had a full plan of action in place!"

"Yes, that is certainly commendable," James Radcliffe said.

"Especially considering, frankly, how poorly prepared we were before then. I assure you we'll never be caught so again," James Hamilton said. "On Sunday night the Governor ordered the following corps to rendezvous for guard." Hamilton leafed through the papers on his desk. "We had Captain Cattel's Corps of Hussars, Captain Miller's Light Infantry, Captain Martindale's Neck Rangers, the Charleston Riflemen, and city guard."

"I spent that Sunday evening at my sister's on South Bay," James Radcliffe said, "and I must say, each time I looked out the windows or watched from the porticos, the key points along the streets were all well posted."

"The men did excellent duty," Intendant Hamilton said. "The whole of the corps were organized as a detachment and placed under the command of Corneal Hayne. Do you know him?"

"Yes, I know who he is." Radcliffe answered.

"Excellent man, honorable man," said Major Hamilton. "Although there was necessarily great excitement, and among the female part of our community much alarm, the night passed without anything like commotion or disturbance. Yes, it is particularly honorable to the corps on service that in a populous town, the streets filled until a late hour with persons uncertain whether it was safe to go to rest or not, not a single false alarm was excited. It showed a steadiness, altogether praiseworthy, in troops unaccustomed to guard duty, at least on an occasion involving such deep interest and distressing anxiety.

"So, James Radcliffe, the conspirators, finding the whole town encompassed at 10 o'clock by the most vigilant patrols, did not dare show themselves, whatever may have been their plans."

"Thanks be unto the Lord," James Radcliffe said soberly.

"The African Church is somehow part of all this, I'm sure of it," the Intendant said. "Morris Brown is in the North in Philadelphia. The moment he returns, I intend to appoint with him. I know he is engaged one way or another. The whole African Church is involved, James, I am certain of it."

Intendant Hamilton picked up the papers on his desk and tapped them on their sides to make a neat square, placed them in a desk drawer, and locked it with a key.

"That's where we are as of this moment," the Intendant said. "I'll ensure to keep you further informed." Intendant Hamilton stood and extended his hand. James Radcliffe took it, responding with a firm shake.

"Thank you again," Intendant Hamilton said. "I will speak with His Excellency, the Governor and inform him I was able to meet with you."

"Give Thomas my regards and congratulations."

"I shall," James Hamilton said, "but we yet have much to do."

"Please feel free to call on me if I can be of any service in this," Radcliffe said.

"I may very well accept your offer," Major Hamilton responded. "We have but three days according to the Slave Law of 1740 to call court for the trial of the insurrectionists. Your name has more than once been suggested as a freeman member of the Court."

"We usually travel to our summer home this time of year," James Radcliffe said. "Keep me informed of the developments. I shall modify my plans if need be."

"I may let you know as early as tomorrow," said the Major, as he saw James Radcliffe on his way.

Later, as the afternoon sun cast blue shadows along the street, the Intendant stood and looked out the window of his bureau. He was proud of his city, this old harbor town. This was what he had strived for; this was the lot he had hoped for, the opportunity to prove his worth. He would locate and capture and punish every guilty slave, a punishment so severe no slave would ever again attempt to rebel. He was ready to do battle. Tomorrow he would request the City Convention create a Committee of Vigilance and Safety to follow through with his plans. He would organize a slave court. The duel had begun.

Altars in the Dust

Those first taken up by the Charleston authorities under the supervision of Intendant James Hamilton and the city's Committee of Vigilance and Safety were Rolla, Ned, Mathias, and Batteau Bennett, men of Governor Thomas Bennett, and Peter Poyas, Mungo Poyas, Stephen Smith, and Amherst Lining. They were arrested on Tuesday, 18th June 1822, two days after the intended insurrection. Denmark Vesey went into hiding the same day.

Tuesday evening near sunset, Denmark Vesey entered the city and cautiously stole his way toward the cabin of one of his wives. He had spent the day hidden in the woods near Bulkley's Farm. He reckoned the Patrol by now likely knew of his involvement. He examined the darkening street to see if he was being followed. He saw no one. He trudged along the dusty road, his shoulders stooped, his head bowed downward. Suddenly he felt old, like a worn blade dull and worthless. He flushed with anger. He swore, if he could ever get his hands on them, he would cut out the tongues of William Paul and Peter Desverneys Prioleau. He worked his way slowly through the alleyways and narrow side streets toward his wife Beck's, hiding from sight when he saw anyone in the street.

He knew it was early for Beck to be home. He determined to wait for her. He must not be seen, he must not be found, he realized. He entered the cabin and sat with no lit candle, his mind tormented at his plans gone astray. Fierce pride does not allow for sad endings, he consoled himself, trying to rid himself of his torture.

A fire-orange glow from the dying light in the western sky pressed through the cracks of the cabin's shuttered window, forming narrow slats of light that moved slowly along the wooden floor. When it was past dark, he heard Beck come upon the porch, then feel for the outside latch on the door. She stopped when she realized the door was unfastened.

"Who there?" she called.

"Me," Denmark Vesey said, alone in the dark room.

"Denmark," she said, putting her tote on the table. "What you doin' here?"

She could not see the big tears build up in the corners of his eyes and run down his cheeks, falling on his arms and hands.

"It's ended, Beck," he said softly.

"What be ended?" she asked, still standing, looking at him barely visible in the dark.

"My life's work." He stopped and wiped his eyes with his hands. "It's over."

She lit a candle. He turned his head so his face was in partial shadow.

"What you talkin' 'bout, Denmark?"

"We've been found out."

"You sho'?"

"Oh, yes."

"How you know?"

"Peter and Rolla and Batteau have been taken up."

"Oh God!" There was alarm in her voice. "What you gonna do now, Denmark?"

"What I must do."

"What's that?"

"Escape. Catch sail to Santo Domingo. Or to Africa."

"What happen?"

"Someone told everything. Our army was so strong," he said. She sat down beside him and placed her hand on top of his. She had never seen him cry. "I trusted 'em, Beck. I trusted each and every one of 'em. God spoke to me, Beck. God spoke to me."

"Maybe it been the devil spoke to you."

His big hand, with the lightning quickness of a snake bite, hit her hard on her face. She drew back in fear, raising her arms in front of her.

"No, Denmark, no!" she cried.

He sank back into the chair. "It was God, Beck. It was God." And he cried like a child.

"Come, Denmark," she said soothingly. "Come rest. I make you something to eat. You can stay here 'til you find a ship to Santo Domingo or Africa, wherever you gonna go. The thing you got to do now is save yo' own skin and get out o' Charleston. You be safe here till then."

"If I could just. If I could just," he said pleadingly. The tears built up again in his eyes.

Intendant James Hamilton sat at his desk. James Radcliffe sat in the leather chair across from him.

"Thank you for seeing me again so soon, James," the Intendant said. "I regret this may keep you from your summer retreat."

"I'm obliged to do my duty for the city," declared James Radcliffe.

"Where is it you usually go?" Hamilton asked.

"Flat Rock, in western North Carolina. We have a summer home there."

"I've never had the pleasure to visit the land of the Cherokees."

"Beautiful country," James Radcliffe replied. "Just the other side of the mountains."

"James," Intendant Hamilton suddenly drew serious. "As you know from the letter City Council had delivered to you this morning, seven gentlemen freeholders will serve as members of the Court for the trials of those against whom insurrection and treason charges have been made. The Governor has asked me to solicit your participation as a Freeman member of this Court. We want to be purposeful in our requests, for we wish for each man to possess in an eminent degree the confidence of the community and the highest approval. Governor Bennett kindly sends his regards and offers his apology that he could not make this request himself but affairs in the Capitol have mandated his presence there. He did request I inform you he asks this as a personal favor. Although your plantation is located outside the jurisdiction of Charleston, as a property holder here in the city, you fulfil the requirements of a resident freeman."

The Intendant had quickly seen the slave insurrection charges and trials as a means to advance his career. Now it became the duty of the civil authority, as the Intendant later expressed it in his published report on the conspiracy, "to take immediate steps for the apprehension, commitment, and trial of those who were in possession of information. City Council was accordingly convened, and as a preliminary measure, it was deemed expedient, that a court of the highest respectability, for the talents and integrity of its members, should be assembled, and that, whilst the requisitions of the act of the assembly, of 1740, should be strictly complied with, in devolving the warrant of summons on the magistrates, the corporation saw no impropriety in affording these officers a list of such names of freeholders, as they knew would meet in a preeminent degree the publick approbation; and to these persons private letters were written by the authority of the council, strongly soliciting their acceptance of a trust, involving indeed the most irksome labour, as well as the deepest responsibility with these arrangements."

"We're uncertain what number of future arrests and charges may be made," the Intendant continued to James Radcliffe. "Our investigation is, as you understand, James, a continuous one. We've uncovered new information on the conspirators almost daily. Your service may be needed for a number of weeks. Due to the particular nature of the charges, this isn't a customary criminal court, but rather is dictated by the various slave laws and crimes of insurrection which govern such special circumstances, primarily the Slave Act of 1740, enacted after the Stono Rebellion of September of 1739.

"I can tell you," the Intendant said, "the other members of the Court are William Drayton, Nathanael Heyward, Colonel J. R. Pringle, Jasper Legare, Robert J. Turnbull, and Major Henry Deas, fine gentlemen all. Lionel Kennedy and Thomas Parker, Esquires, will serve as Magistrates."

"Yes, I know most of them," James Radcliffe said. "I certainly will not shirk my duty, Major, especially in such a grave situation as this." James Radcliffe hesitated for a brief moment, before he asked, "Are any of my slaves involved?"

"I don't know, James," the Intendant replied. "I've heard nothing so far. Our authority extends only to the limits of the city lines, as you know. The plantations in the countryside reside beyond our jurisdiction. I encourage you to make your own inquiry."

"Certainly," James Radcliffe said. "The Court will convene when?"

"Tomorrow at noon," James Hamilton replied. "Please forgive such short notice, James, but time is of the essence. As I explained to you earlier, we have but three days to bring forth the accused to trial based on the 1740 Act, which governs this.

"I should also inform you that contemporaneous with the organization of this court, a Committee of Vigilance and Safety has been appointed from among the members of the City Council to aid me in the execution of the laws and to cooperate with me during the recess of the council. This committee will serve to help coordinate all those measures necessary for exploring the causes and character of the existing disturbance, and bringing to light and punishment of the suspecting and guilty.

"We've taken up some conspirators already and will have others in the Work House tonight," the Intendant said confidently.

"I've informed Magistrates Kennedy and Parker that there are several colored persons in confinement charged with an attempt 'to excite an insurrection among the blacks against the whites,' as the Slave Act of 1740 reads," James Hamilton explained. "With your participation, the necessary steps to organize a court for the trial of those criminals are now complete."

"I shall see you tomorrow morning before noon then," James Radcliffe said as he stood to leave.

"I'll notify the Governor and the Magistrates you've made yourself available," the Intendant said. "The Court will be held in the Work House. We're all extremely appreciative of your service. Good evening, James. God be with you."

Wednesday, 19th June 1822, the semi-tropical sun blazed yellow hot as it rose above the Charleston harbor. Late morning, as his sister's livery servant, Tuesday, delivered James Radcliffe to the Charleston Work House, the air was already insufferably humid and sticky. The interior of the black coach was most uncomfortable.

The carriage rattled down Magazine Street to within several blocks of the Work House. An armed guard stood in front of a barrier blocking the street.

"Halt!" the guard called out, raising his long-barreled musket into position. Tuesday quickly pulled the horses and carriage to a stop. "You'll have to turn around," the Guard commanded loudly, as he eyeballed down the musket barrel. "No blacks allowed beyond this point!"

The public was prevented by the Court and the Charleston Intendant from attending the trials. Those who had no specific interest in the slaves accused could not be present. Only their owners, their counsel, and the owners of those slaves who were used as witnesses were allowed. The Court extended the invitation to attend to the Governor, and the Wardens of Charleston. No blacks were permitted to come day or night within two blocks of the Work House.

James Radcliffe stuck his head out the carriage window.

"I'm one of the Court Freemen," he explained to the guard. "James Radcliffe."

"I'm sorry, sir. Just following my orders," the guard said. He came closer, lowering his gun. "Major Hamilton strictly said no Negroes allowed within two blocks of the Work House. You'll have to go the rest of the way on foot. I'll get someone to escort you." The guard gestured, shouting for one of the other guards.

Tuesday climbed down from the carriage buckboard and opened the door for James Radcliffe to dismount. Radcliffe followed his armed guide in the shadows of the palmetto palms. He could see a cordon of troops in position all around the Work House. He had seen a few slaves wearing sackcloth to protest the trials as he had ridden across town from South Bay, and they were being gathered up by the Patrols and taken to the Guard House in chains. What's the world coming to, James Radcliffe thought.

A room within the Charleston Work House was chosen by Intendant Hamilton for the trials. A high ceiling and iron-barred windows constituted the only flair. The Major determined the trials should not be held in the Courthouse at the busy corner of Meeting and Broad streets. These trials demanded absolute secrecy, he defended to the City Council and Magistrates Kennedy and Parker. The trials served for a special set of circumstances and for a particular class of offenders. The less the public knew of the proceedings, the better. There was no need to alarm the residents of the city without necessity. Even the Charleston newspapers were requested by the Intendant to severely limit their treatment. The Work House suited perfectly. It was the place where slaves arrested by the police, or slaves sent by their masters for punishment, were imprisoned and flogged by black overseers with cowhide whips, or sentenced to walk on the treadmill, providing the power to grind corn, the place slaves were sent for "a little sugar."

The guard accompanied James Radcliffe through a narrow corridor and into the cramped room converted for the trials. The chamber's whale-oil lamps burned brightly. The glass of the barred windows had been scrubbed, and light from the crisp sun added a metallic sheen to the chamber. A Colonel William Moultrie flag, blue with white image of the crescent moon, draped from a staff in one corner. Several armed guards posted at attention. The Intendant had taken every precaution to protect against any attempt by the slaves to storm the Work House and free the prisoners.

Two of Charleston's most prominent attorneys and members of the Charleston Bar, Thomas Parker and Lionel H. Kennedy, as presiding Magistrates selected by the Intendant and Charleston City Council, sat behind a bench on a raised platform facing the center of the room. The Freemen across faced the bench. Between them, two wooden chairs reserved for barristers and owners occupied the space beside where prisoners and witnesses stood. William Drayton, a lowcountry planter, served as Court Recorder, and sat fidgeting at a writing table near the front, a war chest of quills and jars of black ink and stacks of paper at hand. James Radcliffe nodded in recognition to his fellow freemen: planters, merchants, custom collector, lawyers. Intendant Hamilton and Governor Bennett returned the nod. A row of top hats hung on hat racks at the chamber door, installed under the suggestion and careful attention to detail by the Intendant. James Radcliffe hung his hat among them before taking his seat.

Magistrate Parker placed his reading spectacles at the tip of his nose and removed his gold watch from his waistcoat pocket beneath his black robe. He turned and looked at Magistrate Kennedy, who nodded his head. Through the open windows, the bell in the steeple of St. Michael's church began to toll twelve times. Magistrate Parker banged a gavel on the bench. "This court is now in session," he proclaimed. The Freemen immediately grew quiet.

"Gentlemen, the City of Charleston and the State of South Carolina extend their sincerest appreciation for your service here today. Your duty as Freemen is a serious obligation, and especially so in such grave circumstances as these. Our city and our state cannot protect its citizens and execute its laws without such service as you are rendering here today. We know the heat will make things uncomfortable during our session here. You should have found a fan in your chair. Due to the season of the year, you're free to use the fan during the testimony and the proceedings of this Court." The fans began to wave. "We want to also remind you gentlemen you are requested to maintain complete silence in public about these proceedings. We do not wish to add to the rumors already circulating about an intended insurrection. The Court instructs you not to speak to anyone outside this courtroom about the trials."

Magistrate Kennedy then spoke: "We now ask that each of you swear the following oath for your participation in these proceedings. If you will raise your right hand." All hands were raised. "You do solemnly swear in the presence of Almighty God, that you will truly and impartially try and adjudge the prisoners who shall be brought before you upon their trials, and honestly and duly, on your part, put in execution, on these trials, an act, entitled an act for the better ordering and governing of Negroes, and other slaves in this state, according to the best of your skill and knowledge. So help you God."

The freeholders together said: "I do."

Intendant Hamilton had early determined the charges levied and the trials conducted against Denmark Vesey and his co-insurrectionists were to be based upon the May 10, 1740 Act of the Charles Town colony entitled "For the better ordering and Governing Negroes and other slaves in this province." Most of the Act had been adopted from the slave law of the original British settlers in Barbados. The West Indian island of Barbados is a small one. Within a few generations, land for plantations there became scarce. As the sons of the planter class in Barbados began to migrate to the Charles Town colony in search of available land and riches, and began slave-labor plantations in the lowcountry, it was natural they adopted the slave laws for the Carolina colony from those established in Barbados. The Preamble to the 1740 Act read: "Whereas, in his Majesty's plantations in America, slavery has been introduced and allowed, and the people commonly called negroes, Indians, mulattoes and mustizoes, have been deemed absolute slaves, and the subjects of property in the hands of particular persons, the extent of whose power over such slaves ought to be settled and limited by positive laws, so that the slave may be kept in due subjection and obedience, and the owners and other persons having the care and government of slaves may be restrained from exercising too great rigour and cruelty over them, and that the public peace and order of this Province may be preserved: We pray your most sacred Majesty that it may be enacted."

The Act of 1740 provided all crimes committed by slaves in the Carolina Province where capital punishments could be inflicted were to be tried by two Justices assigned to keep the peace, with three to seven jurors selected from freemen in the community. The Act required the trial to take place within three days of the apprehending of the offending slaves. Witnesses were to be called and examined, evidence presented, guilt determined, and sentences given. The Act distinguished between cases of capital sentences and other non-capital charges and punishment.

Magistrate Parker then addressed the members of the Court, "Let the record show the prisoners brought before this Court are charged under the section of the Slave Law of 1740, which reads as follows: *Every slave who shall raise, or attempt to raise an insurrection, in this province, or shall endeavour to delude or entice any slave to run away and leave the province, every such slave and slaves, and his and their accomplices, aiders and abetters shall, on conviction thereof, as aforesaid, suffer death. Provided always, that it shall and may be lawful, to and for the justices who shall pronounce sentence against such slaves, by and with the advise and consent of the freeholders as aforesaid, if several slaves shall receive sentence at one time, to mitigate and alter the sentence of any slave, other than such as shall be convicted of homicide of a white person, who they shall think may deserve mercy, and may inflict such corporal punishment (other than death) on any such slave, as they in discretion shall think fit, anything herein contained to the contrary thereof, in any wise notwithstanding. Provided, that one or more of the said slaves who shall be convicted of the crimes or offence aforesaid, where several are concerned, shall be executed, for example, to deter others from offending in the like kind."*

The Slave Act of 1740 varied in "many essential features from the principles of the common law, and in some of the settled rules of evidence," according to the Court of 1822. The federal constitutional guarantee of trial by a jury of one's peers and a unanimous jury decision did not apply to crimes by slaves. There was no right of appeal. Only three of the freemen and magistrates were required for conviction. All decisions were final. Trials were to be disposed of "in the most summary and expeditious manner," as the Act read, leaving little time for the defense to prepare its case. Unsworn slave testimony was allowed. To protect against any error of procedure, decisions were not to "be reversed, avoided or in any way impeached by reason of and default in form." Free Negroes, such as Denmark Vesey, who were charged with such crimes, were tried not under the laws which applied to white men, but the same laws which applied to slaves.

"In addition to the provisions of the Slave Act of 1740," Magistrate Parker explained, "it is agreed by this Court and the Intendant and the Council of the City of Charleston that a select number of other conditions will apply. For the record, the following are laid down for the governing of these proceedings: first, no slave shall be tried except in the presence of his owner, or his counsel. Second, the testimony of one witness unsupported by additional evidence, or by circumstances, should lead to no conviction of a capital nature. Third, the witness should be confronted with the accused, and with each other, in every case, except where testimony is given under a solemn pledge that the names of the witnesses should not be divulged, as they declare in some instances, that they apprehend being murdered by the blacks, if it is known they volunteered their evidence. Fourth, the prisoners may be represented by counsel, whenever this is requested by the owners of the slaves or by the prisoners themselves, if free. Fifth, the statements or defense of the accused should be heard in every case, and they be permitted themselves to examine any witness they think proper."

The courtroom drew silent, save for the sounds of the city through the open windows, the hubbub of dray wagons and carriages, the muffled boom of a signal cannon from the harbor, the distant chatter of voices in the streets, humming faintly, the windblown song of a street merchant, before being sucked back into the din. The Freemen shifted in their chairs, fanning themselves in the heat.

"Let's begin," Magistrate Kennedy said, "with Intendant Hamilton providing us with a statement. Major, if you would, please inform the Freeholders and the Court how the City Council learned of this plot and the nature of the charges."

Intendant Hamilton pushed back his chair and stood up, his lanky frame fastidiously appareled like his fellow planters and citizens. The freemen each wore the prevailing suits of lowcountry Carolina planters: wool or silk redingote jacket, waistcoat even in summer heat, fawn colored matching or contrasting long trousers, shirt with high collar, silk cravat tied about the neck, all carefully crafted and fitted, and cowhide shoes polished daily by slave hands. The men with whom the Intendant sat were his peers, his colleagues, and controlled the politics of the city as much as the Major did. They were his source of power. The Major stepped and positioned himself so he could see both the Magistrates and the Freemen.

"On Friday, May 31st last," Intendant Hamilton began, "I was visited by Colonel John C. Piroleau, a prominent freeholder and prestigious member of this community, who related to me that a trustworthy slave of his household, Colonel Piroleau's cook, a mulatto named Peter Desverneys, had several days before been approached by a black man at the wharves in the city. This black man asked Colonel Piroleau's Peter if he had heard news that the blacks of Charleston were plotting to rise up against the whites. Peter was encouraged to join in the plot.

"With further questioning of Colonel Piroleau's man, we determined the slave who expressed this news was a William, belonging to the Paul's. William Paul was immediately taken into custody and after a number of days in solitary confinement informed us as to the nature of the plot and the names of some of the conspirators. We learned of more of the plot when the slave of another prominent member of the Charleston community came to his master and said the plot was to be executed at midnight on the 16th of June. This led us to the discoveries, which bring this Court into session today.

"This is a calendar containing the names of all the prisoners currently ascertained, the charges on which they have been committed, and the names of the witnesses who will testify against them." The Intendant held up the papers for all to see, and stepped to the Bench and handed the calendar to Magistrate Kennedy. One thing the Intendant knew: the better he performed his responsibilities during the crises, the more promising his own future.

"We have spent much time," the Intendant continued, "examining all the testimony we could obtain in order to ascertain how far a conspiracy has actually been formed. We are convinced of the existence of a plot." James Hamilton returned to his seat.

"Thank you, Major Hamilton. Is the court ready for the trial of the first prisoner?" Magistrate Parker asked, and he surveyed about the room to make certain all agreed. He studied the calendar given to him by the Intendant. "William, servant of Mr. John Paul, will be the first to be examined."

Chained at both his arms and legs, the prisoner was brought into the courtroom by an armed guard, and positioned between the Magistrates and the Freemen. William's reddened eyes looked about with fear. Sweat beaded on his forehead and ran down his face; his drab grey slave cloth shirt blotched with dark sweat marks under his armpits and at his stomach.

"I have heard something about an insurrection of the blacks," William answered in a nervous whisper the opening question by Magistrate Kennedy, "but was not concerned in it."

"Speak up!" Magistrate Kennedy admonished the prisoner.

William loudly cleared his throat.

"Mr. Harth's Negro man Mingo told me about it and referred me to Peter Poyas for further information, who he said had a list with 9,000 names upon it, and that he was still taking down names. On the week I was to see Peter, I was apprehended. Mingo said that 600 men on the bay was already down on the list in Peter's possession. Mingo would not before the Wardens own what he had told me. I never had any conversation with Peter. Mingo said his name was not yet down, and he would not put it down, until he knew all that was to be done, that Ned Bennett knew all about it, and told it all to Mr. Bennett's people. And that letters were now passing between those concerned. I can read and count printed characters, but not written.

"One Saturday afternoon as I was going to market, I met a brown man belonging to Colonel Prioleau in Meeting Street named, I believe Peter, and walked with him down to the market wharf, where he called my attention to a pendant on a vessel's mast, and said it was numbered 95, to which I said 'twas not, 'tis numbered 76. He then showed me a small privateer in the stream and told me of the distress in which she had arrived here. I asked him for news, and if he had heard anything strange, when he replied he had heard that there would be a disturbance and interruption shortly between the blacks and whites. I told him I did not understand such talk, and stopped the conversation."

Intendant Hamilton grimaced at William Paul's change in details from his earlier confession to the Major, and his attempt to place the guilt on Peter Desverneys. The Intendant turned to catch the eye of James Radcliffe. The Intendant too tried to exchange looks with the Governor to gauge his reaction, but Thomas Bennett only stared straight ahead.

"I did not endeavor to get Colonel Prioleau's man to join the rising of the blacks," William Paul was saying. "On Saturday night Mingo told me as we were going toward his wife's house, that very day at 2 o'clock, Peter went to Mr. Harth's lumber yard and talked to the other men about this matter, to make them sensible of the plan. Mingo said that all those belonging to the African Church are engaged in the insurrection from the country to the town, that there is a little man amongst them who can't be killed, shot, or caught, who was to be their General and who would provide them with arms, that some arms were provided, but did not tell me where they were, and that Ned Bennett and Charles Shubrick are Officers. Peter, Ned, and Charles are Class Leaders in the African Church. The African Association have also a church in Anson Street near Boundary Street and one in Cow Alley, where they have service. I first spoke to Mr. Prioleau's man Peter about the rising. I believe that Mingo was endeavoring to get me to join them in the rising, and from his conversation I have no doubt, but that he was engaged in the conspiracy, and that all he said to me was to get me to join them."

William Paul rambled on, prodded by repeated questions by the Magistrates. "It was also told to me our color from the North to the South had combined together to fight against New Orleans. Mingo was no doubt satisfied that I would join. I never had any conversation with anyone about the rising, but with Mingo and Colonel Prioleau's man. Mingo said that Peter Poyas would tell me when the rising would take place, that Mr. Bennett's man Ned was one of them, that Denmark Vesey was the Chiefest Man and more concerned than anyone else.

"Denmark Vesey is an old man, in whose yard my master's Negro woman Sarah cooks," William Paul continued. "He was her father in law, having married her mother Beck. They've been parted some time, but he visited her at her house near the Intendant Major Hamilton's, where I have often heard him speak of the rising.

"I beg you won't take up Sarah, for no woman knows anything about it. Mingo said that letters were passing between Peter Poyas and Ned Bennett and Charles Shubrick. I'm persuaded that Denmark Vesey was chiefly concerned in this business. Mingo said that the country places were engaged in the plot, and also the Islands, that he knows the little man who can't be shot, who told him there was a Gullah Society going on which met once a month, that all the orders he got, he got from Peter. Mingo always denied that he was engaged, but yet always talked to me as if he wanted me to join."

The digressive testimony of William Paul complete, the guard returned the prisoner to his cell. Guilty, the Freemen all agreed. The question was, did his crime merit death by hanging? A poll was taken by the Magistrates. Only one Freeman endorsed death. William Paul received a sentence of removal outside the limits of the United States, never to return upon penalty of death.

"The next prisoner, Rolla Bennett, slave of his Excellency Thomas Bennett," Magistrate Parker announced. He reviewed the calendar supplied by the Intendant. "Five witnesses will testify on behalf of the prosecution. Their testimony will be taken *in absentia* of the prisoner. These witnesses are covered by the exclusion clause because should it become known they have testified they fear for their lives. For the record, this first witness came forth voluntarily, and gave information of the intended insurrection, and of the places and those concerned, as far as his information extended. Joe, belonging to Mr. La Roche, has asked that his name not be divulged, which this Court pledges to conceal as far as it depends upon us. His name is therefore suppressed from the record. Guard!"

The witness was brought into the courtroom, a blue-black man with skin so dark his features sank into the color of his face save for the whites of his eyes and the gleam of his white teeth. The Governor had hired the services of one of Charleston's most respected lawyers, Jacob Axson, to represent his interest as property holder of Rolla, and J. Axson, Esquire took a seat in the chair in front of the Freemen reserved for the prisoner's council, the empty defendant's standing space beside him. The witness squeezed to one side in front of the Magistrates.

"Tell the Court," Magistrate Kennedy said to the witness, "what you know about Rolla Bennett and this conspiracy of the blacks to rise up against the whites."

"I know Rolla, belonging to Mr. Thomas Bennett," Joe began nervously as he stood stiffly. "We're intimate friends and eat our meals together. All that I know about the intended insurrection I got from him."

"Continue," Magistrate Kennedy encouraged the witness.

"He asked me about three months ago to join with him in slaying the whites. I asked him to give me time to consider it. A week after, he put the same question to me, and at the end of another week, he again came to me on this same subject. I told him take care, for God says we must not kill. You're a coward said he and laughed at me. He said he would tell me how it was to be done. There are white men who have come from afar and who say that St. Domingo and Africa will assist us to get our liberty, if we'll only make the motion first.

"I advised him to let it alone, and told him I'd oppose them if they came to kill my mistress, and he again laughed at me as a coward. He summoned me to go to the meetings where, said he, you'll hear what is going on and be better informed. I told him yes, I'd go. Friday about three weeks ago, he appointed to take me to this meeting. At that night, he came to me and again called me to go. I went away from him. The next day he came to me and said the meeting had been expecting me, and I must send my name to be put down as one of the band.

"This thing has been going on for four months," Joe said in answer to the Magistrates. "Rolla told me that at the meetings 'twas said that some white men said our Legislature had set us free, and that the white people here wouldn't let us go, that Santo Domingo and Africa would come over and cut up the white people if we only made the motion here first. He said that last Saturday night might be the last he had to live as they were determined to break open the thing on Sunday night.

"I told him it could not be done, it couldn't succeed, that our parents for generations back had been slaves, and we'd better be contented. He desired me to tell George Wilson on Sunday last, our Class Leader at the

African Church, to come up to him. George went up after church in the evening. Rolla told George in my presence what he was going to do. George told him let it alone, he would not succeed and wept. Rolla replied 'twas now gone too far to stop it. He told George to go out of town on Sunday night, as he didn't wish him to be hurt. I told George to sound the alarm, and if he didn't, I would.

"I asked Rolla what was to be done with the women and children. He said 'when we've done with the fellows, we know what to do with the wenches.'

"There are a great many involved in it in the Country. Mingo from James' Island was to come over to Charleston with four thousand men, land on South Bay, march up and seize the Arsenal by the Guard House and kill the City guard. Another body of men was to seize upon the powder magazine and another body to seize the Arsenal on the Neck, then march to town and destroy the inhabitants who could only escape by jumping into the river. My army, Rolla said, will first fix my old Buck, the Governor, and then the Intendant. I asked if he could bind his master or kill him. He laughed at me again. I then told him I would have nothing to do with him. He begged me to lend him my boat to go into the country and hasten down the county Negroes, as he feared they would not come. I lent it to him, but again charged him to let it alone. He was going to John's Island, where he wanted me to enlist people, as I knew the country. He went to John's Island at Christmas, but then this business was not in train. He only went to get acquainted with the people."

The dark black man stood for a long moment without speaking, looking down at the floor before he said, "I felt that it was a bad thing to disclose what a bosom friend had confided, that it was wicked to betray him. But then I thought on the other hand that by doing so, I would save so many lives, and prevent the horrible acts in contemplation, that 'twas over balanced, and my duty was to inform.

"I refused to go to the meetings as Rolla wished, as I feared if I opposed them there, they might make away with me to prevent me from betraying them. I don't know where the meetings were held but I believe it was Bull Street in which street Denmark Vesey lives."

"Who else do you know was a member of the conspiracy?" Magistrate Parker posed.

"Rolla said that Ned and Mathias were concerned. I'm well acquainted with Stephen Smith. I believe him to be a worthy, good man, and in conversation with him on the subject he agreed with me that this was an abominable plot. I have not seen him for the last four weeks."

"What can you tell the Court about Denmark Vesey," asked Magistrate Kennedy.

Joe shifted on his feet and looked about the room as if making certain Denmark Vesey was nowhere to be seen before he began. "I know Denmark Vesey. I was one day on horseback when I met him on foot. He asked me if I was satisfied in my present situation, if I remembered the Fable of Hercules' wagon that was stalled, when he began to pray and that God said you fool, put your shoulder to the wheel, whip up the horses, and your wagon will be pulled out, that if we did not put our hand to the work and deliver ourselves, we would never come out of slavery, that the Legislature had made us free. I know Vesey is intimately acquainted with Rolla. Rolla said that there had been a sort of disagreement and confusion at their place of meeting, and that they meant to meet at Vesey's. Vesey told me that a large army from Santo Domingo and Africa were coming to help us, and that we must not stand with our hands in our pocket. He was bitter toward the whites."

"What else do you know," Magistrate Kennedy asked.

"Rolla has a wife in my mistress' yard. Sambo, the brother of Rolla's wife and who stays at the plantation, sent word by his sister to Rolla, that he'd be in town on Sunday night last. Rolla said that they would have a countersign to be known to their friends and in the action, those blacks who couldn't give it, would be killed. Rolla said they would fire the town. His threats are that if any black person is found out giving information or evidence against them, they'll watch for them night and day and kill them certainly, that even now the friends of these in prison are trying about the streets to find who has given information. If my name was known, I would certainly be killed. I advised Rolla to let it alone, but told him that as they passed by my house, I'd fall in behind with my line and grains, which was all I had."

The courtroom was eerily silent. Expressions of incredulousness showed on the faces of the Freemen, disbelief that slowly began to assume the look of fear, pale and wide-eyed, as the reality of the witness' testimony took hold. Intendant Hamilton observed their faces. It was hard for him to hide his own look of satisfaction. The witness had made more of an impression than the Intendant had hoped. The Governor sat fixed, stunned that Rolla had bragged of his plans to murder his master.

One by one, the other witnesses were brought in and questioned without Rolla's presence.

"Will the guard bring in Rolla, servant of His Excellency, Governor Thomas Bennett," Magistrate Kennedy said when the testimony of the five witnesses against Rolla had been heard.

An armed guard escorted the prisoner into the court chamber. Rolla's hands and feet were shackled, connected by chain around his neck and waist. He stood straight as a soldier at the side of his counsel, his black beard thicker from several days without shaving; otherwise, to the Magistrates' and Freemen's surprise, Rolla appeared composed and showed no fear.

Five witnesses were called by Jacob Axson on Rolla's behalf with the intent to impeach the credibility of one of the unidentified witnesses against the prisoner. Instead, their testimony strengthened the witnesses' statements.

Jacob Axson gestured for Rolla to step closer and whispered in Rolla's ear. The Intendant sat nearest the prisoner and his counsel, and thought he heard Axson say, "five witnesses testified to your guilt. This way the Court might spare your life." Rolla bowed his head for a long moment. He then whispered back. Jacob Axson caught the eyes of the Governor before he turned to address the Court.

"The prisoner would like to make a voluntary statement of confession," Jacob Axson announced.

A mummer of surprise sounded from the Freemen. Rolla stepped and stood in the prisoner's spot on the chamber floor. He lifted his chin, his eyes hard and clear. Intendant Hamilton leaned forward, listening carefully. Thomas Bennett had long past assumed a blank, stoic expression and the Intendant could garner no trace of the Governor's feelings.

"I know Denmark Vesey," Rolla Bennett began slowly. "On one occasion he asked me what news. I told him none. He replied we are free but the white people here won't let us be so, and the only way is to rise up and fight the whites.

"I went to his house one night to learn where the meetings were held. I never conversed on this subject with Batteau or Ned. Vesey told me he was the leader of this plot. I never conversed either with Peter or Mingo. Vesey induced me to join.

"When I went to Vesey's house there was a meeting there. The room was full of people, but none of them white. That night at Vesey's we determined to have arms made, and each man put in 12 ½ cents towards that purpose. Though Vesey's room was full, I did not know one individual there. At this meeting, Vesey said we were to take the Guard House and Magazine to get arms; that we ought to rise up and fight for our liberties against the whites.

"He was the first to rise up and speak, and he read to us from the Bible, how the Children of Israel were delivered out of Egypt from bondage. He said that the rising would take place last Sunday night week, the 16th of June and that Peter Poyas was one."

Rolla's words trailed off. He hung his head down.

"Anything else?" Magistrate Kennedy asked.

"No, sir."

The Intendant scrutinized the faces of the Freemen. Denmark Vesey! So he *was* the chief mastermind of the conspiracy! William Paul and the witnesses against Rolla had testified as such, and now Rolla Bennett himself provided the corroborating evidence. The Intendant earlier had doubted William Paul's claim. After all, Denmark Vesey was a long-time resident of the city, widely known by both blacks and whites. The Intendant knew that for a free black man, Vesey's reputation as a dependable, energetic carpenter was unblemished. The Major knew of Denmark Vesey's former master, the old mariner and slave trader from Bermuda, Joseph Vesey.

Now that the Intendant was certain, he swore to himself to have every slave hovel in the city searched and ransacked until Denmark Vesey was found and captured. The Intendant knew it had to be done quickly. Beginning tonight, he resolved, he would assign patrols to watch the docks for every ship departing for Santo Domingo, or Africa. Those were likely the targets for any attempt by Vesey to escape. He would have Vesey's house searched and watched. He determined to know if Vesey was married and where his wife might live. Wherever he was hiding, the Intendant vowed, they would find Vesey, like a fox sniffed out of his lair by the hunting hounds.

The Court unanimously ruled Rolla guilty. A sentence of death by hanging passed upon him. Throughout his trial, until his confession to the Court, Rolla had denied his guilt and feigned ignorance of the plot. After the sentence of death, he broke down in tears in his prison cell, and made a second confession to Reverend Dr. Hall who had, at the Governor's behest, sought to serve as spiritual councilor to His Excellency's condemned chattel. Dr. Hall furnished the confession to the Court in writing:

I was invited by Denmark Vesey to his house where I found Ned

Bennett, Peter Poyas, and others. Some were strangers to me. They said they were from the country.

Denmark told us it was high time we had our liberty, and he could show us how to obtain it. He said we must unite together as the Santo Domingo people did, never to betray one another, and to die before we would tell upon one another. He also said he expected the Santo Domingo people would send some troops to help us. The best way, said he, for us to conquer the whites is to set the town on fire in several places, at the Governor's Mills, and near the Docks, and for every servant in the yards to be ready with axes, knives, and clubs and kill every man as he came out when the alarm bells began to ring. He then read in the Bible where God commanded that all should be cut off, both men, women and children. He said he believed it was no sin to do so for the Lord had commanded us to do it.

But if I had read these Psalms, Doctor, which I have read since I have been in this prison, they would never have got me to join them.

At another meeting, some of the company were opposed to killing the Ministers, and the women and children, but Denmark said it was not safe to keep one alive, but to destroy them totally, for you see, said he, the Lord has commanded it. When I heard this, Master Hall, my heart pained me within, and I said to myself, I cannot kill my master and mistress, for they use me more like a son than a slave.

I then concluded in my mind that I would go into the country on Saturday evening before they were to commence on Sunday, that I might not see it. Some of the company at Denmark Vesey's house asked if they were to stay in Charleston after the killings and were free. Denmark said no, as soon as they could get the money from the banks, and the goods from the stores, they would hoist sail for Santo Domingo, for he expected some armed vessels would meet them to conduct and protect them.

"The next prisoner on the trial calendar is Peter Poyas, property of Mr. James Poyas, Mr. Poyas with James Bentham, Esquire as his counsel attending," Magistrate Parker announced to the Court. "Guard?"

Peter Poyas, in chains from head to foot, entered into the court chamber accompanied by the guard. Of all the conspirators, Peter proved one of the most active and most loyal to Denmark Vesey. "Do not open your lips. Die silent as you shall see me do," Peter admonished his comrades in the cell before their trails. And die silent he did. Although Peter signed the largest number of recruits of any of Denmark Vesey's followers, Peter was so cautious, and so silent, not one of his recruits' names was ever found out by the Intendant and the Wardens of the city.

Like the trial of Rolla Bennett, unidentified witnesses testified against Peter Poyas, witnesses given anonymity because of their claim of fear of retribution for their testimony, witnesses Peter Poyas did not get to face.

"Tell us everything you know regarding Peter Poyas," said Magistrate Parker to one of the anonymous witnesses, the slave Robert Harth, "and all he said to you of the conspiracy of the blacks to rise up against the whites."

"I know Peter Poyas," the witness told the Court. "In May last Peter and myself met in Legare Street, at the corner of Lambol Street, when the following conversation took place. He asked me the news. I replied none that I know of. He said by George we can't live so. I replied how well we do. He said we can do very well; if you can find anyone to assist us will you join? I asked him, how do you mean? He said why to break the yoke. I replied I don't know. He asked me, suppose you were to hear that the whites are going to kill you, would you defend yourself? I replied I'd try to escape. He asked have you lately seen Denmark Vesey, and has he spoken to you particularly? I said no. Well then he said that's all now, but call at the shop tomorrow after knocking off work and I'll tell you more. We then parted.

"I met him the next day according to appointment, when he said we intend to see if we can't do something for ourselves. We then left his shop and walked toward Broad Street, when he said I want you to take notice of all the shops and stores in town with arms in them. Take down the numbers and give them to me. I said I'll see to it and then we parted.

"About the 1st of June I saw in the public papers a statement that the white people were going to build Missionary Houses for the blacks, which I carried and showed to Peter and said to him, you see the good they are going to do for us, when he said, what of that, have you not heard that on the 4th of July the whites are going to create a false alarm of fire and every black that comes out will be killed in order to thin them.

"Do you think that they would be so barbarous, said I. Yes, said he, I do. I fear they have knowledge of an army from Santo Domingo, and they would be right to do it, to prevent us from joining that army if it should march towards this land. I was then very much alarmed.

"We then parted and I saw no more of him until about a fortnight ago. At that time, I saw Peter and Ned Bennett standing and talking together at the corner of Lambol and Legare Streets. They crossed over and met me by Mrs. Myles, and Ned Bennett said to me, did you hear why those boys were taken up the other day. I replied, no, but some say 'twas for stealing. Ned asked me if I was sure I had never said anything to the whites about what Peter Poyas had spoken to me about. I replied, no. Says Peter, you never did? No, I answered. Says Ned to me, how do you stand, at which I struck the tree box with my knuckles and said, as firm as this box. I'll never say one word against you. Ned then smiled and nodded his head and said, that will do, when we all separated.

"Last Tuesday or Wednesday week Peter said to me, you see my lad how the white people have got to windward of us. You won't, said I, be able to do anything. Oh yes, said he, we will. By George we're obliged to. He said all down this way ought to meet and have a collection to purchase powder. What, said I, is the use of powder? The whites can fire three times to our once. He said, but 'twill be such a dead time of night they won't know what is the matter, and our Horse Companies will go about the streets and prevent the whites from assembling. I asked him where will you get horses? Why, said he, there are many butcher boys with horses, and there are the public Livery Stables, where we have several candidates and the waiting men belonging to the white people of the Horse Companies will be told to take away their master's horses. He asked me if my master was not a horseman. I said yes. Has he got arms at his house? I answered yes. Can't they be got at? I said yes. Then, said he, 'tis good to have them.

"I asked him what was the plan? Why, said he, after we have taken the Arsenal and Guard Houses, then we will set the town on fire from different places, and as the whites come out we will slay them. If we were to set fire to the town first, the man in the steeple would give the alarm too soon. I am the Captain, said he, to take the lower Guard House and Arsenal. But, I replied, when you are coming up the centinel will give the alarm. He said he would advance a little distance ahead and if he could only get a grip at his throat he was a gone man, for his sword was very sharp. He had sharpened it and had made it so sharp it had cut his finger, which he showed me.

"As to the Arsenal on the Neck he said that is gone as sure as fate. Ned Bennett would manage that with the people from the country, and the people between Hibben's Ferry and Santee would land and take the upper Guard House. I then said, then this thing seems true. My man, said he, God has a hand in it. We have been meeting for four years and are not yet betrayed. I told him I was afraid after all of the white people from the back country and Virginia. He said that the blacks would collect so numerous from the country we need not fear from other parts, for when we have once got the city we can keep them all out. He asked if I had told my boys. I said no. Then said he, you should do it, for Ned Bennett has his people pretty well ranged, but, said he, take care and don't mention it to those waiting men who receive presents of old coats from their masters or they'll betray us. I will speak to them.

"We then parted and I have not conversed with him. He said the rising was to take place last Sunday night, 16th June; that any of the colored people who said a word about this matter would be killed by the others. The little man who can't be killed, shot, or taken is named Jack, a Gullah Negro. Peter said there was a French company in town of three hundred men fully armed, that he was to see Monday Gell about exciting the uprising. I know that Mingo went often to Mr. Paul's to see Edwin, but don't know if he spoke with William. Peter said he has a sword and I ought to get one. He said he had a letter from the country, I think from St. Thomas, from a Negro man who belonged to the Captain of a Militia Company who said he could easily get the key of the house where the Company's arms were put after muster, and take them all out and help in that way. This business originates all together with the African Congregation in which Peter is a member. When Bennett's Ned asked about those taken up, he alluded particularly to Mr. Paul's William, and asked me if I had said anything to him about it."

The testimony of the anonymous witness completed, the Court then called the owner of the witness. He too testified in Peter Poyas' absence.

"My servant bears a good character," the witness' master stated to the Court. "His general conduct is good. He was raised up in my family, and I would place my life in his hands."

The final witness called to testify against Peter Poyas was William Paul.

The Court unanimously found Peter guilty, and passed upon him a sentence of death. "I suppose you'll let me see my wife and family before I die," said Peter calmly as he stood before the Court. Those were the only words he spoke during the entire trial.

And so it was, with utmost expediency and efficiency, the special slave Court of Charleston during the summer of 1822 proceeded to try the others. Ned and Batteau Bennett were found guilty and sentenced to hang until dead. Two slaves, Stephen Smith and Amherst Lining, were found not guilty based on no or insufficient evidence.

Each man faces death in his own way, the Intendant ruminated as he studied the faces of the convicted slaves. Some were repentant with deathbed confessions and pleas of forgiveness. Such had been the case with Rolla Bennett. Some prayed to God for strength, not a few for the first real time in their lives. Others faced death with fear and trepidation, horrified at the prospect of confronting the Great Unknown. Some went quietly, resigned to the fact that every man in time must meet his end; others comfortable their soul was ready to meet their Maker. Others departed in rage, battling angrily until the end. And a few, like Peter Poyas, were resilient and strong, prideful even at the hand of mighty Death. Peter had given his admonition to "die silent." Had the others adhered to Peter's charge, the Intendant recognized the arrests and the trials would have ended then. But it was not to be. The fear of death, and the fear of an eternity in a hell of everlasting fire and brimstone, broke the will of the weak and less courageous rebels.

Sunday morning, June 23rd 1822, James Radcliffe sat with Intendant James Hamilton in the parlor room of the Major's Charleston home. They were served tea and rice cakes by one of the Intendant's house servants, a plump Negress dressed in the extravagant livery worn by all the Intendant's domestics.

"We apprehended the arch villain conspirator last night," said the Intendant, barely concealing his excitement.

"Denmark Vesey!" James Radcliffe exclaimed.

The Intendant carefully placed his teacup and saucer on the side table. "The Committee of Vigilance had a time of it, tracking down this Vesey." The Intendant scowled. "Four days to find and apprehend him! Finally flushed him out like a fox chased from his lair by hounds. I'm certain he was unable to escape the city because the Patrol has been so vigilant. We're holding him at the Guard House. His trial will begin at our afternoon session today."

"That should be most interesting," James Radcliffe said.

There was a hard knock beyond the room from the Intendant's foyer door. The house servant returned to address the Major.

"Massa Hamilton, Cap'n Dove say you sent for him."

"Yes, Charisa, show him in."

"Oh, excuse me, Major. I didn't realize you had someone with you," the Warden said, stopping at the drawing room entrance. "Good morning, Mister Radcliffe."

"Captain Dove," Intendant Hamilton said, delighted at his good fortune that the Warden had appeared so opportunely. "I was just about to tell Mister Radcliffe about your apprehension last night of another one of the conspirators. Tell him what you were relaying to me earlier."

"Well, sir," Captain Dove said, fingering his hat held in his hand as he took two steps into the room, "it happened during last night's perfect tempest. I haven't seen so much rain in so short a time since the hurricane way back in 1804. Quite a storm! The wind blowing! Lighting flaring overhead! The rumble of thunder over the city and out over the harbor. I know you got your share of it."

"Get on with it, Captain." Hamilton reproved.

"Yes, sir," Captain Dove replied. "Well, the storm was in real earnest when Mr. Wesner, who kept on the trail of Vesey for over three days and explored every possible clue, came pounding on my door. He was soaked to the bone.

"'Dove,' says he, 'I've uncovered where Denmark Vesey's hiding! He's at the cabin of one of his wives. Not far from here! It's rumored he intends to board a ship bound for Santo Domingo early tomorrow morning.'"

"'We must apprehend him tonight. Right now,' I told Wesner, and reached for my hat and coat by the door as he described the particular yard and cabin. 'You stay here,' I said to him. 'Dry out. I'll round up some of my men and we'll be back with this Denmark Vesey.'

"I found three others to accompany me, and we hastened along the deserted streets drenched to the skin, sir, the rain pouring down in great sheets. The palmetto trees bent in the wind, reeling to and fro like a drunkard. Vesey's wife's cabin is a little wooden shack in the yard of her master's house.

"'Go to the back,' I ordered one of the men. 'Don't let him escape under any circumstances. Shoot to kill if you must.'

"The men moved in place to surround the house. Then I banged hard on the door between the thunders."

"'Open up!' I shouted. 'It's the Patrol!'"

"Sir, the door cracked open and Vesey's wife stared out at us, the whites of her eyes big as my fist. Her face had such a look of fear you'd have thought I was the devil himself standing at her door."

"'Where is he?' I roared at her."

"'Who?'"

"'Don't pretend to be ignorant with me, you wench,' I said as we forced our way into the cabin, weapons drawn and ready to fire."

"'Denmark Vesey, where are you?' I called out. 'The house is surrounded. Come out now!'"

"Vesey's wife screamed, 'Don't kill him.' She kept screaming, 'Lord. Don't kill him! Lord, don't kill him!'"

"'Shut up woman,' I said to her. Well, sir, the raindrops hammered on the roof like a smith forging a set of hoof irons for a horse and a great spark of lightning flashed blue through a small window and through the open front door and the boom of thunder like a cannon shot rolled across the sky. A stirring noise came from the back of the cabin and Denmark Vesey walked out of the shadows."

"'What's this about,' he asked. He had a surprising calm in his voice, sir. Surprising."

"'Denmark Vesey,' I ordered him, 'come with us. You're under arrest.'"

"'What charge?' he asked, almost politely, sir. I declare, t'was strange."

"'Never mind that,' I said to him, and I turned to the others. 'Take him to the Guard House. Lock him up with the others. Vesey, put your pants and shoes on,' I told him, for I swear he was in his under drawers and stocking feet, sir. Yes, he was, in his drawers and stocking feet."

Intendant Hamilton's droopy eyes brightened. He leaned forward perched on the edge of his chair. He cocked a faint smile and his face glowed with pride as he turned to look at James Radcliffe.

"Was he armed?" James Radcliffe asked.

"He didn't have an arm on him," Intendant Hamilton answered, "but we found a pistol on a table in the cabin. I was surprised he didn't try to use it till we discovered it was unloaded."

"That's quite a tale," James Radcliffe said. His heart had jumped in his chest just at the hearing of it.

"Yes, it is," James Hamilton said. "And we're just beginning. Before this thing is concluded, we'll have every guilty nigger hanging by the gallows or banished beyond the borders of the state." The Intendant leaned back in his chair and propped a boot on the ottoman on the floor. "I've apprehended some of the suspects myself," Intendant Hamilton said proudly.

"You must exercise caution, Major," James Radcliffe warned him.

"Oh, I do," the Intendant said, and opened his vest pocket, took out a dueling pistol, and placed it on the side table. "Always enough to safeguard myself. I spent a whole afternoon hidden in a slave shack. The nigger finally came in after sundown. Gave me no trouble at all. Not when I put this is his face," and the Intendant's face lighted up with a big toothy grin. James Radcliffe and Warden Dove said nothing. The Intendant assumed a more serious tone. "Here's my report to the Governor on the apprehension of Vesey," the Intendant addressed the Warden, handing him a collection of papers which rested on the table. "I gave you and your men full recognition."

"Thank you, sir."

"Please deliver it to His Excellency promptly. He's expecting it this afternoon."

"Yes sir." The Warden turned to James Radcliffe. "Nice seeing you again, sir."

"Congratulations, Warden," James Radcliffe said warmly. "Admirable work."

"Thank you, sir," the Warden said. "Oh, no need to stand, Major. I can see my way out on my own."

The Intendant leaned back in his chair. Success. He loved success above all things. Success led to recognition. Success led to glory.

The servant returned with more rice cakes and poured the two men fresh tea.

"Did you see the *Courier*, what was it, two days ago now? Last Friday?" Major Hamilton asked.

"Indeed I did!" James Radcliffe said with sudden force. "An unsigned *Communication*! *Melancholy Effect of Popular Excitement*. Who would have written such a thing?"

"I already know," the Intendant answered. "A certain party at the *Courier* who shall remain unnamed alerted me. Justice William Johnson."

"Johnson! What audacity!" James Radcliffe straightened up in his chair. "To question the integrity and behaviour of the Slave Court. And from a member of the federal Supreme Court! It's beyond belief."

"I spoke with some of the other members of the Slave Court. Like you, they're none too happy," said the Intendant.

"I imagine not."

"The way I see it," said the Intendant, "Johnson has insinuated that the Court, under the influence of popular prejudice, is capable of committing perjury and murder."

"Perjury and murder!" Radcliffe said bitterly. "Hogwash."

"We cannot stand idly by," the Intendant continued. "We must strike back, James. I'm prepared to do what we can. What we must. The Court has been injured and defamed. The ones I have consulted are open to resigning and dissolving the Court if need be in order to show our displeasure.

"I agree," said James Radcliffe.

"I'm preparing a response now to be published in the *Courier* if necessary," James Hamilton said.

"Good," James Radcliffe encouraged.

"We must be prepared to influence the Judge to issue a denial of his attempt to imply bad motives or unfair procedure on the part of the special Court. I'll speak to the remaining Freeholders today."

James Hamilton called for Warden Dove.

"I want the Committee of Vigilance to bring in that Morris Brown of the African Church," the Intendant said.

"Do you want us to arrest him, sir?" Warden Dove asked.

"Just tell him I wish to speak with him," the Intendant answered. "Tell him he may come voluntarily, but if he refuses the city will be compelled to bring him in by force." The Warden turned to leave. "Oh, Lieutenant Dove," Major Hamilton stopped him, "I know he's been out of town, but I was told he has returned. He'll likely be at his cobbler shop in Meeting Street. You know the place?"

"Yes, sir," the Warden answered. "Intendant, when do you want him here?"

"Immediately," James Hamilton said. "Bring him back with you."

Within an hour, the Warden arrived with Morris Brown. He was shown to the Intendant.

"Morris," the Intendant addressed the free black man by his first name, as he would a slave, ignoring his standing as minister of the African Church, and not inviting him to sit down in the empty chair. "I suppose you've heard of the goings on which were to take place during your journey up North."

"I heard some rumors," Reverend Brown said, "that be all. I don't know if what I heard be true."

"Oh, I'm certain you've heard some truth." The Intendant stared with cold eyes at the brown man. "The question is what you heard before the

16th June." He carefully emphasized the word *before*.

"What I heard be after that time."

"You've heard, I'm certain, that members of your church were involved in the plot?" The Intendant did not give Morris Brown time to respond. "Ned and Rolla and Batteau Bennett of the Governor, and Peter Poyas and Denmark Vesey are all members of the African Church. Some of them are what you call 'Class Leaders,' are they not?"

"Yes, that be true," Morris Brown said. "But that don't mean . . ."

"It means," the Intendant interrupted him and leaned forward toward Morris Brown, "it means if it becomes known that you participated in this horrific and ungodly plan, you will, like the others, meet your Maker when you are sentenced to hang at the end of a noose."

Morris Brown said nothing.

"Morris," said Major Hamilton threateningly, "When I'm convinced you're involved in this in some way, I'll do everything within my power to see that justice is attained. Everything." Morris Brown remained silent. "My recommendation to you is to leave this town. You're not wanted here. Go back up North and remain there."

"Am I free to go?" Morris Brown asked. Brown's benign appearance was misleading; he was not readily intimidated, more resilient and determined than the Intendant had anticipated.

"You may go," the Intendant said to him, "but this will not be our last interview on this issue."

"Lucinda!" Her mama hurried up the stairs. "Massa Radcliffe wanna see you," she whispered. "What this about?"

"I don't know, Mama." Lucinda's heart pounded. She thought it was going to burst in her chest.

Master Radcliffe and Intendant Hamilton sat in the downstairs parlor room.

"Mary, stay here." Master Radcliffe said. "Lucinda, my sister tells me the two of you know this Denmark Vesey."

"Yes, Master Radcliffe," Lucinda said. She could hear her voice quiver. "Mama and myself met him when we went to the African Church. He's a Class Leader there."

"And you went to his house?"

"He invited us to attend the prayer meetings and Bible study at his shop with some members of the church. Mistress Johnson said . . ."

Master Radcliffe cut her off: "Did he ever talk about any insurrection of the blacks against the whites?"

"No, Master Radcliffe. He never said anything like that."

"What did he talk about?"

"He read to us from the Bible. He preached about Moses delivering the Children of Israel out of their bondage in Egypt to the Promised Land. We prayed and sang Negro spirituals, Master Radcliffe."

James Radcliffe turned to look at Lucinda's mama.

"Is that right, Mary?"

"Yes, Massa Radcliffe. That be exactly what happen."

"That's good enough," James Hamilton said. "I've got five other witnesses. One of them is a white boy about her age. He's to testify about Vesey's complaining of the hardships suffered by the blacks and how the Bible says slavery is wrong. Her testimony will help support that."

Master Radcliffe turned back to Lucinda.

"You'll testify at Denmark Vesey's trial," Master Radcliffe told her.

"What am I to say, Master Radcliffe?" she asked, trying to hide her surprise.

"The truth. What you just told us," he said. "You may leave."

Denmark Vesey was apprehended Saturday night, 22nd June 1822. The next day he was led before the Special Court to have the charges against him read. He stood in chains, his shoulders lifted back, his head held up. He stared straight ahead, meeting in turn the eyes of the Magistrates and the Freemen. They could detect no fear on his face.

"Denmark Vesey," Magistrate Parker said, "You are charged by this Court with treason. The Carolina colony slave law of 1740 states 'every slave who shall raise, or attempt to raise an insurrection, in this province, or shall endeavor to delude or entice any slave to run away and leave the province, every such slave and slaves, and his and their accomplices, aiders and abettors shall, on conviction thereof, as aforesaid, suffer death.' These are the crimes for which you're to be tried."

The eyes of the Freemen of the Court fixed on the stout-chested, white-haired man in front of them. Denmark Vesey's own eyes burned with a dark light.

"I wish to be represented by counsel," Denmark Vesey said.

"Who would you like for the Court to contact on your behalf?" Magistrate Parker asked.

"Colonel Gross." Denmark Vesey did not know him, but remembered Captain Joseph Vesey had once retained his services when Denmark Vesey was still a slave of the Captain.

"He will be contacted. You understand his fees are to be paid by you?"

"I understand." Denmark Vesey said. "I expect to confront all witnesses." There was firmness in his voice.

The Magistrates shifted their focus to the Intendant sitting with the Freemen. Major Hamilton shook his head.

"This Court has witnesses who have agreed to testify only if their identity is kept secret due to fear of their lives," Major Kennedy said.

"Then this Court is not fair," Denmark Vesey said.

His words were ignored.

"Guard," Magistrate Parker said. "Take this prisoner back to his cell."

Thursday, 27th June 1822, Denmark Vesey's trial began. At the behest of his counsel, Colonel G. W. Gross, and reluctantly approved by the Magistrates, Denmark Vesey's chains were removed, and a chair put in place so that Vesey could sit during witnesses' testimony.

During the entire trial, Denmark Vesey sat with his arms folded and his head bowed. He stared at the floor, unmoving. Only once during the testimony of the witnesses did he look up. He appeared to pay great attention to the words given against him, but throughout remained head down and immobile. The cramped chamber of the Work House was unbearably hot and stuffy. The summer Charleston climate could be the most egregiously uncomfortable known to man: humid, hot, the air thick and stuffy. Sweat rolled off Vesey's head, and the members of the Court repeatedly wiped their brow with their handkerchiefs and worked their hand-fans to stir the air. Cups of water were passed around for all, but Vesey ignored his.

"What church membership do you have?" Magistrate Parker asked.

"None," was Denmark Vesey's answer.

He's trying to protect those at the African Church, the Intendant surmised.

The first witness called by the Court was William Paul.

"William, the slave of Mr. J. Paul," Magistrate Kennedy announced. "Tell the Court what you know about this prisoner."

"Mingo Harth told me that Denmark Vesey was the chief man," William Paul began, "and more concerned than anyone else." William then repeated the same testimony he had given in his own trial. "My master's Negro woman Sarah cooks in Vesey's yard." William paused and looked at Denmark Vesey. Vesey continued to stare at the floor. "He was Sarah's father-in-law, married to her mother Beck, and though Denmark and Beck have been parted some time, yet he visited her at her house near the Intendant's, where I've often heard him speak of the rising."

"What did Denmark Vesey say to you about an uprising?" Magistrate Parker asked.

"He said he did not like to have a white man in his presence. He said that he had a great hatred for the whites, and that if all were like him they would resist the whites. He studied all he could to put it into the heads of the blacks to have a rising against the whites, and tried to induce me to join. He tried to induce all of his acquaintances. This has been his chief study and delight for some time. My last conversation with him was in April. He studied the Bible a great deal and tried to prove from it that slavery and bondage is against the Bible."

"Anything else?" Magistrate Kennedy looked about the room as he asked, intending his question for the Freemen of the Court.

"I am persuaded that Denmark Vesey was chiefly concerned in this business," William Paul answered.

The room was hushed. Denmark Vesey continued to sit with his head bowed, staring down at the floor.

James Radcliffe looked at the other Freemen in the room. Did all Negro servants feel this way about their masters, he wondered. A serious effort by more than just the planters in the lowcountry was going to be necessary to ensure the Africans were held in check. A new era had arrived, he concluded. Congressman Pinckney was right. Free blacks were a serious and alarming threat. The town slaves, those who hired themselves out, those who fancied themselves as almost free: they were the most dangerous. They were the ones most influenced by the free blacks.

"Guard!" Magistrate Kennedy called, "Take this witness back to his cell." The Magistrate then continued, "For the record, the next witness is to testify in the absence of Denmark Vesey as he has been promised anonymity to protect his life."

Denmark Vesey had not looked up during the entirety of William Paul's testimony. Now, while led from the courtroom, he continued to stare straight ahead, his black eyes glimmering with a hard light. He did not look at the Magistrates. He did not look at the Freemen. The Intendant tried to gage Vesey's thoughts, but was unable to penetrate his impassive stare.

The Magistrates repeated their questions to the anonymous witness, Joe La Roche, the same dark-skinned African who had testified against Rolla Bennett. "I know Denmark Vesey," the witness said, rubbing the pink palms of his black hands nervously against the upper legs of his soiled pants. He then repeated the testimony regarding Denmark Vesey, which he had earlier given when testifying against Rolla. He had one day on horseback come across Denmark Vesey on foot, he said, that Vesey had asked if he was satisfied with his condition, then related the fable of Hercules whose wagon was stuck.

Satisfied with his testimony, the Court removed the witness from the room. Denmark Vesey was returned to the court chamber. His face was unchanged. He assumed the same stare at the floor.

The next witness called by the Court was Frank Ferguson. He stood nervously, his face damp with sweat. Intendant Hamilton felt a special pleasure that the Committee of Vigilance had tracked down and apprehended this slave, for the Major had participated in the hunt and the arrest.

"I know Denmark Vesey and have been to his house," Frank said in answer to the Magistrates' questions. "I've heard him say that the Negroes' situation was so bad he did not know how they could endure it, and was astonished they did not rise and fend for themselves. He advised me to join and rise. He said he was going about seeing different people and mentioned the names of Ned Bennett and Peter Poyas as concerned with him. He said that he had spoken to Ned and Peter on this subject, and that they were to go about and tell the blacks that they were free, and must rise and fight for themselves, that they would take the Magazines and Guard Houses, and the city and be free, that he was going to send into the country to inform the people there too.

"Denmark Vesey said he wanted me to join them. I said I couldn't answer. He said if I wouldn't go into the country for him he could get others. He said himself, Ned Bennett, Peter Poyas, and Monday Gell were the principal men and himself the head man. He said they were the principal men to go about and inform the people and fix them, that one party would land on South Bay, one about Wappoo, and about the farms, that the party which was to land on South Bay was to take the Guard House and get arms and then they would be able to go on, that the attack was to commence about twelve o'clock at night, that great numbers would come from all about, and that it must succeed as so many were engaged in it. They would all kill the whites. They would have their masters' horses and assemble together near the Lines, march down and meet the party which would land on South Bay. He said that he was going to send a man into the country on a horse to bring down the country people and that he would pay for the horse. He gave $2 to Jesse to get the horse on Saturday week, the 15th of June, about one o'clock in the day, and myself and Adam, also put in 25 cents apiece, and he told Jesse, if he could not go he must send someone else."

By this point in the trials, the Magistrates knew which questions to ask and they proceeded in rapid order.

"I've seen Ned Bennett at Vesey's," Frank submitted. "One night, I met at Vesey's a great number of men, and as they came in each handed him some money. Vesey said there was a little man named Jack who could not be killed, and who would furnish them with arms, that he had a charm and he would lead them. Vesey said that Charles Drayton had promised to be engaged with them. He said the Negroes were living such an abominable life, they ought to rise. I said I was living well. He said though I was, others were not, and that 'twas such fools as I, that were in the way and would not help them, and that after all things were well he would mark me. He said he didn't go with George Creighton to Africa, because he had not a will, he wanted to stay and see what he could do for his fellow creatures."

"Who were at the meetings at Denmark Vesey's?" Magistrate Parker asked.

"I met Ned, Monday, and others there where they were talking about the business. The first time I spoke with Monday Gell 'twas one night at Denmark Vesey's house, where I heard Vesey tell Monday that he must send someone into the country to bring the people down. Monday said he had sent up Jack and told him to tell the people to come down and join the fight against the whites and also to ascertain and inform him how many people he could get.

"A few days after, I met Vesey, Monday, and Jack, in the streets under Mr. Duncan's trees at night where Jack stated that he had been into the country round by Goose Creek and Dorchester, and that he had spoken to 6,600 persons who had agreed to join them. Monday said to Vesey that if Jack had so many men they had better wait no longer but begin the business at once and others would join. The first time I saw Monday at Vesey's. he was going away early, when Vesey asked him to stay, to which

Monday replied, he expected that night a meeting at his house to fix upon and mature the plan, and that he could stay no longer. I afterwards conversed with Monday in his shop, where he asked me if I'd heard that Bennett's and Poyas' people were taken up, that 'twas a great pity. He said he had joined in the business. I told him to take care he wasn't taken up. Whenever I talked with Vesey, he always spoke of Monday Gell as being his principal and active man in the business."

One by one, like the workings of a well-ordered plantation task system, the other witnesses testified against Denmark Vesey. Adam, a Negro man belonging to Mr. Ferguson, testified to the Court: "Denmark Vesey one day asked me to walk to his house, and there asked me for 25 cents to hire a horse to send up into the country. I put down the money on the table and asked what he was going to send into the country for. He said 'twould be for my benefit. As he would tell me no more, I took up the money and put it back into my pocket again. I afterwards met the man who was to go into the country, who told me he had set off, but had been brought back by the Patrol. He said he was going up to bring down the black people to take this country from the whites. I've been at Vesey's house and there it was I met the man who was to go into the country. He was a yellowish man." The witness pointed at Jesse Blackwood, who had been brought into the court chamber, "That is the man who was to go into the country."

Benjamin Ford, a white lad, about 15 or 16 years, gave the following testimony: "Denmark Vesey frequently came into our shop which is near his house, and always complained of the hardships of the blacks. He said the laws were very rigid and strict and that the blacks had not their rights, that everyone had his time, and that his would come around too. His general conversation was about religion, which he would apply to slavery. For instance, he would speak of the creation of the world, in which he would say all men had equal rights, blacks as well as whites. All his religious remarks were mingled with slavery."

Lucinda was next brought into the Court. She avoided the eyes of her master.

"How is it you know Denmark Vesey," she was asked.

"I got to know Uncle Denmark December last when my mama and myself went to the African Church." The Freemen broke into a subdued laughter when Lucinda said "Uncle Denmark" before quickly containing themselves. Denmark Vesey did not flinch.

"Go on," Magistrate Kennedy said, trying to hide his own smile.

"He asked us to his house and shop for Wednesday night prayer meetings and Bible study," Lucinda said.

"How many times did you go there?"

"Maybe a dozen times."

"Who was there?"

"Some other members of the African Church," Lucinda answered.

"What did Denmark Vesey say about a plot to rise up against the whites?"

"He never said anything. He read from the Bible, like the story of Moses leading the Israelites out of their bondage in Egypt."

Lucinda did her best not to endanger Denmark Vesey. She was emphatic about Vesey never telling her of a plot. The entire time she gave her testimony, Denmark Vesey still sat with his head lowered, staring at the floor. She could not see his face. When she stood up from the witness chair provided for her, Denmark Vesey lifted his head slightly. For the briefest moment, his eyes met hers. He again lowered his head. She knew from his look she had done the best she could.

The final witness in the trial of Denmark Vesey was Jack Purcell. He stood with his face turned so that he did not have to look at Denmark Vesey, although Vesey still had his head downward, staring at the floor. The fear for their lives that the trials created in the hearts of those charged who also served as witnesses left no possibility for Peter Poyas' dictate, "be silent." Jack Purcell needed no prompting by the Magistrates. The Intendant listened carefully, his own heart gladdened at the day's testimony.

"If it hadn't been for the cunning of that old villain Vesey," Jack Purcell sobbed, big tears in his eyes, "I wouldn't now be in my present situation. He employed every stratagem to induce me to join him. He was in the habit of reading to me all the passages in the newspapers that related to Santo Domingo, and apparently every pamphlet he could lay his hands on that had any connection to slavery.

"He one day brought me a speech which he told me had been delivered in Congress by a Mr. King on the subject of slavery. He told me this Mr. King was the black man's friend, and that Mr. King had declared he would continue to speak, write, and publish pamphlets against slavery as long as he lived, until the Southern States consented to emancipate their slaves, for that slavery was a disgrace to the country."

The testimony of Jack Purcell concluded the evidence presented by the special Court against Denmark Vesey for the charge of treason and instigating an insurrection of the slaves against the whites. Vesey's counsel, Colonel G. W. Gross, cross-examined each witness, but drew nothing that served to mitigate the Court's charges. Denmark Vesey raised his head and looked up only when his counsel had completed with the witnesses.

"I wish to examine these witnesses myself," Vesey said, turning his eyes from his counsel to the Freemen, and to Magistrates Kennedy and Parker.

The Freemen exchanged questioning looks but Magistrate Parker spoke up quickly, "Yes, permission granted. Go ahead."

Each witness, but for the one who testified in Denmark Vesey's absence, was brought back into in the court chamber and stood crowded together at the witnesses' spot. The Governor and the Intendant traded glances. The Freemen shuffled noisily in their chairs and fanned themselves vigorously. The day had been a long one, and their discomfort from the heat of the congested room was evident on their clammy faces.

Denmark Vesey stood and glowered at the witnesses, his bulging eyes set against the leathered skin of his black face. He watched slowly, like a trader inspecting details of the goods he is to buy. He trusted he could manipulate the fear in which he was held by these men in order to compel them to recant the testimony they had given against him. The guards standing in the room straightened stiffly, rifles ready at their side. Each time Vesey faced another witness, several minutes would pass before he spoke. Then he would thrust his round torso forward threateningly as he questioned them.

"Do you actually think these fantasies which you have concocted about me will be believed?" Vesey asked. No witness responded, but to the Intendant's pleasure each man met Denmark Vesey's stare. "William Paul, you say Monday Gell said this or said that about me, but what have you heard me say? Anyone can make claims about what someone else said or did, just as you have.

"You said the Bible teaches against slavery, and the blacks suffer so that if they were like you they would rise up against the whites," William Paul answered defensively, emboldened by his life having been spared by the Court.

"Yes, I have often expressed my views on religion and on slavery," Denmark Vesey said. "That I do not deny. What crime is in that? You say I study the Bible. Should not each one of us study God's Word to learn what we can? Do you read God's Word? You say I am an old man. Then what gain could I achieve from these accusations you make?" Denmark Vesey had often assumed a dictatorial, despotic manner with the slaves in order to get his way with them, but now the witnesses remained firm and answered him no differently that they had his counsel.

Denmark Vesey's tone changed. He began to implore the men.

"I'm surprised you make such claims. Why do you bear such false testimony against me?" Vesey stopped. Again, his eyes roamed the face of each of those who testified against him.

"You are a slave," he said. "Yes, I'm a free man. Is it your jealousy that makes you lie so?" He reached and took a drink of water from his cup. "Have I ever done anything to harm you?" he began again. "I've always been open to pray for each of you, to pray with you, to help lead you in the Lord's word. Is this the way you repay my kindness and concern and care for you?"

Denmark Vesey then questioned each man as to the dates when the various events or conversations took place, trying to get them to contradict themselves.

"Frank Ferguson, when did I ask you to join me? What were the dates, the times, and the places I supposedly said the things you claim?"

Frustrated that he was unable to catch the men in contradictions or conflicts in their earlier testimony, Vesey then questioned Lucinda.

"Did I ever say anything to you about a plot to overthrow the whites?" he asked her.

"No, you never did," she said. Her voice was shaky. Then she blurted out, as she began to sob, "You shouldn't have to die, Uncle Denmark. You didn't do anything wrong. You didn't harm anybody."

Magistrate Parker looked at the Freemen and banged his gavel. "This witness is finished."

"I have no more questions," Denmark Vesey said calmly.

Lucinda and the others were led by the guards from the courtroom.

"Do you have anything you'd like to say to the Court before judgment is made?" Magistrate Parker asked the prisoner.

Denmark Vesey looked about the courtroom, lingering as if lost in thought as he stared out the iron-barred windows. Sunlight filled the chamber, golden and iridescent. He stood so that he could see the Magistrates and Freemen, his thick chest and burly arms and legs vigorous and muscular even through his clothes, at odds with his leathered face, the balding white of his head, the white beard now thick and heavy.

"I am innocent of all charges which have been brought against me." Denmark Vesey waited some time before he continued. "What earthly reasons could I have to be engaged in such a course of action?" he asked. "Do you think I would risk my life and property, my possessions to join in such a plan?" He examined the faces of the members of the Court, his eyes steadfastly focused on each one before moving on. "I'm not a slave. I am a free man of color. Why would I do something so foolish, something to endanger my life, in order to achieve what I already have? My children, on the other hand, are all slaves. Perhaps they wish to be free. There is no advantage to me.

"Some of you know my reputation. I was for many years a slave of the sea captain Joseph Vesey. I was brought by him here to Charleston when he left a life at sea. By the Providence of God, I was able to buy my freedom from him. I have worked the trade of a carpenter in this city well over two score years. I've always done my work to the best of my talents. I have my own shop. Ask about the town regarding my standing. Yes, anyone who knows me knows I'm against slavery. Any man who was ever a slave feels that way. Is there a crime there?"

It was true. Denmark Vesey's reputation among the whites for his carpentry trade was such that when his name began to surface by the witnesses, even the Intendant did not at first think Vesey could be involved.

"I've lived in relative comfort and freedom, almost as you have. I'm far from being a young man. I could easily live out my days in the security of my craft and my belongings. Do you think I would risk all, give up my position, what I've worked so hard to earn in my life, with no promise of gain? What possible reasons would I have to do so? I have no inducement to join any such attempt, no advantage, no gain, no benefit. As this is so," and Denmark Vesey paused and stared hard into the eyes of the men in the room, "the charges these men make against me must inevitably be false. That is the only conclusion the circumstances support."

He paused again. The court chamber was silent, save for the buzzing of a horsefly which had flown through the open window.

"Each one of you surely knows what envy and jealously will lead a man to say or do." Denmark Vesey gestured toward the door used to bring in the witnesses. "Is it not obvious the acute jealously these men who have testified against me have for my status and my freedom? My accomplishments, my status, have produced such hatred, such a covetousness of me in their hearts, that they would say anything to harm and hurt me. Hatred and resentment and envy, these evil passions are the motives for the words spoken out against me here today, false witness and untrue accusations all. There is no truth in them, only lies."

Denmark Vesey stopped. He dropped his head toward the floor, then, again looked up. "As I said, I am innocent of all charges." He sat down heavily.

Magistrates Kennedy and Parker examined the Freemen for questions. The silence of the court chamber was thick as the stuffy heat. Magistrate Lionel Kennedy then addressed the prisoner.

"Denmark Vesey, the Court will deliberate on your verdict and announce judgment on you tomorrow morning." He then addressed the guard. "Take the prisoner back to his cell."

"Should the Court interview Captain Joseph Vesey?" Intendant Hamilton asked after Denmark Vesey was removed.

Magistrates Kennedy and Parker polled the Freemen. All agreed to have Captain Vesey appear, and the Intendant sent Warden Dove and two members of the Committee of Vigilance with a letter requesting the old guinea captain's presence. Joseph Vesey arrived late in the afternoon dressed in his finest apparel: black top hat, black redingote jacket, a silk cravat, black polished boots, and crisply ironed white pants. Well into his eighties, the Captain moved slowly in short, shuffling steps, supported by a long fancy gold-tipped walking stick; his body stiffly bent forward at the waist as from rheumatism. The skin of his face was pale white, spotted with red blotches where years of harsh ocean sun and wind had scarred him. But his bright blue eyes burned with a fiery fierceness and he was as alert as any man half his age.

The oath was administered to the captain, and questioning began.

"Captain Vesey," Magistrate Parker said. "The Court greatly appreciates your presence and apologizes for any inconvenience originating from our request. You have perhaps heard of the circumstances which induce us to seek your appearance before this Court?"

"I have heard but little, likely just rumors," said Joseph Vesey in his strong Bermudian accent.

"Suffice it to say this city has not seen the likes of which since the Stono rebellion in 1739. You once owned a slave named Denmark?"

"I did, many years ago now."

"Tell the Court if you would the nature of how he came to be your servant."

"During the Revolutionary War," the old slave trader related as he settled into the comfortable chair that had been provided for him, "I commanded a schooner, *Rebecca* her name, which traded between the West Indian islands of St. Thomas and *Cap Français* on St. Dominique. Santo Domingo you call it here."

"Traded . . . ?"

"Supplied the French of the island with slaves."

"Continue, Captain."

"In the year 1781, I believe it was, I took on board at the market of St. Thomas 390 slaves and sailed for the Cape. On that passage, I and some of my officers were struck with what I can only describe as the beauty, alertness, and intelligence of a slave boy we estimated to be about fourteen years of age."

"Fourteen years of age?"

"That's correct."

"And?"

"Life at sea, gentlemen, as you might well imagine," Joseph Vesey directed toward the Freemen, "can be very lonely and very dreary. Especially on a slave trader." The old man spoke slowly, as if choosing his words carefully. "Men will do most anything to entertain themselves." Joseph Vesey cleared his throat. "Some of my officers took the boy and on the voyage made what I would describe as a pet of him."

"A pet?"

"Yes, a pet. A companion, a . . . the boy was taken from the cargo hull and wet down with sea water as a wash and given new apparel. We called him *Telemaque* . . ."

"Telemaque?"

"The son of Odysseus in Homer's *Iliad*."

"Yes, of course."

"That name slowly became corrupted by the Negroes to how he is known today . . . *Denmark* or *Telemak*." The old mariner focused his sharp blue eyes on the Magistrates and Freemen. The room was nearly unbearably stuffy and hot, but Joseph Vesey showed no signs of discomfort. "When we arrived at the Cape, having no further use for the boy, he was put back with those in the cargo hull and sold along with the others. We returned sail to St. Thomas. Imagine my surprise when two months later on our next voyage to the Cape I learned from my consignee that Telemaque would be returned to my hands."

"What reason?" Magistrate Kennedy asked.

"The planter who had purchased him represented Telemaque as unsound and subject to epileptic fits."

"So you bought him back?"

"I had no choice," Captain Vesey said. "As was the custom of trade in that place, the boy was placed in the hands of the king's physician who determined that he was unsound. I was compelled to take him back and return the purchase price to the planter." The old man cleared his throat and again coughed, opened a handkerchief and spit into it.

"Guard, could you bring the Captain some water." Magistrate Parker said. Joseph Vesey took a long drink. "Then what happened?" Magistrate Kennedy asked.

"I had no reason to repent, gentlemen. For twenty years, Telemaque proved a most faithful servant. He sailed with me as part of my crew to the African Gold Coast in the purchase of cargos of slaves. We made deliveries of slave cargo to various ports in the West Indies, including here to Charleston. When I retired to the Carolina lowcountry and Charleston, he lived as a member of my household and served as my personal servant, always doing my bidding without complaint."

"How was it that he became a free man of color?"

"I guess it was God's work," the Captain replied, "or fate, if you don't believe in God. In 1799, he drew a prize in the East Bay Street Lottery. He then petitioned my wife and me to let him purchase his freedom. After much deliberation, I elected to grant his request. He had always served me well. I had no grievances. I let him buy his freedom for $600."

"$600!"

"I knew it was less than his real worth," Captain Vesey said, "especially for a man of his strength and intelligence. He began about that time the trade of a carpenter. I have heard he distinguished himself by his great strength and activity, just some talk here and there over the years by those who knew he was once my slave. That's all I can tell, gentlemen. I have not seen Telemaque in years. And that was all a long time ago now, over twenty years I reckon."

"Magistrates Kennedy and Parker, Gentlemen Freemen," Intendant James Hamilton addressed the Court, "may I ask the Captain a few questions?"

"Certainly, Major."

"Captain Vesey, what do you know of his wives and children?"

"I know he had several wives . . . if that's what you want to call the wenches . . . while he was my servant. But I don't recall ever actually encountering any of them. I believe they were all domestics here. And he may have had some relations with women in the West Indies before Charleston. I've also heard he had some children, but I don't know the particulars. Frankly, Major, it made no difference to me what he did in his private life, if you will. As long as he did his tasks, he was free on Sundays to do as he wished. I never had reason not to trust him."

"Do you have any speculation as to what brought him to the point of advancing an armed rebellion among the slaves?"

"Not a single conjecture, Major. It is an enigma I cannot fathom." The old man made a smacking sound with his lips. "He had a good life for a slave," Joseph Vesey added as in afterthought. "I never had reason to have him whipped. Perhaps the only mistake I made was treating him as an equal. And I sold him his freedom. I thought I knew him better than anyone, but I guess that was not the case. There must be another side to him he kept hidden all these years."

Intendant Hamilton seemed satisfied.

"Anything else?" Magistrate Kennedy asked. No one spoke. "Captain Vesey, the Court again expresses its sincere appreciation for your testimony to us today. Due to the character of this Court and the serious nature of the charges against those on trial your strictest confidence is required and you are asked not to discuss your testimony with anyone."

"Certainly," Captain Vesey said. He stood with a guard's assistance, and walked slowly using his cane into the dark corridor, which led from the chamber through the Work House and out into the brilliant Charleston sun.

Friday, 28th June 1822 Denmark Vesey remained imprisoned in a cell as he waited to be called back to the court chamber to hear the verdict. Even in the cells, the prisoners were chained. The guard brought him a plate of cold food. He refused to eat. The others had already been convicted and the judgment of death by hanging passed upon them. Their faces wore the stress of fear. Only Peter Poyas remained fervent in his determination to maintain silence.

"Be strong, Denmark," Peter told his friend. "That's what you said to us, remember?"

In the middle of the afternoon, the guard returned to escort Denmark

Vesey to the courtroom. The prisoner remained in chains, given no special consideration.

Denmark Vesey stood solitary and motionless before the Court. If a man's face can show no emotion, his showed none. He stared straight ahead, his eyes focused on some place beyond the room. The Freemen sat still, not even fanning themselves in the stifling heat of the late June afternoon. Reaching out from the Work House, the streets of Charleston droned with the din of voices, the clamor of slaves scurrying back and forth on their tasks. The wharves of the harbor spurred with water traffic, bright white clipper and schooner sails, black faces and black backs glistening with streaks of sweat, the sweep of wind, while off in the distance the rumble of a growing thunderstorm charged the air with an electric edge.

Magistrate Lionel Kennedy read the verdict: "Denmark Vesey, the Court, on mature consideration, has pronounced you guilty. You have enjoyed the advantage of able Counsel, and were also heard in your own defense, in which you endeavored, with great art and plausibility, to impress a belief of your innocence. After the most patient deliberation, however, the Court was not only satisfied with your guilt, but that you were the author and original instigator of this diabolical plot. Your professed design was to trample on all laws, human and divine, to riot in blood, outrage, rapine, and conflagration and to introduce anarchy and confusion in their most horrid forms.

"Your life has become, therefore, a just and necessary sacrifice, at the shrine of indignant justice.

"It is difficult to imagine what infatuation could have prompted you to attempt an enterprise so wild and visionary. You were a free man; were comparatively wealthy, and enjoyed every comfort compatible with your situation. You had, therefore, much to risk, and little to gain. From your age and experience, you ought to have known that success was impracticable.

"A moment of reflection must have convinced you that the ruin of your race would be the probable result, and that years would have rolled away before they could have recovered that confidence which they have enjoyed in this community. The only reparation in your power is a full disclosure of the truth. In addition to treason, you have committed the grossest impiety in attempting to pervert the sacred words of God into a sanction for crimes of the blackest hue. It is evident that you are totally insensible of the divine influence of that Gospel "all whose paths are peace." It was to reconcile us to our destinies on earth, and to enable us to discharge with fidelity all the duties of life, that those holy precepts were imparted by Heaven to fallen man.

"If you had searched them with sincerity, you would have discovered instructions, immediately applicable to the deluded victims of your artful wiles: 'Servants,' says St. Paul, 'obey in all things your masters, according to the flesh, not with eye service, as menpleasers, but in singleness of heart, fearing God.' And again, 'Servants,' says St. Peter, 'be subject to your masters with all fear, not only to the good and gentle, but also to the forward.' On such texts comment is unnecessary.

"Your 'lamp of life' is nearly extinguished; your race is run, and you must shortly pass 'from time to eternity.' Let me then conjure you to devote the remnant of your existence in solemn preparation for the awful doom that awaits you. Your situation is deplorable, but not destitute of spiritual consolation. To that Almighty Being alone, whose Holy Ordinances you have trampled in the dust, you can now look for mercy, and although 'your sins be as scarlet,' the tears of sincere penitence may obtain forgiveness at the 'Throne of Grace.' You cannot have forgotten the history of the malefactor on the Cross, who, like yourself, was the wretched and deluded victim of offended justice. His conscience was awakened in the pangs of dissolution, and yet there is reason to believe, that his spirit was received into the realms of bliss. May you imitate his example, and may your last moments prove like his."

The Court sat in silence after the pronouncement by Magistrate Kennedy. Denmark Vesey stood as he had before the reading of the sentence, but in the lamplights of the chamber the Magistrates and Freemen could see a small trail of tears trickle down the prisoner's cheeks. The men in the courtroom did not understand. They thought the tears from fear of death. Only the Intendant recognized they were something else. He had seen fear often enough before. But if not fear, or regret, what were they, the Intendant questioned?

They were tears of pride. His labor had been for a glorious cause, Denmark Vesey vowed to himself. He was an agent in God's work, not the toil of man. He had not failed. He had stood on the mountain top and looked off in the distance where he could see the Promised Land. Others would follow in his footsteps. His people would one day be free.

"Do you have anything to say to the Court?" Magistrate Parker asked.

Denmark Vesey shook his head no and continued to stare somewhere beyond them.

"Then you are sentenced to die by hanging the morning of July 2nd. May God see fit to watch over your soul. Guard, return the prisoner to his cell," the Magistrate concluded.

The armed guard poked his musket in Denmark Vesey's back, prodding him to the chamber door in short steps due to the chains on his ankles. Denmark Vesey halted midway, and turned to face the Magistrates and Freemen.

"I would like a Bible brought to my cell," he said.

The Magistrates looked from their bench down at the Freemen. No one countered the request.

"Guard," said Magistrate Parker, "and get the prisoner a Bible."

"What horror to think these wretched fellows thought for an instant their wicked plan would breed success," James Radcliffe said to James Hamilton as the two men sat in the Intendant's parlor room at the end of the day's court proceedings. "I must admit, Major, I never thought the day would come when I would see such a threat. There've been other attempts at revolt over the generations, but certainly not in the fashion as this one."

The Intendant reflected on his new friend's words as the tobacco smoke from the Major's pipe curled upward toward the room's high ceiling. "All this talk with Missouri coming into the Union of the beautiful propositions of civil and natural freedom was made with a wanton recklessness of their consequences when applied to the condition of a certain portion of our common country," the Intendant said philosophically. "Too many of us have indulged our slaves with freedom of movement and instruction, and allowing them to conduct church services on their own. In that setting, Denmark Vesey's mad ambition and hatred for the whites spread like a fever."

"How many slaves hate their masters," James Radcliffe shared the thoughts he had earlier considered to himself, "enough to rise up and murder them in cold blood? We must exercise grave caution, Major. Charles Pinckney many times said the free blacks pose a serious and dangerous threat. I now see how right he was."

"That is the very reason we must be ever vigilant now and in the future." the Intendant said. "This Denmark Vesey, without question, the plot originated with him. Imagine! Four years they say he went about his crusade to agitate the blacks against the whites. And we heard not a word. The African Church was his means to congregate the blacks. I am certain of it.

"Vesey gave but one indication of his guilt while he was held in his cell before trial," the Intendant said, and he stood and opened the desk in the room, pulling out for display the wigs and whiskers the blacks were to wear the night of the insurrection in order to disguise themselves and look like white men. "It was the single time he was caught unawares. We discovered the French hairdresser Vesey employed to make these. I took the barber to Vesey in his cell. 'Do you know this man?' I asked Vesey. With the greatest effrontery and composure Vesey denied ever having ever seen him. I then took from my pocket the very wig made for Vesey himself. This one right here." The Intendant pointed to one of the wigs exhibited on the desk. "Vesey was stunned. 'Good God!' he said and remained silent for a moment or two. Then he admitted the wig was made for him and that he knew the hair dresser."

James Hamilton returned the hairpieces to the drawer of his desk. "I regret we placed all the prisoners together in one cell while they were held in the Work House," James Hamilton said. "I would change that if we could go back over events again. Vesey and the others adhered to Peter Poyas' directive to "die silent." Otherwise we might have broken Vesey's will and got him to talk. There are so many things, James, so many things we may never know. I'm convinced all decisions and control were in Vesey's hands. Only he can provide the information we don't have. But I know one thing, the more conspirators we charge and convict and hang, the more we'll guarantee it never happens again."

July in Charleston was usually the quietest time of the year. The planter class took refuge from the tropical humidity, the heat of summer, and the threat of swamp fever by escaping from their lowcountry plantations, some to destinations as far away as aristocratic Nantucket, Rhode Island, others like the Radcliffes to Flat Rock in the mountains of western North Carolina. Some journeyed the twenty miles from Charleston to their summer homes in Summerville, or Saint John's or Sullivan's Islands where the breezes from the ocean helped reduce the discomfort of the heat. But the summer of 1822 was not a quiet or typical Charleston July. The city was abuzz with rumor and speculation. As reports of the uprising and trials spread, a climate of fear, a threat of danger, pervaded the city. The enslavement of a majority of the city's inhabitants created an underlying tension, a subject rarely spoken of but always present, submerged just beneath the surface like a vicious shark swimming below the waves, prowling for prey. The whites' worst fears seemed to be coming true. The streets were lined with armed Patrols after dark. Governor Bennett and Intendant Hamilton ordered a strong display of local and state militia and letters were written to Secretary of War and South Carolina native John C. Calhoun requesting the support of heavily armed federal troops. The city was on alert, on edge. And each day the trials continued.

A platform with gallows for the hangings was constructed on Blake's Lands, a filled-in marsh lowland beside the Cooper River, near Hampstead beyond the city lines of Charleston. Tuesday, 2nd July 1822 at dawn the six convicted insurrectionists, Denmark Vesey, Rolla Bennett, Batteau Bennett, Ned Bennett, Peter Poyas, and Jesse Blackwood were chained and force marched from the Work House across the city to the gallows. Guards on horseback and on foot armed with long-barreled rifles, pistols, and bayonets, surrounded the condemned men, wary of any impending attack from blacks intent on attempting to free the prisoners. The crowd that gathered along the route to watch was forced to stand far back. No blacks were allowed to get anywhere near the prisoners.

The *City Gazette* carried a notice of the scheduled executions. A large crowd, black and white, pressed against the line of guards to see the hangings. The blacks who had come to watch were ordered to the rear. The sun burned down from the sky, already at early morning a yellow fireball of heat. A handful of young boys, white and black, climbed the oak trees at the edge of the crowd and perched on the limbs to watch. On the raised-up platform at each end of the gallows, members of the militia stood with their guns held in place surveying the crowd. The convicted men's hands were bound and their legs shackled with chains. They were led one at a time onto the scaffold. The crowd clamored with excitement. Someone in the front whooped loudly. Several people whistled.

The ropes for the hangings were thick and braided together like an arbor-choking vine, a noose knotted at the end of each rope. The rebels were led by the Negro hangman across the platform into position, a noose ringed about their necks and tightened into place. No black-flocked minister in a white collar stood hatless at the edge of the platform, or approached each prisoner and spoke softly so the crowd could not hear. No clergyman gestured the shape of the cross in the front of the convicted men's faces or looked heavenward as he mouthed a silent prayer. The

Intendant had ordered the fated men to have no last minute rights of prayer or confession.

The muttering of the crowd grew hushed in anticipation. In the distance, faintly from the heart of the city, the bells tolled the hours from Saint Michael's steeple. A collective gasp went up from the onlookers as the trap doors under the convicted men were released and swung open, the sound ricocheting across the field. Each man's body suddenly dropped heavily through the yawning port and the ropes snapped into place at their throats, tugging their heads to a quick stop. There was the crack of broken necks, a horrible, painful sound, and an involuntary unified moan issued from the crowd. Several of the men's legs began to kick in a violent spasm, momentarily active in futile response.

A guard on horseback with a rifle at his shoulder rode in front of the gallows as the crowd pushed forward and he took his gun and with one single shot fired into the chest of each hanging man. The limp bodies hung from the ropes like counter-weights on the lock pump of a rice-pond. Somewhere in the crowd a hoarse call rose up and the din from the throng seemed to take on a life of its own, a life of groans and cheers and wails.

Armed guards remained stationed around the gallows and the bodies hung on display as examples to the slaves. At sundown the bodies were taken down and thrown in a mule cart to be delivered to the surgeons to conduct autopsies or for use in medical classes, before burial in unmarked graves in unsanctified swamp land.

The hanging of Denmark Vesey was held for last. He was forced up the steps of the gallows, a guard's rifle digging him in the back, his feet, waist, arms, and hands shackled by chains that clanked with each step, scraping noisily against the wooden floor of the scaffold. The oppressive heat of the July sun scorched the damp air. Beads of sweat glistened in luxuriant sheen and ran down Denmark Vesey's face. He squinted his eyes in the harsh morning sunlight that fell across his face. He looked out above the crowd, like a sailor in the crow's nest staring out over a great stretch of sea trying to spy a speck of land at the far edge of the waterline. The crowd fell silent. Hidden in the shade of a nearby palmetto palm, a solitary mockingbird sang foolishly. The hangman lifted the noose over Denmark Vesey's head and fitted the loop around his thick neck, slipping the knot tighter. The hangman stepped back. The lever on the trap door was pulled and the door dropped open beneath Denmark Vesey's feet.

Lucinda stood on tiptoe near the back of the crowd. She strained to see over the heads of those in front of her, but as the retort of the trap door thudded dully in her ears, her heart sank and she struggled not to be sick. The white observers of the hanging at the front shouted out in celebration. The blacks all around her were stone silent. The sound of the rifle shot reverberated through the crowd as the guard on horseback raised his gun and fired into the body of Denmark Vesey. A dark cloud moved across the sky blocking the sun, and the shadow covered the crowd. She realized hot tears wet her face.

Denmark Vesey was dead.

Lucinda elbowed her way slowly out of the crowd and vomited on the ground. She stood crying hysterically, gasping for air.

A thin, slightly-built black man come up to her, leaning his face close to her ear.

"Lucinda," he said faintly, "It's me." She did not recognize him until he spoke.

"Gullah . . . ?"

"Shhhh." he whispered, looking frantically over his shoulders.

The man before her did not look like the Gullah Jack she knew. The big side whiskers were gone. A black patch covered his bad eye. "This way," he said, tilting his head, directing her away from the crowd.

They walked away and stepped behind a tree so as not be seen or heard.

"He's dead, Gullah Jack," Lucinda whimpered between her sobs. "They killed him."

"Revenge," Gullah Jack said to her in a fierce whisper. "We must seek revenge."

She tried to control her tears. "What are you doing here?" she finally asked.

"I'm in disguise," he said softly, still looking about to make certain he was not heard.

"I didn't recognize you."

"Good." He looked around again. "I tried to put together an army to storm the gallows and save Rolla and Denmark but the others are cowards."

"They made me testify at Denmark Vesey's trial," she said, and began crying again.

"What did you say?"

"I told them Uncle Denmark preached against slavery but never said anything of a plot to rise up against the whites."

"Did they ask about me?" Gullah Jack questioned her.

"Not to me, no," Lucinda said. "Come. We shouldn't stand here. You might be recognized."

They tramped together from the hanging fields, the crowd thinning behind them. They did not speak until they were close to the city. "I have to get some papers from Uncle Denmark's. I promised him," Lucinda said.

"He told me before he was taken up," Gullah Jack said. "He said for you to be careful."

"I pray now's the suited hour," she said. "I might never have another. Watch for me, Gullah Jack. Conjure a charm to hold me safe."

She had double tied the key to Denmark Vesey's shop at the waist of her clothes to keep it safe. The gate in front of the shop was unlatched. Gullah Jack stood away and looked up and down the street to be certain no one was watching. He whistled like a bird to her. She quickly entered the door to the false front and disappeared. She unlocked the shop door and entered, going straight to the wall where Denmark Vesey had showed her where his journal was hidden. She listened closely to make sure she heard no sounds from the street. The small blade to pull the nails from the wall was in its place under the work bench. The trap door in the wall sprang open. She took the journal and slid it under her apron, closed the trap door, and returned the small nails. She stepped out of the shop, locking the door behind her. She saw as she peeked from the false front Gullah Jack standing down the street. She looked up and down Bull Street. The street was empty. Gullah Jack joined her as she closed the front gate.

"Did you get the vial of poison I gave Denmark?" Gullah Jack asked.

"I have it hidden in a safe place," she answered.

"You may yet have need for it," he said. "We're still set to rise up against the whites."

"I must get back to Mistress Johnson's," she said, quickening her pace.

Gullah Jack stole down a side alleyway and disappeared. The next time she saw him he stood on a scaffold with a rope around his neck.

Thursday, 4th July 1822, Charleston celebrated the independence of the United States of America from the tyranny of the British Crown. There was a parade of brigade troops from Broad Street at Meeting to South Bay, where they were reviewed by the Governor. Then they proceeded to the Battery for salutes fired by the cavalry and infantry. The Declaration of Independence was read to the public at Saint Michael's church. The city's Intendant was one of the most visible figures at the day-long celebrations. The Major graciously accepted the praises he received from his fellow planters and freemen for the accomplishments of the special Court. He promised continued diligence until all the insurrectionists and malcontents were brought to justice.

"This Denmark Vesey," Master Johnson said to Lucinda, "I understand you knew him."

"Yes, I knew who he was. Mama and myself met him at the African Church. That's why Master Radcliffe had me testify at the trial. I told them Denmark Vesey never said anything to us about a plot for the slaves to rise up."

"My mother tells me you went to his house."

"With Mama for Bible study and prayer meetings. There were other people from the church there."

"Bible study and prayer meetings!"

"He talked about how the Bible teaches of the wrongs of slavery."

"What did he teach you, how to murder?"

She gave him no answer.

"So you believe slavery is wrong?" he asked.

"No one wants to be a slave," she said boldly. "Especially if you're already a slave. I've talked to other slaves at the markets and at church. Some of the wealthiest families I've learnt of from Miss Elizabeth treat their slaves the worse. They mistreat and torture them, Master Johnson."

"We're here now due to slavery," he said pointedly.

Again, she said nothing.

"My mother treats you and your mama well?"

"Mistress Johnson is most kind."

"I've tried to be good to you, Lucinda," he said.

"You have been good to me," she said. "No one's ever been as good to me as you have. Not even Miss Elizabeth. Every day when I wake in the morning until I go to sleep at night I think of being with you. Then I want to be your slave," she said with a sad smile. She began to remove her clothes. When she had finished, she sat facing him.

"Purchase me, Master Johnson, purchase me and set me free."

"I'm afraid I cannot."

"Why?" she asked pleadingly. "I'll be yours day or night, as often as you wish."

"As much as I might wish to do so, I cannot obtain your freedom,

Lucinda. First, I doubt my uncle would sell you. Certainly not to me. And if I made any inquiries to him he would immediately become suspicious as to why I would want to purchase you.

"Second, I could not set you free even if I did purchase you. This state has recently made it law that no slave can be granted freedom by their master without approval of the Legislature. No slave can now be freed simply by an act of manumission by their master.

"And you seem to have forgotten, Lucinda. I have a wife and a child. It's not easy for me to be with you now as it is. You must be satisfied with how things are. You're better off than any slave could ever hope to be."

"Don't you see," she said, the tears blurring her eyes, "a slave will risk all to be free. That's why Denmark Vesey is dead. He was a free black man yet he gave his life to try to make the slaves free."

"He was a monster! Lucinda, he intended to kill every white person in Charleston!"

She sat crying.

"If you're ever put up for sale, I'll purchase you and do everything I can to set you free,"

"Do you promise, Master?" She tried to dry her tears.

"Yes, I promise. Should I send you back now?" he asked.

"No,' she said, wiping her eyes. "I want to be with you."

"And you'll do anything I ask?"

"Yes, Master."

"Anything?"

"Yes."

When she did not bleed for a second month, she said to him matter-of-factly, "I'm with child, Master." His face showed no surprise. She thought when he learned she was to have his child he would no longer desire her, but instead it seemed to enflame his appetite. He sent her to the apartment two times without any discussion of the change in her state. Each time she wore her necklace. He was rough with her and struck her *derriere* with the crop whip. The room was hot and their skin wet with sweat. When she was leaving, he gave her an unexpected money note.

He said to her, "My uncle will send you back to Radcliffe Place as soon as he learns you're to have a child. You should do everything you can to hide your condition and delay their discovery for as long as possible. Once you return, I'll not be able to be with you, even as much as I'd like to do so." He reached up with his hand and pushed his fair hair off his forehead. "It's too dangerous for me. My uncle would never forgive me. He would disinherit me. Do you want to visit here again before you're sent back to Radcliffe Place?"

"Yes, Master."

"I'll see what I can do," he said. "We've at best but a week or two."

"The first time, Master," she said. "Take me as you did the first time."

She wickedly longed to be forced to submit to him. She was captivated by the detritus of the city, sinking deeper into the recesses of desire. The burden of the city's excess was like an iron chain gripped about her throat. The heartbeat of Charleston beat as her own heart, the rhythm, the movement, the tide. She was violated by her own will. She knew for her survival she had but one source of influence over him. She could not escape her fate. He exercised his power over her and she released herself to him. There was a part of her that loathed that she was a sinful nigger girl, filled with perverse lust. She wondered if she would ever be able to seek God's forgiveness. Would she ever be free, or would she always be a slave ready to submit? As she walked back to South Bay, her body shivered in the warm sun, shivers of craving, shivers of passion, shivers of torment constant in her thoughts.

Friday, 5th July 1822 Gullah Jack was taken up by the Committee of Vigilance and the City Guard at the wharves on the Cooper River. He immediately feigned the role of the ignorant fool, the way he always acted when around the whites. His charade continued when his trial began. Brought in chains into the court chamber, he stood limply at the prisoner's spot. His head swung uncontrollably back and forth like an imbecile. His eyes stared madly from his face, one eye set in one direction, his other eye looking off in another. Spit gathered at the corners of his mouth.

"Dearly beloved," Gullah Jack muttered almost unintelligibly, "we're gathered here today in the face of this company to join this man and this woman in holy matrimony . . ."

Magistrates Kennedy and Parker exchanged glances. Intendant Major Hamilton and the Freemen stared at Gullah Jack, and then turned to one another with expressions ranging from astonishment to feeble efforts to control their laughter. Who was this little black man before them who was muttering the hallowed ceremony of matrimony? Could this actually be the powerful witchdoctor and conjurer of the black Voodoo arts so feared by the African slaves?

". . . which is an honorable and solemn estate and not to be entered into unadvisedly or lightly but reverently and soberly."

Lionel Kennedy banged his gravel on the bench. "The prisoner will cease this foolishness!" the Magistrate cried.

"Where are the bride and the groom?" Gullah Jack asked, searching with his wild eyes about the room. He leaned down and looked under the table where the Magistrates sat. "Do you have them hidden under there? The Grim Reaper's looking for his bride, gentlemen. Have you seen her?"

Magistrate Kennedy banged the gavel again.

"If anyone can show just cause why they may not be lawfully joined together, let them speak now or forever hold their peace." Gullah Jack swung around and stared at the Freeman. "All right, men, now's the time to speak up if you got anything to say!"

"Guard, have this man gagged," Magistrate Parker shouted, his face red with anger.

The guard, a big burley fellow who, when he stepped beside Gullah Jack, made the conjurer appear almost tiny, took a handkerchief from his back pocket, folded it lengthwise, placed it across the face and in the mouth of Gullah Jack, and tied it tightly in the back. Gullah Jack continued to look wild-eyed about the room, moaning words no one could understand.

"Jack, unless you respect the decorum of this Court, you'll be gagged for the entire proceedings of your trail," Magistrate Parker said. "The choice is yours." The Magistrate looked at Gullah Jack's owner. "Mr. Pritchard, before we begin I'll give you the opportunity to speak with your slave for a minute and convince him to end this false madness. One minute only." The Magistrate looked at his watch. Gullah Jack's owner leaned over and whispered in Gullah Jack's ear. Jack nodded his head up and down.

"My slave will remain silent."

"Good," Magistrate Parker said. "Guard, remove his gag. The Court now calls the first witness." Magistrate Kennedy leaned over and whispered to his colleague. "Oh, yes." Magistrate Parker said. "Guard, remove this prisoner from the chamber and return him to his cell. Let him remain gaged. This first witness will testify *in absentia* to protect his identity." The Guard led Gullah Jack away.

Like numerous other revolutionaries tried by the special Court of Charleston in the summer of 1822, Gullah Jack was not allowed to face all those who testified against him. The Charleston authorities' iron fist of might that beat down against the perpetrators, the swiftness of the Court proceedings, and the severity of the sentences lodged against those found guilty, created an atmosphere of intimidation, of terror, a crushing weight that saddled the shoulders of every slave in the city.

"Jack Pritchard also called on me about this business," the anonymous witnesses testified to the Court. "He is sometimes called Gullah Jack, sometimes Cooter Jack. He gave me some dry food consisting of parched corn and ground nuts, and said to eat that and nothing else on the morning the uprising breaks out. When you join us as we pass put into your mouth this crab-claw and you can't be wounded, he said. He said, I give the same to the rest of my troops. If you drop the large crab-claw out of your mouth, then put in the small one."

The Magistrates, Freemen, Intendant, even the Governor, could not refrain from exhibiting a smile at this description of the superstitious nature of the Africans. Did the slaves actually believe, Intendant Hamilton asked himself, that they could make themselves invulnerable by such cookery?

The witness stood silent, confused at the sudden reaction of the Court.

"Continue," Magistrate Kennedy said, collecting himself. "What happened then?"

"Said I, when do you break out, and have you got arms? He said, arms a plenty, but they're over on Boundary Street, and we can't get at them now, but as soon as the Patrol is slack, we can get 'em."

"When did this conversation take place?" asked Thomas Parker.

"That was previous to the 16th June, on which day he said they were to break out. On that day, he came to me and said they would not break out that night as the Patrol was too strong. He said he would let me know when they were ready. That Sunday fortnight, the 30th June, he came to me and said I must lay by, they would not break out then, that he had been round to all his company and found them cowards. I said thank God then. He said give me back my corn and culah, that is crab-claw. I said I would not and upbraided him for having deluded so many. He said all his country-born promised to join because he was a doctor, a conjurer. He said all the white people were looking for him and he was afraid of being taken up, that two men came to his master's wharf and asked him if he knew Gullah Jack, and that he told them no. He said his charms would not protect him from the treachery of his own color. He went away and I have not seen him since."

"Did Jack Pritchard . . . Gullah Jack . . . say anything else?"

"On the 16th June, Jack requested me to let twelve men sleep at my wife's, as they were to break out that night and he wanted them to be near Boundary Street, near to King Street where my wife lives. On being refused he departed in anger and reproached me."

"What else can you tell the Court? Do you know of any others who are involved?"

"George Vanderhorst called on me yesterday morning and asked if I knew that Charles Drayton was taken up, and he was afraid Charles would name him, not because he was on his list, for he had joined Jack's company, but because Charles had met him at Gullah Jack's when they were consulting on the subject. He said if he heard that Charles had named him, he would run off. On Monday, 1st July, Charles Dayton told me that there would be an insurrection on the morning of 6th July, as soon as the Guards turned in. He said he commanded the country born company. Jack told me on the 1st of July the same thing and in addition that they were to rush with their dirks, guns, and swords they had got, kill the City Guard, and take all the arms in the Arsenal. He also said there were some arms in King Street beyond Boundary Street, in possession of a white man, which they intended to take, alluding to the arms of the Charleston Neck Company, deposited at Mr. Wharton's in King Street.

"The blacks would have risen on the night of the 16th June, had not the Guards been too strong. This I know from Gullah Jack and Harry Haig, who said that if the Guards were not too strong they would get the arms near the Lines, but if the Guards were out they could not get them to break out with."

"Any other questions," Magistrate Kenney inquired to the Freemen. "Do you have any other knowledge or testimony," he asked the witness.

"No, sir."

Gullah Jack did get to confront the next witness called by the Court, a slave named George, owned by the Vanderhorts. The moment the witness entered the court chamber and saw Gullah Jack staring at him from where Jack stood on the floor, George cried out in a loud voice, "Lord help! I'll be killed!"

Magistrate Parker placed his hand wearily on his forehead, dropping his head down toward the bench. Upon regaining his composure, he said to the witness, "You've nothing to fear. This man can't harm you."

"No, no, you wrong," shrieked George. "Gullah Jack, he a Voodoo doctor. He can kill with his conjurations!"

Gullah Jack did not speak, but his face suddenly set afire as with a flash of lightning, and he stared at George with a look of animal wildness, as a savage trapped but untamed. His face was one of intense hatred. He grimaced and glowered, clenched his teeth. He stared at George, the Magistrates, and the Freemen with his evil eye, as if trying to cast a hex on each of them with his stare.

"Help me!" George cried in terror. "Look!" and he pointed at Gullah Jack, then squeezed his eyes shut tight and turned his shaking head away.

"George!" Magistrate Parker said. "Listen to me! This man can't hurt you. He's in chains. The guards will protect you. There's nothing he can do. Now let's get on with this."

"Are you sho', Massa?" George begged fearfully, the whites of his eyes big on his face as he fleetingly glanced at Gullah Jack and then turned back to Magistrate Parker. Gullah Jack glared menacingly at the witness.

"Yes, we're certain. You've nothing to fear. Now give us your testimony!"

Finally calmer, although refusing to look at Gullah Jack, George began. "Gullah Jack's an enemy of the white people. I attended a meeting of several at his house, and he was the headman there. All present agreed to join and come against the whites. Jack was my leader. He's the head of the Gullah Company. I heard that among them they had charms."

Gullah Jack glared, his jaw set hard in place. He ground his teeth. He gave his countenance a look of the devil, or some beast, a wolf or wild boar, an animal on the hunt for prey. But he spoke not a word.

George continued to avoid looking at Gullah Jack. "Jack said if any man betrayed them, they would injure him, and I was afraid to inform. The little man standing before me is Gullah Jack, who had large black whiskers, which he has cut since I saw him last." Tears began rolling down George's face. "If I'm accepted as a witness and my life spared, I must beg the Court to send me away from this place, as I consider my life in danger from having given testimony. I have heard it said all about the streets, generally, I can't name anyone in particular, that whoever is the white man's friend, God help them; from which I understand they would be killed. I was afraid of Gullah Jack as a conjurer."

With the witness removed from the chamber, Gullah Jack remained standing in the prisoners' space, visible to all in the room.

"Did you wear big side whiskers up until just a few days ago?" Magistrate Parker asked.

"No," Gullah Jack said. "I ain't never wore side whiskers."

"Please observe, gentlemen," Magistrate Parker said to the Freemen, refuting Gullah Jack's assertion, "the map of where his whiskers were is clearly discernible on his face." Gullah Jack seemed to have heard nothing of the Magistrate's observation. He twisted his head back and forth, saliva dribbling from the edge of his mouth down his chin.

"Jack Pritchard," Magistrate Parker said quite loudly, "do you or have you ever pretended to be a Negro doctor or conjurer?"

Gullah Jack ceased the contortions of his head and suddenly stared wide-eyed at the Magistrate. "No," Gullah Jack said. "Sure ain't."

"Are you absolutely certain?" Magistrate Parker pressed him.

"Certain as these here chains be round my hands and feet." Gullah Jack shook his limbs, clanking the iron shackles.

The Magistrates then called Jack's owner, Paul Pritchard, who testified, "My slave Jack always wore a very large pair of whiskers which he prized very much, and which nothing could induce him to cut off. I often threatened to shave these as a punishment when he misbehaved. These whiskers I found to my surprise he had cut off about three days ago, and I wondered at the cause of it, little dreaming that it was to prevent his being apprehended by a description of him. I did hear some years ago that Jack was a doctor or conjurer. He is called Gullah Jack and Cooter Jack."

The Court heard other testimony used to confirm the guilt of Gullah Jack. Frank, slave of Mr. Ferguson, answered the Magistrates' questions by saying: "The first time I spoke with Monday Gell was one night at Denmark Vesey's house, where I heard Vesey tell Monday that he must send someone into the country to bring the people down. Monday said he had sent up Gullah Jack and told him to tell the people to come down and join in the fight against the whites, and also to ascertain and inform him how many people he could get.

"A few days after, I met Vesey, Monday, and Jack in the street, under Mr Duncan's trees at night where Jack stated he had been into the country round by Goose Creek and Dorchester, and that he had spoken to 6,600 persons who had agreed to join."

Harry Haig, another slave found guilty by the Court, confessed after his conviction his own guilt, and this witness's testimony was used against Gullah Jack, although by this time Jack had already been executed by hanging. "Julius Forest and myself always worked together," Harry Haig had stated. "Gullah Jack called himself a Doctor Negro. He induced Julius and myself to join at last, but at first we refused. Before the 16th of June,

Jack appointed to meet us at Buckley's Farm. When we got there, Denmark Vesey and Gullah Jack were already there. We broke up at daylight.

"Not quite a month before the 16th of June, Jack met us and talked about war. I asked Jack what he would do for arms. Bye and bye, said Jack, we'll have arms. He said he would have some arms made at the blacksmith's. Until Jack was taken up and condemned to death, I felt as if I was bound up, and had not the power to speak one word about it. Jack charmed Julius and myself at last, and we then consented to join. Tom Russell the blacksmith and Jack were partners in conjuring, and Jack taught him to be a doctor. Tom talked to Jack about the fighting and agreed to join, and these two brought Julius and myself to agree to it. Jack said Tom was his second and "when you don't see me, and see Tom, you see me." Jack said Tom was making arms for the black people. Jack said he could not be killed, nor could a white man take him."

Tuesday, 9th July 1822, the special Court of Charleston unanimously found Gullah Jack guilty. Magistrate Kennedy read the sentence as the convicted prisoner stood before the Court in chains.

"Gullah Jack, the Court after deliberately considering all the circumstances of your case, is perfectly satisfied of your guilt. In the prosecution of your wicked designs, you were not satisfied with resorting to natural and ordinary means, but endeavored to enlist on your behalf, all the powers of darkness, and employed for that purpose, the most disgusting mummery and superstition. You represented yourself as invulnerable; that you could neither be taken nor destroyed, and that all who fought under your banners would be invincible.

"While such wretched expedients are calculated to excite the confidence, or to alarm the fears of the ignorant and credulous, they produce no other emotion in the minds of the intelligent and the enlightened, but contempt and disgust. Your boasted charms have not preserved yourself, and of course could not protect others. Your altars and your Gods have sunk together in the dust. The airy specters, conjured by you, have been chased away by the superior light of Truth, and you stand exposed the miserable and deluded victim of offended justice.

"Your days are literally numbered. You will shortly be consigned to the cold and silent grave; and all the Powers of Darkness cannot rescue you from your approaching Fate! Let me then, conjure you to devote the remnant of your miserable existence in fleeing from the wrath to come. This can only be done by a full disclosure of the truth. The Court is willing to afford you all the aid in their power, and to permit any Minister of the Gospel, whom you may select to have free access to you. To him you may unburden your guilty conscience. Neglect not the opportunity, for there is no device nor art in the grave, to which you must shortly be consigned."

Gullah Jack Pritchard was sentence to die by hanging. The sentence was carried out Friday, 12th July 1822.

"How could Gullah Jack have known the words of the marriage ceremony?" James Radcliffe questioned the Intendant.

"Why, isn't it obvious, James?" the Intendant replied. "Morris Brown of the African Church taught it to him."

"That would explain it," James Radcliffe said. "Yes, that makes perfect sense. It did not occur to me."

"The Africans have begun to conduct their own marriage services," James Hamilton said. "Not that it makes any difference. Slaves can't legally marry, as you well know. But wherever that fool Gullah Jack learned of it, I remain convinced Morris Brown was involved in this plot somehow. As soon as the trials are over, I am going to drive him from this town. Whatever it takes. That will then be one less free nigger we have to worry about."

"And make it easier to close down that African Church," James Radcliffe said.

"I'm working on that," Major Hamilton said. "In confidence, James, I've got men who are ready to raze the church as an assault by a public mob the moment I give my word of approval."

Tuesday, 9th July 1822 the other convicted conspirators . . . Monday Gell, Charles Drayton, John Horry, and Harry Haig . . . were called before the Court to receive their sentences. "Death by hanging," the Magistrates read. At this point, the efforts of the Intendant, the Committee of Vigilance, and the special Court had resulted in the arrests, trials, and convictions of ten insurgents.

After receiving their verdicts, the four men were imprisoned in a common ward in the Work House while separate cells could be prepared for them. In this crowded single cell, the fear and frustration building up in every man began to show.

"Damn you, Monday Gell," Charles Drayton cursed his cellmate, "You're the one who led me to this most perilous and miserable condition.

You're the one who convinced me to join in this plot! A plot I must now pay for with my life!"

"Yes," Monday Gell replied without animus, "I'm guilty of you losing your life. And I'm guilty for the loss of my own. If we were not prepared to die we should have never joined in this business."

"Why should we be the only ones to die?" Charles Drayton wailed. "When there are so many others who are just as guilty." He wept openly, the tears on his cheeks.

Monday Gell agreed with his fellow conspirator. "Yes, there are," Monday said, "Lot Forrester, Bacchus Hammett, Tom Russell, Smart Anderson, Jack Glen, Adam Robertson, Polydore Faber, and all the others. We're all guilty. Don't you see, Charles, our sentence of death is what we deserve." Monday had resigned himself that he was going to die. "I'm strong enough to face it. You should be. Our fate is justly and precisely what we have the right to expect after our detected and defeated project."

The fear of death put a sickening taste in the mouth of Charles Drayton. He spat on the jail cell floor. He knew most of the men Monday had named, yet he had no idea they were as involved in the plot as he was. Just as Charles was about to question Monday further, the blacksmith arrived to place them in irons and chains, and take them to their separate cells. Charles cursed his fate aloud. Why was he to die when others would live?

The names of other conspirators who remained unknown to the Charleston authorities tore at the fragile and weakened spirit of Charles Drayton. No sleep came to him. He turned and tossed on the dirty straw mattress on the jail cell floor. The city outside his Work House cell was dark and silent. He could hear the scurry of rats in the corners of his cell. He thought he could feel the rats nibbling at his toes through the worn leather of his brogans. Worse, he imagined the hangman's noose about his neck. He knelt in prayer. "Lord," he prayed, "I'm Daniel thrown in the lions' den. I'm tormented and sore afraid. My soul is doomed to burn in a hell of everlasting fire. I beg forgiveness, Lord. Let me be forgiven like the thief on the cross next to Christ."

He feared his soul was damned.

"Guard! Guard!" Charles Drayton called out in desperation. "Send for Mr. Gordon."

Gordon, in charge of the Work House, came.

"I'm most anxious to see the Intendant," Charles Drayton cried, his voice quivering, his face still wet with tears. "I've some important disclosures to make."

A guard was quickly dispatched to inform Intendant Hamilton. The Major arrived at the Work House as the sun rose over the Charleston harbor on the morning of Wednesday, 10th July 1822.

The prisoner sat dejectedly on the hard jail floor, his legs and arms bound in chains. "I'm in a state of the most lamentable depression and panic," Charles Drayton sobbed to the Intendant. The prisoner's eyes were red and his hands trembled. "I'm prepared to make the most ample declarations. I'm afeard of death and the consequences of an hereafter if I go out of this world without revealing all that I know in relation to the conspiracy in which I have been so active an agent. All this past night, Master, I tried to pray for forgiveness. I tried but my prayers have not lifted up." He wept again, the tears on his cheeks.

"I'm prepared to hear your declarations," Intendant Hamilton said coldly and with calculation as he stood over the prisoner, "but you must be put on guard that no promises can be made to you of a reversal of your fate. Your everlasting soul might rest satisfied, and your situation cannot be worse by you coming out with a full disclosure of all you know."

Plagued by guilt and fear, feverish with desire to empty his torment, hopeful his secrets might yet spare his life, Charles' words erupted from him. "I've known of the plot for some time. It is bigger and more extensive than you've imagined, Intendant. Many are involved. I can tell you the names of those I know," Charles continued. "When Monday Gell and myself were placed together in the same cell after our sentences were read, he named others that I didn't know were involved. I can also tell you those names." The Intendant's pulse quickened. He could hardly believe his good fortune. The results of his persistence were beginning to pay their rewards.

The Intendant had paper, quill, and ink brought, and a list of names told by Charles Drayton written down.

"Those are all I know." Charles said when he had finished. "Monday Gell knows more than I do."

"We'll intern you in a cell with him today and leave you there until tomorrow," Intendant Hamilton said. "We'll say we're overcrowded with new prisoners and short of cell space. Be cautious. Don't give him any reason to be suspicious you're jailed with him merely for the purpose of getting information from him."

"Yes, Master," Charles Drayton complied. In his heart, he prayed his confession and sacrifice of others would save his own life.

The confession of Charles Drayton, and the names of others by Monday Gell which Charles passed on to the Intendant and the Court, opened a new chapter in the arrests and proceedings against the conspirators in the Denmark Vesey affair. Had it not been for this turn of fate and circumstance, the charges and the trials may have ground to a halt for lack of evidence and suspects. Peter Poyas, who remained silent from the moment of his arrest until his death, had not a single member of his party discovered. Such was the intent of Denmark Vesey when he charged his men to maintain utter silence, and threatened all others to be silent at the peril of death. But not all of Vesey's followers had the strength and resolve of Peter Poyas.

"Monday Gell knows more than he's told the Court," the Intendant confided to James Radcliffe as they sat in the Major's parlor discussing the day's testimony. "I'm absolutely assured of it."

"What can you do to get him to talk?" James Radcliffe asked. "He's already been convicted to hang until dead." There was a long silence before James Radcliffe then questioned, "Would it help to have him whipped until his will is broken?"

"He's one of the few on whom I don't believe torture would be effective," the Intendant answered. "He strikes me as far too strong willed."

James Radcliffe reflected on the Intendant's opinion. "This is not my first choice," James Radcliffe finally said, "and I do not wish to speak for the other Freemen, but if you're certain Monday's knowledge is truly valuable to the Court, even if he has already been found guilty, spare his life as an incentive to talk."

"It is not my first choice either, James, but it may be the only means we have," the Major replied. As was his habit, he pulled at his beard in thought. "He could offer a great deal to our efforts if he would but reveal what he knows, for I'm convinced he knows more about the plot than any one now alive, as well as the names of numerous members of the conspiracy. One of other convicted conspirators has confessed to us some names Monday revealed to him."

"What does the governor say?"

"I've not yet communicated with him regarding this," the Intendant answered.

"What do Magistrates Kennedy and Parker say?"

"I have not polled them either. James, please keep this private until I present my beliefs to the Court."

The arrest on Wednesday, 10th July of Perault Strohecker, and the confession and disclosures he made to his master, added to the Intendant's muscle. As it was, in three to four days, upwards of sixty slaves were taken up by James Hamilton's Committee of Vigilance.

As the Intendant had speculated, the most valuable testimony proved to be that of Monday Gell, who helped turn the Intendant's efforts into assured success, and served as the prime mover in the renewed mass arrests of conspirators. The crafty African realized he had something the Intendant, the authorities of Charleston, and the Court wanted. Monday knew it placed him in a position to bargain for his life. For fifteen years, he had survived the vagaries of life as a Carolina lowcountry slave. He knew he now had to be both subtle and shrewd. He could not give away his knowledge. He had to entice and tantalize the authorities, make their effort worthwhile to bargain with him. He held on to the most precious facts, dealt them out in small portions to build his value. When he testified against a newly charged conspirator, he introduced some small new bit of information, a detail that he guessed the Court could not know. Monday Gell's scheme began to have effect.

The Intendant requested a special meeting with the Magistrates. "He knows more than he's given us." Major Hamilton told them. "I've carefully studied the transcripts of his testimony. I have noted each time Monday testifies there is new information presented."

"What are you suggesting be done, Major?" Magistrate Parker asked.

"I'm simply saying we have to be realistic, Gentlemen. If we're going to root out this evil from among us we must sacrifice perfect punishment for a more perfect knowledge. This may be the only way we can learn of the complete nature of the plot."

"What sentence then?"

"I'm not implying we commute his sentence altogether," the Intendant said. "But in exchange for his continued and detailed testimony, I propose that instead of death by hanging his sentence be commuted to banishment beyond the borders of the United States."

"What is the Governor's view?"

"I shall write to him immediately based on your approval. But I thought it best to seek your opinion first."

The truth was as the Intendant claimed. Other than Denmark Vesey, Monday Gell knew more about the plot than anyone else, except perhaps

Peter Poyas, who had refused to talk and was now dead, and Gullah Jack, who was soon to be dead. Meetings to advance the plot had been held at Monday's master's harness shop. Monday and Vesey had written letters to President Jean-Pierre Boyer of the Republic of Hayti. When Monday learned Charles Drayton had informed the Court of what Monday had told him, and the Intendant hinted to Monday promises of a commuted sentence of death, Monday volunteered to confess his own guilt. He knew he had nothing to lose and his life to gain.

The courtroom had not been so overwrought since the trials of Denmark Vesey and Gullah Jack. Additional armed guards were placed on duty both inside the chamber and outside the Work House. The Intendant had ensured the Governor's presence, and His Excellency sat with a drawn melancholy expression fixed upon his face. The journals of the Northern states had been harsh in their treatment of the news of the trials and the initial hangings, and the Governor stung with a sullen sensitivity.

Somehow to the chagrin of the Court, a rumor had spread throughout the city that a major conspirator was to testify and reveal the names of a thousand rebels. Crowds of people filled the Charleston streets, pressing up to the edge of the barricades established around the Work House. A cavalry of mounted horses, summoned by the Intendant by sending members of the Patrol who were proficient riders to the stables to appropriate horses, patrolled the streets. Rifles were discharged in the air to discourage the crowd, whips used to push any blacks in the crowd back and maintain control. Two slaves were shot and killed. The throng was finally dispersed.

Monday Gell stood straight and tall in the center of the courtroom. Always clean-shaven before being taken up, his black beard had grown out during the time he had been held in the Work House, and added a round softness to his lean hard features. His eyes shone bright as polished onyx, No fear could be heard in his voice.

"I come out as a man who knows he is about to die," Monday Gell said to the Court. "Sometime after Christmas, Vesey passed my door. He called in and said to me that he was trying to gather the blacks to try and see if anything could be done to overcome the whites.

"He asked me to join.

"I asked him his plan and his numbers. He said he had Peter Poyas, Ned Bennett, and Jack Purcell. He asked me to join. I said no. He left me and I saw him not for some time. About four or five weeks ago as I went up Wentworth Street, Frank Ferguson met me and he said he had four plantations of people who he was to go for on Saturday, 15th of June. How, said I, will you bring them down? He said through the woods. He asked me if I was towards Vesey's to ask Vesey to be at home that evening. He said he would be there to tell me his success.

"I asked Jack Purcell to carry this message. He said he would. That same evening at my house I met Vesey's boy. He told me Vesey wished to see me. I went with him. When I went into Vesey's I met Ned Bennett, Peter Poyas, Frank Ferguson, Adam Ferguson, and Gullah Jack. They were consulting about the plan.

"Frank told Vesey on Saturday 15th, he would go and bring down the people and lodge them near town in the woods. The plan was to arm themselves by breaking open the stores with arms. One evening, Peirault Strohecker and Bacchus Hammett brought to my shop a keg, and asked me to let it stay there till they sent for it. I said yes, but did not know the contents. The next evening Gullah Jack came and took away the keg. This was before the 16th June. Since I have been in prison, I learned that the keg contained powder.

"Pharo Thompson is concerned, and he told me a day or two after Ned and Peter were taken up, if he could get a fifty dollar bill, he would run away. About two Sundays before I was brought here, he asked me, in Archdale Street, when shall we be like those white people in the Church. I said when it pleased God. Sunday before I was taken up, he met me as I came out of Archdale Church, and took me in a stable in said street, and told me he told his master, who had asked him, that he had nothing to do with this affair, which was a lie. William Colcock came to my shop once and said a brother told him that five hundred men were making up for the same purpose. Frank said he was to send to Hell-Hole Swamp to get men.

"Peter Strohecker is engaged. He used to go of a Sunday on horseback up the road to a man he knows in the same errand. One Sunday he asked me to go with him. I went and Smart Anderson. We went to a small house a little way from the road after you turn into the shipyard road, on its left hand. They two went into the stable with an old man that lived there. I remained in the yard. They remained in the stable about half an hour. As soon as they came out, Peirault and I started to town to go to church, and left Smart there. I was told by Denbow Martin, who has a wife in Mr. Smith's house, that Stephen Smith belonged to some of the gangs.

"Saby Gaillard is concerned. He met me on the Bay before the 16th June and gave me a piece of paper from his pocket. This paper was about the battle that Boyer had in Santo Domingo. In a day or two he called on me and asked if I had read it, and said if he had as many men he would do the same too, as he could whip ten white men himself. He frequently came to me to speak about this matter, and at last I had to insult him out of the shop. He and Paris Ball were often together. A week before I was taken up, Paris told me that my name was called.

"Billy Palmer and Vesey were constantly together. There was once in my shop a long talk between them about this matter. I begged them to stop it. Vesey told him to try to get as many as he could, and he said he would.

"John Vincent told me that Edward Johnson, a free man, had said, as a free man he would have nothing to do with slaves, but the night they began he would join them.

"I told Charles Drayton what uproar there was about this business, and since we have been here we have talked together.

"Albert Ingles came to me and asked if I knew anything about it, and I said yes. He asked me if I had joined. I said yes. He said he was one also. He said Adam, a free man, wanted to see me so I went with him one night. Adam asked me how many men had joined. I told him what Frank Ferguson had said. He asked me if I believed it. I said yes. He said if he could only find men behind him he would go before. Previous to the 16th, Albert said to me quit this business. I told him I was too far into it, so I must stick to it."

In his confession, Monday Gell still did not tell the Court everything he knew. He cautiously created the impression he knew less, and was a less active participant, than he was in truth. He lied and said, "I never wrote to Santo Domingo or anywhere else on this subject, nor kept a list or books, nor saw any such things, but heard that Paul's William had a list. Nor did I hear anything about arms being in the possession of blacks. I didn't know that Tom Russell made pikes, nor that Gullah Jack had any of them."

These false statements proved a fortunate gamble by Monday Gell. The Intendant was taking notes and scribbled furiously as the names of the conspirators spilled from Monday's lips: "Lewis Remoussin called at my shop and asked me to call at his house, that he had something to tell me, but I did not go. Jack Glen told me he was engaged.

"I met Scipio Simms one Sunday, coming from the country, who said he had been near the Savannah's to Mr. Middleton's place. I heard afterwards that his errand was on this business.

"I know John the cooper, who said he was engaged too in this business.

"William Garner said he was engaged in it and had got twelve or thirteen draymen to join.

"Sandy Vesey told me he belonged too.

"At Vesey's house, Frank told Gullah Jack to put one ball and three buck shot in each cartridge.

"Mingo Harth acknowledged to me that he had joined, and Peter Poyas told me so too. Mingo told me so several times. Mingo said he was to have his master's horse on the night of the 16th.

"Lot Forrestor told me frequently that he was one of the company, and I know that he had joined in the business myself. Issac Harth told me once that he had joined. He knew I was in the business.

"Morris Brown knew nothing of it, and we agreed not to let him or Harry Drayton or Charles Corr know anything about it. Bacchus Hammett told me in my store that he was to get some powder from his master and give it to Peter Poyas. He seemed to be a long time engaged in it, and to know a great deal. Joe Jore acknowledged to me once or twice that he had joined. He said he knew some of the Frenchmen concerned. He knew I was in it."

Monday's voice trailed off. He stood silent, his dark eyes as enigmatic as the nighttime sky on a moonless night.

"Is that all you have to say?" Magistrate Kennedy asked.

"Yes," Monday answered. "That's all."

The Guard led him out of the courtroom through the narrow corridor to his cell. The Intendant slipped a note to the Court Reporter, William Drayton, requesting he be allowed to review the court record to ensure he missed nothing.

After his confession before the Court, Monday Gell testified at future trials, and stated many things he had not earlier said. His testimony confirmed the Magistrates' and Intendant Hamilton's belief that Monday knew more about the insurrection than any other then alive. As a result, the Court agreed to recommend to the Governor a conditional pardon if Monday would tell all he knew of the plot and testify against all those charged.

Monday Gell complied with the Court's request. Several days later, he made a second confession to the Court. He stood in chains almost at the same spot on the floor, dressed in the same clothes that for many days had long begun to stink in the humid heat. His thin frame revealed the flesh he had lost since being taken up, his unshaven face gaunt even through his beard.

"The first time I heard of the intended insurrection was about last Christmas from Denmark Vesey who called at my shop, and informed me of it. Vesey said he was satisfied with his own condition, being free, but as all his children were slaves, he wished to see what could be done for them. He asked me to join, but I then positively refused to do so. I inquired of him how many he had enlisted, and he mentioned the names of Peter Poyas, Ned Bennett, Rolla Bennett, and Jack Purcell. I inquired if those were all and he replied yes."

Monday's voice was low and even. Occasionally, he would pause as if collecting his thoughts, and look at the Court Reporter for a cue to continue. He had lived as a slave in Charleston for a decade and a half, and only a trace of his African accent colored his words.

"Vesey then departed, and I had no further correspondence with him until three months ago. I was then walking in Wentworth Street on my way to a see man named Peet Smith, up King Street, and was accosted by Frank Ferguson, who told me he had just returned from the country, and had collected four plantations of Negroes. He requested me to inform Vesey that he would call on him that evening, and give him an account of his operations in the country. I went to Jack Purcell and requested him to carry the message for me, as I was busy. On my return home in the evening, I met Vesey's son-in-law at my door, who said that Vesey wished to see me. I accompanied him to Vesey's, and there found Peter Poyas, Ned Bennett, Gullah Jack, Frank, and his fellow servant, Adam Ferguson.

"Frank then informed Vesey he had collected four plantations of Negroes, and said he would start on Saturday the 15th of June to bring them to town. He said he would conduct them into the woods, and place them about three miles from town until Sunday night. Vesey then urged me to join and I consented. This was about three months prior to the 16th of June."

Monday lied again, for he did not want the Court to know he had been one of Vesey's earliest recruits. "Vesey, from that time, continued to visit the shop in which I worked. Peter, Ned, Vesey, Frank, Rolla, Adam, Gullah Jack, Jack Purcell, and myself were the party at Vesey's, and there agreed to enlist as many as we could. Vesey even ceased working himself at his trade and employed himself exclusively in enlisting men, and continued to do so until he was apprehended.

"Shortly afterwards Vesey said he would endeavor to open a

correspondence with Port-au-Prince, in Santo Domingo, to ascertain whether the inhabitants there would assist us. He said he would send letters there and I advised him to do so, if he could. Sometime after this, he brought a letter to me that was directed to President Boyer, and was enclosed in a cover, which was directed to the uncle of the cook of the vessel by which it was sent. The name of this cook was William. His uncle was to open the envelope and present the letter to Boyer. This vessel, a schooner, had been repaired at the shipyard at Gladston's Wharf, and was afterwards brought to Vanderhort's Wharf, where she was then lying. I walked with Vesey to the wharf. Peirault was in company with us, at the time. Vesey asked William the cook if he would carry the letter for him, and he consented to do so.

"We then returned, each of us to his respective home. Nothing extraordinary took place after this, and I met no band or association after this time, but Vesey's particular company. Bacchus Hammett brought a keg of powder to my shop, and said he would procure five hundred muskets from his master's store on the night of the 15th June. Bacchus also told me, that he would procure more powder, but he did not say where.

"The plan was to break open all the stores where guns were deposited, and seize them after they had procured the five hundred muskets above-mentioned. Vesey said he would appoint his leaders and places of meeting about one week before the 16th of June, but the meeting for this purpose was prevented by the capture of some of the principles before that period. Vesey determined to kill both the women and children, but I opposed him and offended him in doing so. Peter and the rest agreed to the opinion of Vesey in the murder of all. Sometime before any discoveries or apprehensions were made, myself and Peirault wished to drop the business, but thought we had gone too far to retreat. I knew personally of no arms, except six pikes, shown to me by Gullah Jack, which were made by Tom Russell. I knew of no lists except the one which I kept, containing about forty names, and which I destroyed after the first interruption and alarm. It was said that William Paul had a list but I never saw it. William Garner told me that he was to command the draymen, and that he had procured twelve or thirteen horses. Jack Purcell told me that Scipio Simms had been at the Savannah's, in the neighborhood of Bacon's Bridge, to obtain men. Denbo Martin belonged to the party and informed me that Stephen Smith acknowledged that he was one. Charles Drayton and Peirault have both seen Denbo at my shop.

"Vesey originally proposed the second Sunday or the 14th of July, as the day for the rising, but afterwards changed it to the 16th June. After the plot was discovered, Vesey said it was all over unless an attempt was made to rescue those who might be condemned by rushing on the people and saving the prisoners, or all dying together. Vesey said that as Peter and Ned were accustomed to go into the country, they must go there and recruit men. Vesey was in the habit of going to Bulkley's Farm. William Palmer and Vesey were very intimate. Jack Purcell knew of this conspiracy before myself. I do not recollect any person who refused when I applied to him. Some took time to consider, but they all finally agreed.

"Vesey was considered by the whole party as a man of great capacity, and was also thought to possess a bloody disposition. He had, I am told, in the course of his life, seven wives, and had travelled through almost every part of the world with his former master Captain Vesey, and spoke French with fluency. Morris Brown, Harry Drayton, and Charles Corr, and other influential leaders of the African Church, were never consulted on this subject, for fear they would betray us to the whites. Vesey had many years ago a pamphlet on the slave trade. Vesey said that his eldest stepson was engaged in this affair."

Prior to this second confession by Monday Gell, the Court had twice applied for and obtained from Governor Thomas Bennett a respite for Monday, Charles Drayton, and Harry Hiag

in order to secure from them the testimony they appeared so willing to give. On the 24th of July, after Monday Gell's final confession, the Court sent to Governor Bennett the following letter:

24 July 1822

Charleston

Sir,

We recommend that Monday Gell, Charles Drayton, and Harry Haig should be pardoned upon condition that they be sent out of the limits of the United States. We feel it our duty to state to your Excellency the reasons which have influenced us in this measure. These men are unquestionably guilty of the offences with which they have been charged; but under the impression that they would ultimately have their lives spared, they have made to us disclosures not only important in the detection of the general plan of the conspiracy, but enabling the Court to convict a number of the principal offenders. Having used these individuals as witnesses and obtained from them the knowledge they could communicate, we deemed it unnecessarily harsh and amounting almost to treachery, afterwards to sacrifice their lives. In addition to this inducement, we regard it to be politic that the Negroes should know that even their principal advisors and ringleaders cannot be confided in, and that under the temptation of exemption from capital punishment they will betray the common cause.

The Governor responded promptly, the Court receiving his answer the next day. His Excellency declined to conditionally pardon the prisoners, stating "the cases of Monday Gell, Charles Drayton, and Harry Haig would produce me considerable embarrassment, were you not clothed with authority to carry your recommendation to full effect."

The Court then reconsidered the sentences, unanimously altered them, and passed upon the three "that they be imprisoned in the Work House of Charleston, until their masters, under the direction of the City Council of Charleston, shall send them out of the limits of the United States, into which they are not to return under penalty of death."

Monday Gell testified against thirty-three insurgents. Nineteen were sent to the gallows and hanged. After the trials, he was held in the Work House until he was sold to a slaveholder from the Mexican province of Texas visiting Charleston to purchase slaves at the auctions.

The first executions, including the hanging of Denmark Vesey, had taken place at Blake's Fields on Tuesday, July 2nd. The other hangings of those convicted by the special Courts of Charleston in 1822 took place on Friday, 12th July; Friday, 26th July; Tuesday, 30th July; and Friday, 9th August. The site for the hangings was the upper end of the Charleston peninsula at the Lines.

Friday, 26th July 1822, the Court executed twenty-two convicted blacks, the largest mass execution in the history of the city. The Intendant, the Magistrates, and the Freemen desired to show what Major James Hamilton later categorized as "they cannot do what we can stop." The Charleston authorities had but one goal, to so terrorize the slaves of the city that no slave would ever again attempt such a rebellion.

"Captain Dove," the Intendant charged the Warden the evening before the hangings, "tonight at midnight, have all the prisoners from the Work House, the Jail, and those in the cells in the Poor House transferred to the vault under City Hall with the prisoners already there." The Intendant knew so many prisoners were slated to be hanged only the dungeon vault of City Hall could house them all. "Employ an excess number of guards,

Captain. All well armed," the Intendant emphasized. "Place every prisoner in chains. Tell the guards not to speak of this transfer to anyone," Intendant Hamilton said. "I want this done in secret."

"Yes, Major."

"For your own safety, Captain." The Intendant said, "in case the blacks have some secret plans of their own."

"I understand, Major Hamilton."

"And Warden . . . "

"Yes, sir."

"I want a rifle trained on every prisoner at all times. Tell your men shoot to kill at the first sign of an attempt to escape or an attempt by the blacks to free the prisoners. "

The following morning at dawn, the guards trooped the twenty-two doomed, chained men at gun point from the vault below City Hall out onto Meeting Street. Militia on foot and horseback crowded the streets with aimed rifles. The Intendant commanded from his mount as guards forced each fated man to sit upon his coffin set upon a mule-drawn cart driven by a slave. The grisly parade of death proceeded slowly up Meeting Street to the Lines. A huge crowd of whites as well as blacks gathered to watch the convicted prisoners.

Lucinda woke well before sunrise. The night before, she had begged Mama to let her steal away to witness the executions. She could not sleep, horrified and fascinated at the prospect of the hangings.

"Why you wanna see them men die?" Mama asked, but she told Lucinda she would look out for her while she was gone.

As Lucinda made her way from South Bay, cavalry patrols positioned along the streets and at every corner to prevent any riots or disturbance.

The city had never seen anything like the brutal horror of the scaffolds. Twenty-two monstrous gallows, twenty-two thickly braided ropes, twenty-two hangmen's nooses, twenty-two trap doors waiting for death to strike terror into the heart of every slave. Days and scores of slave labor had been used to construct the gallows.

The early morning glistened with a translucent softness, unusual for July, and the golden sunlight fell gently on the faces of the condemned men. In an eerie and surrealistic scene, Bacchus Hammett rode atop his coffin laughing madly, bidding his acquaintances in the streets 'goodbye'. Many waved back to him as he passed. The Guards with long-barreled rifles were everywhere. Some in the noisy crowd whooped and hollered in excitement as the row of mules and carts, and coffins, and criminals queued up at the Lines. Bacchus Hammett continued to laugh hysterically. His insane guffaws rang out and echoed in Lucinda's ears, impossible to forget. Each prisoner was shackled at wrists, waist, and feet, and the dang of the chains could be heard above the noise of the crowd. The Intendant, dressed in military finery, a royal blue jacket ornamented with numerous medals, brass buttons, and shoulder epaulets, led his steed in a canter between the spectators and the condemned. The Intendant looked for the Governor but did not find him in the crowd. One by one, the condemned men's chains were unloosed from the iron ring on their coffins, and the Guards shouted at the men to climb down and prodded them to line up at gunpoint. The sun began to glow hot. Sweat covered the brows of the men. Some of the doomed men began to shed tears. Some mumbled near silent prayers, begging God to save them. Others moaned and shivered in fear. One by one, the men were forced into place on the scaffolds. As the hanging rope was put about his neck, Bacchus Hammett continued to laugh luridly.

The Intendant knew hanging was a gruesome way to die, and it was especially horrendous that hot and muggy Tuesday morning in late-July in the year of 1822. The foot doors of the scaffolds released, but the Negro hangman had not tied the ropes properly around the necks and the hanged men twisted and agonized while they slowly strangled to death, groaning and choking as they begged to be dispatched to end their misery. Bacchus Hammett threw himself forward off the scaffold platform floor and as he swayed back, he lifted up his feet so that his knees did not touch the board of the gallows. In the mayhem of the crowd, a small slave boy was trampled to death by horses. Whimpers of gaging and suffocating delivered up from the men. Silence overtook the crowd. Intendant Hamilton caught the eyes of Warden Dove and signaled with a nod of his head. The Warden rode down the Line, loaded and discharged his rifle into the struggling, twisting bodies.

The special Court of Charleston adjourned with these executions, although four more slaves were hanged on July 30th.

A letter from Sara Johnson (Charleston) to Anna Moore (Savannah) :

27th July 1822

My dearest Anna,

You have by now certainly heard of the late unfortunate circumstances of our city. Yesterday we had another Act in this awful Tragedy—22 unfortunate wenches were at one fatal moment sent to render up their dread account—29 had been sentenced to be hanged but some were respited til 9th of August and 3 had their sentence commuted to perpetual banishment—the night was such as you may picture from a large number of Cavalry passing back and forth the whole of it—Gracious heavens to what all this will lead—certainly it will throw our city back at least ten years—28 have now been executed, and I am told that there are an awful number yet to be tried. Do not think I saw them hung myself—But I can imagine and feel. I understand they behaved with great firmness—A deathlike silence reigned in the City at that time.

Gracious Heavens, when I think what I have escaped & what I may yet suffer my blood curdles. Alas! Some too truly said, "Slavery was a bitter draught"—and I am afraid we shall in this country know it to our bitter cost some day or other. The plot was only found out by the noble interposition of a Negro whom they wanted to join them—he instantly with the subtlety of his class drew from his acquaintance the design plan and time & carried them with trembling anxiety informed his master, who instantly informed the Intendant and the Governor. Every means was then taken to protect the city—for the information was given only a few days before the insurrection was to have taken place! Their plans were simply these—they were to have set fire to the town, as the whites were endeavoring to out it, they were to have commenced their horrid depredations—it seems that the Governor and Intendant were to be the first victims. It is true that in our city the White & Black population is equal. I imagine the same are true for Savanah. I am told that the number in the plot is computed to be about 3000.

My brother was one of the Freemen members of the Court with other of the important and honorable men of our city. As he was sworn to secrecy, he has told me but little -- the streets are filled with rumors. James said no women knew of the conspiracy. But to think, I permitted two of my domestics to attend the services of the African Church, and I believe it is the generally received opinion that this church commenced this awful business or at any rate they took this for their rallying point. My servants even visited the house of the Chief of the plot, Denmark Vesey, a Free Negro Carpenter, who was a Class Leader of the Church and considered the Champion in the African Church business. He was among the first hanged with five other Chiefs 2 July. James says the plot was so secret it was in consideration for over four years without any whites being aware. My youngest servant testified at the trial of this villainous Chief.

The children were to have been spiked & murdered and I am told the words from a free black man taken up before the first hangings were, "I feel a little sorry for the children, but they must go, as to those already condemned, it is no matter that some must die for the cause—you have still many brave spirits among you—go on—booty Beauty & Glory"—this from a free born American—I thought not to hearing such a villain breathing the pure air of a free born America.

I believe all danger for the present season is over—but to any one at all disposed to reflect, or feel for others as well as their own interests, these recent events were calculated to excite much painful and bitter reflection. Nothing but the merciful interposition of our own God has saved us from horrors equal if not superior to the scenes acted in Santo Domingo. I never heard in my life more of a deeply laid plot or plots more likely to succeed, indeed "twas a plot, a good plot—an excellent plot."

"Did you receive the message my sister's livery servant delivered to you this morning?" James Radcliffe asked the Intendant as the two men sat in the Intendant's bureau.

"I did," James Hamilton replied. "And I'm happy to see you, James. I regret we were unable to speak before your departure for Radcliffe Place after the trials. We had to quickly call a second Court to attend to some unresolved charges, as I'm sure you've heard."

"I had to return to Radcliffe Place," James Radcliff said, "for I had been absent for a long while."

"Serving on the Court was burdensome for all of us," the Intendant said. "Thank you again for your service, James. We could not have done without you." The Intendant rang a bell to call for a servant. "I hope all is well on the plantation?"

"Things would be better if the price of cotton would hold up," James Radcliffe complained.

"How well I know," the Intendant agreed. "It affects all of us." The servant appeared and the Major ordered tea for his guest. "Any spread of the insurrection among your own slaves?"

"That was the other purpose for my hurried return to my plantation," James Radcliffe explained. "I wanted to ensure the plot hadn't spread from the city to the country. The slaves I believe to be my most trustworthy say not, if they can be believed. I'm no longer certain now if any can be trusted."

"I have something that will interest you," James Hamilton said, and he reached and retrieved a collection of papers along with his spectacles from the desk. "Magistrates Parker and Kennedy and I have prepared a calendar comprising those arrested, their owner's names, the time of their commitment, and the manner in which they were disposed of. I had the printer prepare copies for each of the Freemen. Here are yours."

James Radcliffe pulled his spectacles from his jacket.

"This first page lists Class Number 1, the prisoners found guilty and executed. This next sheet lists Class Number 2, those found guilty and sentenced to death, but recommended to the Governor they be pardoned upon condition they be sent beyond the limits of the United States."

"I see," James Radcliffe said.

"And so on," James Hamilton said, "Class 3, guilty and sentenced to death but respited by the Executive until 25th of October with a view to banishment out of the limits of the United States. Class 4, found guilty and sentenced to be transported by their masters beyond the limits of the United States. This Class Number 5 is the prisoners found guilty and transported beyond the limits of this State. Class 6, those acquitted by the Court, their guilt not fully proved, but suggested to their owners of transporting them beyond the limits of the United States. Number 7, acquitted and discharged. And Class 8 those discharged after being arrested, testimony against them not being sufficient to bring them to trial.

"And this final sheet is a recapitulation," said James Hamilton. "Thirty-five were executed. Twelve respited with a view to their transportation. Nineteen sentenced to be transported by their owners beyond the limits of the United States. One transported out of State. Eleven acquitted but suggested to their owners to transport. Fifteen acquitted and thirty-eight discharged. The whole number arrested was one-hundred-thirty-one."

James Hamilton removed his spectacles from the tip of his nose and leaned back in his chair.

"That includes the figures from the second Court convened 1st August to try William Garner, who had gone to Columbia before it became apparent of his involvement in the plot, He was to be Vesey's leader of the horseman and recruited blacks among the draymen. Found guilty and hanged 9th August. The second court heard thirteen other cases, James, with seven defendants convicted and banished beyond the limits of the States. Six were acquitted. The second Court adjourned 8th August."

"Extraordinary work," James Radcliffe complemented the Major. "You have every right

for the City to be most proud of you."

"Thank you," the Intendant affected modesty. "I'm almost complete with my pamphlet on the plot entitled *1822 Negro Plot: An Account of the Late Intended Insurrection among a Portion of the Blacks of the City of Charleston, South Carolina*."

"I look forward to reading it," said James Radcliffe.

"I'll be certain to get you a copy," the Intendant promised. "The price is one dollar."

Not everyone was as convinced as Intendant James Hamilton that the plot was as elaborate and fully-developed as claimed by the Court. And not all agreed with the procedure of the Slave Court. The most prominent of those who questioned the Court's character were Governor Thomas Bennett, and U S Supreme Court Judge William Johnson, Bennett's bother-in-law and a native and resident of Charleston.

On the morning of 21st June, an unsigned "Communication" was published in the *Charleston Courier*, which indirectly questioned the impartiality of the Special Court's slave trials. The communication was entitled "Melancholy Effect of Popular Excitement" and before long, it became known the author was Judge Johnson. The Justice told the story of an earlier hanging of a slave at the demand of a furious mob, a slave whose innocence was clearly irrefutable. Johnson warned of the potential dangers of rumors and false charges, of the danger inherent in mob behavior.

"You created quite a controversy with your anonymous 'Communication' published in the *Courier*," the Governor said to Judge Johnson, emphasizing the word anonymous partially in jest, although both men well understood the serious nature of the Governor's remark. The communication had resulted in a bitter public exchange between the members of the Slave Court and the Supreme Court judge.

"Not so anonymous, I would think," William Johnson replied, and he smiled a sheepish grin. "It certainly didn't take the proponents of the Intendant and the Court very long to figure out who the author was." The judge pulled at his slight chin in thought before he continued. "Do you agree with my points in the 'Communication,' Thomas?"

"Let's say I certainly don't disagree with you," the Governor said slowly, drawing out his answer. "The members of the Special Court, on the other hand, claim you insinuated the Court was capable of committing perjury and murder.'"

"Yes, yes, I read their response in the *Courier*. I know, they felt 'injured and defamed.'" The fair-skinned putty face of the Supreme Court Justice suddenly drew into a grimace. "That was not my intent, Thomas. The *Courier* chose to publish my communication. I simply sent it to them. I stand by my contention that hysteria and rumormongering are dangerous things. Don't misunderstand, from what you tell me, I recognize there was something of a plot affront. But the causes are infinitely exaggerated. With the lack of resources and organization, the uprising simply could never have ever gotten very far. A trifling cabal of a few ignorant, penniless, unarmed, uncombined fanatics . . . that's what this plot was all about, Thomas. Then a few timid and precipitate men managed to disseminate their fears and their feelings and inflated the strength of the conspiracy. You know that popular panics spread with the expansive force of vapor. "

"I concur with you, William," the Governor said, as if to apologize for the Court's actions.

"I didn't even know of the establishment of the Court when I sent my communication to the *Courier*, and doubted a Court would be necessary," Johnson continued. "I had no intention of interfering with the state authorities, and meant no reflection on the character or the reputation of the judges." The Judge's face began to turn red. "And then the Court sends a constable who hands me a peremptory demand for satisfaction! The Intendant has this honor or duel deportment. I'm washing my hands of this. The *Courier* has published my response, all sixteen pages." The Justice reached for his rum and swallowed a gulp. "I have lived to see what I never really believed possible. Courts with closed doors, and men dying by scores who have never seen nor heard the voices of their accusers. Trails must be fair, Thomas. Even slave trials must have some rudiments of fairness."

"I agree, William," Governor Bennett said again. "I'm equally committed to due process. My opinion is once the plot was uncovered the risk of danger was greatly reduced. Nonetheless, I have written two letters to Secretary of War John C. Calhoun, requesting federal militia be sent to Charleston."

"Well, no harm done in that I suppose," Justice Johnson said. "As long as federal forces are held in control."

"Listen to this," Governor Bennett said, and he removed a folded broadsheet from his vest. "I want your opinion. I also wrote a letter in the form of a printed circular which will be distributed to the general press. In it I say, "Servility, long continued, debases the mind and abstracts it from that energy of character, which is fitted to great exploits. It cannot be supposed, therefore, without a violation of the immutable laws of nature that a transition from slavery and degradation to authority and power, could instantly occur."

"Exactly, Thomas," Justice William said.

"I simply refuse to believe," the Governor said as he returned the paper to his pocket, "that the slaves of Charleston, including my own, could organize, and even in bitter hatred of the whites, seek murderous retribution and revenge."

"Why do the others not see this?" Judge Johnson asked.

"This affair has cast a shadow on the reputation of my governorship . . ."

"And this state," Justice Johnson interjected.

"One northern newspaper, the New York *Daily Advertiser*, described our events as 'the bloody sacrifice,'" Governor Bennett said. "Add to that my loss of three of my own slave chattel. I wrote a letter to the Court asking that a review be made of the decision regarding my slave Batteau and requested his sentence of death by hanging be mitigated."

"What happened?" William Johnson asked.

'The Court reviewed the sentence, but unanimously determined to maintain the decree of death."

Both Justice Johnson and the Governor were slave holders. Thomas Bennett was one of the wealthiest men in Charleston. Bennett's palatial home was situated neighboring his lumber and rice mills, where he employed not only more than sixty of his own slaves but hired numerous others from their owners on an annual basis. He had made his fortune by supplying timber and financing the development of the new residential areas of Charleston.

"I even requested that Colonel Robert Hayne, as Attorney General of the State and legal advisor for the special Courts, issue an opinion on the lawfulness of the trials," the Governor explained. "Intendant Hamilton did the same."

"What was Hayne's opinion?" William Johnson asked.

"The Attorney General expressed his opinion that the trials were lawful."

Bennett had conceded the ability and integrity of the judges. Instead, his emphasis was on the importance of the rules of procedure. The governor issued a message to the legislature, which described the procedural deficiencies of the trials, but it was shelved and remained unpublished. In it, the governor wrote, "the rules which universally obtain among civilized nations, in the judicial investigation of crime, are not merely hypothetical, or simply matter of opinion, but the result of the highest intelligence, instructed and matured by experience. They are given as guides, to assist the imperfections of human reason, and to enable it to combine and compare the various circumstances and probabilities, which occur in every case. Few minds are competent without these aids, to develop the intricate affections of the heart."

Bennett's plea was ignored.

Intendant James Hamilton, Jr. captured the most representative opinion of the public and press in Charleston about the Denmark Vesey conspiracy when he wrote in the introduction to his published report on the insurrection, "among a certain portion of our population, there is nothing they are bad enough to do, that we are not powerful enough to punish."

"Morris," James Hamilton addressed the free black man who stood before him, having the Reverend summoned to the Intendant's workplace on Broad, "As I'm certain you've heard, the trials of the conspirators in the Denmark Vesey plot are now completed." The Intendant leaned forward and fixed his stare straight into Morris Brown's brown-black eyes. "Do you know how many of them were members of your church?"

"Well, no sir, I don't rightly know."

"Let's just say it was a large number, a very large number. Virtually all the leaders were members and what you call Class Leaders."

Morris Brown said nothing.

"Let me get straight to the point," the Intendant said firmly. "Monday Gell testified that you were not consulted on the question of the revolt and knew nothing of it. I've decided to accept that as fact until I have evidence otherwise.

"There were others who testified you were aware of the plot and gave it your blessing. That you swore on the Bible not to divulge the secret, even if suffering death. They testified you said you were going to the North during the time of the planned insurrection and told the men not to mention your name." The Intendant did not give Morris Brown the opportunity to respond. "Regardless, Magistrate John White has come to me. He has issued a warrant for your appearance before him for violating the Act of 1820. Free Negroes formerly in residence here who leave cannot return to this state."

"But I was away on Church business . . ."

"It doesn't really matter whether the act applies to your situation or not," declared the Intendant. "You're not wanted here. I advised you of this when I had you in here before. You have five days in which to leave this city. Otherwise, you'll be convicted and banished."

"If you have any concern for me, promise you'll do all you can for our child," Lucinda implored Master Johnson. He had told her this was to be their final time together in Charleston.

"You cannot expect me to do more than I am able," he said. "I've told you, should the Radcliffes ever discover I'm the father of your child, it would destroy their confidence and trust in me. Would you prefer to see me lose everything? Neither can I talk with Elizabeth, as it's best she doesn't know. Use your influence with her. If the child is a girl, seek for her to become a house slave with you, if a boy, a livery man who works with my uncle's horses and carriages."

"I could not bear it if our child was forced to work in the fields," Lucinda said. "What if the child were to be sold? What could I do?"

"There's nothing either of us can do," he said dryly. "You're not my slave. If you were, things would be very different. I've talked with you of this. You belong to my uncle. He can do with you and your child as he wishes. I don't believe Elizabeth would let her father, or her mother for that matter, sell your child. Elizabeth is very fond of you, regardless of what you may think. Lucinda, there is no point worrying about things over which you have no control."

"That's what it means to be a slave," she cried. Tears blurred her eyes.

Master Johnson placed his open palm against her stomach. "It's not yet so when you're in your clothes, but without them you show you're with child. They will notice soon."

"I've been most careful Mama does not see," Lucinda said shyly. "I've told no one about us, Master Johnson. I'll never tell." She looked down away from him. "When we return to Radcliffe Place, I'll slip away and meet you at the spring house or in the flower gardens, where ever I can, whenever you wish."

She lay naked on the bed. She shut her eyes and whimpered as he released his power on her. She was a sinful nigger girl. Like a swarm of mad hornets the thought teemed in her brain. Afterwards she lay breathless and spent; the weight of Master Johnson heavy upon her. The necklace hung about her throat twinkling like a bright star in the nighttime sky.

She promised herself she would change. *I was a young girl when Jesus came into my heart and I know he will forgive my sins. I'll be cleansed by His blood, and on the Day of Judgment when He comes again I'll be resurrected in His glory.* But when night came and she was alone on her pallet, the craving of desire burned inside her. Temptation drew her like an undertow. She could not bear that she might never be with him again.

Images of the city troubled her fitful sleep. Buzzards fed off dead carrion. The bloody whip scarred the backs of slaves. Dead bodies slumped from the scaffold gallows. Young slave girls were shamed by lust. The grand houses of Charleston constructed in the darkest regions of the human heart.

By the Waters of Zion

No one told Lucinda and Mama they were to be taken back to Radcliffe Place Plantation until the day they were to leave. Not even Mistress Johnson gave them a warning. Master Johnson appeared about noon with Abraham and two other slaves from Radcliffe Place; with them were Ruth and Phoebe, the new house slaves for Mistress Johnson.

"Abraham and the men will get your trunks," Master Johnson said to Lucinda. His face was a blank. She had never seen him this way before. She could not tell what he was thinking. She tried to get him alone for a moment but could not do so.

No one even asked Lucinda who was the daddy of her expectant child. Not even Mama questioned her. Lucinda was certain Mama thought the papa was David Walker.

"I ain't always gonna be 'round fo' you, chile," Mama said as they rode in a dray wagon to the wharves. The slave men walked along beside the wagon. Abraham sat up front steering the mule. Master Johnson sat on the driver's rack. Her mama spoke Gullah so Master Johnson would not understand. Lucinda looked out over the silted brown water of the Cooper River.

"You's ain't a li'l girl no mo'," Mama went on. "So you can do wha' ever you wants, I reckon."

"I'm a woman now, Mama," Lucinda said. "I can make my own choices."

"Ain't no slave that can make their own choice," Mama said. "Work 'n' serve, serve 'n' work, that be all we's can do." Then more softly Mama said, "If you don't love me no mo', least I got a gran' baby a comin'."

"You know I love you, Mama," Lucinda said. She put her face up against her mama's and reached to give her a hug.

"I hope you 'nuff full o' this town life," Mama said, hiding the tears in her eyes.

Lucinda did not answer.

"The only thing I likes 'bout Charlestown be the African Church," Mama continued, "An' now they gone and shut it up. Tore it to the ground. Po' Rev'nd Brown be run out o' town. Better than hangin', I reckon. Wha' you know 'bout the uprisin'?" Mama suddenly asked in a low whisper.

"Nothing, Mama," Lucinda said. She tried not to appear surprised.

"Does you think you can fool me, chile?" Mama said. "You and that Denmark Vesey, y'all been too much like peas in a pod fo' you not to know somethin'. Oh, you ain't got no fret. I ain't gonna say nothin'. Denmark Vesey been a mighty brave man tryin' fo' somethin' like that . . . free all the slaves in Charleston. Yes'm, he be a mighty brave man. He be right 'bout the whites, how cruel they's be and how much they hate de blacks. Ain't no tellin' how many black men they hang jus' to sho' de ain't gonna let no black man be free. Denmark Vesey been full o' pride, chile. Full o' pride like a fat tick full o' blood on a ole coon dog. Too much pride get a man kill't."

"That's what I'm going to call him, Mama."

"What that?"

"My baby, if it's a boy, no matter what name Master Radcliffe gives him, I'm going to call him Denmark."

Mama pretended she did not hear her. "Soon you has yo' baby," Mama said, "You be workin' in the chillens' house. Massa Radcliffe have ever baby chile on the plantation pullin' at yo' pap day 'n' night."

"How do you know, Mama?" Lucinda asked.

"Jus' do. I see it times afore. Been do it afore when you come along."

The dusty grey wagon pulled by the dusty grey mule stopped on the dusty road at the wharf. Lucinda looked back at Charleston as she climbed down from the wagon. She wished she could fly like a bird over the city.

Abraham and the other slaves unloaded the provisions for the plantation from the dray wagon and loaded Lucinda's and Mama's trunks into the boat. No one spoke, not even Mama. In no time, they were sailing briskly through the harbor, gaining speed. The wind blew in Lucinda's face. She looked back over her shoulder. Behind her between the sky and the sea, growing smaller and more distant, the jeweled city receded into the line of the horizon. Only the tips of the church steeples could be seen. She shifted to look out over the choppy water before them. The wind picked up and began to blow hard. Huge black clouds gathered and darkened the sky above them.

"Abraham! A squall!" Master Johnson called out, pointing up at the threatening sky. The wind muffled his words.

"Yessa, Massa," Abraham hollered.

The wind gusted, whistling and whining shrilly, flapping the cloth of the sails. Huge drops of rain splattered on Lucinda's face before torrents quickly began dropping in thick sheets. Her clothes and hair were drenched. The clouds were black, massive, and weighed down on the water, like a throng of ravenous vultures ready to deploy, blocking the sun. The wind blew the boat uncontrollably toward the Bar. The sky turned eerily purple-black. The swells splashed higher, rocking the boat at a sharp pitch. A jagged line of blue lightning flashed in the near distance from cloud to sea. A boom of thunder clapped deafeningly above their heads. Lucinda's heart leapt in fright and pounded in her chest. The schooner rolled and tilted as the men fought the oars and tried to upright the boat. Lucinda was sore afraid. Abraham stood unsteadily and tugged with all his strength at the ropes on the sails. The rain poured down. Lucinda could no longer see anything in any direction, blocked by the grey curtain of rain. She shivered in her wet clothes, was jostled and banged about by the rolling of the boat.

"Abraham, go back!" Master Johnson shouted above the storm as he held tightly with both hands to the mast, his wet clothes stuck to his body.

"We's be tryin', Massa," Abraham yelled back as the men tugged and struggled with the ropes trying to reverse the wet, rain-heavy sails. The wind whipped and tore at the sails. The two slaves, one on each side, struggled with their oars to stabilize the boat, but with no success. One of the oars snapped and broke in two, falling into the water. Master Johnson stepped toward Abraham, almost falling down as he did so, grabbed the rope on the sails and tried to help turn the boat back toward the harbor.

Mama whimpered in terror, the whites of her eyes protruding from her face. She stood up like a drunkard on weak legs, staggered to the rail of the ship, and was sick. Lucinda felt a big wave rock the boat from the other side, and in a sharp shift of the schooner, Mama fell on the rail toward the sea. Another huge wave tilted the boat and Mama tumbled over the railing. Lucinda had tried to grab hold of her mama, but the roll of the boat knocked Lucinda down and she fell hard banging her head on the wood floor. She saw stars and fainted away for a moment. A wave washed over the railing of the boat, drenched her, and splashed on her face, stinging her eyes. She choked and coughed, spitting out the salty spray.

"Mama! Mama!" Lucinda screamed, as she was tossed across the floor of the rocking boat. She grabbed at the empty air, struggled to get on her feet. "Mama fell!" she screamed. "Master Johnson! Abraham! Help! Help!"

The men turned toward Lucinda, terror on their faces. Lucinda's mama floundered and bounced in the water, then disappeared underneath. Master Johnson stumbled toward Lucinda and tried to help her stand. The rain lashed down. Thunder rumbled above, the sky dark like dusk.

"Do something!" Lucinda screamed. "Abraham! Save her!"

"Ain't nobody can swim," Abraham cried to Lucinda.

The men yanked at the sails and finally turned the boat around.

Lucinda clung to the rail with one hand and frantically searched the waves, rubbing with her other hand the burning water from her eyes. Everything was all upside down. Mama was nowhere to be seen.

"No, God, no!" she screamed. "No, God, no!"

The squall began to break as the schooner made its way from the Charleston Bar back toward the harbor and the wharf. Lucinda could not speak. She could not remember where she was. She shivered in her wet clothes.

Master Johnson leapt from the boat and ran to the Custom House. Lucinda leaned weakly against the railing and was sick. Abraham and the other slaves shivered in fear, huddled in a corner.

"What's the fuss about, sir? It's just a nigger dead," said the port official to Master Johnson.

The rest of the day until dark a search was made at the Bar, but no body was ever found.

"We must get back to Radcliffe Place," Master Johnson said to Lucinda the next morning. "There's nothing else we can do."

Sailing up river, she sat in the boat, quiet and unmoving, dazed, almost unaware of where she was. Finally, she looked up just as the boat came to a bend in the river and revealed Radcliffe Place spread out before them. Lucinda recalled the bright November morning they had journeyed down the river the year before, and how the lumber mill and the cotton fields and the rice ponds, the slave quarters, and the plantation Big House, had slowly disappeared in the distance, just as they were appearing to her now. She could barely believe what she saw in front of her was real. She felt like she was in a dream and could not wake up. She was numb and cold. She saw Miss Elizabeth come from the Big House toward them as the slave men worked to secure the boat to the river dock. Elizabeth said not a word, but gave Lucinda her hand, and helped her from the boat, big tears on Elizabeth's cheeks as she hugged Lucinda tightly. Lucinda's eyes were red from weeping but she had no more tears to shed. Elizabeth led her to the Big House.

"Father says you don't have to work until the day after tomorrow," Elizabeth said to her. "Your tasks will now be at the children's cabin. You'll sleep in a cabin with the old mid-wife Aunt Hattie." Elizabeth's eyes moved to look at Lucinda's belly. "At leasr until sometime after your child is born."

That night under the stars, the Africans gathered in the yard of the Settlement. A huge bonfire burned, with flames flying upward like orange hands clasp in prayer. Lucinda watched the evening star rise above the lip of the western horizon, shining steady and bright. She heard the woods ring with sounds of the night. Fresh tears gathered in her eyes. She prayed Mama had joined her grand mammy and her grand pappy and her pappy, her mama's spirit journeying to their ancient African home, soaring like a gull across the sea. She prayed Mama's spirit hastened unto the realms of time and memory and passing. One day, she prayed, one day I will journey to Africa and dwell again with my grand mammy and my mama. These were her only thoughts of solace.

That there was no body for the funeral ritual made for a problem. The shaman of the plantation consulted the omens. There was deemed only one solution. Under the cover of darkness, a kid was filched from the goat pen, its mouth wrapped shut with a rope strap to hush its cries, and sacrificed so all could see, the flowing blood from the cut throat captured in an earthen bowl and drunk by the shaman to serve as the host body of the lost loved one. Lucinda prayed hard with her eyes squeezed shut for the African gods to grant their plea, prayed the gods would honor their sacrifice, prayed the gods would guide home her mama's soul.

The Africans danced in a circle around her. They sang a mournful chant, their dirge rising up like a soul departing from a dead body, escaping skyward away from the dark earth. The slaves clapped their hands together in the rhythm of a heartbeat. Lucinda rocked gently, surrounded by the Africans as they swayed and danced, carrying her back and forth with their bodies. Her voice was hoarse and low from her crying as she closed her eyes and joined in the chant.

Lucinda opened her eyes and looked all around. She felt strange. Her grand mammy had told her all things have spirits. She felt the spirits of the night envelope her, the spirits of the earth, the sky, and the stars. She felt the dancers wrap around her like a blanket, their spirits move from the ground beneath her feet up her legs, through her womb growing with life, up through her body, into her breasts and her arms and burst from the top of her head, then swirl in a whirl storm of shifting, changing faces. The eyes of the black faces glistened with reflections from the firelight, the black faces wet with glistening sweat, the moans of their chant flowing out like heat from the bonfire. She seemed to withdraw from her body, to separate and join with the spirits that surrounded her. She was consumed by the dance and the chant, swallowed up by the darkness of the night. Her body could no longer feel. She was one with the stars and the dancers, the flames and the spirits of her ancestors. The African women began to wail and shriek, call out in cries of lamentation. Lucinda's heart throbbed in escalating time to the dance, the repeating clap of hands, the rhythmic clip, repeating, echoing, filling her and the yard and the fields and the woods. As she became part of everything, her legs gave way, and she fell to the ground. The world around her was swallowed up by a gaping black hole, and the rhythm of the chants faded into a buzzing drone like a swarm of bees alive in her head.

When she woke, she was on a pallet on the floor of Aunt Hattie's cabin. The old Negress sat in a straight wooden chair next to the hearth watching the fire burn, dipping snuff with her toothless gums and spitting into an earthen jar. Lucinda could smell a hoecake and a pot of rice cooking in the fireplace. When the Negress realized Lucinda was awake, the old woman rose and shuffled over to Lucinda with the corn cake and rice and a cup of clabber. She handed them to Lucinda without speaking.

Lucinda tried to recall what happened. She remembered the night sky, the fire, the chants, and the dancers; she remembered her spirit taken up out of her body. She could not remember beyond that.

"Ye best eat somethin' chile," the old woman said encouragingly.

Lucinda's round stomach slowed her as she got up and took the food.

At first, she refused to accept Mama and Denmark Vesey were dead. For days on end, her thoughts were confused, her body numb. No, it can't be true, she thought over and over to herself. She would wake early each morning expecting to see her mama, but as she opened her eyes, and the trail of sleep began to fade from her brain, her thoughts would slowly form and she would feel the sorrow and sadness, the loss weighed heavy upon her, pressing down, sucking her breath away, suffocating her like she was the one drowning in the sea, chocking her like a hangman's noose tugging at her neck. She pulled the blanket over her head and closed her eyes, wished desperately to be alone. She struggled to get up, her spirit desperate and dark at dawn, longing for sleep and escape. At the end of the day when her tasks at the chillens' house were done she shied away from the company of others, returned to the cabin she shared with the old woman, ate a scant meal, and slept. Days on end passed in gloom.

Then she was angry and hated everything and everyone. She was angry most of all with God. Why were the people she loved taken from her, she wondered. She blamed Abraham that the schooner was caught in the storm. She blamed Master Johnson for being unable to save Mama. No one on the plantation seemed to understand. She blamed the men in Charleston like Master Radcliffe for hanging Denmark Vesey. Most of all she blamed herself. She was angry and hated herself. God was punishing her for her sins.

The nasty old woman, Aunt Hattie, said to her, "Ain't a one o' us that know when we's be called home. Ain't right fo' us to question the Lord, chile."

She detested the old Negro woman. She hated her smell, her constant spitting of snuff, her toothless gums, the way her lips peeled back when she spoke.

Slowly the anger which burned inside her began to fade. She was learning to consider, learning to traverse trials. She was renewed from the inside out. She went at suppertime alone toward the springhouse and the rice fields and sat near the edge of the woods, watching the crimson sun color the place where the trees and the river converged with the blazing sky. She watched as the birds winged their way to their night retreats. She had no more tears. In her loneliness, she promised God she would nurture and protect the child she carried within her. She sang softly to herself:

"*Down by the river Zion, I laid my burden down.*"

She saw a red fox far on the other side of the riverbank. She blinked. When her eyes opened, the fox had disappeared. A spirit! There were spirits everywhere: spirits of the dead, the spirit of her mama, the spirit of Denmark Vesey.

"Girl, best ye get the root doctor concoct a charm fo' ye," Aunt Hattie said to Lucinda one evening. The old woman stirred a steaming pot over the fireplace. "Sho' nuff better get the haints 'way from ye." Hattie directed her reddened eyes on Lucinda. "The dead ain't 'posed to live with the quick."

The wrinkled face of the ancient Negress was silent for several minutes. Then she said: "The root doctor me tell ye best drop by 'morrow evenin.'" She turned back to stare at the fire and dribbled a big spit of snuff into her spittoon jar.

The root doctor's cabin was at the other end of the Settlement, and the next evening the sun was beginning to set as Lucinda drew close enough to see in the darkening light the root doctor's open cabin door. She stepped up on the porch and tapped on the doorframe. The root doctor sat at a wooden table; a woman, his wife Lucinda supposed, was cooking over the fire and the smell of hoecake greeted Lucinda from the room.

"You can come on in," the root doctor said.

Hanging from pegs on one wall Lucinda saw thin lines of rope threaded through an array of dried plants and roots. On the crude pine table were laid out fresh roots and herbs, blue-grey, yellow, red, and bright green.

"Aunt Hattie sent me," Lucinda explained. "She said you'd know I was coming." The root doctor nodded his head but said nothing. The woman in the cabin did not look up and continued to bake the hoecake and work the hearth-place fire.

"Aunt Hattie say haints be a tr'ublin' ye," the man finally said.

"The spirits of the dead have taken hold of me," Lucinda told him, unsure what to say.

"The haints be lost 'n can't find their way," he said to her. "They feed off the livin'. They got be set free, 'n' find their way home."

He stood and with his left hand reached across for a dark blue root hanging on the wall. He handed the root to her. As he turned, she saw in the reflected firelight on his face the African tribal scars, which marked his cheeks. Then she noticed his left ear was missing; it had been cut off.

"This root here be fo' ye 'n' ye chile," the root doctor said. "The night o' the new moon take this 'n' put in yo' pot 'n' boil 'til de water be dark. Black as the dark rain cloud. Then let sit 'til day clean and drink then. Take nottin' else that day 'til de sun be high in the sky." The root doctor paused and studied Lucinda's face to make certain she understood. "Come back 'morrow 'bout this time," he then continued. "I then have de charm fo' rid ye o' the haint o' the hag."

Lucinda clung tightly in her closed fist to a dollar coin she brought from the money she had gotten from Master Johnson, the amount Aunt Hattie told her to pay. She suddenly asked, "Root Doctor, do you have a charm that'll bring back my lover to me?"

"That be extry," the root doctor said guardedly.

"Oh, I know," Lucinda said. "How much for everything, the root for me and my baby, the charm to rid of the haints, and a love charm?"

"Two dolla' that be," the root doctor said firmly.

She fished in the pocket of her clothes and drew out enough two-bit coins, handing them with the dollar coin to the root doctor.

"'Morrow 'bout this time," the root doctor repeated, "'round sundown."

A still hot orange sun sat on the edge of the evening sky as Lucinda walked through the Settlement the next day. When she worked in the Big House, she always wore the leather shoes Mistress Nelly had given her, but now at the chillens' house she often went barefoot. The soft sandy soil squeezed up between her toes, warming her feet. The root doctor again sat at the wood table, the woman preparing their meal.

"Root Doctor," Lucinda called as she tapped on the door.

"Come in, come in," he answered. "Sit down, chile." Lucinda dropped her round burdened body into the empty chair at the table. "This be fo' the haints," the root doctor said. He placed in the palm of her hand a small piece of brown burlap tied into a knot, a bone stuck through two ends, with buzzard's feathers protruding. He waved his hand back and forth over her hand and mumbled some words she could not make out.

"Take this 'n' the night o' the nex' full moon bury it at the edge o' the Afric' grave yard," the root doctor instructed her.

"No!" Lucinda cried and she leaned back from the root doctor, dropping the charm on the table. "No. I can't!"

"Huh?" the root doctor grunted.

"I'm afeard of grave yard haints and hags!" she exclaimed.

"They be no other way," the root doctor said sternly. "Ye want the haints be no mo'?"

"Yes," Lucinda answered him, "but . . ."

"Then ye got to do it," the root doctor told her. He thought for a long moment. "I go with you to de graveya'd 'n' watch out fo' ye."

"Root Doctor, I can't!" Lucinda said pleadingly. "There's got to be another way,"

"Ain't none," the root doctor said, as if that settled it. He looked at her with a fixed stare. "Listen gul! Now take this with ye." He picked up the charm from the table and put it back in her hand. "Be careful fo' it hold mighty powa'. Come back the night o' the nex' full moon. Then I make a special charm take with us that night to protect ye."

She was scared, but she was desperate. She looked about the cabin's shadowed room. The root doctor's woman bent down at the hearth, saying nothing, tending to a pot that smelled of rice and beans.

Lucinda hesitated. "You'll go with me to the grave yard?"

"Yes, chile."

"What about the love charm?" Lucinda asked hesitantly.

"This be that," the root doctor said, with satisfaction in his voice.

He gave Lucinda a small sack about the size of her hand. She opened it and looked in. It held dried herbs and flowers. She placed her nose to the opened top and sniffed; the smell was sweet like the meadows between the woods in the spring.

"Ye got a snip o' he hair?" the root doctor asked.

Lucinda shook her head no.

"Some he clothes?"

She continued to shake her head.

"What he touch? Give ye?"

Lucinda thought of the necklace.

"Yes," she said. "I have something he gave me."

"Then ever night put what he give ye under ye whiles ye sleep 'n' sprinkle two pinch o' this 'round it. Be sho' to take up ever mornin'. Do that fo' five night in a row. Does ye dream 'bout 'im?"

"Sometimes," Lucinda answered. The root doctor's questions made her uncomfortable.

"If's ye do," the root doctor said, "be sho' save this that mornin' and throw it in the wind when ye go out yo' cabin."

She decided to rid herself of the haints before she used the love charm. The full moon was a fortnight away. Her dread grew greater with each passing day. She was the most frightened she had ever been. Even when she sneaked through the alleyways of Charleston to warn Denmark Vesey about the visit to Master Radcliffe by the Intendant and the Governor, even during the squall when Mama had fallen overboard, Lucinda did not think she had ever been this afeard. She took the charm from her trunk, whispered repeated prayers asking God to keep her safe, and set out in the dark.

She walked swiftly across the Settlement to the root doctor's cabin, silently mouthing her prayers. The face of the full moon, harvest orange above the tops of the trees, stared down at her. She thought of turning back. Then she renewed her prayer asking for strength and walked on.

The root doctor sat on his porch step bathed in moonlight, waiting for her. He held a hoe in his hand. He stood as she approached.

"Got the charm with ye?" he asked.

"Yes," she whispered.

"Then stay the back o' me," he said and set out toward the Africans' graveyard, the hoe held like a weapon upright in his hand.

Lucinda struggled to keep up. "Root Doctor, will we be safe?" she asked.

"Long as ye do 'zackly like I say do," he said firmly.

"What if a hag rips my belly open and steals my baby?" Lucinda's voice shook.

The root doctor turned and glared at her in the moonlight. "Say nuttin'" he instructed her forcibly.

The fields beyond in the distance glowed ghostly white in the moonlight, and they passed the barns, the animal pens, and the lumber mill standing quiet in the dark. The root doctor must have placed a hex on the hunting dogs, for Lucinda heard not the slightest whimper from their pen. She saw the black outline of tree limbs stretch skyward at the border of the woods and fields, and the limbs seemed to her like a clutching hag's hands. Ghostly beards of Spanish moss hung in spidery webs from the oak trees. She knew the graveyard was near. Her heart pounded with fear.

The root doctor stopped. "Be full o' care," he whispered. "Step on no grave." He handed the hoe to her. "I need de charm." She had held it tightly in her hand and now gave it to him. She shut her eyes, afraid to look. She heard the root doctor mumble a Voodoo plea.

"Dig with the hoe," the root doctor told her.

She opened her eyes.

"Where?" she asked.

"There," he said pointing to the ground. "Wha ye be standin'."

She awkwardly took the hoe in her hands and struck clumsily at the ground.

"Ain't ye ever hoed nuttin?" he asked.

"No," she said. "I'm a house slave." She thought she saw him grin in the moonlight.

"Jis' keep diggin'. Ye's getting' there."

She hit and chopped and chopped and hit with the hoe against the ground, each strike a little deeper, until the hole was almost a foot deep and the root doctor said, "That be 'nuff." He dropped the charm into the ground. "Now cover it with the dirt."

Lucinda scraped the loose dirt into the hole with the hoe as fast as she could.

"Now step on hit," the root doctor said. "Cover hit good."

Suddenly the call of a question came from the woods: "whoo? whoo?" Lucinda stopped. "A hag!" she whispered to the root doctor. She raised the hoe to protect herself. The call came again: "whoo? whoo?"

"Root doctor, a hag's gonna get us!"

The moon had climbed higher in the blue-black sky and glowed pearly white, skirted with a puff of clouds. Lucinda frantically worked the hoe to finish her task.

"Ye's done?" the root doctor questioned, and he looked back and forth from her to the woods.

"Is that enough?" Lucinda asked.

"That be good," the root doctor said and he stomped the dirt on the buried charm with his foot. He grabbed the hoe from her hand and moved quickly away from the graveyard toward the plantation. Lucinda followed close behind. She was afraid to look back, fearful the hag might be shadowing them.

The rapid knock of her terrified heart thumped loudly in her ears all the way back to Aunt Hattie's cabin and continued to thump as she lay shivering on her pallet. She had done it. She had buried the charm to rid her of the horrible haints.

Thank you, Lord, Lucinda said in her evening prayers. She rose from her knees.

She had come to where she no longer had to deny the deaths of Mama and Denmark Vesey. She was no longer rent by anger, no longer obsessed by hate. Slowly as her belly grew full, her sadness began to ebb and her thoughts of the ghostly dead began to wane. There came a time when she was at peace, when her sadness and gloom were gone. Those evenings she sat silently with Aunt Hattie and watched the fire. She began to look forward to seeing the children each morning with their bright smiles, to hear their excited cries and laughter. There was not great feeling in her heart, but she was calm. Her ordeal was over. The haints were sent to their final resting place. She was free from torment by the dead.

Still, sometimes in her dreams Mama came to her like her grand mammy had, and she talked with her mama in the dreams, lengthy, intricate, mesmerizing talks, stories of her childhood, tales that brought them to laughter and tears, but when she woke she could not remember what they said, no matter how hard she tried. Or Denmark Vesey would appear to her. He struggled to speak, the hangman's noose tight about his neck, choking him. No words came from his mouth, only the silent movement of his lips. Only in her memory did she hear him incite with words the call of freedom for the slaves. Words she would never forget.

Elizabeth sent for her. Lucinda walked the path to the back door of the Big House. The new house servant greeted her when she knocked on the doorframe.

"Miss 'Liz'beth be 'spectin' you," the girl said, opening the screen door for Lucinda. "Lord, you be gettin' big girl," she exclaimed when Lucinda entered the house. "That baby be bakin' in the oven, eh?" Lucinda said nothing. "Miss 'Liz'beth say go on upstairs. She be in her chamber."

Elizabeth sat on the divan in her room. One of the other female house slaves stood behind, brushing Elizabeth's hair.

"That's enough," Elizabeth said, dismissing the girl. "Leave us. Come in, Lucinda."

Lucinda stood facing Elizabeth. She watched as Elizabeth's eyes inspected the round bulge, which showed at Lucinda's front.

"My cousin tells me my aunt was pleased with your performance. It's unfortunate you had to be brought back."

"Yes'm."

"Father says after you've fed the mouths of the little pickaninnies for a while, perhaps when you dry up you can be returned here to the Big House."

"Yes'm."

"What was it like?" Elizabeth asked sharply, her blue eyes staring straight into Lucinda's black ones.

"What?"

"You know, becoming with child." Lucinda gave no answer. "Anyway," Elizabeth said dismissively, "things are as they are, regardless of who the father is." There was a long silence until Elizabeth then said, "Someday I shall marry."

"May it be soon to some lucky man, lovely as you are, Miss Elizabeth."

"Do not flatter me. I am plain, Lucinda. But I am white, and I shall be rich, rich with land and rice and cotton and slaves. Better to be plain and wealthy than beautiful as a Helen of Troy among slaves."

She did not seem to expect an answer so Lucinda made none.

"I was told you knew this Denmark Vesey, the leader of this horrible insurrection conspiracy."

"I told Master Radcliffe Mama and myself met him when we went to the African Church in Charleston. That's all. I testified such at his trial."

"Was he the horrible beast I have heard he was?" Miss Elizabeth asked.

"He cared about the slaves," Lucinda said meekly, and regretted her words as she said them.

Elizabeth's blue eyes flashed. "He was a monster," she cried. "And unless you want to be whipped at my command, you'll never refer to him as anything otherwise! Father said to report to him at once the slightest suggestion of insurrection. I recommend you forget all this foolishness. God made the blacks slaves. And it will be up to God to set them free."

Lucinda stared down at the floor. Tears wet her eyes.

"I do not want to be misunderstood," Elizabeth said with a hint of regret in her voice. "I'm glad you're well and I'm glad you're back. Things just did not turn out as planned. You were always special, Lucinda. You know that. You have no reason for your tears."

Lucinda turned to go.

"Lucinda."

"Yes'm."

"I have something for you." Elizabeth stood, and reached for a white paper box on her bed. She walked over to Lucinda and handed it to her. "Go ahead," Elizabeth said, sitting down again on the divan. "Open it."

Lucinda carefully pulled the lid from the box. Inside, wrapped in a soft white paper was a delicate, lavender-colored baby's gown.

"Oh, Miss Elizabeth." Lucinda's tears began again.

"That's all. You may leave," Elizabeth said, and before she turned to the door, Lucinda was certain she saw the light from the window reflect on tears in Miss Elizabeth's eyes.

Each night when Lucinda went to sleep she took the necklace from her trunk, secretly placed it under her pallet, and sprinkled around it two pinches of the love charm the root doctor made for her. Each night she had a dream, but not with Master Johnson in it. In her dream, she was back in Charleston. She was on her way to the apartment to meet Master Johnson but the man who tried to trap her between the two buildings was suddenly behind her. She turned to look over her shoulder at him. His yellow eyes glared at her. She began to run, and ran and ran and ran, staying just beyond his reach. "Master Johnson!" she cried out. He did not come. Her heart beat wildly in terror and she suddenly awoke. She could feel her child move within her.

The final night she placed the necklace and the charm under her pallet like the root doctor said. Her dream was different from the other nights. She dreamt of Master Johnson. This time she went straight to the apartment. No one was behind her. The streets were empty and she was alone. Master Johnson was waiting for her and he took her in his arms and kissed her. Their love in her dream was unlike anything she had felt before.

The next morning she took the necklace and carefully hid it away, swept the charm herbs into the palm of her hand, stepped out onto the cabin porch and threw them into the wind. That night she walked from the Settlement along the path to the springhouse. Master Johnson was coming toward her on horseback on the trail beside the Ashley.

"Lucinda," he called to her as he approached.

"Master Johnson." She tried to hide her surprise.

He dismounted and tied the horse just inside the woods.

"The springhouse," he said to her. "I'll meet you there."

She looked to make certain no one was watching from the plantation as she walked in the darkening shadows to the springhouse. She went inside. She sat on the stone wall that surrounded the spring. She listened for him.

The wooden door creaked as it opened and she could see his outline in the doorway.

"Are you here," he asked softly.

"Yes."

He placed the palm of his open hand on her stomach. "By your size it must be a boy," he said. She sat back down on the stone wall. "Elizabeth said she spoke with you."

"She sent for me," Lucinda said. "Does she know, master?"

"Know? No," he answered, as he suddenly understood her question. "But she may suspect something. I'm not sure. When your child is born the whole plantation will be speculating." He was quiet for a time, the gurgle of the spring the only sound. "She said you're doing well."

"Yes, master," she said.

"It's hard," he said. "I'm hopeful later, after you have your child . . ." His voice trailed off. He then said, "I have plans for us, all of us."

He stood close to her.

"Master, what do you want me to do?" she whispered.

He did not answer.

Coming back to Radcliffe Place was like starting all over again. Starting over with a new round of seasons: the bright flowers of spring, the birth of new calves and folds and piglets; summer hot, rich, and green; the gold harvest and plenty of autumn; the quiet grey stillness of winter. She was reabsorbed into the pattern of the plantation. Her wish had come true. She had lived in Charleston. Now she had a baby boy she called Denmark. Mama was dead. Denmark Vesey was dead. Was it the work of God, or the work of man, she wondered?

Epilogue

Exodus

James Radcliffe died from a riding accident in 1828. Mistress Nelly followed two years later. While her parents still lived, Miss Elizabeth married a Carolina lowcountry planter's son. After their deaths, she inherited Radcliffe Place Plantation and purchased from her cousin the Johnson share. She and her husband lived on Radcliffe Place until the end of the Civil War. Mistress Johnson, Master Johnson's mother, died in Charleston seven years after Lucinda was moved back to the plantation. Jimmy Johnson sold the mansion in Charleston and in 1837 moved to the new Republic of Texas with his family, where he quickly made a fortune in cotton. He purchased twenty-two slaves from his cousin Elizabeth to take with him when he left the lowcountry of South Carolina, including Lucinda and the child.

25th August 1838
Mistress Elizabeth:

Our ship sailed south along the coast of Florida, and in the most beautiful blue water, we journeyed into the Gulf of Mexico. We reached New Orleans, a city that stirred within me all my old memories of Charleston. We then departed New Orleans by steamboat up the Mississippi, a great muddy river many times bigger and more powerful than the Ashley River. Next our steamboat traveled the Red River to a place called Shreveport, Louisiana, a bustling, noisy place packed with people and wagons and horses heading west on the Texas Trail like us. Our wagons were loaded with provisions and after but three days in Shreveport, we began a journey of many days and many nights, the slaves and myself and my child walking the entire distance on foot. Finally, we came to Master Johnson's plantation on a great plain in Texas.

The Indians in Texas ride horses with great skill and hunt a huge beast called the buffalo. The cows here have long horns, each horn on the side of their head, longer, they seem, than I am tall. They are the fiercest looking creatures you could ever picture in your mind, Miss Elizabeth, except for the buffalo!

The land here for cotton lays flat like Radcliffe Place Plantation and is easy to plow and plant and hoe. Master Johnson says the land is good, Black Prairie he says it is called. The balls on the cotton plants are now as fluffy and white as the whitest cloud in the sky. Rain days are fewer than at Radcliffe Place. When it does rain, it comes in great torrents, huge storms with black clouds and wind, which blow in from the south. This past winter the wind blew cold out of the north for a week or more and the water in the mule and horse troughs turned to hard ice.

We first all lived in cabins built by the Africans, but now Master Johnson's Big House is complete and the furnishings for the house have arrived from New Orleans.

I do tasks for Master Johnson and Mistress Ruth raising their children and my boy has grown up with Jerimiah as I did with you. I write down records for Master Johnson of the plantation's cotton crop, how many acres were planted, and how many bales picked and when the land was plowed, planted, and hoed. Sometimes I am very sad that I will never get to see you again. I miss you very much, Miss Elizabeth, and think of you often. Write to me when you can.

Your faithful servant,

Lucinda

2nd July 1840

Mistress Elizabeth:

Mistress Ruth told me she wrote to you of Master Johnson's sudden and horrible death. Sad and dreadful now are the days here. I tended to Master Johnson during his sickness. I cooked his meals and fed him, for he became too weak to nourish himself. Mistress Elizabeth, only a few weeks before he turned sick, Master Johnson showed me his will where Li'l Denmark and myself were to be set free upon his death! The Lord knows I would prefer to have remained a slave until I died rather than see Master Johnson pass away so young and in such agony.

But we are now free! Freedom is a glorious feeling after being a slave.

Mistress Ruth says she is going to sell the plantation and return to South Carolina. She says it is too much for her to bear. I cannot return to Charleston as much as I would like, for I would be sold back into slavery.

I am going to take Li'l Denmark with me and go to New Orleans. There are many free blacks there. If the Lord wills it, perhaps I can find a free black man as a husband.

The world is strange, Miss Elizabeth. Fate has its way with each of us.

Lucinda

She folded the page, poured a thimble-size of wax from the burning candle and sealed the letter with Master Johnson's seal. Before she hid them again in her trunk, she took the emerald and diamond necklace from the silk purse and inspected the shimmering jewels carefully, turned the ribbon of gold over in her black, pink-palm hands, fingered the necklace like a blind person, a mark of a time past, spread between a dream and a truth. She looked at the empty un-stoppered bottle which had held the poison she had saved for so long.

"Revenge," Gullah Jack had told her, "We must seek revenge."

She had slipped and called her son Li'l Denmark in Master Johnson's presence.

"I warned you if I ever heard you use that name, I would whip you myself, and I meant it," he had cried angrily. He ripped her shirt from her body, chained her arms to the slave whipping post, and struck her repeatedly until she bleed and cried out for mercy.

She picked up Denmark Vesey's journal, held to it like the precious raiment of a sacred saint, opened it carefully, and read aloud to herself in the empty room, "*I know I am placing myself in grave danger by taking up this quill . . .* "

Afterword

Although a work of fiction, *The Death of Denmark Vesey* incorporates substantial historical bases obtained chiefly from the primary source materials (the Slave Courts' trial transcripts, a narrative of the conspiracy published by the Court Magistrates Parker and Kennedy, a published description of the plot by Charleston Intendant James H. Hamilton, Jr., a published commentary on the plot by Governor Thomas Bennett, and private letters from the period). Some of Intendant James Hamilton's dialogue in the novel uses wording from his published report. The Major's writing style is affected, archaic even for his time, and certainly so to the modern ear. But I elected to occasionally use his writings with few changes with the view that it likely approximates his actual spoken words, especially those spoken in a formal setting, as when he explains the status of the investigation to the fictitious James Radcliffe. Portions of the chapter *Altars in the Dust* use verbatim testimony by witnesses as recorded in the trial transcript, and the sentencing pronouncements by the Court of Vesey and Gullah Jack. Parts of the letter by the fictional Sara Johnson to the fictional Anna Moore in the chapter *Altars in the Dust* include some wording from actual historical letters dated 28 June, 1822 by Anna Johnson of Charleston to Elizabeth Haywood of Raleigh, NC (Ernest Haywood Papers, Southern Historical Collection, Wilson Library, University of North Carolina, Chapel Hill); and 18 July 1822 by Anna Johnson, Charleston, to Elizabeth Haywood, Raleigh, (South Carolina Historical Society, Charleston, South Carolina); a letter dated 27July, 1822 by Anna Johnson, Charleston, to Elizabeth Haywood of Raleigh, NC (Southern Historical Collection, Wilson Library, University of North Carolina, Chapel Hill); and from a letter dated 25 July with postscript dated 27, July 1822 by Mary Beach, Charleston, to Elizabeth Gilchrist (Mary Lamboll, Thomas Beach Papers, South Carolina Historical Society, Charleston, South Carolina). The quotes of David Walker which appear in the chapter *Denmark Vesey's Journal*, and some of the dialogue of David Walker in the chapter *The Holy City* are from David Walker's *Appeal in Four Articles; Together with a Preamble, to the Coloured Citizens of the World, but in Particular and Very Expressly to Those of the United States of America*, first published in September 1829. A portion of Federal

Supreme Court Justice William Johnson's comments on the plot are taken from a letter from the Justice to Thomas Jefferson.

I have taken various liberties from the historical record when it suits my needs. For example, it is not known where or precisely when Denmark Vesey was born, where he traveled after becoming a slave of Captain Joseph Vesey before settling with the captain in Charleston, or details on Vesey's wives. Monday Gell testified Vesey had seven wives, although some historians have argued the court reporter made a mistake and Monday actually testified "several wives." Intendant James Hamilton, Jr. stated in his published overview of the plot "numerous wives." Only one wife, Beck, is named in the trial transcript, found in the testimony of William Paul. In another example of my liberties, there were no riotous gatherings in the streets during Monday Gell's first testimony and confession, but I have created this to dramatize the turmoil of emotions in the city at the time. The Act of 1740 under which the Vesey conspirators were tried provided the Court be composed of 3 to 6 jurors of selected Freemen in the community. I expanded the number to provide the reader with the names of the historical six jurors plus the fictitious James Radcliffe as the 7th juror.

The trial transcript does not record any testimony spoken by Denmark Vesey, perhaps to keep Vesey's incendiary rhetoric from the slaves of Charleston after his death. The narrative of the plot in the published report by the Magistrates provides synopses of some of Vesey's comments, but no actual quotes. Some of the blacks on trial, or those testifying against the insurgents, told of statements made by Denmark Vesey. I have incorporated these into the novel at various points as part of Denmark Vesey's dialogue or writings in his journal. Interestingly, perhaps motivated by the slaves' fear of retribution, the hangings on July 2, 1822, including that of Denmark Vesey, were sparsely attended by Charlestonians, black or white.

No images of Denmark Vesey exist, as Vesey died in 1822, and Louis Jacques Mandé Daguerre did not invent his daguerreotype photographic process until 1839. There are however photographic images of James H. Hamilton, Jr., Morris Brown, and Thomas Bennet made later in their lives. The identity of the black man whose image is used on the cover of *The Death of Denmark Vesey* is unknown, although a few historians speculate it may be a young Frederick Douglass. This image, although factually inaccurate, is frequently found on websites representing Vesey.

For more on Gullah language and culture, see *Down by the Riverside:*

A South Carolina Slave Community by Charles W. Joyner; *Africanisms in the Gullah Dialect* by Lorenzo Dow Turner; *Gullah Folktales from the Georgia Coast* by Charles Colcock Jones, Jr.; and *The Black Border of the Carolina Coast* by Ambrose E. Gonzales.

All of the characters on Radcliffe Place Plantation and the members of the extended Radcliffe family and slaves, are fictional. Any resemblance to actual persons, living or dead is unintended and completely coincidental.

About the Author

JAMES PAUL RICE is a life-long native of South Carolina, the Palmetto State, in the USA and studied English literature and Aesthetics at the University of South Carolina. After reading a newspaper article about the 1822 Denmark Vesey slave revolt in Charleston, SC, James began to envision an historical novel with the Vesey affair at its core. He initiated the process by feeding on a steady diet of Graham Greene, Robert Penn Warren, Lawrence Durrell, Gore Vidal, and William Styron to build up writing muscle. The end result was The Death of Denmark Vesey. This is James' first novel. James is a voracious reader of literature, poetry, history, cultural history, and art history. He is at work on his new novel, loosely based on the life of the French painter Henri Matisse, and set in Tunisia of the 1920's with time shifts to ancient Carthage. The novel is also a treatise on aesthetics.

CPSIA information can be obtained
at www.ICGtesting.com
Printed in the USA
LVOW11*1440090517
533871LV00005B/90/P